City Girls

Having it all—on their terms?

By Request

Praise for three best-selling authors – Penny Jordan, Liz Fielding and Jessica Hart

About Penny Jordan
'Women everywhere will find pieces of themselves in Jordan's characters.'
—*Publishers Weekly*

About THE THREE-YEAR ITCH
'Liz Fielding delivers a brilliant story chock full of poignant scenes…'
—*Romantic Times*

About WORKING GIRL
'Jessica Hart delivers delightful reading, creating intense characters and an intriguing plot.'
—*Romantic Times*

City Girls

WANTING HIS CHILD

by

Penny Jordan

THE THREE-YEAR ITCH

by

Liz Fielding

WORKING GIRL

by

Jessica Hart

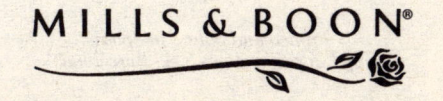

MILLS & BOON®

DID YOU PURCHASE THIS BOOK WITHOUT A COVER?
If you did, you should be aware it is **stolen property** as it was reported *unsold and destroyed* by a retailer. Neither the author nor the publisher has received any payment for this book.

All the characters in this book have no existence outside the imagination of the author, and have no relation whatsoever to anyone bearing the same name or names. They are not even distantly inspired by any individual known or unknown to the author, and all the incidents are pure invention.

All Rights Reserved including the right of reproduction in whole or in part in any form. This edition is published by arrangement with Harlequin Enterprises II B.V. The text of this publication or any part thereof may not be reproduced or transmitted in any form or by any means, electronic or mechanical, including photocopying, recording, storage in an information retrieval system, or otherwise, without the written permission of the publisher.

This book is sold subject to the condition that it shall not, by way of trade or otherwise, be lent, resold, hired out or otherwise circulated without the prior consent of the publisher in any form of binding or cover other than that in which it is published and without a similar condition including this condition being imposed on the subsequent purchaser.

MILLS & BOON and MILLS & BOON with the Rose Device are registered trademarks of the publisher.
Harlequin Mills & Boon Limited,
Eton House, 18-24 Paradise Road, Richmond, Surrey, TW9 1SR

CITY GIRLS
© by Harlequin Enterprises II B.V., 2002

Wanting His Child, The Three-Year Itch and *Working Girl* were first published in Great Britain by Harlequin Mills & Boon Limited in separate, single volumes.

Wanting His Child © Penny Jordan 1999
The Three-Year Itch © Liz Fielding 1997
Working Girl © Jessica Hart 1996

ISBN 0 263 83153 1

05-0202

*Printed and bound in Spain
by Litografia Rosés S.A., Barcelona*

Born in Preston, Lancashire, **Penny Jordan** now lives with her husband in a beautiful fourteenth-century house in rural Cheshire. Penny has been writing for over ten years and now has over one hundred and twenty novels to her name including the phenomenally successful POWER PLAY and SILVER. With over thirty million copies of her books in print and translations into seventeen languages, she has firmly established herself as a novelist of great scope.

Look out for:
The Blackmail Baby **by Penny Jordan in Modern Romance™, April 2002**

WANTING HIS CHILD

by
Penny Jordan

CHAPTER ONE

VERITY MAITLAND grimaced as she directed the long nose of the top-of-the-range BMW sports car she was driving through the outskirts of what had once been her home town.

It may have been over a decade since she had originally left but, from what she could see, nothing much seemed to have changed—but then why should it have done? Just because so much had changed in *her* life, that didn't mean...

The car was attracting a good deal of covert attention, and no wonder: from its immaculate shiny paintwork to its sporty wheels and its sleek soft-top hood it screamed look at me...admire me...*want* me.

She would never in a thousand years have deliberately chosen a car so blatantly attention seeking and expensive and had, in fact, only bought it as a favour to a friend. Her friend, a modern wunderkind spawned by the eighties, had recently taken the decision to 'downsize' and move herself, her man, and her two children to a remote area of the Scottish Highlands where, as she had explained ruefully to Verity, the BMW would be a luxury she simply couldn't afford. What she had also not been able to afford had been the time to look around for a private buyer prepared to pay a good price for the almost new vehicle and so, heroically, Verity had stepped in and offered to buy the car from her. After all, it was hardly as though she couldn't afford to—she could have afforded a round dozen or so new cars had she wished.

Along with the nearly new car she had also acquired from the same friend a nearly-new wardrobe of clothes, all purchased from Bond Street's finest.

'I'm hardly going to be wearing Gucci, Lauren, Prada or Donna Karan where we're going,' Charlotte had sighed, 'and we are the same size.'

Well aware, although her friend hadn't said so and despite her cheerful optimistic attitude, that her 'downsizing' had not been totally voluntary and that money was going to be tight for her, Verity had equably picked up on Charlotte's hints about selling off her wardrobe and had stepped in as purchaser.

She could, of course, have simply offered to give her friend the money; as a multimillionairess, even if only on a temporary basis, she could after all afford it, but she knew how Charlotte's pride would be hurt by such an offer and their friendship meant too much to her for her to risk damaging it.

'After all, it isn't just *me* who's being done a favour,' Charlotte had commented enthusiastically as they had stood together in the large bedroom of her soon to be ex-Knightsbridge house, viewing Verity's appearance in the white Gucci trouser suit she had just pulled on.

'Now that you've sold the business and you aren't going to be working non-stop virtually twenty-four hours a day, you're going to need a decent wardrobe. You're going to have to watch out for fortune hunters, though,' she warned Verity sternly. 'I know you're in your thirties now, but you're still a very attractive woman…'

'And the fact that I'm currently worth over forty million pounds makes me even more attractive,' Verity suggested dryly.

'Not to me, it doesn't,' Charlotte assured her with a warm hug. 'But there are men...'

'*Please*... You sound just like my uncle,' Verity told her.

Her uncle. Verity was thinking about him now as she drove through the town and headed out towards her destination. It had been an ironic touch of fate that the very house where she had grown up under the guardianship of her late uncle should have been one of the ones the estate agent had sent her details of as a possible house for her to rent.

When people had asked her what she intended to do, having finally taken the decision to sell off the business she had inherited from her uncle—a business which she had been groomed by him to manage and run virtually from the moment she had gone to live with him following her parents' death; a business which she had been brought up by him to look upon as a sacred trust, as the whole focus of her life and as something far, far more important than any personal desires or needs she might have—she had told them, with the calmness for which she was fabled, that so far she had made no plans. That she simply intended to take some time out in order to give proper consideration to what she wanted to do with the rest of her life. After all, at thirty-three she might not be old, but then neither was she young, and she was certainly wise enough to be able to keep her own counsel—it was not completely true that she hadn't made any plans. She had. It was just that she knew exactly how her advisers, both financial and emotional, would look upon them.

To divest herself of virtually all of the money she had received from the sale of the company was not a step they would consider well thought out or logical, but for once in her life she wanted to do what felt right for *her*, to be motivated by her *own* judgement rather than simply complying with the needs and demands of others.

She had fought a long battle to retain ownership of the business—not because she had particularly wanted to, but because she had known it was what her late uncle would have expected—but that battle was now over. As she herself had known and her financial advisers had warned her, there had been a very great danger that, if she had not accepted one of the excellent offers she had received for the sale of the business, she could have found herself in a position where a sale had been forced upon her. She had at least managed to ensure that her uncle's name remained linked to that of the business for perpetuity.

Verity frowned, automatically checking her speed as she realised she was approaching the local school and that it was that time in the afternoon when the children were coming out.

It was the same school she had attended herself, although her memories of being there were not entirely happy due, in the main, to the fact that her uncle's strictness and obsession with her school grades had meant that she had not been allowed to mingle freely with her classmates. During the long summer evenings when they had gone out to play, she had had to sit working at home under her uncle's eagle eye.

It had been his intention that her father, who had worked alongside him in the business and who had been his much younger brother, would ultimately take over from him, but her father's untimely death had put an end to that and to the possibility that he might have further children—sons.

Her uncle's own inability to father children had been something that Verity had only discovered after his death and had, she suspected, been the reason why he had never married himself.

She was clear of the school now and the houses had become more widely spaced apart, set in large private gardens.

Knowing that she would shortly be turning off the main road, Verity automatically started to brake and ten seconds later was all too thankful that she had done so as, totally unexpectedly, out of a small newsagent's a young girl suddenly appeared on a pair of roller blades, skidded and shot out into the road right in front of Verity's car.

Instinctively and immediately Verity reacted, braking sharply, turning the car to one side, but sickeningly she still heard the appalling sound of a thud against the front wing of the car as the girl collided with it.

Frantically Verity tugged at her seat belt with trembling fingers, her heart thudding with adrenalin-induced horror and fear as she ran to the front of the car.

The girl was struggling to her feet, her face as ashen as Verity knew her own to be.

'What happened? Are you hurt? Can you walk…?'

As she gabbled the frantic questions, Verity forced herself to take a deep breath.

The girl was on her feet now but leaning over the side of the car. She looked all right, but perhaps she had been hurt internally, Verity worried anxiously as she went to put her arm around her to support her.

She felt heartbreakingly thin beneath the bulkiness of her clothes and Verity guessed that she wouldn't be much above ten. Her grey eyes were huge in her small, pointed white face, and as she raised her hand to push the weight of her long dark hair off her face Verity saw with a thrill of fear that there was blood on her hand.

'It's okay,' the girl told her hesitantly, 'it's just a scratch. I'm fine really... It was all my fault... I didn't look. Dad's always telling me...'

She stopped talking, her eyes suddenly brimming with tears, her whole body starting to shake with sobs.

'It's all right,' Verity assured her, instinctively taking her in her arms and holding her tight. 'You're in shock. Come and sit in the car...'

Glancing up towards the shop the girl had just come from, she asked her gently, 'Is your mother with you? Shall I...?'

'I don't have a mother,' the girl told her, allowing Verity to help her into the passenger seat of the car where she slumped back, her eyes closed, before adding, 'She's dead. She died when I was born. You don't have to feel sorry for me,' she added without opening her eyes. 'I don't mind because I never knew her and I've got Dad and he's...'

'*I* don't feel sorry for you,' Verity assured her, adding with an openness that she could only put down to the fact that she too was suffering the disorientating and disturbing effects of shock, 'I lost *both* my parents in a car accident when I was six.'

The girl opened her eyes and looked thoughtfully at her. Now that she was beginning to get over her ordeal she looked very alert and intelligent and, in some odd way that Verity couldn't quite put her finger on, slightly familiar.

'It's horrid having people feeling sorry for you, isn't it?' the girl said with evident emotion.

'People don't mean to be patronising,' Verity responded. 'But I do know what you mean...'

'Dad told me I wasn't to go outside the garden on my rollers.' She gave Verity an assessing look. 'He'll ground me for ages—probably for ever.' Verity waited, guessing what was coming next.

'I don't suppose... Well, he doesn't *have* to know, does he...? I could pay for the damage to your car from my pocket money and...'

What kind of man was he, this father, who so patently made his daughter feel unloved and afraid? A man like her uncle, perhaps? A man who, whilst providing a child with all the material benefits he or she could possibly want, did not provide the far more important emotional ones?

'No, he doesn't *have* to know,' Verity agreed, 'as long as the hospital gives you the all clear.'

'The *hospital*?' The girl's eyes widened apprehensively.

'Yes, the hospital,' Verity said firmly, closing her own door and re-starting the car.

She would be being extremely negligent in her duty as a responsible adult if she didn't do everything within her power to make sure the girl was as physically undamaged as she looked.

'You have to turn left here,' the girl began and then looked closely at Verity as she realised she had started to turn without her directions. 'Do you know the way?'

'Yes. I know it,' Verity agreed.

She ought to. She had gone there often enough with her uncle. Before he had moved the company's headquarters to London, the highly specialised medical equipment he had invented and designed had been tried out in their local hospital and Verity had often accompanied him on his visits there.

One of the things she intended to do with the money from the sale of the company was to finance a special ward at the hospital named after her uncle. The rest of it… The rest of it would be used in equally philanthropic ways. That was why she had come back here to her old home town, to take time out to think about what she wanted to do with the rest of her life and to decide how other people could benefit the most from her late uncle's money.

When they arrived at the casualty department of the hospital they were lucky in that there was no one else waiting to be seen.

The nurse, who frowned whilst Verity explained what had happened, then turned to Verity's companion and asked her, 'Right… Let's start with your name.'

'It's… It's Honor—Honor Stevens.'

Honor Stevens. Verity felt her heart start to plummet with the sickening speed of an out-of-control lift.

She was being stupid, of course. Stevens wasn't that unusual a name, and she was taking her own apprehension and coincidence too far to assume that just because of a shared surname that meant…

'Address?' the nurse asked crisply.

Dutifully Honor gave it.

'Parents?' she demanded.

'Parent. I only have one—my father,' Honor began weakly. 'His name's Silas. Well, really Silas Stevens.' She pulled a face and looked at Verity, and unexpectedly told her, 'You look…' She stopped, looked at her again speculatively, but Verity didn't notice.

Silas Stevens. Honor was Silas' daughter. Why on earth hadn't she known? Guessed? She could see so clearly now that the reason she had found Honor's features so oddly familiar was because she was Silas' daughter. She even had his thick, dark, unruly hair, for heaven's sake, and those long-lashed grey eyes—*they* were his, no doubts about it. That disconcertingly level look was his as well and…

'Are you feeling all right?'

Verity flushed as she realised that both Honor and the nurse were watching her.

'I'm fine,' she fibbed, adding dryly, 'but it isn't every day that I get an out-of-control roller blader courting death under my car wheels.'

And it certainly wasn't every day that she learned that that child was the daughter of a man…of *the* man… What would Honor think if she knew that once Verity had believed that Silas' children would be hers, that *she* would be the one to bear his babies, wear his ring, share his life…? But that had been before… Before her uncle had reminded her of where her real duty lay, and before Silas had told her so unequivocally that he had his own plans for his life and that they did not include playing second fiddle to another's wishes, another man's rules, another man's business.

'But I can't just walk away and leave him, leave *it*,' Verity had protested shakily when Silas had delivered an ultimatum to her. 'He needs me, Silas, he expects me to take over the business...'

'And what of my needs, my expectations?' Silas had asked her angrily.

In the end they had made up their quarrel, but six weeks later her uncle had announced that he had made arrangements for her to go to America where she would work for a firm manufacturing a similar range of medical equipment to their own, since he believed the experience would stand her in good stead when she took over his own business. She had been tempted to refuse, to rebel, but the strictness with which he had brought her up had stopped her—that and her sense of responsibility and duty towards not just him but the business as well. The twenty-year gap which had existed between him and her father, despite the fact that they had been brothers, had meant that her father himself had been a little in awe of him, and Verity, entering his household as a shy six-year-old suddenly bereft of her parents, had been too nervous, too despairingly unhappy over the loss of her mother and father, too intimidated to even think of rebelling against his stern dictatorship so that the seeds had been sown then for her to be taught by him to obey.

Later, away from his oppressive presence, she had started to mature into her own person, to feel able to make her own judgements and have her own values and she had known then, tried then...but it had been too late...

Quickly she veiled her eyes with her lashes just in case either Honor or the nurse might read what she was feeling.

'We'll need to take some X-rays and of course she'll have to see the doctor, although it doesn't look as though anything's wrong,' the nurse assured Verity.

'You'll wait here for me. You won't leave without me, will you?' Honor begged Verity as the nurse indicated that she was to follow her.

'I...' Verity hesitated. She too knew what it was like to feel alone, to feel abandoned, to feel that you had no one.

'Your father—' the nurse was beginning firmly, but Honor shook her head.

'No,' she said quickly. 'I don't want... He's away...on business and he won't be back until...until next week,' she responded.

The nurse was pursing her lips.

'Look, if it helps, I'll wait...and take full responsibility,' Verity offered.

'Well, I don't really know. It is most unorthodox,' the nurse began. 'Are you a relative, or—?'

'She's...she's going to be my new mother,' Honor cut in before Verity could say anything, and then looked pleadingly at her as the nurse looked questioningly at Verity, seeking confirmation of what she had just been told.

'I...I'll, er...I'll just wait here for you,' Verity responded, knowing that she ought by rights to have corrected Honor's outrageous untruth, but suspecting that there was more to the girl's fib than a mere desire to short-circuit officialdom and avoid waiting whilst the hospital contacted whoever it was that her father had left in official charge of her.

It baffled Verity that a parent—any parent, male or female—could be so grossly neglectful of their child's welfare, but she knew, of course, that it did happen, and one of the things she intended to do with her new-found wealth was to make sure that children in Honor's situation were not exposed to the kind of danger Honor had just suffered. What Verity wanted to do was to establish a network of secure, outside-school, protective care for children whose parents for one reason or another simply could not be there for them. She knew that what she was taking on was a mammoth task, but she was determined and it was also one that was extremely dear to her heart.

It was almost an hour before the nurse returned with Honor, pronouncing briskly that she was fine.

'I'll run you home,' Verity offered as they walked back out into the early summer sunshine.

Honor had paused and was drawing a picture in the dust with the toe of her shoe.

'What is it? What's wrong?' Verity asked her.

'Er... Dad doesn't have to know about any of this, does he?' Honor asked her uncomfortably. 'It's just... Well...'

Verity watched her gravely for a few seconds, her heart going out to her, although she kept her feelings to herself as she told her quietly, 'Well, *I'm* certainly not going to say anything to him.'

Wasn't that the truth? The thought of having anything...*anything* whatsoever to do with Silas Stevens was enough to bring her out in a cold panic-induced sweat, despite the fact that she would dearly have loved to have given him a piece of her mind about his appalling neglect of his daughter's welfare.

'You're not. That's great...' A huge smile split Honor's face as she started to hurry towards Verity's car.

When they did get there, though, her face fell a little as she saw the dent and scraped paintwork where she had collided with the car.

'It's a BMW, isn't it? That means it's going to be expensive to repair...'

'I'm afraid it does,' Verity agreed cordially.

She sternly refused to allow her mouth to twitch into anything remotely suspicious of a smile as Honor told her gravely, 'I *will* pay you back for however much it costs, but it could take an awfully long time. Dad's always docking my pocket money,' she added with an aggrieved expression. 'It isn't fair. He can be really mean...'

You too, Verity wanted to sympathise. She knew all about that kind of meanness. Her uncle had kept her very short of money when she'd been growing up, and even now she often found it difficult to spend money on herself without imagining his reaction—which was why her cupboards had been so bare of designer clothes and the car she had driven before kind-heartedness had driven her to purchase Charlotte's BMW had been a second-hand run-of-the-mill compact model.

'I get my spending money every week. I wanted to have a proper allowance but Dad says I'm still too young... Where do you live?' she asked Verity.

Calmly Verity told her, watching as she carefully memorised the address.

'Can you stop here?' Honor suddenly demanded urgently, adding, when Verity looked quizzically at her, 'I...I'd rather you didn't take me all the way home...just in case...well...'

'I won't take you all the way home,' Verity agreed, 'but I'm not going to stop until I can see that you get home safely from where I'm parked.'

To her relief Honor seemed to accept this ruling, allowing Verity to pull into the side of the road within eyesight of her drive.

'Will there be someone there?' Verity felt bound to ask her.

'Oh, yes,' Honor assured her sunnily. 'Anna will be there. Anna looks after me...us... She works for Dad at the garden centre when I'm at school... I won't forget about the money,' she promised Verity solemnly as she got out of the car.

'I'm sure you won't,' Verity agreed, equally seriously.

So Silas still had the garden centre.

She remembered how full of plans he had been for it when he had first managed to raise the money to buy it. Her uncle had been scornful of what Silas had planned to do.

'A gardener?' he had demanded when Verity had first told him about Silas' plans. 'You're dating a gardener? Where did you meet him?'

Verity could remember how her heart had sunk when she had been forced to admit that she had met Silas when he had come to do the gardens at the house. She had hung her head in shame and distress when her uncle had demanded to know what on earth she, with her background and her education, could possibly see in someone who mowed lawns for a living.

'It isn't like that,' Verity had protested, flying to the protection of her new-found love and her new-found lover. 'He's been to university but...'

'But what?' her uncle had demanded tersely.

'He...he found out when he was there that it wasn't what he wanted to do...'

'What university has taught me more than anything else,' Silas had told her, 'is to know myself, and what I know is that I would hate to be stuck in some stuffy office somewhere. I want to be in the fresh air, growing things... It's in my blood, after all. My great-grandfather was a gardener. He worked for the Duke of Hartbourne as his head gardener. I don't *want* to work for someone else, though—I want to work for myself. I want to buy a plot of land, develop it, build a garden centre...'

Enthusiastically he had started to tell Verity all about his plans. Six years older than her, he had possessed a maturity, a masculinity, which had alternately enthralled and enticed her. He had represented everything that she had not had in her own life and she had fallen completely and utterly in love with him.

Automatically, she turned the car into the narrow road that led to the house originally owned by her uncle—the house where she had grown up; the house where she had first met Silas; the house where she had tearfully told him that her responsibility, her duty towards her uncle had to take precedence over their love. And so he had married someone else.

The someone else who must have been Honor's mother. He must have loved her a great deal not to have married for a second time. And he had quite obviously cherished her memory and his love for her far longer than he had cherished his much-proclaimed love for *her,* Verity acknowledged tiredly as she reached her destination and drove in through the ornate wrought-iron gates which were a new feature since she had lived in the house. Outwardly, though, in other ways, it remained very much the same. A large, turn-of-the-century house, of no particular aesthetic appeal or design.

Both her uncle and her father had spent their childhood in it but it had never, to Verity, seemed to be a family house, despite its size. Her uncle had changed very little in it since his own parents' death, and to Verity it had always possessed a dark, semi-brooding, solitary air, totally unlike the pretty warmth she remembered from the much smaller but far happier home she had shared with her parents.

After her return from America her uncle had sold the house. His own health had started to deteriorate, during Verity's absence, so he had set in motion arrangements to move the manufacturing side of the business to London. It had seemed to make good sense for both he and Verity to move there as well, Verity to her small mews house close to the river and her uncle to a comfortable apartment and the care of a devoted housekeeper.

Stopping her car, she reached into her handbag for the keys the letting agent had given her and then, taking a deep breath, she got out and headed for the house.

She wasn't really sure herself just why she had chosen to come back, not just to this house but to this town. There was, after all, nothing here for her, no one here for her.

Perhaps one of the reasons was to reassure herself that she *was* now her own person—that she had her own life; that she was finally free; that she had the right to make her own decision. She had done her duty to her uncle and to the business and now, at thirty-three, she stood on the threshold of a whole new way of life, even if she had not decided, as yet, quite what form or shape that life would take.

'What you need is a man...to fall in love,' Charlotte had teasingly advised her the previous summer when Verity had protested that it was impossible for her to take time off to go on holiday with her friend and her family. 'If you fell in love then you would have to find time...'

'Fall in love? Me? Don't be ridiculous,' Verity had chided her.

'Why not?' Charlotte had countered. 'Other people do—even other workaholics like you. You're an attractive, loving, lovable woman, Verity,' she had told her determinedly.

'Tell that to my shareholders,' Verity had joked, adding more seriously, 'I don't *need* any more complications in my life Charlie. I've already got enough and, besides, the men I get to meet aren't interested in the real me. They're only interested in the Verity Maitland who's the head of Maitland Medical...'

'Has there *ever* been anyone, Verity?' Charlotte had asked her gently. 'Any special someone...an old flame...?'

'No. No one,' Verity had lied, hardening her heart against the memories she'd been able to feel threatening to push past the barriers she had put in place against them.

She'd had her share of opportunities, of course—dates...men who had wanted to get to know her better—but...but she had never really been sure whether it had been her they had wanted or the business, and she had simply never cared enough to take the risk of finding out. She had already been hurt once by believing a man who had told her that he loved her. She wasn't going to allow it to happen a second time.

Squaring her shoulders, she inserted the key into the lock and turned the handle.

CHAPTER TWO

AS SHE stepped into the house's long narrow hallway, Verity blinked in astonished surprise. Gone was the dark paint and equally dark carpet she remembered, the air of cold unwelcome and austere disapproval, and in their place the hallway glowed with soft warm colours, natural creams warmed by the sunlight pouring in through the window halfway up the stairs. The house felt different, she acknowledged.

Half an hour later, having subjected it to a thorough inspection, she had to admit that its present owners had done a wonderful job of transforming it. Her uncle would, of course, have been horrified both by the luxury and the total impracticality of the warm cream carpet that covered virtually every floor surface. Verity, on the other hand, found it both heart-warming and deliciously sensual, if one could use such a word about something so mundane as mere carpet. The bedroom carpet, for instance, with its particularly thick and soft pile, was so warm-looking that she had had to fight an urge to slip off her shoes and curl her bare toes into it. And as for the wonderful pseudo-Victorian bathroom with its huge, deep tub and luxurious fitments, not to mention the separate shower room that went with it—it was a feast for the eyes.

'It's the best we've got on our books,' the agent had told her. 'The couple who own it had it renovated to the highest standard and if his company hadn't transferred him to California they would still be living there themselves.'

Well, at least she had plenty of wardrobe space, Verity acknowledged a couple of hours later, having lugged the last of her suitcases up the stairs and started to remove their contents.

It had been Charlotte who had decided that they should have a ceremonial clear-out of all the plain, businesslike suits Verity had worn during her years as Chief Executive and Chairperson of the company.

'Throw them out!'

Verity gasped in shock as she listened to what Charlotte was proposing.

'They're far too good for that. That cloth…'

'…will last forever. I know. I remember you telling me so when you originally ordered them—and that was five years ago.'

'Just after Uncle Toby died, yes, I know,' Verity agreed sombrely.

'I hated them on you then and they don't have any place in your life now,' Charlotte reminded her, adding, 'and, whilst we're on the subject, I just never, ever, want to see you wearing your hair up again—especially when it looks so wonderful down. Nature is very, very unfair,' she continued. 'Not only has she given you the most wonderful skin, a profile to die for and naturally navy blue eyes, she's also given you the most glorious honey-blonde hair. It's every bit as thick and gorgeous-looking as Cindy Crawford's and it curls naturally…'

'Cindy who?' Verity teased, laughing when Charlotte began to look appalled and holding her hands up in defeat as she admitted, 'It's okay. I do know who she is...'

'What *you* need to do is to cultivate a more natural, approachable look,' Charlotte counselled her. 'Think jeans and white tees, a navy blazer and loafers, with your hair left down and just a smidgen of make-up.'

'Charlie,' Verity warned, telling her friend, 'I've been in business far too long not to recognise someone trying to package an item for sale.'

'The only person *you* need selling to is yourself,' Charlotte countered. 'I've lost count of the number of men I've introduced you to who you've simply frozen out... One day you're going to wake up on your own heading for forty and—'

'Is that such a very bad deal?' Verity objected.

'Well, there *are* other things in life,' Charlotte reminded her, 'and I've watched you often enough with my two to know how good you are with children.'

It wasn't a subject which Verity wanted to pursue. Not even Charlie, who was arguably her closest friend, knew about Silas and the pain he had caused her, the hopes she had once had...the love she had once given him, only to have it thrown back in her face when he had married someone else, despite telling her... But what was the point in going back over old ground?

She had been nineteen when she and Silas had first met; twenty-two when he had married—someone else—and what time they had had together had been snatched between her years at university, followed by a brief halcyon period of less than six months between her finishing university and being sent to America by her uncle. Halcyon to her, that was. For Silas?

Face it, she told herself sternly now as she hung the last of her spectacular new clothes into the wardrobe. He was never really serious about you, despite everything he said. If he had been he'd have done as he promised.

'I'll love you forever,' he had told her the first time they had made love. 'You're everything I've ever wanted, everything I *will* ever want...'

But he had been lying to her, Verity acknowledged dry-eyed. He had never really loved her at all. And why on earth he had encouraged her to believe that he did, she really could not understand. He had never struck her as the kind of man who needed the ego-boost of making sexual conquests. He was tall, brown-haired and grey-eyed, with the kind of physique that came from working hard out of doors, and Verity had fallen in love with him without needing any encouragement or coaxing. She had just finished her first year at university and come home for the holidays to find him working in her uncle's garden. He had introduced himself to her and had watched her quizzically as she had been too inexperienced, too besotted, to hide her immediate reaction to him, her face and her body blushing a deep vivid pink.

Verity tensed, remembering just how betrayingly her over-sensitive young body *had* revealed her reaction to him, her nipples underneath the thin tee shirt she had been wearing hardening so that she had instinctively crossed her arms over her breasts to hide their flaunting wantonness. He, Silas, had affected not to notice what had happened to her or how embarrassed she had been by it, tactfully turning his head and gently directing her attention to the flower bed he had been weeding, making some easy, relaxed comment about the design of the garden, giving her time to recover her equilibrium and yet, somehow, at the same time, closing the distance between them so that when he'd started to draw her attention to another part of the garden he'd been close enough to her to be able to touch her bare arm with his hand.

Verity could remember even now how violently she had quivered in immediate reaction to his touch.

Fatefully she had turned her head to look at him, her wide-eyed gaze going first to his eyes and then helplessly to his mouth.

He had told her later that the only thing that had stopped him from snatching her up and kissing her there and then had been his fear of frightening her away.

'You looked so young and innocent that I was afraid you might... I was afraid that if I let you see just how much I wanted you, I'd frighten you, terrify the life out of you,' he had told her rawly, weeks later, as he'd held her in his arms and kissed her over and over again, the way she had secretly wanted him to and equally secretly been afraid that he might that first day in the garden.

Looking back with the maturity she had since gained, she could still see no signs, no warnings of what was to be or the full enormity of how badly she was going to be hurt.

She had believed Silas implicitly when he had told her that he loved her. Why should she not have done? *He*, after all, had been the one who had pursued her, courted her, laid seige to her heart and her emotions, her life.

That first summer had been a brilliant kaleidoscope of warmth, love and laughter, or so it seemed looking back on it. She had still been talking to Silas hours later when her uncle had returned home, her bags still standing on the drive where the taxi driver had dropped them and her off. She had been blissfully unaware of just how late it had been until she'd seen her uncle draw up.

'Still here?' he asked Silas curtly, nodding dismissively to him as he turned to Verity and demanded frowningly, 'I should have thought you'd have too much studying to do to waste your time out here, Verity…'

Chastened, Verity bade Silas a mumbled 'goodbye' and turned to follow her uncle into the house. But when she went to pick up her bags, Silas had got there first, gathering up the two heaviest cases as though they weighed a mere nothing.

To Verity, used as she was to the far more frail frame of her elderly uncle, the sight of so much raw, sexual, male strength was dizzyingly exciting.

Her uncle lectured her over supper about the need for her to allocate time during her summer vacation for working hard at her studies.

'Of course, you'll come to the factory with me during the day,' he informed her, and Verity did not attempt to argue. Every holiday since she had turned sixteen had been spent thus, with her learning every aspect of the business from the factory floor upwards, under her uncle's critical eye.

But fate, it seemed, had had other plans for her. The following morning when she went downstairs— her uncle always insisted on leaving for the factory well before seven so that he could be there before the first workers arrived at eight—she learned that her uncle had received a telephone call late the previous evening informing him that the firm's Sales Director had been taken to hospital with acute appendicitis, which meant that her uncle was going to have to step into his shoes and fly to the Middle East to head a sales delegation.

He would, he informed Verity, be gone for almost a month.

'I shall have to leave you here to your own devices,' he told her. 'I can't have you going into the factory without my supervision. Had this happened a little earlier I could have made arrangements for you to come with me. It would have been excellent experience for you but, unfortunately, it's far too late now for you to have the necessary inoculations and for me to get a visa for you. Still, you must have brought work home with you from university.'

'Yes,' she agreed meekly, eyes downcast, her heart suddenly bounding so frantically fast against her chest wall that she felt positively light-headed.

Even with her uncle gone she was still unable to acknowledge the real reason for her excitement and sense of freedom, nor for her sudden decision to work in the sitting room which overlooked the part of the garden which Silas had been working on the previous day and to wear a pair of cotton shorts which showed off her long slim legs.

Silas arrived within an hour of her uncle's departure, and from her strategic position in the sitting room Verity was able to discreetly watch him as he worked. As the day grew hotter he stopped working and stood up, stretching his back before removing his soft cotton tee shirt.

Dry-mouthed, Verity watched him, her body shaking with the most disturbing sensation she had ever experienced.

'Lust,' she told herself angrily now as she folded the last few pairs of briefs and put them neatly into one of the wardrobe drawers.

Lust: she had been too naive to know just what that was or how powerful it could be *then*. All she *had* known was that, no matter how hard she tried to concentrate on her work and the words on the paper in front of her, all that she could really see was Silas' image imprinted on her eyeball.

At lunch time she had gone outside to offer him a cold drink and something to eat. Gravely he had accepted, following her into the kitchen, and it had only been later that he had admitted to her that he had brought his own refreshments with him but that the opportunity to spend some time with her had been too much of a temptation for him to resist.

Over the light salad lunch she had quickly and nervously prepared for him—Verity had possessed very few domestic skills in those days; her uncle had considered that learning them was a waste of time when she was going to take over his business and they had a housekeeper who lived in, but who fortuitously was away at that time taking her annual period of leave—Verity had listened wide-eyed whilst Silas had described to her his work and his plans.

'That's enough about me,' he announced gruffly when they had both finished eating. 'What about you? What do you intend to do with your life?'

'Me? I'm going to take over my uncle's business,' Verity told him gravely. 'That's what he's training me for. I'm the only person he's got to inherit it, you see. It's his life's work and—'

'*His* life's work, but *you* have your own life and the right to make your own choices, surely?' Silas interrupted her sharply, before telling her pointedly, '*My* parents originally wanted me to train as a doctor like my father, but they would never impose that kind of decision on me, nor would I allow them to…'

'I…my uncle… My uncle took me in when my parents were killed,' Verity explained low-voiced to him. 'I've always known that he expects me…that he wants me… I'm very lucky, really, it's a wonderful opportunity…'

'It's a wonderful opportunity if it's what you really want,' Silas agreed, 'otherwise it's… *Is* it what you want, Verity?'

'I… I… It's what's expected of me,' Verity told him a little unsteadily. It was proving virtually impossible to concentrate on what he was saying with him sitting so close to her—close enough for her to be intensely, embarrassingly aware of his body and its evident physical masculinity, its tantalising male scent. He had asked her permission to 'clean up' before sitting down to lunch with her and his discarded shirt was now back on.

Every time she dared to look at him she was swept with such an intense and heightened awareness of him that she could feel her face starting to flush with hot self-consciousness.

'What's *expected* of you? Listen,' Silas commanded her, reaching out and taking hold of her hand, keeping it between his own with an open easiness which robbed her of the ability to object or protest. 'No one has the right to *expect* anything of you. *You* have the right to choose for yourself what you do with your life. It is *your* life you're living you know, and not your uncle's...'

Verity bit her lip.

'I... I know,' she responded uncertainly, 'but...'

'I'm having a day off tomorrow,' Silas told her, changing the subject. 'There's a garden that's open to the public twenty miles away—I was planning to go and see it. Would you like to come with me?'

Shiny-eyed and flushed with delighted happiness, Verity nodded.

'Good,' he told her. 'I'll pick you up at nine, if that's okay.'

Once again Verity nodded, not trusting herself to speak.

Silas was still holding her hand and she had to tug it before he released it, giving her a rueful smile as he did so.

Of course, she didn't do any work for the rest of the day, nor did she sleep that night.

Three outfits were tried on and discarded before Silas arrived to pick her up, and she blushed betrayingly at the appraising look he gave her as he studied her jeans-clad figure and the neat way the denim hugged her small firm bottom.

Jeans. How long had it been since she had worn a pair of those? Verity wondered grimly now, as the rest of her underwear joined the items she had already put away.

She had acquired a couple of pairs from Charlotte, designer labelled and immaculately tailored.

'You could have taken these with you,' Verity had protested when Charlotte had handed them over to her.

'What? Wear Lauren where *we're* going? Do you mind? The jeans *I'll* be wearing now are a pair of sturdy 501s,' she had told Verity, her face breaking into a wide grin as she had caught sight of the raised-eyebrowed look her friend had been giving her.

'Oh, 501s. Poor you,' Verity had commented dryly.

'Well, they might be "in" fashion-wise but they are also ideally designed for working in and, besides, the Lauren ones are too tight. I can barely move in them. They'll fit you much better—you're slimmer than I am right now.'

Jeans. Verity went to the wardrobe and pulled them out, touching the fabric exploratively, smoothing it beneath her fingertips.

The jeans she had worn on that first date with Silas had been a pair she had bought from her allowance. Thus far, she had not worn them in front of her uncle, knowing that he would not have approved. He had been a rather old-fashioned man who had not liked to see women wearing 'trousers'—of any kind.

Courteously Silas had held the door open for her on the passenger side of his small pick-up. The inside of the vehicle had been spotlessly clean, Verity had noticed, just as she had noticed that Silas was a good and considerate driver.

The gardens they had gone to see had been spectacularly beautiful, she acknowledged, but she had to admit that she had not paid as much attention as she ought to have done to them, nor to Silas' explanation of how the borders had been planted and the colour combinations in them constructed. She had been far too busy studying how he was constructed, far too busy noticing just how wonderfully dedicated to her task nature had been when she had put *him* together with such spectacular sensuality. Even the way he'd walked had made her heart lurch against her ribs, and just to look at his mouth, never mind imagining how it might feel to be kissed by it...by him...

'What's wrong? Are you feeling okay?' Silas asked her at one point.

'I'm fine,' Verity managed to croak, petrified of him guessing what she was really feeling.

He had brought them both a packed lunch—far more tasty and enjoyable than the meal *she* had prepared for him the previous day, Verity acknowledged, assuming, until he told her otherwise, that his mother had prepared it for them.

'Ma? No way,' he told her. 'She believes in us all being self-sufficient and, besides, she works—she's a nurse. My two brothers are both married now and I'm the only one left at home, but Ma still insists on me making my own packed lunches. One thing she did teach us all as a nurse, though, was the importance of good nutrition. Take these sandwiches. They're on wholemeal bread with a low-fat spread, the tuna provides very important nutrients and the salad I've put with it is good and healthy.'

'Like these,' Verity teased him, waving in front of him the two chocolate bars he had packed.

Silas laughed.

'Chocolate *is* good for you,' he told her solemnly,

adding with a wicked smile, 'It's the food of love, did you know that...?'

'Want me to prove it?' he tempted when Verity shook her head.

He enjoyed teasing her, he admitted later, but what he enjoyed even more, he added, was the discovery that beneath her shyness she possessed not just intelligence but, even more importantly, a good sense of humour.

They certainly laughed a lot together that first summer; laughed a lot and loved a lot too.

She could still remember the first time he kissed her. It wasn't sunny that day. There was thunder in the air, the sky brassy and overcast, and then late in the afternoon it suddenly came on to rain, huge, pelting drops, causing them to take refuge in the small summer house several yards away at the bottom of the garden.

They ran there, Silas holding her hand, both of them bursting into the small, stuffy room, out of breath and laughing.

As the door swung closed behind them, enclosing them in the half-light of the small, airless room, Silas turned towards her, brushing her hair off her face. His hands were cool and wet and, without thinking what she was doing, she turned her head to lick a raindrop off him, an instinctive, almost childish gesture, but one which marked the end of her childhood, turning her within the space of an afternoon from a child to a woman.

Even without closing her eyes she could still visualise the expression in Silas' eyes, feel the tension that suddenly gripped his body. Outwardly, nothing had changed. He was still cupping her face, they were still standing with their bodies apart, but inwardly *everything* had changed, Verity acknowledged.

Looking into Silas' eyes, she felt herself starting to tremble—not with cold and certainly not with fear.

'Verity.'

Her name, which Silas started saying inches from her face, he finished mouthing with his lips against her own, his *body* against her own. And there was nothing remotely childish about the way she reached out to him—for him—Verity remembered; nothing remotely childish at all in the way she opened her mouth beneath his and deliberately invited him to explore its intimacy. They kissed frantically, feverishly, whispering incomprehensible words of love and praise to one another, she making small keening sounds of pleasure against Silas' skin, he muttering rawly to her that he loved her, adored her, wanted her. Over and over again they kissed and touched and Verity felt incandescent with the joy of what she was experiencing; of being loved; of knowing that Silas loved her as much as she knew she loved him.

They weren't lovers that day. She wanted to but Silas shook his head, telling her huskily, 'We can't... I can't... I don't have... I could make you pregnant,' he explained to her, adding gruffly, 'The truth is I would *want* to make you pregnant, Verity. That's how much I love you and I know that once I had you in my arms, once my body was inside yours, there's no way I could... I want to come inside you,' he told her openly when she looked uncertainly at him, explaining in a low, emotional voice, 'I want to have that kind of intimacy with you. It's man's most basic instinct to regenerate himself, to seed the fertility of his woman, especially when he loves her as much as I love you.'

'I... I could go on the pill...' Verity offered, but Silas shook his head.

'No,' he told her gently, 'taking care of that side of things is *my* responsibility. And besides,' he continued softly, looking around the cramped, stuffy summer house, 'this isn't really the right place. When you and I make love I want it to be...I want it to be special for you...perfect.'

Verity moistened her lips.

'My uncle is still away,' she offered awkwardly. 'We could...'

'No. Not here in another man's house. Yes, I know that it's your home, but no, not here,' Silas said quietly.

'Where, then?' Verity breathed eagerly.

'Leave it to me,' Silas told her. 'Leave everything to me...'

And like the dutiful person she had been raised to be she dipped her head and agreed.

CHAPTER THREE

THE doorbell rang just as Verity had finished her unpacking. Frowning, she went downstairs to answer it. Who on earth could that be? She certainly wasn't expecting anyone.

She was still frowning when she opened the door, a small gasp of shock escaping her lips as she saw who was standing there and recognised him immediately.

'Silas!'

Instinctively her hand went to her throat as she tried, too late, to suppress that betraying whisper of sound.

'Verity,' her visitor responded grimly. 'May I come in?'

Without waiting for her assent he was shouldering his way into the hallway.

'How...how did you know I was back?' Verity managed to ask him huskily. Was it possible that he had actually grown taller *and* broader in the years they had been apart? Surely not, and yet she couldn't remember him ever filling the space of the hallway quite so imposingly before. He might be over ten years older but he was *still* as magnetically male as she remembered, she recognised unwillingly, and perhaps even more so—as a young man he had worn his sexuality very carelessly, softening it with the tenderness and consideration he had shown her.

Now... She took a deep breath and tried to steady her jittery nerves. Now there was *nothing* remotely soft nor tender about the way he was looking at her. Far from it.

'I didn't until I did a check at the hospital and found out that *you* had accompanied Honor there. What the hell kind of person *are* you, Verity? First you damn near run my daughter over and then you don't even bother to let *me* know that she's had an accident. What am I saying? I know *exactly* what kind of woman you are, don't I? Why should I be surprised at *anything* you might choose to do, after all I know?'

Verity couldn't utter a word. What was he saying? What was he trying to accuse her of doing? She... He made it sound as though she had deliberately tried to hit Honor, when the truth was...

'I did what I thought was best,' she told him coolly. There was no way she was going to let him see just how much he had caught her off guard, or how agitated and ill-equipped to deal with him she actually felt.

Thinking about him earlier had done nothing to prepare her for the reality of him. She had been thinking about, remembering, a young man in his twenties. *This* was a mature adult male in his late thirties and a man who...

'What *you* thought was best?' He gave her an incredulously angry look as he repeated her words. 'Didn't it strike you that as Honor's father *I* had the right to know what had happened? Didn't it cross that cold little mind of yours that *you* had a responsibility to let me know what had happened? After all, you used to be very big on responsibility, didn't you? Oh, but I was forgetting, the kind of responsibility you favoured was the kind that meant—'

'I didn't get in touch with you because I had no idea that you were Honor's father until we got to the hospital,' Verity interrupted him quickly, 'and by then…'

By then Honor had begged her not to let her father know what had happened and, additionally, untruthfully told both her and the nurse that Silas was unavailable and out of the country. But she certainly wasn't going to tell Silas *that*. Against all the odds, and ridiculously, she felt a certain sense of kinship, of female bonding with Honor.

Female *bonding* with a *ten*-year-old? And she was supposed to be intelligent? Charlotte was right—she *did* need to get a grip on her life.

'Presumably, though, you knew by the time Honor had informed the nurse that *you* were going to be her stepmother,' he informed her with deadly acidness.

She was surely far too old and had far too much self-control to be betrayed now by the kind of hot-faced blush which had betrayed her so readily all those years ago, but nonetheless Verity found herself hurriedly looking away from the anger she could see in Silas' eyes and curling her toes into her shoes as she fibbed, 'Uh…did she…? I really don't remember…the casualty department was busy,' she embroidered. 'I just wanted to make sure that Honor got some medical attention—'

'Liar.' Silas cut across her stumbled explanation in a brutally incisive voice that made her wince. 'And don't think I don't know *exactly* why you laid claim to a non-existent relationship between us.'

This was worse than her worst possible nightmare, worse by far than the most embarrassing and humiliating thing she could ever have imagined happening to her, Verity decided. She could *never* remember feeling so exposed and vulnerable, so horribly conscious of having her deepest and most private emotions laid bare to be derided and scorned. No, not even the first time she had had to stand up in front of her late uncle's board of directors, knowing how much each and every one of them must secretly have been resenting her appointment as their leader, as the person to whom they would have to defer.

In that one sentence Silas had torn down, trampled, flattened, all the delicate defences she had worked so hard to weave together to protect herself with—defences she had created with patience and teeth-gritting determination; defences she had bonded together with good humour and cheerful smiles, determined never to allow *anyone* to guess what she was really feeling, or to guess how empty her life sometimes felt, how far short of her once idealistic expectations it had fallen. Other people's compassion and pity were something she had always shrunk from and gently rejected. Her lack of a man to share her life, a child to share her love—these had been things she had determinedly told herself she was not going to allow herself to yearn for. She had her *life*, her *friends*, her *health*.

But now, pitilessly and brutally, Silas had destroyed that precious, fragile peace of mind she had worked with gentle determination to achieve.

Silas had guessed, unearthed, exhumed the pitiful little secret she had so safely hidden from other eyes.

Bravely Verity lifted her head. She wasn't going to let him have a *total* victory. Something could be salvaged from the wreckage, the destruction he had caused, even if it was only her pride.

'Contrary to what you seem to think—' she began, but once again Silas wouldn't let her finish.

He cut her off with a furious, 'I don't *think*. I *know*. You let the nurse believe that you had the right to sign Honor's consent form because you thought it would get you off the hook, that that way you wouldn't have to face up to what you had done, nor suffer any potential legal consequences.

'My God, what kind of woman are you to be driving so carelessly in a built-up area in the first place, and at school-leaving time? But, then, we both already know the answer to that, don't we? Such mundane matters as children's safety, children's lives, simply don't matter to you, do they? You've got far more important things to concern yourself with. How many millions are you worth these days, Verity? No doubt that car outside is just *one* of the perks that comes with being a very rich woman.

'Funny—I knew, of course, that the business came first, second and third with you, but I never had you down as a woman who needed to surround herself with all the trappings of a materialistic lifestyle.'

Verity gave him a dazed, almost semi-blind look. What was he saying—something about her car? About her wealth? It didn't matter. All that mattered was the intense feeling of relief she felt on realising that he hadn't, after all, meant what she had thought he had meant by that comment about knowing why she had not refuted Honor's outrageous claim that she was soon to become her stepmother. That he had thought she had allowed his daughter's fib to stand so that no questions could be asked about the accident, not because secretly she still yearned for...still wanted...

'My God, but you've changed,' she heard him breathing angrily. 'That car...this house...those clothes...'

Her clothes... Verity pushed aside her euphoric sense of relief—there would be time for her to luxuriate in that later when she was on her own.

'I'm wearing jeans,' she managed to point out in quiet self-defence.

'Designer jeans,' Silas told her curtly, nodding in the direction of the logo sewn on them.

Designer jeans? How had Silas known that? The Silas she remembered simply wouldn't have known or cared where her clothes had come from. The Silas *she* knew and remembered would, in fact, have been far more interested in what lay beneath her clothes rather than the name of the design house they had originated from.

Quickly, Verity redirected her thoughts, telling him dryly what her own quick eye had already noticed.

'Your own clothes are hardly basic chain store stuff.'

Was that just a hint of betraying caught-out colour seeping up under his skin? Verity wondered triumphantly.

'I didn't choose them,' he told her stiffly.

Then who had? A woman? For some reason his admission took all her original pleasure at catching him out away from her, Verity acknowledged dismally.

'I suppose you thought you were being pretty clever and that you'd got away with damn near killing my daughter,' Silas was demanding to know, back on the attack again. 'Well, unfortunately for you a...a friend of mine just happened to see you at the scene of the accident and she took a note of your car's registration number.'

'Really? How very neighbourly of her,' Verity gritted. 'I don't suppose it occurred to her that she might have been more usefully employed trying to help Honor rather than playing at amateur detective?'

'Myra was on her way to a very important meeting. She's on the board of several local charities and, as she said, she could hardly expect busy business people who are already giving their time to feel inclined to make a generous cash donation to a charity when its chairperson can't even be on time for a meeting...'

Whoever this Myra was, Silas obviously thought an awful lot of her, Verity reflected. He made her sound like a positive angel.

'You aren't going to deny that you *were* responsible for Honor's accident, I hope?' Silas continued, returning to the attack.

Verity was beginning to get angry herself now. How dared he speak to her like this? Would he have done so had he not already known her, judged her...had she been a stranger? Somehow she doubted it. He was being unfairly critical of her, unfairly caustic towards her because of who she was, because once she had been foolish enough to love him, and he had been— Quickly she gathered up her dangerously out-of-control thoughts.

Deny that she was responsible? But she *hadn't* been

responsible. It was... On the point of opening her mouth to vigorously inform him just how wrong he was, Verity abruptly remembered her conversation with Honor and the little girl's anxiety. Quickly she closed it again.

'It *was* an *accident*,' was all she could permit herself to say.

'An accident caused by the fact that *you* were driving too selfishly and too fast along a suburban road, in a car more properly designed for fast driving on an *autobahn*, or in your case, probably more truthfully, for showing off amongst your friends.'

Verity gasped.

'For your information,' she began, 'I bought that car...' On the point of telling him just why she had bought the BMW, she suddenly changed her mind. After all, what explanations did she possibly owe *him*? None. None at all.

'I bought that car because I wanted to buy it—because I liked it. No doubt your *friend* prefers to drive something ecologically sound, modest and economical. She has a Beetle, perhaps, or maybe a carefully looked after Morris Minor which she inherited from some aged aunt...' she suggested acidly.

'As a matter of fact—not that it's any business of yours, Myra drives a Jaguar. It was part of the settlement she received when she divorced her husband... But I'm not here to talk about my friends or my private life. You do realise, don't you, that I could report you to the police for dangerous driving?'

Immediately Verity froze, unable to control her expression.

'Yes, you may well look shocked,' Silas told her grimly.

'You can't do that,' Verity protested, thinking of Honor.

'Can't I? I've certainly got a damned good mind to, although, given your cavalier attitude towards the truth and the fact that there were no witnesses to the *whole* event, no doubt you'd manage to find a way of extricating yourself.'

'*Me* cavalier with the truth? That's rich coming from you,' Verity retorted bitterly.

'What the hell do you mean by that?' Silas challenged her.

Verity glared at him, her own temper as hot as his now. After all, she could hardly remind him that he had once told her he loved her; that he would always love her; that there would never be anyone else.

'Why have you come back here?' he demanded abruptly.

Verity turned her face away from him so that he couldn't fully see her expression.

'I grew up here. It's my home town,' she reminded him quietly.

'Sentiment. You've come back out of sentiment. My God, now I really have heard everything!'

'My roots are here,' Verity continued, praying that nothing in her voice or her expression would reveal to him how very, very much his cruelty was hurting her.

'Roots, maybe,' Silas allowed in a biting voice. 'But if you're hoping to revisit the past or resurrect old—'

'I'm not hoping to do any such thing,' Verity interrupted him passionately. 'So far as I'm concerned, the past is the past and that's exactly how I intend it to stay. There's *nothing* in it that I miss.'

'Nothing in it that you miss and certainly nothing in it that you ever valued,' Silas agreed.

And then to Verity's shock he suddenly took a step towards her.

'Silas.' Dizzily Verity moved too, but not back away from him putting more distance between them as she had planned. No. Instead what she actually did was take a step towards him. A step that brought her within intimate reach of his body, within his private body space, and close enough to him not just to see the dark shadowing along his jaw where his beard would grow but also to reach out and touch it, to feel it prickling against her palm as she had done all those years ago, the first time they had shared a bed together, and she had woken up in the opalescent light of a summer morning in the euphoric knowledge that he was there beside her, that she had the blissful, awesome right to simply turn her head and watch him as he slept, knowing that he was *hers*; that *she* was his, that nothing and no one could cause them to part—ever.

Silas!

Verity closed her eyes. She could feel the deep, uneven, heavy thud thud of her own heartbeat, pounding through her body in urgent summons. Was it *that* that was making her feel so weak, so...?

'I'm warning you, Verity, stay away from me. Stay out of my life...'

The ugly words hit her like blows aimed viciously into her unprotected vulnerable emotions. Instinctively she tried to protect herself from them by wrapping her arms around her body, but Silas was already turning away from her and heading for the door.

'I mean it,' he warned her as he paused to open it. 'Stay out of my life.'

She must be suffering some kind of shock, Verity decided dazedly ten minutes later as she slowly made her way back upstairs.

Stay out of *his* life? Did he *really* think he needed to warn her off, that she didn't *know* that there was no place there for her, no love there for her?

Numbly she stared out of her bedroom window and into the garden below. From this window she could just about see the roof of the little summer house where they had sheltered from the rain, and it had been here in this room, if not on this bed, that she had lain dreaming her foolish, idealistic, heated, adoring, loving, girlish dreams of him.

And it had been here too that she had lain in the days after he had fully made love to her, feeling and believing that the reality of his lovemaking had far, far outstripped even her most feverish and sensually exciting daydreams.

It had been here too in this room, this sanctuary, that she had come after that dreadful quarrel when he had challenged her to choose between her love for him and her duty to her uncle, and here too that she had cried her tears of relief and happiness when he had told her, with remorse and regret, that the last thing he had wanted to do was to hurt her; that hurting her had hurt him even more and that, of course, he had understood that she had to at least attempt, as a matter of duty and honour, to accede to her uncle's wishes.

'It won't be for long,' she had promised him as he had held her face and her tears had flowed down onto his hands. 'America isn't really so very far away and when I come back...'

'When you come back I'm never ever going to let you out of my sight again,' he had told her savagely. 'If you weren't so damned stubborn I wouldn't be letting you go now.'

'I have to go,' she had wept. 'I owe it to my uncle...' And yet she had known even as she had said the words that a part of her had longed for him to snatch her away, to refuse to allow her to leave him, to, however implausible it would have been, insist.

'You could come with me,' she had even suggested. 'You could work over there...'

'Come with you? As what?' He had balked immediately, telling her, 'I'm a independent man, Verity. I *can't* live on your coat tails and, besides, what about our plans to buy the small holding we visited last week—to develop the garden centre...?

Verity closed her eyes now and leant her hot face against the cool glass.

'I'll wait for you,' he had promised her when she had left. 'I'll wait for you, no matter how long it takes...'

Only he hadn't...he hadn't waited. Hadn't loved her. Hadn't given her the wedding ring nor the child he had promised her so passionately and, she had believed, so meaningfully.

Oh, God! Had he guessed just now in the hallway,

when she had stepped towards him instead of stepping away, just what was going through her mind, her body? How *easy* it would have been for her to…? Had he known that a foolish, idiotic part of her had actually thought that he *was* going to kiss her, that he had *wanted* to kiss her? That that same foolish, idiotic part of her remembered with such aching intensity that that was exactly how he used to move towards her when…?

'No,' Verity protested despairingly beneath her breath. 'No…please, no…' But it was already too late, already the memories were flooding back, swamping her. The first time he had made love to her… She could remember it as clearly and intensely as though it had only happened yesterday.

They had been out together for the day. Another visit to a famous garden—Silas, as she had discovered by this time, was a passionate advocate of the importance of good garden structure.

'Not having a proper structure to me is like…like…well, imagine trying to clothe a human body if all the limbs had simply been stuck on haphazardly here and there and everywhere, or if a house had been designed simply by adding one room next to another…'

And he produced books and then drawings to show Verity to reinforce his point. Completely head over heels in love with him by this stage, Verity acknowledged that she was probably spending longer gazing adoringly at the way his hair curled into his collar and flopped over his forehead than studying the designs he was showing her, but she took on board all that he was saying and she was as impressed and excited as he was by the elegant simplicity of the gardens they went to see.

'Every garden has a right to be properly designed,' he told her passionately, 'and you only have to read one of Sir Roy Strong's books to see just how the concept of good architectural design can be transferred to even the smallest urban garden.'

They were sitting eating their sandwiches at the time.

'Mmm…' Verity agreed, smiling lovingly at him.

And then he put down his sandwich and removed hers from her, and took her in his arms and kissed her lingeringly and very, very thoroughly, but very gently, before lifting his head and looking from her love-dazed eyes to her kiss softened mouth before telling her rawly, 'You don't know what I'd give right now to be somewhere alone with you and private…'

Very slowly he reached out and traced the shape of her lips with his fingertip.

'Perfect,' he whispered tenderly.

'Good architectural design,' Verity whispered teasingly back.

'Better than that. The best,' Silas told her solemnly, but then the laughter died out of his eyes as the tip of his finger touched the centre of her bottom lip and Verity could feel it and him starting to shake with need—a need which she fully reciprocated.

'Couldn't we do that—be together?' Verity asked him huskily.

They talked about becoming lovers but Silas told her that he had applied the brakes to his plans to find them the perfect hideaway because he wanted to wait until he was sure it was what she wanted—he was what she wanted—and that he didn't want to rush her.

'We could…there's my bedroom,' Verity boldly offered her home again. Her uncle was away on another trip. The Sales Director's appendicitis had proved more problematic than his doctors had first expected, causing a delay in his recovery, and her uncle had had to take over his duties and was consequently away on business far more than usual.

'No, not there,' Silas answered firmly, 'but if you're sure…'

His hand was holding the back of her head, caressing her scalp through her hair. Shivering with excitement and emotion, Verity smiled tremulously at him. The look in his eyes made her face burn—and not with the embarrassment of coy self-consciousness of a young woman who was still a virgin.

'I'm sure,' she told him positively. 'Oh, Silas, I'm so sure…'

'I want everything to be right—special,' he told her gruffly. 'I've looked into some of the hotels in the area and I could book us a room—for tonight…'

'Oh, yes, yes,' Verity breathed.

Tenderly she reached out and touched his face, feeling the warmth of his skin beneath her fingertips, the hard firmness of the bones and muscles that lay below it. She might not have been physically experienced, might never have had a previous lover, but she had no sense of fear nor trepidation, simply a deep inner knowledge of how right this was, of how right Silas was!

Silas found them a hotel several miles away from the garden they had visited. Small and privately owned, it was set in its own gardens but, for once, after they had booked in, Silas showed no inclination to explore.

'I...I thought you might like to...to see the gardens,' Verity had protested a little uncertainly once they were alone in the room.

Silas shook his head quietly, locking the door before turning back to her.

'No. Right now there's only one thing I want to do, one garden I want to explore,' he said softly, and Verity knew from the way he looked at her, his glance slowly caressing every inch of her, just exactly what he meant.

'I...what...? I don't know what to do,' she told him finally and honestly, blushing and then laughing. 'Well, I do, at least I think I do, but...'

'Come here,' Silas commanded her and, her colour still high, Verity walked unsteadily into his arms.

They had kissed before of course, and touched intimately so, but never like this, Verity acknowledged as Silas kissed his way slowly along the soft line of her lips and then, repeating the gesture he had made earlier, pressed the pad of his thumb to the centre of her bottom lip, hungrily nibbling the tender flesh he had exposed, his arms tightening possessively around her as Verity trembled in response to his touch. His tongue slowly caressed the inner sweetness of her mouth as hers did his and then he slowly and rhythmically sucked on her tongue and taught her to do the same to his.

As she repeated his sensual, intimate caress, Verity could feel the jolt that ran through his body and the sexual hardening and arousal that went with it.

Wrapping her arms around him, she pressed herself just as close to him as she could get, instinctively rubbing her body lovingly against his and making little purring sounds of pleasure as she did so, her eyes closing.

'Verity, Verity,' she heard Silas groaning as his hands gripped her waist half as though he was going to put her slightly away from him, but then he changed his mind, his hands sliding down her body to cup her buttocks and grind his own hips into her receptive body.

A delicious shiver of pleasure convulsed her and Silas removed one of his hands from her bottom to gently rub and knead the length of her spine in a caress that was so tenderly soothing that it made Verity open her eyes and look dazedly up at him.

'I don't want to take things too fast,' Silas told her rawly in response to her unspoken question. 'This will be your first time and I want…I want to make it perfect for you—in every way, Verity.'

'It will be,' she promised him, knowing as she spoke the words that they were true, with some deep rooted primal feminine wisdom that didn't need to be analysed or questioned.

Gently and lovingly, Silas undressed her, pausing to caress and kiss each bit of flesh he exposed, but once he got to her breasts, Verity felt his self-control beginning to slip away. As he slowly circled one taut, hard, flushed nipple with the pad of his thumb she knew it wasn't just her who was trembling so violently in sensual reaction.

'These are the most beautiful…you are the most perfect thing I have ever seen,' he whispered throatily as he picked her up and carried her over to the huge king-sized bed.

'More perfect than one of Sir Roy Strong's gardens,' Verity teased him remembering their earlier shared humour.

An answering smile crinkled the corners of his mouth and momentarily lightened the passion that had darkened his eyes as he teased back, 'Who's Sir Roy Strong?'

Their laughter immediately banished whatever small feeling of self-consciousness Verity felt she might otherwise have had and very soon her fingers were equally busy as Silas', if not perhaps quite as patient, as she tugged at the buttons of his shirt and then closed her eyes in mute pleasure when she had finally revealed the tanned male expanse of his chest.

Lovingly she buried her face against him, closing her eyes and breathing in his scent before delicately licking at the small indentation in the middle of his chest, discovering the faintly salty male taste that was exclusively his.

'Verity,' Silas groaned.

'I want to,' Verity protested. 'I want to know every bit of you, Silas. I want to hold you, touch you, taste you. I want…'

'You don't know what you're saying,' Silas warned her.

But gravely and seriously and suddenly completely adult and mature, suddenly totally sensually a woman, Verity told him quietly, 'Oh, yes, I do. I want you, Silas,' she told him, lifting one of his hands and placing it first against her heart and then against her sex, saying, 'Here,' and 'here,' and then finally lifting his hand to her temple and repeating softly, 'and here.'

'With all my heart I thee love,' Silas whispered back, taking hold of her hand and pressing a kiss into the palm before placing it against his chest. 'With my body I thee worship.'

Watching her eyes, he placed her hand intimately on his own body. Verity drew in a quick sharp breath of feminine appreciation and urgency, the pulse in her wrist thudding every bit as fiercely as the pulse she could feel throbbing through the urgent shaft of male flesh she was touching. Instinctively her fingers closed over him, delicately learning and knowing him, whilst Silas continued in a thickly changed voice, lifting not the hand that was holding his sex with such feminine tenderness and love, but her other to his own forehead. 'With my mind I thee honour, with everything that is me I commit myself to you now, Verity. Nothing ever can and ever will break the bond we are forming between us tonight. Nothing...'

'Nothing...' Verity repeated softly, and beneath her fingertips she could feel the hot, hard shaft of his sex harden even further and begin to pulse in ever fiercer demand.

The first time he entered her Verity cried out, not in pain but in exultation, clinging passionately to him, welcoming him within her with a heart full of love and joy, her emotions so charged and heightened that the feel of him within her, the knowledge of the intimacy, the love they were sharing, the bond they were creating, brought quick, emotional tears to her eyes.

Seeing them, Silas immediately cursed himself under his breath and started to withdraw from her, believing that he had hurt her. Quickly Verity reassured him, explaining in a choked voice that it was the pleasure of having him within her that had caused them, and not the pain.

Later he told her that what they had shared was just the beginning of the pleasure he intended to give her, the special sensual intimacy they would share.

'*You* are my *special* garden, Verity,' he told her as he lovingly caressed her warmly naked body. 'My most private, secret garden where what flowers between us is special and magical and for us alone.'

'And which, one day, hopefully will bear fruit,' Verity continued, picking up on his theme as she blissfully ran her fingertips down his spine, revelling in her right to touch him and to be with him. 'But not for a long time yet,' she added drowsily. 'And I don't suppose that Uncle Toby will want me to have more than the most basic maternity leave…'

'Maternity leave?' Silas checked her, his body suddenly tensing as he started to frown. 'I know you've said that your uncle expects you to work in the business once you've finished university, but surely what's happened between us changes that? I'm not so sexist that I'd want to prevent you from working if that's what you want, but…'

'It isn't a matter of what *I* want, Silas,' Verity told him slowly. 'My uncle *expects* me to work alongside him in the business and then to take over from him. It means *everything* to him…'

'More than *you* or *your* happiness,' Silas challenged her. 'Or are you trying to tell me that it and he mean more to you than me and our children…?'

'No, of course not...but I owe him so much and he...'

'More than you owe our love?' Silas demanded.

They were on the verge of quarrelling and Verity's eyes filled with hot, hurt tears. Couldn't Silas understand how *difficult* things were for her? Of course she wanted to be with him. How could she not do?

'Please, don't let's spoil things by fighting,' she begged him. Although she sensed that he wanted to continue their discussion, instead he gave a small sigh and said, 'No, you're right. This isn't the time...nor the place...'

'Make love to me again, Silas,' she urged him, and it wasn't until many, many months later that she was mature enough to recognise how dangerously she had begun the habit then—a way of avoiding the issue and sidelining it, and Silas, by distracting his attention away from the future through lovemaking. In fact, it wasn't until Silas himself accused her of it that she was forced to recognise just what she was doing and by then...

'I'll love you for ever. You're everything I've ever wanted, everything I *will* ever want,' Silas promised her the following morning as they lay entwined with one another in bed, her body still sleek and damp from the passion of their recent lovemaking.

Only it hadn't been a promise which he had kept. It had been a promise he had broken, just as he had broken her heart and almost broken her.

CHAPTER FOUR

HER first impression that the town hadn't changed had been an erroneous one, Verity acknowledged as she dumped the supermarket carrier bags on the kitchen table.

She had spent the afternoon exploring her old environment before calling in at an out-of-town supermarket to fill her car with petrol and buy some food.

The layout of the town centre might essentially be the same but many of the small shops she remembered from her girlhood had gone, to be replaced with what she privately considered to be an over-representation of building society and estate agents offices. The pedestrianisation of the town centre itself, though, she had to admit, was an improvement, and she had particularly liked the way shady trees had been planted and huge tubs of brightly coloured tumbling summer bedding plants grouped artistically around them. Along with the strategically placed benches, they had created a relaxed, informal, almost continental air to the town centre, which today had been heightened by the fact that the warm summer weather had meant that people had been able to eat outside the square's several restaurants and cafés under the umbrellas decorating the tables and chairs on the pavement. It had been disconcerting, though, to read from a small plaque that the square had been re-designed by Silas as a gift to the town.

If the town centre itself had looked disconcertingly unfamiliar, then so had the faces of the people she had seen around her. She had never made any really close friends during her school-days. The regime imposed by her uncle had prevented that, but there had been girls whose company she could have enjoyed.

Tonight she would ring Charlotte, she promised herself as she started to unpack her provisions. It would be good to hear a friendly voice. She didn't want to think about the consequences of the fact that one of the few adult voices she had heard since her return had been that of her ex-lover and that it had been far from friendly.

A 'friend' had told him about the accident, he had told her tersely. What exactly did *that* mean? The term 'friend' applied to a member of the opposite sex could cover so many possibilities. Anyway, why should *she* care who or what this woman was to Silas?

Removing the jacket of the Gucci trouser suit she was wearing, she opened the fridge door.

Wearing Gucci to do the supermarket shopping was perhaps a trifle over the top, especially outside Knightsbridge, and even more especially when the suit in question was white and had featured extremely prominently in all the glossies early on in the season, but having given into Charlotte's pleas and bought the dratted thing she could hardly leave it hanging in her wardrobe... Even so... She had fully registered the several double takes she had received from other shoppers, women clad in the main in the busy suburban women's uniform of immaculate neat jeans, white shirt and navy blazer.

She supposed her hair didn't help either, she acknowledged, flipping it back over her shoulder, then taking a clip from her pocket and pinning it up. She had worn it long ever since she could remember. As a teenager she had wanted to have it cut but for once her uncle and Silas had been unanimous in their veto—albeit for very different reasons. Her uncle had always insisted that her hair was neatly tucked into an old-fashioned bun—the kind he remembered his mother wearing—whilst Silas... Silas had whispered to her that first night they had shared together that he had fantasised about taking her hair and wrapping it around his body, feeling its supple silkiness caressing his skin.

She had made that fantasy come true for him, even if she had blushed a little to do so that very first time.

In the years that had passed since then, she had still not had her hair cut—trimmed occasionally, yes, but cut, never—and, until she had sold the company, in obedience to her uncle's wishes she had always worn it rolled into an elegant knot.

She had lost count of the times Charlotte had tried to persuade her to wear it down.

'I'm too old for long, loose hair,' she had protested determinedly.

'Are you crazy?' Charlotte had argued back, adding, 'Have you seen the latest round of jeans ads—the one featuring the back view of a woman with hair down to her waist? She's seventy and she's making one hell of a positive statement about the way women have the right to view ourselves, besides which she looks absolutely stunning. If I had hair like yours—thick, wavy—there's no way you'd ever get me to hide it away.'

'In business, big business, men view long hair on a woman as a sign of weakness. It's probably some kind of Narcissus complex,' Verity had remarked wryly. 'They see long hair and immediately they think, Ah ha...gotcha...she's going to be spending more time in front of the mirror than in front of any sales figures, and then they start rubbing their hands together in glee because they think they're going to put one over on you.'

'Oh, yeah. Let me tell you something, lady,' Charlotte had corrected her after she had finished laughing. 'The reason they're rubbing their hands together in glee is because they're thinking, Wow, that's some woman, *I* want to take her to bed...'

'In other words to them long hair equals bimbo, victim...weakness.'

'Why do I get the distinct impression that somewhere, some time, some man has hurt you very badly?' Charlotte had asked intuitively. But Verity had simply shaken her head. The past, her past, was simply something she was not prepared to talk about—not even to her closest friend.

One thing Verity had noticed, though, when she had been out, and it was something that had caught painfully at her unguarded, vulnerable emotions, had been the number of couples shopping together—and not all of them young. Seeing the loving, tenderly amused looks one couple had exchanged, as the man had reached up to a higher shelf for something the woman had wanted and she had surreptitiously stroked his thigh whilst he did so, had made Verity look away in hot-cheeked sharp awareness of the emotional emptiness of her own life. It didn't have to be that way. Once she had had time to think, to assess and to plan; once she became fully involved in the charities she intended to set up with her uncle's money, then there would be no time for painful regrets about what might have been.

It was seeing Silas that had unsettled her so distressingly, she told herself angrily. Seeing him and listening to him making those outrageous accusations against her.

She stiffened as she heard the doorbell ring. There was no reason for her to think that it might be Silas, of course, but just in case... Forcing her face to assume the expression she normally reserved for the boardroom—the one that said 'Don't even *think* about trying to mess with me'—she headed determinedly for the front door and yanked it open.

'Honor,' she squeaked in startled surprise. 'What on earth are you doing here?'

'I got my pocket money today and I've come to pay the first instalment of the money I owe you for the damage to your car,' Honor told her sturdily, adding before Verity could say anything, 'May I come in? It's so hot...'

'Yes. Of course. Let me get you a cold drink,' Verity offered, leading the way to the kitchen. 'Did you walk here?'

'Mmm...' Honor mumbled as she took a deep gulp of the iced orange juice Verity had poured for her.

'Mmm...real juice!' Honor exclaimed blissfully. 'Wonderful, but it's very expensive,' she told Verity sternly. 'Dad won't buy it—he says I waste it because I never finish it and it's too expensive. He buys it when Myra comes round, though.' She pulled a face.

'Apparently she likes it for breakfast—not that she's ever stayed overnight. She'd like to, though. She thinks I don't know what her game is but I do—a woman always knows,' she concluded wisely. 'She wants to get married again and she wants to marry Dad. He'd be mad if he did—she's poison.' Honor pulled an expressive face. 'She didn't even like the new clothes I made him buy, and I know why—she doesn't want any other woman looking at him.'

Honor had chosen Silas' designer clothes! But Verity didn't have time to digest this information properly before Honor was continuing, 'I've tried to warn him but Dad just can't see it... I suppose he can't see the truth beneath all that make-up she wears. She hates kids as well. That's why she left her first husband. I know... But Dad thinks it's because he wouldn't let her get pregnant...'

Verity gave her a wary look.

'Oh, it's okay, Dad didn't tell me that. He's a great father, the best, but we don't have that kind of relationship. He's pretty much for keeping what he thinks of grown-up things to himself, but I'm not a kid...and I've got my ear to the ground. She's just not good enough for him.'

'How old are you exactly, Honor?' Verity asked her faintly, automatically refilling the now empty glass Honor had extended.

'Ten...' Honor told her promptly.

Ten going on ninety, Verity decided. Did Silas have any inkling of how his daughter felt about her prospective stepmother? she wondered. At least she now knew exactly what the word 'friend' meant when applied to Silas' relationship with his tell-tale girlfriend.

'I'm starving,' Honor told her winningly, 'and Dad's gone out for dinner tonight. I don't suppose...?'

Her aplomb really was extraordinary for someone so young, and perhaps Verity ought to very firmly remind her of the age gap that lay between them and the inadvisability of inviting herself into other people's lives—but she *liked* her, Verity acknowledged, and even if it *was* a weakness within herself she simply couldn't bring herself to dent that luminous youthful pride by pointing out such facts to her.

'I'm afraid I *can't* offer you anything to eat,' she replied gravely instead, intending to tell Honor that she rather thought that her father would disapprove of them having any kind of contact with one another—and not just because *he* obviously considered that she had more or less callously practically run Honor down, thanks to the evidence of his 'girlfriend'. She amended her private thoughts to say gently instead, 'I was planning to eat out.'

'Oh, good.' Honor grinned, telling her frankly, 'I hate cooking too.'

Verity blinked.

'Honor, I *don't* hate cooking,' she protested. 'It's just...'

'There's a terrific Italian place just opened up in town. Italian's my favourite, I love their ice cream puddings,' Honor volunteered.

Totally against her better judgement, Verity knew that she was weakening.

'Mmm...' she agreed. 'I like Italian too...'

Woman to woman they looked at one another.

'You're right,' Verity heard herself saying, a little

to her own bemusement. 'Why cook at home when you can eat Italian somewhere else?'

What was she thinking? What was she *doing*? Verity asked herself grimly ten minutes later when she had parked the car in the town centre car park. There would be hell to pay if Silas ever found out, she acknowledged fatalistically, frowning a little as she waited for Honor to get out of the car before activating the central-locking system.

That wasn't by any chance *why* she was doing this, was it? To get at Silas? She was way, way above those kind of childish tit-for-tat manoeuvres, wasn't she? Wasn't she…?

'It's this way,' Honor told her, happily linking her arm through Verity's.

'You should wear your hair down,' she advised Verity seriously as she checked their reflections in a shop window. 'Men like it.'

'Uh-huh…er…do they?'

Heavens, what was wrong with her? *She* shouldn't be the one acting flustered and self-conscious, Verity derided herself.

'The purpose, the point, of being a woman is not to please men or to seek their approval,' she told Honor sternly.

'No, but it sure helps when you want your own way,' Honor told her practically.

Verity gave her an old-fashioned look. 'Your father came to see me,' she told Honor quietly. 'His…friend…Myra…saw the accident and told him about it.'

Honor grimaced. 'Yes, I know. He hasn't grounded me, though, but he was pretty angry about it. He just got angry, though, because he feels guilty that he can't be there all the time for me,' Honor told her with a maturity that caught at Verity's sensitive heart. 'He worries about me—I worry too,' Honor admitted unexpectedly, showing heart-rending vulnerability as she confided reluctantly, 'It isn't much fun—not having a mother. It hurts a lot sometimes.'

'I know,' Verity agreed quietly.

For a moment they looked at one another and then Honor told her quickly, 'Look, the restaurant's here,' directing Verity's attention to the building in front of them. 'Don't let them give us a bad table just because we're two women eating alone without a man,' Honor hissed to Verity as they walked inside.

'Two *what...*?' Verity started to question, but the *maître d'* was already approaching them and, mindful not only of Honor's stern admonition but also of the fact that as a potential mentor—not to mention role model—to the young girl, it behoved her to set a good example, she looked him firmly in the eye and said, 'We'd like a table for two, please. That one over there,' she added, pointing to what was obviously their 'best' table.

Without batting an eyelid the *maître d'* swept them both a small bow and agreed, 'Very well, Madam, if you would just follow me.'

'That was good,' Honor acknowledged gleefully when they had been seated.

'No,' Verity corrected her wryly with a grin, '*that* was Gucci,' she told her flicking her fingertips over her suit. 'It isn't *just* long hair that men are susceptible to, you know,' she pointed out drolly, before picking up her menu.

'Ready to order?' she asked Honor several minutes later.

'Mmm...' the young girl agreed.

Raising her hand discreetly, Verity summoned the *maître d'*, waiting until Honor had given him her order before giving her own.

'Oh, and I'd like a glass of the house red as well,' Honor included decidedly.

The *maître d'* was visibly and seriously impressed, as well he might be, Verity acknowledged as, considerably less so, *she* gave Honor a thoughtful look.

'Er...with water,' Honor amended hastily, obviously sensing the veto that was about to leave Verity's lips.

'It's okay,' she told Verity defensively when the waiter had gone. 'Dad lets me—he says it's important for me to grow up learning how to handle alcohol. He says it makes for less mistakes later.'

'Dad said that you used to live here, in town,' Honor commented to Verity once they were eating their starter.

'Er, yes. Yes, I did,' Verity agreed.

'Did you know him then?' Honor asked her.

Verity paused, the forkful of food she had been lifting towards her mouth suddenly unappetising for all its rich, delicious smell.

'Er...no, I don't think so,' she prevaricated. How much had Silas told his daughter? Not the truth. How could he?

'Did you know my mother?' Honor asked her, startling Verity with the unexpectedness of the question.

'No. No, I didn't,' she told her truthfully. Poor child, and she *was* a child still, for all her quaintly grown-up ways and determined independence, Verity recognised. It couldn't be easy for her, growing up without any real personal knowledge of the woman who had given birth to her.

'She and Dad met when he was staying in London,' Honor told her pragmatically, 'so I didn't think you would. I don't look very much like her.'

'No, you look like your father,' Verity agreed, her heart suddenly jolting against her ribs as the restaurant door opened and the subject of their conversation walked in, accompanied by a woman whom Verity didn't recognise but who she guessed must be his 'friend' Myra.

'What is it?' Honor asked her innocently.

'Your father's just walked in,' Verity told her warningly, but to her surprise, instead of reacting as she had expected, the little girl simply dimpled a wide smile that caused sharp alarm bells to ring in Verity's brain.

'You *knew* he was coming here,' she breathed.

'It's the "in" place to be seen, but Myra won't be very pleased that *we've* got the best table,' Honor told her sunnily.

No, she certainly wasn't, Verity acknowledged, quickly assessing the other woman's angry-mouthed expression, and, what was more, Verity suspected that it wasn't simply the fact that the best table wasn't free that was angering her. *Their* presence—full stop—Verity rather guessed had a very definite something to do with the other woman's ire.

In any other circumstances the sternly condemnatory look Silas was sending her would probably have had her scuttling for the exit, Verity reflected ruefully, but she could hardly leave Honor to face her father's wrath alone, even if perhaps she did semi-deserve it.

Silas was heading for their table, having bent his head to say something first to his girlfriend, who was now standing glaring viciously, not so much at her as at Honor, Verity recognised with a strong surge of protection towards the young girl.

'Mmm, this is yummy... Hi, Dad,' Honor acknowledged her father, turning her head to give him a wide beam.

'Would you like to explain to me what the *hell* you think you're doing?' Silas asked Verity in a dangerously quiet voice, totally ignoring his daughter's sunny greeting.

'Riccardo gave us the best table, Dad,' Honor chattered on, apparently oblivious to both Verity's tension and her father's fury. 'Verity said it was because of her suit. It's Gucci, you know, but I think it was probably because Riccardo fancied her. He likes strawberry blondes,' she added warmly to Verity. 'That's probably why he never gives Myra a good table,' she told her father, whilst Verity closed her eyes and sent up a mental prayer, not just for her own safe deliverance from Silas' very evident ire, but Honor's as well. 'He doesn't like brunettes... Dad...' She paused judiciously before refilling her fork '...do you suppose Myra dyes her hair? *I* think she must because it's such a very hard shade of dark brown. What do you think, Verity?'

Verity gulped and shook her head, totally incapable of making any kind of logical response. She was torn between giving way to the fit of extremely inappropriate giggles of feminine appreciation of Honor's masterly undermining of a woman whom Verity could see quite plainly she considered to be a rival for her father's attention, and a rather more adult awareness of the danger of her own situation and just how little Silas would relish the fact that *she* was the one to witness his daughter's artful stratagems.

'What are you doing here, Honor?' Silas turned to his daughter to ask with awful calmness.

'I...I...er...invited her to have dinner with me,' Verity began, immediately rushing to the little girl's defence, but Honor, it transpired, didn't need any defending—rather she seemed positively to enjoy courting her father's fury, looking him straight in the eye.

'I invited Verity to have dinner with me,' she told her father challengingly. 'It was the least I could do after—'

'The least *you* could do?' Shaking his head, he turned from Honor to Verity and told her acidly, 'First you damn near kill my daughter with your dangerous driving and then you, God alone knows by what means, persuade her to have dinner with you. What were you intending to do? Trick her into changing her story just in case I *did* decide to report you to the police? You run her down and then—'

'No, Dad... It wasn't like that...' Honor pushed away her plate and looked quickly from Verity's white face to her father's. 'I... It wasn't Verity's fault... I...' She swallowed and then continued bravely, 'It was mine...'

'Yours? But Myra said—'

'It happened exactly how you'd warned me it would,' Honor ploughed on doggedly. 'I did just what you told me not to do. I was on my blades and I didn't think to stop or look and then I lost control and—'

'Is this true?' Silas asked Verity coldly.

For a moment Verity was tempted to lie and take the blame, but before she could do so Honor was speaking again, reaching out to touch her father's arm.

'Yes. It is true, Dad,' she told him quietly. 'I...I'm sorry... Please don't be mad. I...I went to see Verity because I want to pay for the damage to her car out of my spending money. It was my idea for us to come out for dinner...'

'Honor. You *know* the rules. What on earth...? You were *supposed* to be going straight to Catherine's from school and staying there tonight.'

'I know that, Dad, but today Catherine said that her aunt and uncle were coming to stay and I knew it was going to be a family sort of thing... I didn't want...' She hung her head before saying gruffly, 'I just wouldn't have felt right being there.'

As she listened to her, Verity's heart went out to her. Underneath her amazingly streetwise exterior she was still, after all, a very vulnerable little girl at heart. A little girl who had never known the love of her mother; a little girl who quite plainly and understandably was jealously protective of her own place in her father's life, to the extent that she quite obviously did not like the woman who she had told Verity was angling to become her father's second wife.

'I think perhaps we should go, Honor,' Verity intervened, gently touching the little girl's arm, summoning the quiet strength of will she had often been forced to use in her boardroom battles. It had never been Verity's style to assume the manner of a 'man'—there *were* other ways of making one's point and any man, anyone, who thought that she could be bullied or pushed around just because she didn't hector or argue very quickly discovered just how wrong they had been.

'I haven't had my pudding,' Honor reminded her stoutly, but Verity could see that she was glad of her protective intervention.

'I've got some fruit and ice cream,' she told her, before turning to Silas and looking him straight in the eye as she said, 'You're quite right, I *should* have checked with you before bringing Honor out—that was *my* mistake. Yours...' She paused and reminded herself that with Honor as an interested audience, never mind the *maître d'* and the now very obviously fuming Myra, this was not the time nor the place to point out where *he* had gone wrong or what his misjudgement had been.

'I'm quite prepared to drive Honor round to her friend's, but I wonder if she might be permitted to finish her supper with me?'

'Oh, yes, Dad. And then you could pick me up from Verity's on the way home,' Honor interrupted her eagerly. 'I'd much rather do that than go to Catherine's.'

'If your pudding is ordered, then I'll ask the *maître d'* to bring another chair and you can stay with Myra and me. I take it *you've* finished your meal,' Silas demanded of Verity coldly.

'No. She hasn't... She hasn't had *her* pudding,' Honor told him indignantly, adding, 'Besides, I don't *want* to be with you and Myra, you know she doesn't like me...'

'Honor,' Silas began warningly, twin bands of anger beginning to burn high on his cheek-bones, although, as Verity could see, she herself was more alarmed by his fury than Honor.

'Look, *what's* going on? When are we going to eat?'

All three of them looked up as Myra finally grew tired of waiting on the sidelines and came to join battle.

'I'm sorry,' Silas apologised, giving her a warm smile. But Myra wasn't looking at him. Instead, her eyes were flashing warning signs in Verity's direction, narrowing angrily as she studied Verity's suit.

'I was just explaining to Honor that she could finish her meal with us,' Silas told Myra.

'What? But you're coming back with me so that I can show you that video I've got of my cousin's wedding...' Myra protested, darting a fulminating look at Honor.

'If I stay with you, can I have cappuccino to finish with?' Honor asked Silas.

'Er...' Silas was looking uncertainly from his daughter's face to his girlfriend's. In any other circumstances and with any other man, Verity knew she would have felt quite sympathetic towards him. As it was, tucking down the corners of her mouth so that no one could see the smile curling there, she caught Honor's attention.

'Remember the Bible story of Solomon?' she asked the little girl *sotto voce*.

'Solomon?' Honor whispered back whilst Silas and Myra removed themselves slightly from the table to engage in what looked like a very heated conversation. 'Oh, you mean the one where the two women both claimed the baby and Solomon threatened to cut it in two and let them have half each?' Honor asked her.

'That's the one,' Verity agreed dulcetly. Honor frowned and then suddenly burst out laughing as she saw Verity glance over towards Silas.

'Oh, but Dad isn't a baby,' she protested.

'No, but he *is* your father and sometimes loving someone means letting them make their own decisions,' Verity told her gently.

'But she's not right for him,' Honor protested, and then shrugged her shoulders. 'Okay.'

'Dad...'

'Honor...'

Verity waited as they both started to speak and then both stopped.

'If you're sure you don't mind giving Honor supper and keeping her with you until I can collect her,' Silas told Verity distantly.

'*I* don't mind at all,' Verity responded truthfully, adding as she smiled at Honor, 'In fact, it will be a pleasure.'

'Goodie... There goes Myra's plan for showing my father the tempting prospect of getting married via her cousin's wedding video,' Honor exulted several minutes later as she and Verity exited the restaurant, Honor clutching a huge double portion of rich ice cream that the now-besotted *maître d'* had insisted on giving her complete with a bowl of ice to keep it chilled until they got home.

'I shouldn't be too sure about that,' Verity warned her. 'Myra looks one very determined lady to me...'

'Determined she might be, but Dad is catastrophically old-fashioned about me going to bed early on school nights. There's no way he's going to be able to go home with Myra tonight.'

Verity stopped walking and swung round to glance incredulously at Honor.

'Did you deliberately plan all of this?' she asked her bluntly.

Honor's face assumed a hurt expression.

'Me... I'm ten years old,' she reminded Verity.

'Yeah...but somehow you seem so much older,' Verity responded feelingly.

As they walked in amicable female companionship towards Verity's parked car, Honor allowed herself to relax.

Part one of her plan was working. What would Verity say, she wondered, if she told her that she had recognised her straight away on the day of the accident from a photograph of her she had found in her father's desk? Her father needed rescuing from Myra and it was high time, Honor had already decided, that she had a mother—one of her own choosing!

She looked sideways at Verity—why had she fibbed about not knowing her father? She was tempted to ask but she decided it might be best not to rush things so much...not yet. Honestly, grown-ups, they were so slow... But it was just as she and her friend Catherine had said earlier this afternoon when she had jubilantly told her all about Verity. Sometimes grown-ups didn't know where their own best interests lay, so it was just as well that she, Honor, was here to show them.

What she needed to do now was to keep her father and Myra apart, but if her plans worked out as she knew they would that shouldn't prove too difficult—Catherine had her instructions!

Verity gave her a surprised look as Honor suddenly slipped a small, slightly grubby hand into her own and beamed a huge smile up at her.

'It's no good trying to get round me like that,' Verity warned her severely, adding untruthfully, 'and, besides, I can't make cappuccino...'

'No, but I bet Myra can,' Honor told her. 'She was *really* frothing at the mouth, wasn't she?' she observed dispassionately.

'Honor...' Verity warned, and then spoiled it by suddenly giving way to an uncontrollable fit of the giggles.

'Verity...just a moment, please...'

Verity's body tensed in shock as she heard Silas calling out curtly from behind her. She had already unlocked the car for Honor to get inside it and now, as she too saw her father, Honor opened the door.

Silas shook his head and told her crisply, 'You stay where you are, please, Honor. I want to have a few words with Verity...in private!'

Verity wasn't sure which of them looked the more wary—herself or Honor. What she *was* sure of, though, was that she could feel her skin turning a very definite shade of mollified pink as Honor, after one look at her father's stern 'I mean business' expression, quietly closed the passenger door of Verity's car.

Equally reprehensibly feebly, Verity discovered that she herself was moving several yards away from her car, mirroring the way that Silas was moving out of Honor's potential earshot. Just to make sure that Silas knew and understood that, unlike his daughter, *she* was not someone he could talk down to or tell what to do, before he could tell her whatever it was that had brought him hotfoot out of the restaurant and away from Myra's side, Verity demanded coldly, 'Please be quick, Silas, I still haven't eaten my pudding.'

'Ice cream?' His mouth took on a mocking twist. 'As *I* remember it you were always more of a cheese and biscuits woman and—'

Immediately Verity's eyes flashed. How dared he remind her of the intimacy they had once shared; of everything they had once been to one another, now when he...?

'Is *that* why you came running after us—to remind me because *I* opted for ice cream over cheese and biscuits? *My* tastes have changed, Silas...just like yours...'

But sharp though her words were, for some unaccountable reason, as she said them, Verity discovered that she was looking at his mouth and remembering...

A shudder of self-contempt shook her as she acknowledged just *what* she was remembering, her eyes darkening as she did so.

Did Silas remember that ice cream they had shared so long ago, and, if he did, did he remember too the way he had teased her by offering her the last mouthful of it and then, when she had taken it, kissing her through the icy-cold taste, his lips, his mouth, his tongue, so velvet-hot and sensuous against her lips, and then when the ice cream had melted his kiss becoming so passionate that *it* had practically melted *her*?

Her face on fire, Verity made to take a step back

from him, but to her consternation Silas immediately reached out to stop her, his hand grasping her upper arm in a grip she knew it would be impossible for her to break.

'Verity,' he began, his voice unexpectedly thick and husky as though...

Quickly Verity cast a lash-veiled look at him. Surely his own colour was slightly higher than it should have been?

Because he was angry? It certainly couldn't be because he was aroused, could it?

Unexpectedly he gave his head a small shake, as though trying to dispel some unwanted thought, and when he spoke again his voice was much crisper.

'Honor is ten years old...a child... I don't want her getting hurt...' he began warningly.

Immediately Verity took umbrage. How dared he suggest that *she* might hurt Honor?

'If you're implying that I might hurt her,' she told him furiously, 'then you're wrong. In fact, if you believe that Honor *is* being hurt I should look far closer to home for the source if I were you.'

There was a moment's shocked pause before he demanded in disbelief, 'Are you trying to say that *I* might hurt her...?'

Taking advantage of his momentary lapse in concentration, Verity pulled herself free of his grip and started to turn towards the car.

'Verity, I haven't finished—' she heard him saying furiously to her, but Verity had had enough—more than enough if the way her body, her senses, were still responding to the memory of that shared ice cream so long ago was anything to go by.

'Oh, but I think you have,' she corrected him through gritted teeth and then stopped abruptly, shocked to discover that for some reason all his attention seemed to be focused on her mouth. Instinctively she raised protective fingers to her lips, her whole body starting to tremble.

'Verity...' she heard him saying roughly, but she shook her head, unable to listen to whatever it was he wanted to say, whatever further contemptuous criticism he wanted to hurl at her unprotected heart.

'Go away, Silas,' she demanded shakily. 'Go back to Myra...'

And without waiting to see his reaction she hurried quickly towards her car and opened the door.

'What did Dad want?' Honor asked uncertainly several minutes later, once Verity had negotiated their way out of the car park.

'Er...he wanted to tell me that you weren't to have too much ice cream,' Verity fibbed, making up the first excuse she could think of.

'Not much chance of that. By the time we get back it will all be melted...gone...' Honor told her in disgust.

Gone...like their love... Verity bit down hard on her bottom lip. Ice cream and Silas' kisses. Funny how sharply painful the sweetest things could sometimes become!

CHAPTER FIVE

'It's gone ten o'clock,' Verity told Honor worriedly. 'I thought your father would have been here by now—you said he wouldn't want you to be out late.'

'Mmm... I know.'

Honor seemed far less perturbed about her father's absence than she was, Verity noticed, which surprised her. She would have thought that, given Honor's obvious dislike of Myra, she would have become at least a little anxious about the fact that Silas was quite obviously lingering with the woman rather longer than Honor had originally intimated.

Perhaps Myra had prevailed on him to take her home after all, and, once there, no doubt she had insisted that he remain for a nightcap and of course, whilst he was drinking it, she had no doubt put on the video. 'Just so that he could see a few minutes of it.' And then, of course, it would be a small step—a *very* small step for her kind of woman—from that to turning down the lights and refilling Silas' glass, insisting that there was no need for him to rush and that surely Honor could miss a morning of school for once...

Verity could virtually hear the enticing personal arguments she would purr into his ear as she slipped onto the sofa beside him and placed her hand on his jacket, supposedly to remove a bit of non-existent fluff, before sliding it up onto his shoulder and then caressing the back of his neck where his hair curled thick and dark. Verity closed her eyes. She could remember so clearly just how that felt—how *she* had felt, how just the intimacy simply of touching him like that had made her go weak at the knees, all melting, yielding, wanting womanhood.

'Verity, are you all right?'

'What…? Er…' guiltily Verity opened her eyes '…er, yes…' she fibbed, hot-cheeked, hurriedly getting up so that she could avoid meeting the innocence of Honor's eyes.

'Perhaps we should ring the restaurant,' she began hurriedly. 'I—'

'No… No… I don't think that would be a good idea,' Honor instantly denied. 'I mean, Dad was so angry, wasn't he? And…' But despite what she had said Verity couldn't help noticing that Honor herself did keep looking at the silent telephone.

'Perhaps he's been delayed…a flat tyre or something like that,' she offered comfortingly.

'How long is your hair?' Honor asked, moving their conversation away from her father's late arrival.

'Er…'

'Take it down now,' Honor urged her, reaching out to tweak some of the constraining pins from Verity's hair before she could stop her.

Suspecting that the little girl was more disturbed by her father's non-appearance than she wanted to admit, Verity gave in.

'Oh, it's lovely,' Honor told her in open and honest admiration when all the pins were finally removed and Verity had quickly pulled the small brush she kept in her handbag through her soft curls.

'It's getting too long. I should really have it cut,' Verity said ruefully.

'Oh, no, you mustn't,' Honor told her, gently stroking her fingers through it.

Verity felt her heart jerk and then almost stop. Once, a long time ago, a *lifetime* ago it seemed now, Silas had touched her hair just like that and spoken similar words to her.

'No, don't ever have it cut,' he had whispered to her. 'I love it so much—I love *you* so much.'

Instinctively she closed her eyes.

'What's the matter? You look awfully sad,' Honor told her.

There was a huge lump in Verity's throat.

'I—' she began, and then stopped as the phone suddenly rang. Honor reached it first but, a little to Verity's surprise, she waited for her to pick up the receiver.

'Verity?'

There was no mistaking the crisp tones of Silas' voice.

'Yes. Yes, Silas...'

'Look, I can't talk now. There's been an emergency. I'm at the garden centre. The police called me out. Someone reported seeing intruders trying to break in. So far we haven't found any signs of anyone but it looks as though I could be tied up here for some time. Honor...'

'Honor's fine with me, unless you want me to take her to her friend's,' Verity assured him as calmly as she could. Why was her heart beating so frantically fast, her pulse racing, her mouth dry, her whole body reacting to the sound of his voice as if... as though...?

'No. It's probably best if she stays with you. I don't know what time I'm going to be through here...'

'Don't worry,' Verity assured him. 'She'll be fine here with me. Would you like to speak with her?'

Without waiting for his response, she handed the receiver over to Honor, before walking over to the window and putting her hands to her suddenly hot face.

What on *earth* was the matter with her? She was reacting like...like a woman in love... A deep shudder ran through her. Impossible. No. No way. Not again. Not a second time.

'Not a second time what?' Honor asked her curiously.

Wide-eyed, Verity turned round and looked at her. She hadn't heard Honor replace the telephone receiver, never mind realised that she had spoken out loud.

'Er...nothing... Look, it could be some time before your father gets here. If you want to go to bed...'

'No. Well, yes, perhaps that might be a good idea,' Honor allowed. 'I haven't got anything to wear, though,' she reminded Verity.

'That's okay, you can sleep in your undies for tonight,' Verity told her practically.

'I don't very much like the dark,' Honor said as they walked upstairs. 'Will you...will you stay with me until I go to sleep?'

Once again Verity was reminded of the fact that Honor was only a very young girl—a motherless young girl—and Verity herself knew what that meant and all about the private desperate tears cried into one's pillow at night. Tears for the love and want of a mother's arms—a mother's care. Honor had her pride, Verity could see, but she could see as well that she also had her vulnerability, her need to be reassured, her need to be mothered.

'Yes, of course I will,' Verity agreed warmly, giving her hand a small squeeze.

'I'm not very keen on the dark myself,' she added.

In the end it was another hour before Honor was finally in bed—Verity's bed, since it was the only one that was made up and since Honor had announced that she liked Verity's room best of all. 'Because it smells of you,' she had so engagingly told Verity.

Who could resist that kind of persuasion? And, for the second time, Verity had been all too intimately reminded of hearing Honor's father make just such a similar comment, although in a vastly different context—a context far too intimate and personal to *even* allow herself to think about in the presence of anyone else, never mind Silas' young daughter.

'Why not? Why don't you want me to?' he had asked her thickly when she had tried to push him away the first time he had bent his head towards the most intimate part of her body.

'Because...because...' Awkwardly she had struggled to explain how both shocked and excited she had felt at the thought of being caressed so, so personally by him, of having his lips, his mouth, kiss the most delicate and sensitive part of her body.

'It just doesn't seem right,' she had told him shakily in the end. 'I mean, it's...' Pleadingly she had lifted her gaze to his. 'Silas, I don't...it's...'

'It's just another way of showing you how much I

love you,' Silas had told her gently. 'If you don't want me to then I won't, but I want to enjoy the scent and taste of you—the real you—so much, Verity. I know what you're thinking...how you're feeling...but I promise you that it will be all right.'

'It seems so... It makes me feel so...so nervous and afraid and so...excited at the same time,' she had confessed. 'All sort of squirmy and...and...'

'It makes me feel the same,' Silas had told her in a deep voice. 'Only even more so. Will you let me, Verity? I promise I'll stop if you want me to. It's just...' He had paused and looked deep into her eyes, making her heart thump against her chest wall in great shuddering thuds.

'I want to make you mine in every way there is. To know you so completely; to love you so completely.'

And when eventually he had lain her tenderly on the bed and bent his head over her body, when she had felt his tongue tip gently rimming the very centre of her sexual being, Verity hadn't wanted him to stop at all, not at all, not ever, as she had cried out frantically to him when the racking paroxysms of pleasure had seized hold of her, caught her up and dislodged from her mind any thought she might ever have had about not wanting the pleasure that Silas had been giving her, the intimacy...

'Verity...'

With a start Verity dragged her mind and her thoughts back to the present.

'It's a very big bed, isn't it?' Honor told her in a small voice. 'Do you always sleep in a big bed like this?'

'M...mostly,' Verity confirmed.

'It must feel very lonely. Haven't you ever wanted to get married, have children?' Honor asked her.

'It's after eleven o'clock,' Verity warned her, side-stepping the question, knowing that the only honest answer she could give her was no answer to give the ten-year-old daughter of the man whose wife she had hoped to be.

'Stay with me,' Honor whispered again, a small hand creeping out from beneath the bedclothes to hold onto Verity's.

Watching her ten minutes later as she lay next to her, Verity felt a tug of love on her heartstrings so strong that Honor's small hand might actually have been physically wrapped around them.

'Stop it,' she warned herself sternly. 'Don't you dare start daydreaming along those lines... Don't you dare!'

Very gingerly Verity eased her arm from beneath Honor's sleeping body. It ached slightly and had started to go a little numb. Disconcertingly, though, she discovered as she slid carefully off the bed, she actually missed the warm young weight of Honor's body.

The knowledge that she would probably never marry and have children of her own had been something she had pushed to the back of her mind in recent years. A child or children that she would have to bring up on her own had never been an option for her—her own childhood had given her extremely strong views about a child's need to feel secure and, to Verity, the kind of security *she* had craved so desperately as a child had come all neatly wrapped up with two parents.

In the early years after her breakup with Silas she'd had virtually only to see a young couple out with a small child to feel pierced with misery and envy.

Another woman, a different woman, might, on learning that the man she had loved, the man who had promised always to love her, had married someone else, have hardened her heart against her own emotions and made herself find someone else, built a new life for herself with a new man in it, but Verity had never been able to do that. For one thing the business had meant that she simply hadn't had the time to form new relationships and for another... For another, for a long time she had felt so hurt and betrayed, so convinced that Silas was the only man she could ever love, that she simply hadn't tried.

But there had still been that sense of loss, that small, sharp ache of envy for other young women who'd had what she hadn't: a man to love and their child.

But now she felt she was far too mature to give in to such feelings.

'What rubbish,' Charlotte had told her forthrightly recently when she had brought up the matter and Verity had said as much to her.

'For one thing you are not even in your late thirties, and for another, women in their early forties are giving birth to their first child nowadays. Neither can you start telling me that you can't spare the time and that the business is too demanding—you don't *have* the business any more.'

'I don't have a partner either,' Verity had felt bound to point out.

'That could easily be remedied,' Charlotte had told her firmly, 'and you know it!'

'Perhaps I'm simply not the maternal type.' Verity had shrugged, anxious to change the subject.

'Come off it,' Charlotte had scoffed. 'You know my two adore you.'

And she loved them, Verity acknowledged now as she tiptoed towards the bedroom door, but something about Honor had touched her heart and her emotions had really shaken her.

Because she was Silas' child?

If anything, surely that should make her resent and dislike her and not...? It was certainly plain that Myra did not feel in the least bit maternal towards her intended future stepdaughter. Was it Honor herself she didn't like, or did she perhaps simply resent the fact that she was the physical evidence that Silas had loved another woman? Myra certainly hadn't struck her as the emotionally insecure type.

As Verity opened the bedroom door, Honor moved in her sleep and muttered something. Holding her breath, Verity waited until she was sure she had settled down again and, leaving the bedroom door open and the landing light on, she went quickly downstairs.

It was gone twelve. How much longer would Silas be?

Her discarded suit jacket was lying on the chair where she had left it. Automatically she picked it up and folded it neatly, smoothing the soft fabric. Her uncle would have thoroughly disapproved of her buying something so impractical in white and in a delicately luxurious fabric. Clothes to him had simply been a necessary practicality. Verity could still remember how surprised and thrilled she had been when she and Silas had been walking through town one day and he had stopped her outside a boutique window and, indicating the dress inside, told her tenderly, 'That would suit you...'

The dress in question had been a silky halter-necked affair, backless, the fabric scattered with pretty feminine flowers, and it had also been a world away from the type of clothes she had normally worn: sturdy jeans, neatly pleated skirts, dully sensible clothes bought under the stern eye of her uncle's sixty-year-old Scottish housekeeper.

'Oh, Silas, it's lovely,' she had breathed, 'but it's far too...too pretty for me...'

'*Nothing* could ever be *too* pretty for you,' Silas had returned softly, adding huskily, 'Not pretty enough, maybe...'

'Oh, Silas...' she had whispered, blushing.

'Oh, Verity,' he had teased her back but, later in the week, when he had arrived with a present for her that had turned out to be the dress, the look in his eyes when he had persuaded her to model it for him had made her blush for a very, very different reason.

She had protested, of course, that he shouldn't have bought her something so personal nor so expensive.

'Why not?' he had countered. 'You're the woman I love, the woman I'm going to marry.'

She had been so young and naive then, assuming that he'd accepted that even as Silas' wife she'd owe it to her uncle to do as he wished and take her place in his business. She had known too, of course, that

Silas hadn't been happy about the silent but ostrich-like way she had convinced herself that it would all work out and had pushed it to the back of her mind. Silas would surely come to respect her point of view. They were young and in love—how could anything so mundane as duty come between them? She had been too dazed with love and happiness to guess that Silas might still see her role as his future wife in a far different light from that in which she did herself.

Through the sitting-room window Verity saw the headlights of a car coming up the drive. Silas! It had to be.

She opened the front door to him, putting her finger to her lips as she warned him, 'Honor's asleep.'

He looked tired, she recognised, deep lines etched either side of his mouth and tension very evident in the way he moved as he followed her into the house. For some inexplicable reason these indications of the fact that he was no longer a carefree young man in his twenties increased rather than detracted from his masculinity, Verity realised, her heartbeat quickening as the adrenalin kicked into her system and sent a surge of dangerous emotion racing through her veins.

'Was everything all right at the garden centre?' she asked him shakily as he followed her into the kitchen.

Best not to look at him. Not yet. Not until she had herself fully and properly under control. Not that that shuddery, all-too-familiar sensation within her body *meant* anything, of course, it was just...just... Well, she certainly didn't want him looking at her face and recognising anything that might possibly be familiar to him.

'Well, there were no signs of anyone having broken

in,' Silas told her tiredly. 'I checked and then double-checked the place and the alarm and everything seemed okay, but the police say that they had a definite tip-off that the place was being broken into and it always leaves you worrying. You know the sort of thing—create a false alarm and then when all the fuss has died down... We've got a hell of a lot of valuable young plants there at the moment, plus a delivery of antique garden statues which I've acquired for one of my clients. It's insured but...' He changed the subject. 'Thanks for looking after Honor for me.' He stopped and grimaced as his obviously empty stomach gave a protesting growl.

'You're hungry.' Verity looked at him. 'Would you like something to eat...?'

He started to shake his head and then stopped as his stomach gave another, louder, protest.

'It isn't anything much,' Verity warned him without waiting for him to make any refusal. 'Just some pâté and French bread...'

Behind her as she busied herself at the fridge, Verity could hear him groan.

'That sounds marvellous,' he told her, admitting, 'I'm famished and I missed out on lunch altogether today.'

'But you *had* dinner,' Verity began as she removed the pâté and some salad, 'and you always used to enjoy Italian.'

'So did you... Remember when I flew out to New York to see you and you took me all around the Italian restaurants you'd discovered...?'

Verity looked at him.

'Yes,' she agreed huskily. 'Yes, I do.'

It had been a brief, a far too brief, visit—a cheap flight he had managed to get, involving only a two-night stay, his visit a surprise to her on her birthday.

She had cried with joy when he'd arrived and she had cried again—*wept* with misery when he had left, but those tears had been nothing to the ones she had cried the day she had read of his marriage to someone else.

'Unfortunately Myra isn't as keen on Italian food as I am and after... Well, we left the restaurant shortly after you—the call came through from the police on my mobile before we could order.'

'It isn't much,' Verity told him again as she put the plate of pâté and salad she had just prepared onto the table in front of him and then went to cut the bread.

'Not much! It's *wonderful*, manna from heaven,' Silas told her fervently.

'Cappuccino?' Verity asked him quizzically as she handed him the bread basket.

It had always been a bit of a joke between them that he had loved the rich chocolate-sprinkled coffee so much. She didn't need to guess where Honor had got *her* sweet tooth from.

'Mmm...this pâté's good. Did you buy it locally?' Silas asked her.

Shaking her head, Verity turned away from him. Despite what Honor had assumed, she was, in fact, a very good self-taught cook.

'Actually, I made it myself,' she told him truthfully, and she could see what he was thinking from the way he looked from his plate to her expensive and impractical white trousers.

'Not wearing this,' she told him slightly tartly.

He had almost finished eating and had started to frown again. 'I'd better go up and get Honor,' he told her. 'I'm sorry you got landed with her this evening... It's one of the trials of being a single parent that...'

'Yes. It must have been hard for you, losing your wife,' Verity forced herself to acknowledge.

'Nowhere near as hard as it was for her to lose her life, nor Honor to lose her mother,' he countered harshly, before adding equally grimly, as he glanced at her unbanded wedding finger. 'Obviously, you've never married.'

'No,' Verity agreed coolly. 'The business—' she began, but Silas wouldn't allow her to finish.

He interrupted her with a harsh, 'Don't tell me. *I* know...remember?'

He started to get up as Verity reached to remove his plate, her hair accidentally falling forward and brushing his face as they both moved at the same time.

Immediately Verity tensed, lifting her hand to push her hair off her face, but Silas, on his feet by this time, got there first. The sensation of his fingers in her hair was so familiar, so intimate, that she instinctively closed her eyes.

'Verity...' she heard Silas groan, and then the next minute she was in his arms and he was kissing her with a fierce, hungry, angry, passion that brought her defences crashing down so that immediately and helplessly she was responding to him, the years rolling back so that she was a girl again, so that they were a couple, a *pair* again, so that there was nowhere that it was more natural for her to be than here in his arms, *nothing* that was more natural for her to *feel* than what she was feeling right now, nothing it was more natural for her to *want* than what she was wanting right now.

Beneath his mouth and hands her body threw off the shackles she had so sternly imposed on it—he was hers again and she was his. Hers to reach out and touch, as she was doing right now, slipping her fingertips into the gap she had miraculously found between the buttons on his shirt, feeling the solid, familiar heat of his skin. Without realising what she was doing, she unfastened one of the shirt buttons that was preventing her from touching him as she wanted to do.

Beneath his mouth she made a small, contented sound of triumph and pleasure at being able to spread her hands fully over his chest with nothing in the way to bar her sensual exploration of his naked skin.

He felt so good, so Silas, so wonderfully familiar. He even tasted just as she had remembered. Automatically Verity pressed closer to him, shuddering deliciously as she felt his hands slide down her back to cup her bottom, lifting her even deeper into his body.

She could feel the urgency, the hunger, the need, in the way he touched her, running his hands over all her body as he continued to kiss her with increasing passion.

The kitchen was full of the sound of their heightened breathing, the electric crackle of hands against cloth, the silky whisper of skin against skin.

'It's been so long,' Verity whispered emotionally between their kisses. 'I've wanted…'

I've wanted you so much, she was just about to say, but suddenly she stiffened. From upstairs Verity heard the bathroom door open. Silas must have heard it too because he immediately released her, saying tautly, 'This shouldn't be happening. Blame it on the frustration of the evening...'

The frustration? Verity's hands were shaking so much she had to hold them out of sight behind her back as she came back down to earth with a sickening jolt.

What was Silas *saying* to her? That it was *his* sexual frustration at having to leave Myra which had caused him to kiss her?

For a moment she thought she was actually going to be sick. A pain, like red-hot twisting knives, was shredding her emotions. Silas hadn't been thinking about *her* at all. All that passion, all that need, all that *wanting* she had felt in him, had *not* been for her at all and she, like a complete idiot, had virtually been on the point of telling him, revealing to him...

Turning away from him so that he couldn't see her face, she told him quietly, 'Honor's obviously awake.'

'I'll go up and get her,' Silas announced curtly. 'Thanks for looking after her for me.'

'I didn't do it for *you*,' Verity told him fiercely. 'I did it for *her*.'

She still couldn't risk turning round. She daredn't, just in case... Just in case what? Just in case Silas guessed what she had been thinking...feeling... wanting...? His pity was something she couldn't bear. His scorn and his rejection would be hard enough to stomach—almost as hard as the knowledge that for the second time he was rejecting her in favour of another woman, letting her *know* that he simply didn't want her—but if she should look at him now and see pity in his eyes...

Quickly she headed for the kitchen door.

'I'll show you which room Honor's in,' she told him without looking at him.

Honor was back in bed when Verity pushed open the bedroom door. When she saw her father she smiled winningly at him.

'Can I stay here with Verity tonight?' she asked.

'No, you can't,' Silas denied sharply, softening his denial by explaining, 'I'm sure Verity's far too busy...'

'You're not, are you, Verity?' Honor appealed.

Verity hesitated. What could she say?

'Perhaps another time,' she offered as Silas gathered up Honor's clothes and stood waiting determinedly with them.

The house felt empty once they had gone.

Oh, but how could she have been so stupid as to overreact like that just because...? No wonder Silas had felt it necessary to make it clear to her that there had been nothing personal in that kiss he had given her. She could feel her face starting to burn with humiliation and pain. As she began to tidy up the kitchen, a small item on the floor caught her eye. Frowning, she bent to pick it up. It was a button—a man's shirt button. Her face burned even more hotly. She must have *ripped* it off when she had... Quickly she swallowed. She had never been driven by her sexuality and even when she and Silas had been lovers she had always been the more passive partner. She could certainly never remember having virtually ripped the shirt off his back before. Angrily she put her hands to her hot face. The last thing she needed was for Silas to start thinking that she was holding some kind of torch for him…that she still *wanted* him, that she was stupid enough to still be hurting over the way he had treated her.

From now on, when they met—*if* they met—she was going to have to make it very clear to him that tonight's kiss was something as little wanted or relished by her as it had been by him!

CHAPTER SIX

'DAD.'

'Mmm...' Silas glanced down at his daughter's head as she sat next to him in the car.

'When Verity lived here before, were you friends?'

'What makes you ask that?' Silas questioned her sharply.

'Nothing.' Honor smiled, looking up at him. 'Well, were you?'

'No.' Silas told her curtly.

'Yes. That's what she said.'

Silas frowned.

'She's very pretty, though, isn't she?' Honor continued sunnily. 'Riccardo certainly thought so.'

'Very,' Silas agreed through gritted teeth. As a young girl Verity has possessed a natural, wholesome, sweet prettiness, but as a woman she had matured into someone whose subtle sensuality...

His favourite plants were always those that took a little bit of knowing; whose attractions were not necessarily flashingly visible at first glance. He had never liked anything overblown nor obvious and Verity... Just now, kissing her, he had been overwhelmed by the urge, by the memory of a certain night they had spent together in the heat of her small New York flat when, during their lovemaking, she had wrapped her legs around him and...

Tonight, watching the way she had moved in that

silky white suit she had been wearing, remembering just how lovely and equally silky and feminine her legs were…

'I really like her and she's going to be *my* friend,' Honor informed him. 'Can I invite her round for tea tomorrow?'

'What? No, you can't. You've got school in the morning and homework.'

'No, I haven't. We're having a leave day—I told you last week.'

'What?' Silas looked at her and groaned.

'Honor, why on earth didn't you remind me of that earlier?' he demanded. 'I've got a site meeting in the morning that I can't put off.'

'You should have left me at Verity's,' Honor told him practically. 'You'll have to ring her and ask her if she can look after me tomorrow.'

'What? No way. What about Catherine?'

'No.' Honor shook her head firmly. 'She's got her aunt and uncle staying, remember?'

Silas groaned again.

When Honor had been a baby he had employed a succession of full-time live-in nannies to take care of her when he wasn't there, also taking her into work with him when he could, but the situation was more complicated now that Honor was growing up. For one thing she was extremely independent and diabolically good at getting her own way so that finding the right kind of person—someone firm enough for her to respect and yet young enough not to be too restrictive with her—was proving increasingly difficult. Anna helped out when he could spare her from the garden centre, but they were too busy just now for her to be away from the centre all day.

His last housekeeper had left after Silas had made it plain that she was employed to take care of Honor's needs and not his own, and since then he had been relying increasingly on a patchwork of haphazard arrangements, getting by on a wing and a prayer and the good offices of kind friends.

If he hadn't hit such a busy patch with the business, he would have had time to advertise and sort something more permanent out, but as it was...

'I expect Myra was really cross when you had to leave to go to the garden centre,' Honor commented.

Silas gave her a wry look.

'Just a little,' he agreed.

The truth was that Myra had been furious. She was not a particularly maternal woman. In fact, her own two sons from her marriage lived with their father and his new partner. Silas knew perfectly well that becoming his wife was Myra's goal but being Honor's doting stepmother was the last thing the woman wanted.

She was a woman who, as she had told him quite openly, had a very high sex drive—so far, despite all the encouragement she had given him, Silas had kept their relationship on a purely platonic footing. Perhaps he was out of step with modern times, but sex for sex's sake was something that didn't appeal to him. It never had, which was why...

Silas looked down again at his daughter's dark head. As always when he thought of Honor's mother he was filled with a mixture of guilt and regret.

Neither of them had ever imagined when Sarah had

conceived Honor that giving birth to her would result in Sarah losing her own life. If they had...

It had been Sarah herself who had suggested that they should have the pregnancy terminated—neither of them, after all, had been thinking of a baby when Honor had been conceived—but Silas had persuaded her not to go ahead with it.

'I can't afford to bring up a baby,' she had told him frantically.

'I can,' Silas had replied.

A week later they had been married and just over seven months after that Honor had been born.

Forty-eight hours after giving birth Sarah had been dead despite everything that the doctors had done to try and save her. Nothing had been able to stop the massive haemorrhaging which had ended her life and, in the end, the doctors had told Silas that there was simply nothing they could do, that no amount of blood transfusions were going to help, that her body was too far in shock for them to be able to risk any kind of emergency surgery.

She had died without ever seeing Honor.

It hadn't been easy in those early years being totally responsible for a motherless girl child. His own parents had been retired and living abroad, and he had been determined that since he was Honor's only parent he was going to be as involved in her life and as much 'there' for her as he possibly could be, and so he had learned to change nappies without flinching, to bring up wind and to correctly interpret what all those different baby cries meant. But then, almost as soon as he had mastered those complexities, Honor had found new ways to tax his parenting skills—was still finding new ways to tax them, he admitted ten minutes later as he ushered her upstairs to her own bedroom, newly decorated last year for her birthday since she had announced that the 'Barbie' colour scheme and decor she had insisted on having for her sixth birthday was now totally passé and far too babyish for a girl of her new maturity.

In its place her room was now resplendent with everything necessary for a devout and ardent fan of the latest popular 'girl band'.

'I really like Verity,' Honor told him drowsily as he was tucking her up. 'I wish...'

'Go to sleep,' Silas said.

He had reached the doorway and was just about to switch off the light when she called out, 'Da-ad.'

'Yes.' Silas waited.

Honor sat bolt upright in her bed and eyed him seriously. 'You do know, don't you, that I'm getting to an age where I need to have a woman to talk to?'

Silas wasn't deceived. Honor, as he well knew, could run rings around a woman four times her age—could and, exasperatingly, very often did.

'You know what I mean,' Honor stressed. 'There are things I need to know...girl-type things...'

Silas gave her a sceptical look. He and Honor had always had a very open and honest relationship, no subject was taboo between them, and he had assumed that when the time came the subject of Honor's burgeoning womanhood and sexuality would be one they would cope with together. Honor, or so she was implying, had other ideas.

'Go to sleep,' he advised his daughter thoughtfully before switching off the light and going downstairs.

He only wished he could go to bed himself, but he had some paperwork to do. The landscaping business, which he had built up from nothing, had thrived—two years running he had won critical acclaim from the judges at the Chelsea Flower Show and he was now fully booked up with design commissions for the next eighteen months.

Add to that the garden centre side of his business and it was no wonder that, increasingly, he was finding it difficult to juggle all the various demands on his time.

It had hurt him more than he liked to think about even now when Verity had made it plain that taking over from her uncle in his business meant more to her than being with him—had *hurt* him and had damn near *destroyed* him. It wasn't that he was arrogant enough to think that a woman, his woman, should not want to have a career or run her own life, it was just... It was just that he had assumed that their relationship, their love, had meant as much to her as it had to him and that...

Plainly, though, he had been wrong.

'Give me time,' she had begged him, and because he had loved her so much he had.

'I have to go to New York,' she had told him. 'But I'll be back... It won't be for ever and there'll be holidays.' But too many months had come and gone without her coming back and in the end he had been the one to go to her. A meagre forty-eight hours was all they had had together—all he'd been able to afford to pay for and he had only managed that because he had picked up the short break as a special tour operator's bargain.

'Don't make me wait too long,' he had begged her.
'Please understand,' she had asked him.

Finally, pushed to the limits of his pride and his love, he had given her an ultimatum.

'Come home, we need to talk,' he had written to her, but she had ignored his letter—and when he had rung her apartment a strange male voice had answered the phone, claiming not to know where she was.

He hadn't rung again and then, four weeks later, he had met Sarah, and the rest, as they said, was history.

The local paper had carried several articles about Verity's uncle five years ago when he had died—he had been, after all, probably the town's most successful and wealthy inhabitant—but Silas had never expected that Verity would come back.

If it hadn't been for that incident with Honor and her roller blades, he doubted that they would even have seen one another. And he wished to God that they hadn't. Tonight had resurrected too many painful memories. Grimly he switched his thoughts back to the present.

He was going to have to find someone to take care of Honor tomorrow. But who? He had used up all his credit with his normal 'babysitters'. If worse came to worst, he would have to take her to the garden centre with him and ask Anna to keep an eye on her.

He groaned. Sometimes she made him feel as old as Methuselah, and at others her maturity filled him with both awe and apprehension.

Earlier this evening, walking into the restaurant and seeing her there with Verity, he had felt such a confusing and powerful mixture of emotions and when they had both looked at him, identical womanly expressions of hauteur and dismissal in their eyes, he had felt, he had felt… Grimly he pushed his hand into his hair. They certainly made a formidable team.

A team… Oh, no. No! No! No way. No way…

Silas looked enquiringly at Honor as she replaced the telephone receiver as he walked into the kitchen.

She looked enviably fresh and alert in view of how late it had been when she had finally gone to bed last night.

'I've just checked with Verity,' she told Silas with a very grown-up air as she poured herself some cereal, 'and she says it's okay for me to stay with her today. I've arranged for her to come and collect me at ten o'clock.'

Silas opened his mouth and then closed it again and, going to make himself a cup of coffee, waited until he had poured the boiling water on the coffee grains before trusting himself to speak.

'Correct me if I'm wrong, Honor,' he began pleasantly, 'but I rather thought that *I* was the adult in this household and that as such *I* am the one who makes the decisions.'

'I knew you probably wouldn't have time to drive me over to Verity's,' Honor told him virtuously, 'that's why I asked *her* if she could come *here* to pick me up.'

'Honor!' Silas warned and then cursed under his breath as the phone rang.

By the time he had dealt with the call, Honor had made a strategic retreat to her bedroom.

The phone rang again as he snatched a quick gulp of his now cold coffee. Sooner rather than later he and Honor were going to have a serious talk—a *very* serious talk.

Honor waited until her father had gone out, leaving her in the temporary care of their cleaning lady, before making her second call of the morning.

'It's me,' she announced when she heard her friend Catherine pick up the receiver. 'Guess what?'

'Is it working?' Catherine asked her excitedly. 'Did your father...did they...?'

'Both of them are pretending that they've never met before,' Honor told her friend. 'I haven't told them about finding that photograph. I got Verity to take me out for supper last night like we planned—to the same place where Dad was taking Myra. You should have seen her face...'

'What, Verity's? Did she look as though she still loved him? Did he—'

'No, not *Verity*,' Honor interrupted her. 'I meant you should have seen *Myra's* face—she was furious.'

'I bet she wasn't too pleased later when your dad got that phone call about the garden centre being broken into either.' Catherine giggled.

'Mmm...that worked really well. Tell your cousin I'll pay him what I owe him when I get more pocket money. I can't stay on the phone too long. Verity's coming round for me at ten. I'm spending the day with her. When she gets here we're going to do some womanly bonding.'

'What's that?' Catherine asked her uncertainly.

'I'm not sure, I read about it in a magazine. I think it's when you sit round and talk about babies and things,' Honor told her grandly.

'Oh. I'd rather talk about the boys,' Catherine informed her. 'Are you sure that your dad's still in love with her?'

'Positive. Last night they were kissing,' Honor informed her smugly.

'What? Did you see them?'

'No, but Dad had got lipstick on his mouth.'

'It could have been Myra's…'

'No. Myra wears red. This was pink…'

'But if they really love one another like you told me, how come he married your mother?'

'I don't know. I suppose they must have fallen out. Just think, if I hadn't found that photograph I'd never have discovered Dad and Verity knew each other before. I can't wait for them to get married.'

'Will you be a bridesmaid?' Catherine asked her wistfully.

'I'll be *the* bridesmaid,' Honor responded firmly, unaware of a touch of wistfulness in her voice too.

'They'll go away on one of those honeymoon things and leave you at home,' Catherine warned her, retaliating for Honor's comment about being 'the' bridesmaid and squashing her own hopes of wafting down the aisle alongside her friend in a cloud of pink tulle. Despite all Honor's chivvying, Catherine still retained regrettable fondness for their shared Barbie days.

'My uncle left Charlie at home when *he* remarried.'

'No, they won't,' Honor said adding, 'Verity would never let Dad leave me behind. She's so exactly right.' She smiled happily. 'I could tell the moment I met her.'

Catherine knew from experience when her friend's mind was on other things.

'I've got a new video,' she told her. 'We could watch it together on Saturday…'

'Maybe,' Honor hedged. 'I might not be very well…'

'Not very well? What do you mean?' Catherine demanded.

'Wait and see,' Honor responded mysteriously, before adding quickly, 'Verity's just driven up, I've got to go…'

'Daddy said to say thank you very much for looking after me,' Honor told Verity in a serious tone when she had opened the front door to her. 'He said he was very, very grateful to you and he couldn't think of anyone he could trust more to look after me.'

Verity blinked. To say she had been surprised to receive a telephone call from Honor asking if she could possibly spend the day with her because she was off school and Silas had to go out was something of an understatement. After what had happened between them last night she would have thought that *she* was the last person Silas would want around his daughter—and around himself.

What kind of a father *was* he exactly, if he could so easily entrust his only child to a woman he himself did not even pretend to like? she wondered critically as Honor skipped off to collect her coat.

Thoughtfully she waited for Honor to return.

'Your father *does* know that you're spending the day with me, doesn't he?' she questioned her dryly.

Honor gave her an injured look.

'Of course he does. You can ring him on his mobile if you like…'

'No. It's all right,' Verity assured her, adding palliatively, 'I'm not used to looking after little...*young* women... What would you like to do?'

'Could you take me shopping?' Honor asked her. 'I don't have any nice clothes,' she confided. 'Dad isn't very good at buying me the right kind of things.' She looked down at her jeans and tee shirt and told Honor, 'I think sometimes he forgets that I'm a girl.'

Honor couldn't have said anything more guaranteed to touch her own heart, Verity acknowledged. She too had suffered from hopelessly inaccurate male assessment of what kind of clothes were suitable for a young girl.

Even so...

'Your father...' she began uncertainly, but Honor shook her head.

'Dad won't mind,' she answered Verity excitedly. 'He'll be pleased. He *hates* taking me shopping. In fact...' She paused and gave Verity an assessing look, wondering how far she should try her luck. Not too far if that unexpectedly shrewd question Verity had asked her earlier was anything to go by. 'Well, he *has* been saying that he would have to try and find someone—a woman—to take me out shopping.' Honor gazed up pleadingly at Verity.

'Wouldn't Myra...?' Verity began cautiously.

But Honor immediately shook her head and pulled a face before informing Verity tremulously, 'Myra doesn't like me... I think she...if she ever married my father, she would try to send me away...'

The horrified look Verity gave her reassured Honor. Everything was going to work out. Verity was going to make the *perfect* mother for her.

Prior to receiving Honor's telephone call Verity had planned to spend the day working, and a couple of hours after she had picked Honor up she was beginning to wonder if working might not have proved to be the easier option.

They were in the pre-teen department of a well-known chain of clothes shops, Verity waiting outside the cubicle area whilst Honor tried on the clothes she had chosen.

'And I thought having *teenagers* was bad,' another woman standing next to Verity groaned. 'My youngest...' she nodded in the direction of one of the changing rooms '...isn't speaking to her father because he refused to allow her to have her navel pierced. She's eleven next week. So far, the only clothes she's said she'll wear are the ones that her father will have forty fits if he sees her in, and I've got to admit he does have a point. Of course, we all know that fathers don't like to see their little girls growing up, but—'

'Verity, what do you think?' Honor demanded, suddenly emerging from the changing cubicle dressed in a tiny cut-off top that clung lovingly to her mercifully still flat chest and a pair of stretch Lycra leggings in a mixture of colours that made Verity's eyeballs ache.

'It's... I don't think your father will like it very much,' Verity began.

But she was out-manoeuvred as Honor informed her sunnily, 'No, I don't suppose he will, but you'll soon be able to talk him round.'

She could talk him round? Verity opened her mouth and then closed it again.

'Honor...' she began, but Honor was already disappearing in the direction of the changing cubicle.

It was another three hours before Honor pronounced herself reasonably satisfied with her purchases, declaring that she was hungry and suggesting that they made their way to the nearest McDonald's.

They were settled at a table when Honor asked Verity her most searching question yet. 'Have you ever been in love?'

Verity put down her cup of coffee.

'Once,' she admitted quietly, after a few long seconds had passed. 'A good many years ago.'

'What happened?' Honor asked her curiously.

Verity focused on her. What on earth was she *doing*? This wasn't a suitable topic of conversation to have with a ten-year-old girl even when the girl was the daughter of the man she had loved—especially when that ten-year-old was the daughter of the man she had loved, she corrected herself quickly—and yet, to her consternation, she still heard herself saying huskily, 'He...He married someone else!'

'Perhaps he married someone else because *he* thought *you'd* stopped loving him,' Honor told her quickly. 'Perhaps he really still loves you,' she said eagerly.

Verity started to frown. It was quite definitely time to change the subject.

'It's half past four,' she told Honor. 'What time did you say your father would be back?'

Silas' meeting had ended a little earlier than he had anticipated, and since he needed petrol he headed for the large out-of-town supermarket where he normally did his grocery shopping.

Catherine's mother was heading for the checkout with a full trolley-load when he walked in. Smiling at him, she asked, 'Did your aunt enjoy seeing Honor? Catherine was disappointed that she couldn't stay with us after all.'

Silas frowned.

'I'm sorry?' he began and then checked. What exactly was going on? Honor had told *him* that she couldn't stay at Catherine's because her friend had family visiting, but from what Catherine's mother had just said she seemed to be under the impression that it was *Honor* who had had the family commitment.

'Oh, and thanks for the invitation to dinner next week, we'd love to come.'

The invitation to dinner...? Next week? Silas opened his mouth and then closed it again. His daughter, he decided grimly, was going to have some serious explaining to do.

It was five o'clock when Verity finally pulled into Silas' drive, empty thankfully of his car, but she knew she couldn't escape until he returned home to care for his daughter. Besides, Honor was not feeling very well.

'My stomach hurts,' she told Verity.

'I'm not surprised. You *did* have two milk shakes,' Verity reminded her.

'It's not that kind of pain,' Honor came back quickly. 'It's the kind you get when you feel sad and...and lonely.'

Once they were inside the house, though, Honor

suddenly remembered something she had to do outside.

'You stay here,' she told Verity, pushing open the kitchen door. 'I won't be long.'

The kitchen was generously proportioned and comfortable. In the adjoining laundry room Verity could see a basket perched on top of the tumble-dryer, a pile of clean laundry next to it as though someone had pulled it from the machine and not had time to fold it.

Automatically she walked through and started to smooth out the crumpled garments. Honor's underwear and school clothes and...

Her fingers tensed as she picked up a pair of soft male briefs, white and well styled. Her hands were trembling so much she almost dropped them. Quickly she put them down as though they had scalded her. She could hear Honor coming back.

'*I* bought Dad those for Christmas,' she told Verity, picking up the briefs.

'I'm learning to cook at school. You should have dinner parties and invite people round.'

Verity looked at her.

'Dinner parties?' she questioned warily.

'Mmm... Catherine's mother has them all the time. Dad was saying last week how embarrassed *he* felt because he wants to invite them round here but he doesn't have anyone to help him. I mean, he's okay really with the food, but it's the other things, isn't it?' Honor asked her earnestly. 'The flowers and the...the placements. Myra says that those are very important.'

The placements. Verity bit her inner lip to keep her mouth straight. It would never do to laugh and hurt

Honor's feelings. The last time she had heard someone referring to the importance of their placements had been at a stuffy Washington diplomatic dinner.

'Er...yes,' she agreed. 'Well, I'm sure that Myra would be only too pleased to act as hostess for your father.'

'She can't,' Honor told her quickly, 'It's... Catherine's mother doesn't like her... Perhaps you could do it?' Honor suggested.

Verity's eyes widened.

'Me? But...'

'I don't know how well you can cook, but I could help.'

Verity automatically continued to fold the laundry. Now she stopped and turned to Honor.

'Honor,' she began gently, 'I don't think—'

'Dad's back, I just heard the car,' Honor interrupted her, adding quickly, 'Don't say anything to him about the dinner party... He doesn't like people thinking that he can't do things.'

Outside the kitchen door Silas hesitated. Just the sight of Verity's BMW had raised his heartbeat. What the hell was the matter with him? Hadn't he learned his lesson the *first* time around? Eleven years ago Verity had rejected him in favour of her uncle's business and he was a fool if he allowed himself to forget that fact.

Even so, the sight that met his eyes when he finally pushed open the kitchen door was one that made him check and curl his hand into a hard warning fist. Verity and Honor were standing in the laundry room deep in conversation, Honor holding the end of the sheet that Verity was busily folding.

'Dad always says that it's a waste of time to iron them because no one but us ever sees them.'

No one! Verity's heart gave a quick thud. Did that mean that Myra and he...? Or was it simply that he discreetly chose not to share a bed with his lover in the same house where his daughter slept?

'Dad!' Honor cried, releasing the sheet as she saw her father and bounding across the kitchen to hug him with such very evident love that Verity's heart gave another and even more painful lurch.

It was so obvious, watching the two of them together, not just that Honor was Silas' daughter but also how much they loved one another. There was nothing false or artificial about the way Silas held his daughter.

'Thank you for helping out,' he told Verity formally. 'I—'

'Dad, Verity took me shopping. Just wait until you see what we bought. I told her you'd pay her,' Honor hurried on, 'but she still wouldn't let me have some of the things I wanted. There was this top and these leggings...' She began enthusiastically explaining the eye-popping ensemble to Silas before adding, 'But Verity didn't think they were my colours.'

Over her head Silas' eyes met Verity's.

Thank you, he mouthed silently before turning his attention back to Honor and telling her gravely, 'I'm sure she was right.'

'Well, that's what I thought because her own clothes are so beautiful,' Honor agreed. 'Don't you think she looks luscious in that suit, Dad?'

Luscious...

Verity could feel her face starting to grow warm as

two identical pairs of eyes studied her Donna-Karan-clad body.

'She certainly looks very...elegant...and successful,' Silas agreed quietly. But somehow, instead of sounding like a compliment, the words sounded much more like condemnation, Verity recognised grimly.

'I was just telling Verity how much you want to have a dinner party,' Honor chattered on, apparently oblivious to the tension growing between the two silent adults. 'She said she'd love to come and help you and it will help her to get to know people as well, won't it?'

'Honor...'

As they both spoke at once, Verity and Silas looked at one another.

'Now you're both cross with me...'

Bright tears shimmered in Honor's hurt eyes as her bottom lip wobbled and she turned her head away.

Verity was immediately filled with guilt and contrition. Out of her own embarrassment and reluctance to have Silas think that she was deliberately inveigling her way back into his life, she had inadvertently hurt Honor.

Silas looked less concerned but he was still frowning.

'This dinner party,' he began, ignoring his daughter's tear-filled eyes. 'It wouldn't be the same one that Catherine's mother informed me she would be delighted to attend, when I bumped into her in the supermarket earlier, would it, Honor?'

Honor gave him a sunny smile.

'Oh, can they come? Good... Catherine's mother is a brilliant cook,' she informed Verity, 'and—'

'Honor!' Silas began warningly.

Quickly Verity picked up her handbag.

'I think I'd better go,' she announced quietly.

'Go? Oh, no, not yet. I wanted you to stay for supper,' Honor pleaded.

'I'm afraid I can't... I... I have another appointment,' Verity fibbed.

Honor's eyes widened.

'But this afternoon you said that you were staying in tonight by yourself,' she reminded Verity in a confused little voice.

'I'll see you out,' Silas told her, shooting Honor a quelling look.

'Thank you once again for looking after Honor,' he told Verity formally as he accompanied her politely to her car.

Verity daredn't allow herself to look at him but suddenly he was striding past her, examining the front wheel of her car.

'You've got a flat tyre,' he told her sharply.

Disbelievingly Verity looked at her car.

'I...I've got a spare,' she told him, but he was shaking his head,

'*That* won't do much good,' he said curtly. 'The back one's flat as well. They've both got nails in them,' he informed her. 'You must have driven over them.'

'Yes, I must,' Verity agreed, shaking her head. 'But I don't know where. If I could use your phone to ring a garage...'

'You can, but I doubt you'll be able to get it fixed until the morning,' he told her dryly. 'It's more likely the garages round here will all be shut now.'

Helplessly Verity studied her now immobile car.

How on earth had she managed to run over two nails—and where? She certainly hadn't been aware of doing so, nor of driving anywhere where she might have expected loose nails to be lying on the ground.

'Let's go back inside. I know the local dealer, I'll give him a ring,' Silas suggested.

Silently Verity followed Silas back into the house.

Watching them from the sitting-room window, Honor surreptitiously crossed her fingers. So far, so good—the plan to get them together was working beautifully. It had been hard work driving those nails into the tyres, though—much harder than she had expected.

'You *can't* do that,' Catherine had protested, her eyes widening in a mixture of shock and excitement when Honor had told her what she had planned to do.

'Watch me,' Honor had challenged her, bravado covering her brief twinge of guilt at what she had to do.

Verity waited in the kitchen with Honor whilst Silas went into his study to ring the garage. When he came back his expression was grave.

'The garage can't come out until tomorrow, I'm afraid, which means that you're going to have to spend the night here.'

Verity opened her mouth to protest and say that if he couldn't run her home she could get a taxi, and then, for some inadmissible and dangerous reason, she found that she was closing it again.

'Oh, good, now we can play Scrabble and you can share my bedroom,' Honor was saying excitedly.

'Verity can sleep in the guest bedroom,' Silas reproved crisply, 'and as for Scrabble—'

Verity smiled. Honor had told her earlier in the day how much she enjoyed the game.

'I'd love to play with her,' she interrupted Silas pacifically, adding truthfully, 'It's always been one of my favourite games.'

'Yes. I... I enjoy it as well,' Silas agreed.

Her heart hammering too fast for comfort, Verity wondered if that slight hesitation in his voice had been her imagination. Had he, as she had momentarily felt, been about to say that he remembered how much she had enjoyed Scrabble?

Ridiculous to feel such a warm, fuzzy, sentimental, inappropriate surge of happiness at the thought.

'I still can't understand where I managed to pick up those nails,' Verity commented, shaking her head.

They had just cleared away after supper and Honor had gone upstairs to get the Scrabble.

'Where they came from is immaterial now,' Silas pointed out. 'The damage is done...'

'Mmm...'

'More wine?' Silas offered her, picking up the still half-full bottle from the kitchen table.

On the point of refusing, Verity changed her mind. What harm could it do, after all, and since she wasn't driving...? The meal they had eaten had been a simple one of chicken and vegetables, prepared by Silas with Honor's rather erratic assistance.

It had touched Verity, though, when Honor had insisted on dragging her out to the garden with her so that they could find some flowers to put on the table.

'Dad, when you have the dinner party, you'll have to use the dining room,' she told her father whilst they were eating. 'I'll show you the dining room afterwards, Verity,' she informed Verity with a woman-to-woman look. 'You'll need to know where everything is.'

'Honor,' Silas began, 'I don't think—'

But Honor refused to listen to him, turning instead to Verity and demanding passionately, 'You will do it, won't you, Verity? Please,' before telling her father, 'You don't understand... I *hate* it at school when the others talk about the parties their mothers give. I can tell that they're all feeling sorry for me. I know that Verity may not be able to cook, but *we* can have just as good a dinner party here as they have.'

After such a passionate outburst, what else could Verity do other than swallow her own feelings and give in? Silas, she suspected, must be swallowing equally hard—harder, perhaps, if the frowning look on his face was anything to go by.

'You had no business inviting Catherine's mother and father round, though, no matter the circumstances...' Pausing, Silas shook his head before adding sternly, 'No business at all. But since you *have*, I agree that we can hardly tell Catherine's mother the truth. Please don't feel that *you* have to get involved, though—' he told Verity.

'I'd be happy to help,' Verity cut him off, looking him straight in the eye as she told him quietly, 'I know how Honor feels, but, of course, if there's someone else you would prefer to act as your hostess...?'

She waited. Would he tell her that, by rights, Myra ought to be the one hostessing his dinner party? And what if he did? Why should that concern *her*?

'No. There's no one,' he denied before adding, 'Besides, this will be *Honor's* dinner party, I suspect, not mine...'

'You can choose the wine, Dad,' Honor informed him in a kind voice. 'That's the man's job. What will we do about food?' she asked Verity excitedly.

'We'll sort something out,' Verity promised her whilst she mentally reviewed which of her favourite dishes she should serve.

In London she had had little time for giving dinner parties, but when she had they had been occasions she had thoroughly enjoyed.

Good food, good wine and good friends—most of all good friends; they were a recipe for the very best kind of entertaining. But she didn't know Silas' friends and the situation was bound to be both uncomfortable and awkward. He was being polite about it now, just as he had been good-mannered about the accident to her tyres and the fact that he had been forced to offer her a bed for the night. But they both knew how he really felt about her.

Quickly now, Verity reached for her wine and took a deep gulp, grimacing a little as the wine's sharpness hit her palate.

'You never did have much of a head for alcohol,' Silas commented, watching her.

Silently their glances met and held.

'That was over ten years ago,' Verity finally managed to tell him huskily. 'My...tastes have changed since then.'

'Here it is...'

Both of them looked round as Honor came bounding into the room carrying the Scrabble.

CHAPTER SEVEN

'RIGHT, time for bed...'

'Oh, Dad, just *one* more game,' Honor protested, but Silas was already shaking his head.

'You said that last time,' he reminded her sternly.

Diplomatically Verity busied herself tidying up the letters and putting everything away. Honor had needed no allowances made for her and she had thoroughly trounced them, not once, but twice—perhaps because in Verity's own case, at least, her concentration had been more on the words that Honor had formed than matching them, she admitted, quickly glancing away from Honor to the board.

Love... Tiff... Quarrel... Mama... Surely she was being over-sensitive in her reaction to seeing those words? After all, Honor knew nothing about the past, their shared past.

Quickly Verity broke up the words and folded the board.

'You will come up and say goodnight to me, won't you?' Honor begged Verity, adding determinedly, 'I want you both to come up...together...'

Verity couldn't bring herself to look at Silas. Instead she went to wash the empty coffee mugs whilst Silas took Honor upstairs.

She was just about to remove their wineglasses when he came back down.

'No, leave those,' he told her. 'We might as well finish off the bottle.'

'I'll just go up and say goodnight to Honor,' Verity told him huskily.

Standing in the kitchen on her own whilst he'd been upstairs with Honor had given her too much time to think, to remember…to regret…

If things had been different Honor could have been *her* child… If things had been different… If Silas had not rejected her… If… If… But what use were 'ifs'? No use whatsoever to an aching, lonely, yearning heart. A heart that still beat ridiculously fast for a man who had hurt it so badly.

Honor was lying flat beneath the bedclothes, her hair a dark mass on the pillow. Automatically as she bent to kiss her Verity smoothed it back off her face.

'I do like you, Verity,' Honor told her softly. 'I wish you could be here with us for always…'

Sharp tears pricked Verity's eyes. She wasn't totally gullible, and she was perfectly well aware that Honor wasn't averse to using soft soap and flattery to get her own way, but for once there was no mistaking the very real emotion in the little girl's voice. The real emotion and the real need, Verity recognised.

Honor was looking, if not for a mother, then certainly for a mentor, a role model, a woman with whom she could bond. None knew better than she herself just how it felt to be on the verge of young womanhood without any guiding female influence in one's life, Verity acknowledged. It was one of the loneliest and most isolated places on earth—almost as lonely and heartache inducing as being without the man you had given your heart to.

Her uncle, although providing for her material welfare, had been oblivious to the emotional needs of a young girl, and Verity remembered with painful clarity how she as a young adolescent had tried desperately to attach herself to the mother of a school friend, and then, when that had been gently discouraged by the woman in question, she had turned instead to one of her schoolteachers. But both women, although kind and caring, had had their own families and their own lives, and their distancing of themselves from her had left Verity feeling even more bereft than before—and not just bereft, but sensitively aware of being gently held at a distance.

Honor, she suspected, although on the surface a very different girl from the one she had been, was going through a similar stage. There was no doubting Silas' love for his daughter, nor his caring paternal concern for her. He was, Verity could see, a father who was very actively involved in his daughter's life, but Honor was making it plain that she wanted a *woman's* influence in her life as well as her father's.

'You will stay the night, won't you?' she whispered now, clutching Verity's hand. 'I want you to be here when I wake up in the morning...'

'I'll be here,' Verity promised her.

'I like your hair best when it's down,' Honor told her sleepily. 'It makes you look...more huggy. Catherine, my friend, has got two brothers and loads and loads of cousins...' Her eyes closed. Very gently, Verity bent and kissed her.

For all her outer layer of sturdy independence, inside she was still very much a little girl. Silas' little girl.

Quietly Verity got up and headed for the bedroom door.

Alone in the kitchen, Silas allowed himself to relax for the first time since he had come home. He didn't know what kind of game Honor thought she was playing by inveigling Verity into agreeing to hosting that damned dinner party, and the only reason he hadn't given her a thorough dressing down over it was because he was well aware that she had reached that sensitive and delicate stage in her development where her burgeoning pride and sense of self could be very easily bruised. He would have to talk to her about it, of course, and explain that she had put Verity in a very embarrassing and difficult position.

It had been hard to guess exactly what Verity's real feelings about the situation were. She had developed a disconcerting, calm, distancing and very womanly maturity which, very effectively, drew a line over which no one was allowed to cross, but he certainly knew how he was going to feel, sitting at the opposite end of the dining table from her whilst she acted as his hostess. It was going to be sheer hell, total purgatory, an evening filled with excruciating pain of 'could have beens' and all because his darling daughter wanted to be on a par with her school friends.

Well, he couldn't blame her for that. It was all part and parcel of growing up. Honor was getting ready to grow into womanhood and she was making it clear to him that she wanted a woman in her life to pattern herself on.

He had, at one stage, wondered if Myra—but the pair of them would never accept one another.

Had Verity been anyone other than who she was he suspected that by now he would have been thanking fate for bringing her into their lives. It was glaringly obvious how Honor felt about her—and not just from the determined way she was attaching herself to Verity. If he was honest with himself, which he always tried to be, without the past to cast its unhappy shadow he knew perfectly well that, had he been meeting Verity for the first time now, he would have been instantly and immediately attracted to her.

She had still, despite the life she had lived, an air of soft and gentle femininity, an aura of natural womanly strength melded with compassion and love.

He found it hard to picture her as the head of a multi-million-pound business making corporate decisions based purely on profits and completely without emotion. It wasn't that he doubted her skills or abilities, it was just that, to him, even now, she still possessed that certain something that made him want to look after her and protect her.

Protect her? Was he crazy? She *had* all the protection she needed in the shape of the material assets she had chosen above their love.

'It's my duty, I owe it to him,' she had told him sadly when she had allowed her uncle to part them and send her away to New York, but those had been words he hadn't wanted to hear.

Last night, holding her in his arms, kissing her... She'd been back less than a week and already... He wasn't going to make the same mistake he had made last time. This time he was going to be on his guard and stay on it...

He had known, of course, of her uncle's plans for

Verity's future and the way her uncle had deliberately fostered and used her strong sense of duty for his own ends.

One of the first things he had decided when he had found himself widowed and the father of a baby girl was that he would never ever manipulate her feelings and cause her to feel that she was in debt to him for anything in the way he had witnessed Verity's uncle manipulating hers.

But, naively perhaps, he had assumed that Verity had shared his feelings, his belief that their future lay together.

'Do you love me?' he had demanded, and shyly she had nodded.

Had she ever loved him or...?

'I'll be back soon from New York and then...then we can be together,' she told him.

And he had taken that to mean that she had wanted to marry him, and share his dream of establishing a business together.

He could still remember the sense of excitement and pride he had felt the day he had first taken her to see the small run-down market garden he had hoped to buy. She had seemed as thrilled and excited as him.

'There's a real market locally for a garden centre and a landscaping service, but it won't be easy,' he warned her. 'I've been through all the figures with the bank and for the first few years we're going to have to plough back every penny we make into the business. I won't be able to buy us a big house or give you a nice car.'

'I don't care about things like that,' Verity assured him softly, making one of those lightning changes she could make from a girl's *naiveté* to a woman's maturity and shaking his heart to its roots in the process. It fascinated and delighted him, held him in thrall with awe to be privileged to see these glimpses of the woman she was going to be. She was so gentle, so loving, so everything that most appealed to him in a woman.

'I don't care where we live just so long as we're together…'

'Well, I should certainly make enough to support a wife and our child, our children…' he had whispered. It was all he wanted then. His parents were away on holiday with friends and he took her home with him, making love to her in the warm shadows of the summer evening. He was twenty-seven and considered himself already a man; she was twenty-one.

'I'm going to see the bank manager tomorrow,' he whispered to her as he slowly licked and then kissed her pretty pink fingertips, 'and then I'm going to put a formal offer in on the business. Once it's ours, we can start to make plans for our wedding.'

He thought that the quick tears that filled her eyes were tears of love and pleasure—she often wept huge silent tears of bliss after their lovemaking—and it was only later that he realised that she had wept because she had known that, by the time he was the owner of the small plot of land, she would be on the other side of the Atlantic.

Silas warned her repeatedly that her uncle was trying to separate them, that he had his own selfish reasons for not wanting them to marry, but Verity refused to listen.

Her uncle wasn't like that, she protested, white-faced. He didn't push the matter, thinking he knew how vulnerable she was, how much she needed to believe that the man who had brought her up did care more about her than his business, not wanting to do anything that might potentially hurt her.

Hurt her! Did *she* care about hurting *him* when she ignored his letter, his pleas to her to come home? She didn't even care enough to write to him and tell him that it was over. She simply ignored his letter.

And then her uncle called round, supposedly to buy some plants but in reality to tell him that Verity had decided to stay on in New York for a further year.

The business wasn't building up as fast as Silas had expected. He was struggling to service the bank borrowing he had taken out to buy and develop the garden centre, and when his bank manager telephoned him a week later to inform him that they had had an anonymous offer from someone wanting to buy the newly established garden centre from him he was so tempted to take it, to move away and make a fresh start somewhere else. What, after all, was there to keep him in the area any longer? His parents had decided to retire to Portugal, and he knew there was no way he could bear to live in the same town as Verity once she *did* return to take over her uncle's business—but then fate stepped in, throwing him a wild card.

He had obtained tickets for the annual prestigious Chelsea Flower Show—two of them—because he had assumed by then that Verity would be back from New York and he had wanted to take her with him.

Almost, he decided not to go. He had lost his love, and it looked very much as if he could soon be losing his business as well, but the tickets were bought and paid for and so he set out for London.

He saw Sarah when he was booking in at his hotel. She was staying there too, a thin, too pale girl who looked nothing like Verity and whom, if he was honest, he felt more sympathy for than desire. Her attempts to pick him up were so obvious and awkward that he had took pity on her and offered to buy her a drink. She was, she told him, originally from Australia where she had lived with foster parents, and she had come to England trying to trace her birth mother.

Whilst living in London she had met and fallen in love with a fellow Australian who had now left the country to continue his round-the-world tour, refusing to take Sarah with him.

'I thought he loved me,' she told Silas sadly, 'but he didn't, he was just using me.'

Her words and her sadness struck a sombre chord within Silas. In an attempt to cheer her up he offered her his spare ticket for the flower show, which she accepted.

They spent all that day together and the next, although there was nothing remotely sexual between them. Silas simply didn't feel that way about her. Verity was the only woman he wanted. Emotionally he might hate her for what she had done to him, but physically, at night alone in his bed, he still ached and yearned for her.

Even now he still didn't know what prompted him to knock on Sarah's door the second night after they had met. She didn't answer his knock but when, driven by some sixth sense, he turned the handle and pushed open the door, he found her seated on the bed, a glass of water in one hand and a bottle of pills on the bed beside her.

He shook her so savagely as he demanded to know how many she had taken that it was a wonder her neck didn't snap, he acknowledged later.

'None,' she told him dull-eyed, 'not yet...'

'Not yet. Not ever!' Silas told her sharply, picking up the bottle and going through to the bathroom to flush the contents down the lavatory.

When he came back she was crying soullessly into her hands.

'Don't go,' she begged him. 'I don't want to be on my own.'

And so he stayed and, inevitably perhaps, they had sex, out of compassion and pity on his part and loneliness and need on hers.

In the morning they went their separate ways, but not before Silas had insisted on giving Sarah his telephone number and getting her own address from her.

He was concerned enough about her to telephone her as soon as he got home and to ring her regularly twice a week after that.

Always, at the back of his mind, was the concern that she might succumb and try a second time to take her own life. She had told him sadly that when her boyfriend had moved on she had felt she had nothing left to live for. His own pain at losing Verity had enabled him to understand what she had been feeling. He had counselled her to think about returning to Australia and her foster parents and friends, and she had promised him she would think about doing so, and then he received the tearful telephone call that was to completely change his life—to change both their lives.

She was pregnant, she told him, an accident. She was on the pill but had forgotten to take it. He was not to worry, she said, she intended to have the pregnancy terminated.

Silas reacted immediately and instinctively, taking the first train to York where she was living.

'I can't afford a baby,' she protested when he told her that he didn't want her to have a termination.

'This is *my* baby as well as yours,' Silas reminded her sombrely. 'We could get married and share the responsibility.'

'Get married? *Us*…? You and me? But you don't… It was just sex,' she protested shakily.

Just sex maybe, but they had still created a new life between them, and in the end she gave way and they were married very quickly and very quietly.

From the start Honor had been an independent, cheerful child. Until she had started school Silas had often taken her to work with him and the bond between them was very close and strong. She had asked about her mother, of course, and Silas had told her what little he knew, but until recently she had always seemed perfectly happy for there just to be the two of them.

He had named her Honor as a form of promise to Sarah that he would always honour the bargain they had made between them to put the welfare of the child they had created first, and he believed that he had always honoured that bargain.

He could hear Verity coming back downstairs now.

'I… I'm sorry about…about the car…' she told him awkwardly as she walked into the kitchen.

'It's hardly your fault,' Silas pointed out.

'Do you plan to stay in town long?' he asked her politely as he handed her the glass of wine he had poured her.

'I… I'm not really sure yet.'

Silas frowned. 'Surely the business—?' he began, but Verity cut him off, shaking her head.

'I sold it… It was either that or risk being forcibly taken over. I plan to use the money to establish a charitable trust in my uncle's name,' she told him.

Silas fought hard not to let his shock show. What had happened to the woman who had put the business before their love? Verity must have changed dramatically—or perhaps weakened. Quickly he caught himself up. There was no point in allowing his thoughts to travel down *that* road, or in hoping, *wishing*— what? That she had had such a change of heart earlier, that their love…that he had been more important to her, that they could have… Stop it, he warned himself.

'It must have been hard for you, making the decision to sell,' he commented as unemotionally as he could. 'After all, it's been your life…'

Her *life*. Had he any idea how cruel he was being? Verity wondered. Did he know what it did to her to be told by him, of all people, that her life was so cold and empty and lacking in real emotion? She stiffened her spine and put down her glass.

'No more than *your* business has been yours,' she pointed out quietly.

It wasn't true, of course—his work had been something that he loved, that he had chosen *freely* for himself, whilst hers... Not even with him could she be able to discuss how it had felt to finally step out from beneath the heavy burden that the business had always been to her, to feel free, to be her own person for the first time in her life.

Verity drew in her breath with a small hiss of pain.

'I think I'd like to go to bed,' she told him shakily. 'It's been a long day.'

Meaning, of course, that she didn't want to spend any time with him, Silas recognised.

'I'll take you up,' he told her curtly.

The guest room, Verity discovered, was more of a small, private suite on the top floor of the house in what must have originally been the attics—a pretty, good-sized bedroom with sloping ceiling and its own bathroom plus a small sitting room.

'I had this conversion done for Honor,' Silas informed her. 'She's getting to an age where she needs her own space and her own privacy.'

As he turned and walked towards the door Verity had a strong compulsion to run after him and stop him.

'Silas...'

He stopped and turned round, waiting in silence.

'Goodnight,' she told him shakily.

'Goodnight,' he returned.

After showering and brushing her hair, Verity crept into bed. It felt so strange being here in Silas' house. During the years they had been apart she had resisted the temptation to think about Silas and what might have been. She thought she had learnt to live with the pain, but seeing him again had reawakened not just the pain she had felt but all her other emotions as well. She couldn't possibly still love him. Hadn't she learned her lesson? Verity could feel the back of her throat beginning to ache with the weight of her suppressed tears as she closed her eyes and willed herself to go to sleep.

CHAPTER EIGHT

SILAS woke up abruptly. There was a sour taste in his mouth from the wine he had drunk and his head ached. Swinging his legs out of bed, he stood up and reached for his robe. His weight was much the same now as it had always been but his body was far more heavily muscled than it had been when he was in his twenties—the work he did was responsible for that, of course. Shaking his head, he padded barefoot out onto the landing and into the bathroom. He needed a glass of water.

He was just reaching into the bathroom cabinet for an aspirin when he heard a familiar sound. Putting down the glass of water he had been holding, he walked quickly towards Honor's door. When she was younger she had often woken in the night in tears, frightened by some bad monster disturbing her dreams, but when he gently opened her bedroom door she was sleeping deeply and peacefully.

Still frowning, he glanced towards the stairs that led to the guest suite.

The noise was clearer now, a soft, heart-tearing sobbing. Verity was crying?

Immediately, taking the stairs two at a time, Silas hurried to her room, pushing open the door.

Like Honor she was asleep, but unlike Honor her sleep wasn't peaceful. The bedclothes were tangled and the duvet half off the bed, exposing the creamy softness of her skin. As he realised that, like him, she slept in the nude, Silas hastily willed himself to ignore the temptation to let his gaze stray to her body, concentrating instead on her pale, tear-stained face.

Without her make-up and with her hair down she looked no different now than she had done at nineteen and, for a moment, the temptation to gather her up in his arms and hold her close was so strong that he had to take a step back from the bed to prevent himself from doing so.

In her sleep Verity gave a small, heartbreaking little cry, fresh tears rolling down her face from her closed eyes.

Silas could remember how rarely she had cried, how brave and independent she had always tried to be. Once, when they had quarrelled about something—he had forgotten what, some minor disagreement—she had turned her face away from him in the car and he had thought she had been sulking until he had looked in the wing mirror and seen the tears streaming from her eyes.

'I didn't want you to see me cry,' she had told him when he had stopped the car and taken her in his arms. 'It hurts so much.'

'The last thing I want to do is hurt you,' Silas had told her and meant it.

In her sleep Verity was reliving the events of the final summer of her relationship with Silas. After the two days they had spent together, New York had seemed even more lonely than ever. The work she had been doing with her uncle's old friend had been mentally and physically demanding and yet, at the same time somehow, very unsatisfying. She hadn't got the heart for it, Verity had acknowledged. Her heart had been given to Silas. Just how empty her life had been without him had been brought home to her during the two days they had spent together. Then, she had felt alive, whole, complete... When he had gone... It had been less than a week since he had flown home, having begged her to tell her uncle that she had changed her mind and that her future now lay with Silas.

'I can't do it,' she protested.

'It's business, Verity,' Silas argued, 'that's all. *We're* human beings with feelings, needs... I miss you and I want us to be together.'

'I miss you too,' Verity told him.

Initially she had been supposed to be spending four months in New York, but the original four had stretched to eight and then twelve, and every time she mentioned coming home her uncle procrastinated and said that, according to his friend, there was a great deal she still had to learn.

Sometimes the temptation to tell him that she simply couldn't do what he wanted her to do was so strong that she almost gave in to it, and then she would remember how he had taken her in.

Although it had never been discussed between them, Verity had the feeling that her uncle blamed her for her father's death. He and her mother had been on their way to collect her from a birthday party she had insisted on going to when they had been involved in the fatal accident which had killed them both, and she felt as though, in taking his place, she was doing some kind of penance, making some kind of restitution.

She had tried to say as much to Silas but he always got so angry when they discussed her uncle that she had simply not been able to do so. And her uncle seemed to dislike and resent Silas as much as Silas did him.

'Have you any idea just how wealthy you are going to be?' he demanded of Verity when she begged him to allow her to return home. 'You must be very careful, Verity,' he warned her. 'There are always going to be hungry and ambitious men out there who will try to convince you that they love you. Don't listen to them.'

'Silas isn't like that,' she protested defensively.

'Isn't he?' her uncle countered grimly. 'Well, he is certainly a young man with an awful lot of debts—far too many to be able to support a wife.'

'Come home,' Silas begged her.

But she said, 'No...not until I have fulfilled my debt to my uncle.'

Shortly after Silas returned to England, the murder of one of her fellow tenants in the block where she rented an apartment resulted in her uncle insisting that she moved to a safer address.

Verity tried to telephone Silas to tell him that she was moving but, when she wasn't able to get any reply either from Silas' home telephone or the garden centre, she had to ask her uncle to pass on to him her new address and telephone number.

She knew from what Silas had told her during his visit that he had several new commissions and was working virtually eighteen hours a day, which explained why she was unable to get hold of him.

A month later when she had still not heard from

him she finally made herself acknowledge the truth. She loved him and missed him—dreadfully. He was the most important thing, the most important person in her life, and even though it meant disappointing her uncle she knew that it was impossible for her to go on denying her feelings, her love, any longer. She wanted to go home.

She rang her uncle, who assured her that he had passed on to Silas her new address and telephone number.

Silas was angry and upset with her, Verity acknowledged. It had taken a lot for him to beg her to come home as he had done and, no doubt, she had hurt his pride when she had been unable to say yes.

She knew how little he had been able to afford either the time or the money for his spur-of-the-moment flying visit to her, and she wished she had been able to tell him then how much she was missing him and how much she wished she could be with him.

When another two months passed without him getting in touch with her, she finally acknowledged the truth. She had lost weight; she couldn't sleep; she thought about him night and day; she ached so badly for him that the pain of missing him was with her all the time. She loved him so much that, even if it meant letting her uncle down, she knew that it was impossible for her to go on denying her feelings. There must surely be a way that she could be with Silas and do as her uncle wished, a way she did not have to choose between them, but if there wasn't...

If there wasn't, then she had made up her mind, selfish though it might be: being with Silas was more important to her than pleasing her uncle. She wanted to go home; she wanted to be with Silas; she wanted to be held in his arms close to his heart; she wanted to hear him telling her in that gruff, sexy voice he used after they had made love that he loved her and needed her and that he would never ever let her go. She wanted to hear him telling her how much he wanted her to be his wife, how much he wanted them to spend their lives together.

Reliving the times they had had together over and over again in the empty loneliness of her apartment was no substitute for the reality of being with him.

Without giving herself time to change her mind, she booked herself on the first available flight home, without telling anyone what she was doing. She wanted to surprise Silas, to see the look in his eyes when she walked into his arms, to show him that he meant more to her than anything else, than anyone else, in the world.

Confronting her uncle wasn't going to be easy, she knew that. She was twenty-two, old enough to know her own mind and to make her own decisions.

She bought a copy of the local newspaper whilst she waited for a taxi to take her from the station to the garden centre. Without that, without seeing that small, bare announcement of Silas' marriage to another woman, she wouldn't have known, would have walked into a situation for which she was totally unprepared.

The taxi driver, seeing her white face, was concerned enough to ask her if she was ill.

Verity looked at him blankly, her gaze returning to the newsprint in front of her. Silas was *married*. How could that be possible? He had been going to marry *her*. Was she suffering from some kind of madness, some kind of delusion? Was it all just a bad dream? How *could* Silas be married to someone else? There must have been a mistake, and yet she knew that there was no mistake, just as she now knew the reason for his silence during these last long weeks.

The pain was like nothing she had ever imagined experiencing: a tearing, wrenching, soul-destroying agony that made her want to scream and howl and tear at herself and her clothes, to ease a grief she could neither control nor contain.

She made the taxi driver take her back to the station. *En route* to Heathrow and a transatlantic flight back to New York she couldn't understand why, despite the heat of the day, her fingers and toes felt as cold as ice, so cold that they hurt, her movements those of a very, very old woman.

Back in New York she applied herself to her work with a grim concentration, throwing up a barrier around herself that she would allow no one to pass through.

Silas hadn't loved her at all. Silas had lied to her. Her uncle was right. From now on she was going to devote herself to the business. What else, after all, was there for her?

Fresh tears rolled down Verity's face—the tears she had never allowed herself to cry during the reality of her heartbreak at losing Silas but which now, reliving those days in her sleep, she had no power to suppress.

Silas. Not even in the privacy of her apartment had she allowed herself the weakness of whispering his name, of reliving all the times they had shared together.

'Silas…'

As he heard her say his name Silas closed his eyes. It hurt him to hear the emotion in her voice and to see the evidence of the distress on her damp face.

Very gently he reached out and touched her wet cheek. Her skin felt cool beneath his fingertips, her eyelashes ridiculously long as they fanned darkly on her cheek. She was lying half on and half off the pillow and automatically he slid his hand beneath the nape of her neck intending to make her more comfortable, just as he often did for Honor. But Verity wasn't Honor, a child…his child… She was a woman…his woman…

The shudder that galvanised his body was its own warning but it was a warning that came far too late. He stiffened as Verity suddenly opened her eyes.

'Silas…'

The husky wonderment in her voice held him spellbound.

'Silas.'

She said his name again, breathing it as unsteadily as an uncertain swimmer gulping air. As she struggled to sit up, the duvet slid further from her body, leaving it clothed only in the soft silver moonlight coming in through the window.

Silas caught his breath. In her early twenties she had had the body of a girl, slender and gently curved, only hinting at what it would be in maturity, but now she was fully a woman, her curves were so richly sensuous that he had to close his eyes to stop himself from reaching out to touch her just to make sure that she was real. He could feel the beads of sweat beginning to pearl his skin as he was flooded with hungry desire for her.

Even though he had looked away immediately, every detail of her was already imprinted on his eyeballs and his emotions. His hands ached to cup the ripe softness of her breasts, to stroke the taut warmth of her belly, to cover the feminine crispness of her pubic curls, to…

The power of his reaction to her, not just sexually but emotionally as well, shocked him into immobility.

'Silas…'

Reluctantly he opened his eyes as she whispered his name. Her mouth looked soft and warm, her eyes confused and unhappy. He lifted his hand to touch her hair and let it slide silkily through his fingers, his body shuddering as he started to release her.

Verity watched wide-eyed, still caught up in the intensity of her dream, her glance following Silas' every movement. Pleadingly she raised her hand to touch the side of his face, her palm flat against his jaw where she could feel his beard prickling her skin.

Silas closed his eyes as he moaned her name, a tortured, haunted sound of denial, but Verity was too lost in what she was doing to respond to it. Her fingertips trembled as she pressed them against his mouth, exploring its familiar shape, feeling them move as he mouthed her name. Instinctively she slipped them between his lips.

Immediately her nipples hardened, the muscles in her belly and thighs tautening as she shook with the force of what she was feeling.

Helplessly Silas opened his mouth, his tongue tip

caressing the smooth warmth of her fingertips. He could see as well as feel her whole body trembling in reaction to his caress. Holding her arm, he sucked slowly on her fingers.

Beneath her breath Verity made a small, familiar keening noise as she lifted her other hand to his face, stroking him with frantic little movements, far more sensual and exciting for all their lack of open sexuality than a more calculatedly sexual caress could ever have been.

His self-control breaking, Silas caught hold of her hands, bearing her back against the softness of the pillow, his hands now cupping her face as he started to kiss her, opening her mouth with his lips, his tongue, feeding rather than satisfying his hunger for her with passionate, deeply intimate kisses.

As she opened her mouth to him, Verity caught back a small sob of relief. It had been so awful, dreaming that she had lost Silas, but here he was, with her, holding her, loving her, showing her that she was safe.

The smell of him, the sight of him, the *feel* of him, totally overwhelmed her starved senses, her body, so sensitive to him that her breasts were aching for his touch even before she felt his hands reaching out to cup them. Eagerly she moved to accommodate and help him, shivering in mute pleasure as she felt the hard familiarity of his palms against the taut peaks of her nipples.

Beneath his robe he was naked and it was heaven to have the luxury of sliding her hands up over his shoulders and down his back, to feel the solid male warmth of his skin, his *body* beneath her hands, to have the longed-for male reality of his flesh against her own, to feel that she was totally and completely surrounded and protected by him.

'Silas.' As she said his name she moved beneath him, silently inviting him to increase the intimacy between them.

As he felt her lifting her body towards his Silas groaned. He could feel her trembling as he touched her and he knew that he was shaking just as much. There hadn't been this much sexual tension between them even the first time they had made love. It felt as though their bodies were waiting to explode, to meld, to come together so completely that they could never be parted again.

She felt so good, so right...so...so Verity. He wanted to touch her, kiss her, possess her so completely that she would never be able to leave him again.

His hand touched her stomach and she rose up eagerly against him. He bent his mouth towards her breast, holding his breath as he started to lick delicately at her nipple, half afraid he might accidentally hurt her as he forced himself to go slowly, but Verity seemed to have no such inhibitions, her hand going to the back of his head as she pulled him closer to her body so that his mouth opened fully over her damp nipple.

Shuddering, he drew it deeply into his mouth and started to suck rhythmically on her. Beneath his hand he could feel the flesh of her belly grow hot and damp. Her face was flushed with desire, her body trembling as she made small, pleading cries deep in her throat.

Wordlessly he parted her thighs. The room was light enough for him to be able to see her naked body, and her sex. He could remember how shy she had been the first time he had whispered to her how much he wanted to see her, to look at her. But she had still let him and he could still remember the sense of awe and love he had felt, knowing just how much she trusted him.

He could see that same trust in her eyes now and, even though he knew he was deluding himself, it was almost as though there had never been anyone else for her but him, as though her body had never known any other lover, as though it had memories of only him, his touch, his need, his love.

Sombrely he parted her soft outer lips, exposing the secret kernel of her sex. His heart was thudding frantically fast, his own body stiff with arousal and need. He could see her looking at him, silent and wide-eyed as she reached out to caress him with her fingertips.

Very gently he touched her, coaxing, caressing.

Verity gave a low, aching groan, her hand tightening around him. She could feel her body responding to him, aching for him. It had been without him for so long that it needed no preliminaries, hungry and eager now for the longed-for feel of him within it.

'I want you, Silas,' she told him jerkily. 'I need you...now... Oh, yes, now...' she whispered frantically. 'Now. Now...now...'

The rhythm of their lovemaking was fast and intense, their shared climax a juddering, explosive catalyst of release that left them both trembling as Silas held Verity in his arms.

'Stay with me,' Verity whispered to him as her exhausted body slid into sleep. 'Don't leave me, Silas. Please don't leave me... Not this time...'

As she slept Silas looked down into her face. She was a woman now, a woman with a woman's needs, a woman's sexuality. If she hadn't loved him enough to put their love first before, she was hardly likely to do so now. She might want him sexually, she might even stay for a while, but it wasn't just his own emotions she was likely to hurt this time, his own heart she could easily break. There was Honor to consider as well.

'Stay with me,' she had begged him. But she was the one who had left *him*. *She* was the one who had refused to stay.

Very slowly he eased himself away from her, picking up his discarded robe as he looked down at her.

'Stay with me,' she had said. As he bent and kissed her cheek a single tear rolled down her face, but it wasn't one of her own.

Clenching his jaw, Silas walked towards the door, closing it quietly behind him without daring to look back.

CHAPTER NINE

VERITY surfaced slowly from the deepest and most relaxing sleep she could remember having in a long time. She stretched luxuriously, a womanly knowing smile curling her mouth. Her body felt deliciously, blissfully satisfied. Even her skin where the sunlight shone warmly on her exposed arm on top of the duvet seemed to have a silken, sensuous shimmer to it. She closed her eyes and made a purring sound of female happiness deep in her throat as she savoured the novelty of feeling so good. It was as if she had opened a present, spilling out from it a glowing, sparkling, magical gift of happiness and love. Mmm... Her eyes still closed, she rolled over and reached out for Silas.

Abruptly, Verity opened her eyes properly, her body tensing as her hand rested on the cold empty space on the other half of the bed. Of course. She had known Silas wouldn't be there in bed beside her—he had Honor to think of, after all—but the pristine smoothness of the unused pillow next to her own suggested that he had left her on her own as speedily as he could, not even pausing for a few moments to savour their closeness, and that hurt!

Her happiness and joy evaporated immediately.

Once before, he had left her like this and she had woken up alone. Then, he had returned carrying arms full of flowers and fresh bagels he had bought from a bakery in her New York neighbourhood.

Then they had shared a breakfast of kisses and bagels in her bed.

Then...

But this was now and instinct told her that the reason for his absence from her bed had nothing to do with any plans he had to surprise her with early morning flowers or other gifts of love.

She could hear footsteps on the stairs leading to her bedroom but she knew, even before the door was pushed open and Honor's dark head appeared around it, that they did not belong to Silas.

'Are you awake?' Honor asked her.

Forcing a smile, Verity nodded.

'I wanted you to sleep with *me* last night,' Honor told her reproachfully as she ran across the room and scrambled up onto the bed next to Verity, snuggling up to her.

Automatically Verity reached out her arm to draw her close and hold her. Her body, which such a short space of time ago had felt so good, so female, so loved, now felt cold and empty, her muscles aching and tense. But it wasn't *Honor's* fault that she wasn't her father.

Verity could hear fresh footsteps on the stairs but, unlike Honor's, these stopped halfway and she heard Silas call out, 'Honor... Breakfast...'

'Coming, Dad,' Honor called back, scrambling off the bed and starting to head for the door, and then unexpectedly turning round and rushing back to fling her arms around Verity's neck and give her a brief little girl kiss.

Blinking fiercely, Verity watched her leave. The fact that Silas had not chosen to come into her room had told her everything she needed to know about how he felt about last night, as though she *needed* any extra underlining of the fact that it had meant so little to him.

Fresh tears welled and once again she forced them back, but these had nothing to do with the tenderness she had felt at Honor's kiss.

She might only have the haziest memory of how she and Silas had come to be making love last night—she could remember waking up to the touch of his fingers on her face, the warmth of his body next to hers. Presumably he must have had some reason to come up to her room.

She might not know what that was, but she certainly knew why he had made love to her—made love! Had *sex*, she told herself brutally. She might not be able to remember what had brought him to her bed, but she could certainly remember what had kept him there. She couldn't have made her feelings, her need of him, more plain if she'd written them on a ten-foot banner, she told herself bitterly. He'd have to be made of granite not to have taken what she had so stupidly put on offer for him.

Sexual desire, sexual frustration, could do all manner of things to a man—even make him feel the need for a woman he did not like, never mind love, and that was quite plainly what had happened last night. Silas had used her to vent his sexual frustration. No *wonder* he hadn't stayed with her. No *wonder* he was keeping his distance from her this morning.

The plain, ugly truth was that he had used her and she had let him—and not merely let him but positively encouraged him. And to think that when she'd woken up she had thought...felt...believed...

Would she *never* learn? She had believed once before that he had loved her, cared for her, *about* her, and she had been wrong. Now, here she was, eleven years down the line, still hoping, still feeling...still *loving*.

Verity closed her eyes. No. She did *not* still love him. She could not still love him. She *would* not still love him. She opened them again and stared dully at the wall. Just who did she think she was kidding? She loved him all right!

Drearily she got out of bed and headed for the bathroom. Coming back to town had been a total mistake. And she was not even convinced any more about her real motives in having done so.

Or perhaps she was. *Had* it been at the back of her mind all the time that she would see Silas? Even though she knew he was married to someone else?

She gave a small, hollow groan. She had come back because this was her home, the place where she had grown up.

Once she had dressed, reluctantly she made her way downstairs.

When she pushed open the kitchen door, Honor was seated at the table eating her cereal whilst Silas stood at the counter making coffee.

As she walked in he turned and looked at her and then looked quickly away again.

'I've just checked with the garage. They're going to make picking up your car a priority,' he told her, his attention on the kettle he was refilling, asking her briefly, 'Tea or coffee?'

'Coffee, please,' Verity responded. Did he really need to ask? Had he really forgotten how he had teased her in the past about her urgent need for her morning caffeine, or was he underlining the fact that, although her preferences mattered, they were of as little importance to him as she was herself.

'I'll drop you off at your place when I take Honor to school,' he told her as he made her coffee.

'Toast...cereal?'

'No, nothing, thanks,' Verity told him coolly.

As he brought the coffee to her she deliberately turned away from him. He smelled of soap and coffee and her stomach muscles churned frantically as he stood next to her. Inside she was trembling and she had to wrap both her hands around the mug of coffee he had brought her, just in case he might see how much he was affecting her.

'When are we going to do the shopping for the dinner party?' Honor was keen to know.

They were in Silas' car on the way to Honor's school, Verity seated in the front passenger seat next to Silas, at Honor's insistence and very much against her own inclinations. The dinner party! Verity had forgotten all about that.

'That's enough, Honor,' Silas told her crisply as he pulled up at the school gate.

As she hopped out of the car Honor said, 'Look, there's my friend Catherine. I want her to meet you,' and then she was tugging open Verity's door and leaving Verity with no alternative other than to unfasten her seat belt and go with her to where the young girl was standing watching.

'Catherine, this is Verity,' Honor announced importantly. Catherine was smaller and fairer than Honor and it was plain to see which of them was the leader of their twosome, Verity acknowledged as Catherine gave her a shy look and started to giggle.

'Goodbye.' Honor reached up and gave Verity a fierce hug before telling her, 'And don't forget, will you, about the dinner party?'

Verity watched her race out of sight with her friend before turning to walk back to the car. Bending down, she told Silas through the open window, 'I can walk home from here, thank you...'

And before he could say anything she turned smartly on her heel and proceeded to do just that.

She wasn't going to give him another opportunity to humiliate her by keeping his distance from her, she decided proudly, as she lifted her chin and willed herself not to look back at him.

As he watched Verity walking away through his rear-view mirror, Silas hit the steering wheel with the flat of his hand.

He was the one who was in danger of being hurt, rejected, used, so how come it was *Verity* who was behaving as though he were the one treating her badly?

He had known all along that last night had been a mistake and there, this morning, was the proof of it. Verity was treating him as distantly as though they were two strangers. It was perfectly obvious that she regretted what had happened between them, and that she intended to make it very plain to him that neither it nor he meant anything to her. Last night she might have wanted him, but this morning...

* * *

'But you promised...' Honor insisted, tears clustering on her lashes as she stared across the table at her father.

'Honor. I've just explained. I don't have the time to get involved in giving dinner parties and—'

'*Verity's* going to do it...'

'*Verity* is far too busy with her own life to want to get involved in ours,' Silas told her curtly. 'And, whilst we're on the subject, I want you to promise me that you won't go round there any more. Verity has her own life to live.'

Watching the tears run pathetically down his daughter's face, Silas cursed silently to himself.

He hated having to disappoint and hurt her like this but what other option did he have? The more he allowed her to get involved with Verity, the more she was going to be hurt in the end.

'Now hurry up and finish your homework,' Silas admonished her sternly. 'I've got to go out at eight and Mrs Simmonds is coming round to babysit you...'

'Mrs Simmonds.' Honor glared at him. She liked the elderly widow who normally came to sit with her on the rare occasions when Silas went out in the evening, but she wasn't Verity.

'Why can't I have Verity? Where are you going anyway?' she demanded suspiciously. 'Not to see Myra?'

Silas gritted his teeth.

'No. I am not.'

He knew perfectly well what was in Honor's mind. She had made it more than plain that she didn't want Myra as a stepmother—not that there had been any real danger of that happening. Myra was not good stepmother material, Silas acknowledged, especially not for Honor who needed a much more compassionate hand on the reins; a much more gentle touch—like Verity's! Now where had that thought come from?

Watching him under her lashes, Honor held her breath. For her, Verity would make the perfect stepmother. She remembered the message she had seen on the back of the photo in her father's desk.

'To my beloved Silas, with all my love for ever and always.'

'Why did they say they didn't know each other, do you suppose?' Catherine had asked, wide-eyed, when Honor had related this interesting fact to her.

Honor had rolled her eyes and told her severely, 'Because they're still in love with one another stupid…'

'How can they be?' Catherine had objected naively. 'Your father married your mother…'

'It happens!' Honor had assured her wisely.

'Maybe they just stopped being in love,' Catherine had suggested, adding, 'Anyway, why do you want to have Verity as your stepmother?'

'Because…' Honor had told her with quelling dismissal.

If she had to have a stepmother, and it seemed that she did, then Verity was quite definitely the one she wanted, and so she had mounted her own special campaign towards that end.

Now, though, things weren't going at all according to plan and the tears filling her eyes weren't entirely manufactured. Cuddled up in Verity's arms this morning, she had experienced an emotion which had broken through the tough, protective outer shell she had created around herself. From being very young she had resented the pity she had seen in the eyes of the women who had cooed at her father and said how hard it must be for him to bring up a little girl like her on his own, scowling horribly at them when she had digested what they'd been saying. Gradually, she had come to see the adult members of her own sex not as potential allies, but as adversaries who wanted to come between her and her father.

With Verity it was different. Honor didn't know why. She just knew that it was, that there was something soft and comforting and lovely about Verity and about being with her. She now wanted Verity as her stepmother, not just to protect her from the likes of Myra, but for herself as herself, and now, just as things were beginning to work out, here was her father being awkward and upsetting all her plans.

His suggestion that Verity might be too busy with her own life to have time for her was one she dismissed out of hand. She knew, of course, that it wasn't true. Verity *liked* her. She could see it in her eyes when she looked at her; there was no mistaking that special loving look. She had seen it in Catherine's mother's eyes when *she* looked at Catherine and felt envious of her because of it.

Silas was driving past Verity's house on his way home. Her BMW was parked in the drive. On impulse he stopped his own car and got out.

The gardens looked very much the same now as they had done when he had worked in them. There was the border he had been working on the first time he had seen Verity. Grimly he looked away and then, almost against his will, he found himself turning back, walking across the lawn.

The house might have changed since she had lived here, but the gardens hadn't, Verity acknowledged as she paused by the fish pond, peering into it in the dusk of the summer's evening.

Her uncle had used to threaten to have it filled in, complaining that the carp attracted the attentions of a local tom-cat, but Verity had pleaded with him not to do so. She used to love sitting here watching the fish. It was one of her favourite places.

From here she could see the small summer house where she and Silas had exchanged their first earth-shattering kiss.

An unexpected miaow made her jump and then put her hand on her heart as, out of the shadows of the shrubbery, a small, black cat stalked, weaving his way towards her to rub purringly against her legs.

Laughing, Verity bent to stroke him.

'Well, *you* certainly aren't old Tom,' she told him as she rubbed behind his ear, 'but you could be one of his offspring.'

Miaowing as if in assent, the cat jumped up onto the stone edge of the pond where she was sitting and peered into the darkness of the water.

'Ah ha. Yes, you definitely *must* be related to him,' Verity teased.

As a child she would have loved a pet but her uncle had always refused, and once she had become adult the business had kept her too busy and away from home too often for her to feel it would be fair for her to have one.

Now, though, things were different. When she finally decided where she was going to spend the rest of her life, there was nothing to stop her having a cat or a dog if she so chose... A cat, I suppose it would have to be, she mused. After all, cats and lonely single women were supposed to go together weren't they? A dog somehow or other suggested someone with friends, a family...a full, vigorous life.

Bending her head over the cat, she tickled behind his ear.

'Verity...'

'Silas...' Quickly Verity stood up, her stance unknowingly defensive as though she was trying to hold him off, Silas noted, as she held her hands up in front of her body.

Immediately he took a step back from her.

He couldn't even bear to be within feet of her, never mind inches, Verity recognised achingly as she saw the way Silas distanced himself from her.

'I was just thinking that this cat could be one of old Tom's descendants,' she told Silas huskily, trying to fill the tensioned silence.

'Mmm...from the looks of him he very probably is,' Silas agreed.

'Look, Verity, I wonder if I could have a few words with you.'

Verity's heart sank.

'Yes... Yes, of course,' she managed to agree. Whatever it was Silas wanted to say to her, she could see from his expression that it wasn't anything particularly pleasant.

'It's about Honor,' Silas told her, still keeping his distance from her. 'I've had a talk with her this evening about...about the way she's...she's been trying to involve you in our lives... I've explained to her that *you* have your own life to live and—'

'You've come here to tell me that you don't want her to see me any more,' Verity interrupted flatly, guessing what he was about to say and praying that he wouldn't be able to tell just how much what he was saying was hurting her.

'I... I think it would be best if she didn't,' Silas agreed heavily. 'She's at a very vulnerable age and...'

'Do you think that *I* don't know that?' Verity told him swiftly, her face paling with the intensity of her emotions. 'I've been there, Silas,' she advised him jerkily, 'remember...?'

It was the wrong thing to say, the very worst thing she could have said, she realised as she saw his mouth twist and heard the inflection in his voice as he told her curtly, 'Yes, *I* remember... Honor's got it into her head that she needs a woman's influence in her life,' Silas admitted slowly, 'but...'

'But there's no way you want that woman to be *me*,' Verity guessed angrily.

'I don't want Honor to be *hurt*,' Silas interrupted her bluntly.

Verity stared at him. She could feel the too-fast beat of her own heart and wondered dizzily if Silas too could hear the sound it made as it thudded against her chest wall.

Was he really trying to imply that *she* would stoop so low as to try to hurt *Honor*? A *child*...? Did he really think...?

For a moment Verity felt too outraged to speak. Quickly she swallowed, drawing herself up to her full height as she challenged him, 'Are you suggesting that *I* would hurt Honor? Is that *really* what you think of me, Silas?' she questioned him carefully. 'Do you really think of me as being so...so *vengeful*?'

Half blinded by the tears that suddenly filled her eyes, she turned away from him and started to walk quickly towards the house, breaking into a run when she heard him calling her name.

'Verity,' Silas protested, cursing himself under his breath. She had every right to be angry with him, he knew that. But surely she could see that he had every right to protect his child?

'Verity,' he protested again, but he knew it was too late. She was already running up the steps and into the house.

Quickly Verity dabbed at her hot face with the cold water she had run to stop her tears.

How *could* Silas imply that she would hurt Honor? How *dared* he imply it after what *he* had done to her, the way *he* had hurt *her*? It must be his own guilty conscience that was motivating him.

She would *never* do anything like that. Not to a child, not to *anyone*... She had wanted to help Honor for Honor's sake alone. Her sense of kinship with her had nothing to do with the fact that she was his daughter.

Hadn't it? Slowly she straightened up and looked at herself in the bathroom mirror. Hadn't a part of her recognised how easily *she* might have been Honor's mother? Hadn't she felt somehow honour-bound herself to reach out and help the girl because of that inner knowledge?

To *help* her, yes, but to *hurt* her, never. Never...never...

She couldn't stay here in this town. Not after this. She would ring the agent tomorrow, tell him that she was terminating her lease on the house; the charitable trust she had wanted to establish in her uncle's name in the town could still go ahead—the details of that could be dealt with as easily from London as from here. She had been a fool ever to have come back. She *was* a fool. A stupid, idiotic, heartbroken fool!

CHAPTER TEN

'Verity... Verity... It is you, isn't it?'

Verity put down the shopping she had just been about to put in the back of the car and looked uncertainly at the woman hailing her, her face breaking into a warm smile as she recognised a girl who had been at school with her.

'Gwen!' she exclaimed warmly. 'Good heavens. How *are* you...?'

'Fine. If you don't count the fact that I'm thirty-three, ten pounds overweight and just about to do a supermarket shop for a husband and three kids,' the other woman groaned. 'When did you get back to town? You look wonderful, by the way...'

'Only very recently. I—'

'Look, I'm in a bit of a rush now. We've got the in-laws coming round for supper.' She pulled a wry face. 'I'd love to have a proper chat with you, catch up on what you've been doing... Can I give you a ring?'

'Yes. Yes, that would be nice,' Verity acknowledged, quickly writing down her telephone number for her before climbing into her car.

It was ironic that she should bump into one of the few girls she had made friends with at school just as she had decided she was going to leave town, she thought as she started her car.

* * *

Honor looked sideways at the telephone in the garden centre office. It was Saturday morning and, instead of going swimming with Catherine and her mother, she had opted to come to work with her father. He was outside dealing with a customer. Glancing over her shoulder, Honor reached for the telephone receiver and quickly punched in Verity's telephone number.

Verity heard the telephone ringing as she unlocked the front door, putting down her bag as she went to answer it.

'Verity, is that you?'

Her heart lurched as she recognised Honor's voice and heard its forlorn note.

'Honor... Where are you? Are you all right?' she asked anxiously.

'Mmm...sort of... I'm at the garden centre. Verity, can I come and see you?'

Verity leaned back against the hall wall and closed her eyes.

'Oh, Honor,' she whispered sadly beneath her breath. Opening her eyes, she said as steadily as she could, 'Honor, I don't think that would be a good idea, do you? I—'

'You've spoken to Dad, haven't you?' Honor demanded in a flat, accusing voice. 'I thought you *liked* me... I thought we were *friends*...'

Verity could hear the tears in her voice.

'Honor,' she pleaded. 'Please...'

'I thought you *liked* me...' Honor was repeating, crying in earnest now.

Verity pushed her hand into her hair. She had left it down this morning, oblivious to the admiring male glances she had attracted as she'd walked across the supermarket car park, the bright sunlight burnishing it to honey-gold.

'Honor. Honor, I do... I do... but I shan't be staying in town very much longer. I only intended to make a very short visit here,' Verity began, but Honor was no longer listening to her.

'You're leaving? No, you can't. You mustn't. I need you, Verity.' Then the phone went down.

Leaning against the wall, Verity took a deep breath.

Honor looked at her father. He was still talking to his customer. Sometimes grown-ups just didn't know what was good for them!

She went up to him.

'Dad, I've changed my mind and I want to go swimming with Catherine after all.'

'All right,' Silas agreed. 'Give me five minutes and then I'll drive you round to Catherine's.'

'I'll need to go home first to get my swimming things,' Honor reminded him.

'Fine...' Silas replied.

He was well aware that he was in his daughter's bad books—and why. His only comfort was that one day she would understand and thank him for protecting her. One day... but quite definitely not *today*.

'So what are you going to do?' Catherine asked Honor interestedly. They were sitting in Catherine's bedroom eating Marmite sandwiches and drying one another's hair after their trip to the leisure centre.

'I don't know yet,' Honor replied in despair.

'You could always try to find someone else to be your stepmother,' Catherine suggested cautiously.

'I don't *want* anyone else,' Honor retorted passionately. 'Would you want to change your mother?'

Catherine looked at her.

'Sometimes I would,' she reflected. 'Specially when she won't let me stay up late to watch television.'

'Goodbye, Honor.'

Honor turned dutifully to smile and wave as she got out of Catherine's mother's car.

The latter had just brought her home and Honor could see her father opening the front door for her. Dragging her bag behind her, she headed towards him.

'No kiss for me...?' Silas asked her with forced joviality as she stalked past him and into the house.

Honor turned to give him a withering, womanly look.

'Honor, I was thinking, you know that puppy you wanted...'

'I don't want a puppy,' Honor told him coldly. 'I want *Verity*.'

Silas gritted his teeth. He knew when he was being punished and given the cold-shoulder treatment. How best to handle it? In situations like this he'd benefit from a woman's advice. Verity's? He checked abruptly. Damn Honor. Now she'd got him doing it.

'I've got your favourite for supper,' he told her heartily as he followed her into the kitchen.

'I'm not hungry,' Honor replied. 'We're having an end-of-term play at school... I'm going to be a pop singer but I'm going to have to have a costume.'

'Well, I'm sure we'll be able to find you one,' Silas

offered, ignoring for the moment the dubious merits of a ten-year-old aping the manners of a much older pop-singer star, sensing that he was being led onto very treacherous ground indeed, but not as yet quite sure just where the danger was coming from. He soon found out.

'All the other girls are having outfits made by their mothers,' Honor informed him.

'Well, perhaps Mrs Simmonds might...' Silas began, but it was obvious that Honor was not going to be so easily put off.

'*Verity* would know how to make mine,' she informed him coldly. Silas held his breath.

'Now, look, Honor—' he began, but as he watched his daughter's eyes fill with tears which then ran slowly down her face he closed his eyes. This was the very situation which he had hoped to avoid.

'Honor,' he began more gently, but his daughter was refusing to listen to him, whirling round and running out of the room and upstairs.

Silas heard the slam of her bedroom door and sighed.

Verity...

God, but even thinking her name hurt, and not just on Honor's account.

Ever since the night she had spent here he had been fighting not to think about her, not to give in to his compelling, compulsive urge to relive every single second of the time he had held her in his arms, every single heartbeat...

Closing his eyes, he acknowledged what he had been fighting to deny ever since he had walked away, leaving her alone in bed.

It was too late to tell himself not to fall into the trap of loving her again. It had always been too late, for the simple reason that he had never stopped.

'Honor, I've got to go out for half an hour. Will you be all right or shall I phone Mrs Simmonds?'

Honor looked up from the book she was reading. It was Monday teatime and Silas had just received a phone call from one of his customers who wanted to see him urgently.

'No, I'll be fine,' Honor assured him instantly.

Honor waited until she was sure her father had gone before going into the study and rifling through his desk until she found what she was looking for. Yes, there it was, the photograph of Verity.

Picking it up, she turned it over, quickly reading the message on the back.

Desperate situations called for desperate measures. Squaring her shoulders, she went upstairs to her bedroom and packed a haversack with a change of clothes. In the kitchen she added a bar of chocolate to it and then, after thoughtful consideration, added another—for Verity.

Having packed her bag, she then sat down and wrote her father a brief note.

Slowly she read it.

'I am going to live with Verity.'

It didn't take her very long to walk round to Verity's, but even her stout heart gave a small bound of relief when she finally got there and saw that Verity's car was outside. She wasn't sure what she would have done if Verity hadn't been in.

The unexpected ring on the doorbell brought Verity to the door with a small frown.

'Honor!' she exclaimed as she saw the small lone figure. 'What...?'

'I've come to live with you,' Honor told her stoically, walking quickly into the hall and then bursting into tears and flinging herself into Verity's arms as she told her between sobs, 'It's horrid not being able to see you.'

By the time Verity had managed to calm her down she was comfortably ensconced in the kitchen eating home-made biscuits and drinking juice whilst the cat, who had decided to adopt Verity, sat purring on her knee.

'Honor, you *know* you can't stay here, don't you?' Verity asked her gently. 'Your father—'

'He doesn't care,' Honor interrupted her.

'You know that isn't true,' Verity chided her. 'He loves you very much...'

'Like you love him?' Honor asked her, looking her straight in the eye.

Verity opened her mouth and then closed it again. Her legs, she discovered, had gone strangely weak. She sat down and was soon extremely glad that she had done so.

Honor was rifling through the haversack she had brought in with her. Triumphantly she produced the photograph she had taken from her father's desk.

'I found this,' she told Verity, watching her.

'Oh, Honor,' was all Verity could say as she stared at the familiar picture. She could remember the day Silas had taken it—it was the day after they had made love for the first time and Silas had told her he would always keep the photograph in memory of all that they had shared.

'Not that I shall ever need any reminding,' he had whispered passionately to her as he had abandoned the camera and taken her in his arms.

'It says "To my beloved Silas, with all my love for ever and always",' Honor told her solemnly.

Verity looked away from her.

'Yes. Yes, I know,' she agreed weakly.

'You said you didn't *know* my father...' Honor reminded her.

'Yes. Yes, I know,' Verity agreed again.

'And *he* said that *he* didn't know you, but you wrote here that you love him. Why did you stop loving him, Verity?'

'I... It wasn't...' Verity shook her head. 'It was all a long time ago, Honor.'

'But I want to know,' Honor persisted stubbornly.

Verity shook her head, but she sensed that Honor wasn't going to be satisfied until she had dragged the whole sorry story out of her.

'There isn't a lot *to* know,' she told her. 'Your father and I were young. I thought... He said... I had to go away to New York to work and whilst I was there your father met someone else—your mother...'

Silas cursed as he found the note Honor had left for him. Angrily he picked up his discarded car keys and headed for the door. She was coming home with him right now and no nonsense, and once he got her home he was going to have a serious talk with her—a *very* serious talk.

Parking his car behind Verity's, Silas got out and

headed for the front door and then, changing his mind, turned to go around the back of the house instead.

The kitchen door was half open—Verity had been outside hanging out some washing when Honor had arrived. Neither of the two occupants of the room could see him and Silas paused in the act of pushing open the door as he heard Verity saying huskily, 'I thought your father loved me. I didn't know about your mother... I suppose I should have guessed that something was wrong when he didn't get in touch with me, but I just thought that he...that he was cross with me because...' She stopped and shook her head. 'I came home to tell him how much I loved him, to tell him that he was right and that our love was more important than any duty I owed my uncle, but I discovered that your father had married your mother.'

Helplessly Verity spread her hands.

'I thought he loved me but he didn't really love me at all.' Her voice shook with emotion and the cat stopped purring.

Honor looked up, her eyes widening as she saw her father standing in the doorway.

Verity turned round to see what had attracted Honor's attention, her face paling as she too saw Silas.

For a moment none of them spoke and then Silas marched across the room and took hold of Honor's arm, saying firmly to her, 'Honor, you're coming with me—right now and no arguments.'

He hadn't said a word to Verity. He hadn't even looked at her, Verity acknowledged as he walked Honor out of the back door, firmly closing it behind him.

She could hear the engine of his car firing. Her hand shook as she reached across the table for the photograph that Honor had left.

Tears blurred her eyes. Tipping back her head, she blinked them away. She was not going to cry...not now, not again...not ever...

Catherine's mother looked surprised when she opened the door to find Silas and Honor outside.

'Jane, I'm sorry to do this to you but something very urgent's cropped up. Can Honor stay with you for...until I can get back for her...?'

'Of course she can,' she agreed warmly, ushering Honor inside. What, she wondered, was going on? There had been a lot of whispering being done between the two girls recently and Catherine was rather obviously 'big with news', as the saying went, announcing importantly to anyone who would listen that she and Honor had a special secret.

Having coldly inclined her cheek for her father to kiss, Honor marched inside with all the regal bearing of a grand dowager—a highly offended grand dowager, Jane Alders reflected ruefully.

Silas, however, was looking far too grim-faced for her to think of questioning him.

Verity was just finishing pegging out the last of the washing she had abandoned when Honor had arrived when Silas came back, walking soft-footed across the grass so that she had no inkling of his presence until she suddenly saw his shadow.

'Si...Silas...' To her chagrin the unexpected shock

of seeing him made her stammer. 'Wha...what do you want? What are you doing here?'

'Do you want the abridged version?' Silas asked her tersely and then, shaking his head without waiting for her to respond, he demanded abruptly, '*Why* did you tell Honor that you came from New York to tell me how much you loved me?'

'Because it was the truth,' Verity admitted huskily. Why on earth was he asking her that? What could it possibly matter now?

'No, it isn't,' Silas argued flatly. 'Your *uncle* told me the *truth*. He told me that you had asked him to tell me that you didn't want to see me again; that it was all over between us.'

Verity stared at him. Suddenly she felt extremely cold.

'No,' she whispered, her hand going to her throat. 'No, that's not true, he *couldn't* have told you that. I don't believe it...'

'Believe it,' Silas told her harshly, 'because I can assure you that he did. Not that I was in any mood to listen to him. Not then. I even wrote to you begging you to change your mind, pleading with you to write back to me, giving what I suppose was an ultimatum in that I wrote that if *I* didn't hear from you then I would have to accept that it was over between us.'

Verity badly needed to sit down.

'Is this some kind of joke?' she asked Silas weakly.

His mouth hardened.

'Can you see me laughing?' he demanded.

Verity shook her head. She could see that he was telling her the truth, but the full enormity of just what her uncle had done, of what he had set in motion, was still too much for her to fully comprehend.

'I never got your letter,' she whispered. 'There was a murder in the apartment block and my uncle insisted that I had to move out. He promised me that he would give you my new address and telephone number. I... I waited and waited for you to get in touch and then, when you didn't...for a while I... You were right. Our love was more important than doing what my uncle wanted. I... I came home to tell you that. To tell you how much I loved you and...' To her horror Verity felt hot tears spill down her cheeks as she relived the full trauma of that time.

'I read about your marriage in the taxi on the way from the station. After that I knew there was no point in trying to see you,' she told him bleakly.

Verity looked down at the ground. *Why* was he doing this to her, dragging her through this...this humiliation? What could it matter now?

'Look, let's put aside the issue of my marriage for the moment,' she heard Silas telling her huskily. 'I want to concentrate on something else, on something far more important... Did you really love me so much, Verity?'

For a moment she was tempted to lie, but why should she? Proudly she lifted her head and looked at him.

'Yes. I did,' she acknowledged. 'I...' Quickly she swallowed, knowing that she could not admit to him that she had never stopped loving him; that she still loved him and that, if anything, that love was even deeper and more painful to her now than it had been then.

'I didn't marry Sarah because I loved her,' she heard Silas telling her rawly. 'I married her because she was pregnant.'

Disbelievingly, Verity focused on him.

'But…' she whispered, shaking her head. 'You would never do something like that. You would never make love to someone you didn't…you didn't care about…'

'I didn't make love to her,' he told her bluntly. 'We just had sex.'

Briefly, without allowing her to stop him, Silas told her exactly what had happened.

After he had finished speaking Verity looked searchingly into his eyes. There was no doubting the veracity of what he had just told her. Her stomach felt as though it had just done a fast cycle in a washing machine, her heart was banging so hard against her ribs she thought it was going to break them, and as for her legs…

'I…I need to sit down,' she told Silas weakly.

'And I need to lie down,' he countered gruffly, 'preferably in bed with you in my arms with nothing between us, with nothing to separate us. Oh, Verity,' he groaned as he suddenly reached for her, wrapping her in his arms as he kissed her eyes, her face, her mouth. 'Oh, Verity, Verity,' he whispered rawly to her. 'You are the only woman I've ever loved, the only woman I ever *will* love…'

'No, that can't be true,' Verity whispered back through kiss-swollen lips. 'It can't be… Not after the way you left me the other night…not after I'd begged you to stay…'

Tears filled her eyes and rolled down her cheeks.

'Oh, no, my darling, don't cry. Please don't cry.' Silas groaned, holding her tight and rocking her in his arms, his cheek pressed against her head. 'It wasn't like that, it really wasn't. I left you because...because I was afraid, not just for myself or for the pain I knew I would feel if I let you back into my life, but for the pain I thought you might cause Honor.'

'I would *never* hurt Honor,' Verity protested fiercely.

'No,' Silas agreed softly. 'Forgive me for that.'

'She reminds me so much of the way I was...' Verity told him shakily. 'Oh, I know how much you love her, Silas...and you *couldn't* be more different from my uncle—'

'But I'm not enough,' Silas interrupted her ruefully, adding before she could protest, 'I know, so my darling daughter has already informed me.'

'Did you really think that of me...that I might hurt you both...?'

'You'd already hurt me very badly once,' Silas reminded her softly. 'Or, at least, so I thought.'

'I felt the same way about you,' Verity admitted. 'It hurt so much knowing that when you'd told me you loved me, when you said that you'd love me for ever, you didn't mean it...'

'I *did* mean it,' Silas corrected her. 'I still mean it, Verity. Is it too late for us to start again?' he asked her seriously.

Verity looked at him, her heart in her eyes.

'I... Oh, Silas...' she whispered.

'Let's go inside,' he whispered back. 'There's a phone call I want to make...'

Even to make his telephone call to Jane Alders, Silas refused to let Verity move out of his arms.

'You stay right where you are,' he mock growled at her when she did try to move away.

'Jane, it's Silas,' he announced when Catherine's mother answered his call, tucking the receiver in the crook of his neck whilst he bent his head to feather a soft kiss against Verity's mouth. 'Would it be asking too much for you to keep Honor there with you tonight? I wouldn't ask but... You don't mind...? No, it's okay, I don't need to speak with her,' he continued, 'but if you could just give her a message from me, if you wouldn't mind. Could you tell her that I think she might be going to get what she wanted? What she wanted more than a puppy,' he stressed, smiling.

'What was all that about?' Verity asked him when he had replaced the receiver.

Smiling at her, Silas said, 'Honor has been begging and pleading with me to let her have a puppy. The other day when I ill-advisedly offered her one as a peace-offering, she informed me that she didn't want a puppy, she wanted you.'

Verity looked at him.

'Oh, Silas,' she protested, torn between laughter and tears.

'I want to take you to bed,' Silas told her huskily, cupping her face in both his hands. 'I want to make love to you, Verity... I want to make love with you. I want to re-affirm all those vows and promises we made to each other years ago, but if you think it is too soon, if you want to wait...if you feel...'

Putting her fingertips against his lips to silence him,

Verity told him softly, 'What I feel right now is that I want you. I want you in all the ways that a woman wants a man she loves, Silas. You can't imagine how empty my life has been without you, how—'

'Can't I?' he checked her gruffly. 'There hasn't been a day in the years we've been apart when *I* haven't thought about you. Even on the day of Sarah's funeral... As I stood at her graveside all I could think was how much I needed and wanted you.'

'Poor girl,' Verity whispered compassionately.

'Yes, poor girl,' Silas agreed.

'Take me to bed,' Verity begged him urgently. 'Take me to bed, Silas, and...'

She didn't have to say any more, *couldn't* have said any more because suddenly he was picking her up and carrying her towards the stairs.

'You are the most beautiful woman on earth,' Silas whispered extravagantly as he threaded his fingers through Verity's hair.

Smiling lazily up at him in the aftermath of their lovemaking, Verity reached out and touched his face, wriggling appreciatively against the muscled warmth of his naked body.

'Hey, don't do that,' Silas warned her as he slowly kissed the palm of her hand. 'At least, not unless you want...'

'Not unless I want what?' Verity teased, deliberately moving even closer.

'Not unless you want this,' Silas told her huskily, taking her hand and placing it against his hardening body.

'Silas, we can't,' Verity protested unconvincingly

as her fingers stroked instinctively down the hard strength of the silky, hot-skinned shaft of male pleasure she was caressing.

It felt so good to be able to touch him like this, to know how much he wanted and needed her, to know how much he loved her.

'Oh, no?' Silas challenged softly, cupping her breast in his hand and bending his head to trail tiny provocative kisses all the way down from her collarbone to her navel.

'Don't...' Verity whispered.

'Don't what?' Silas asked her as he circled her navel with the tip of his tongue, gently biting at her flesh.

'Don't...don't stop,' Verity breathed.

'I'm not going to,' Silas assured her as his head dipped lower and his hand slid between her thighs.

This was bliss, heaven, every delight she had ever known or imagined knowing, Verity decided shakily as she gave in to the gentle caress of Silas' hand against her body and the slow, sensual search of his mouth as it homed in on the sensitive female heart of her.

The orgasmic contractions gripping her body were, if anything, even stronger this second time. Just for a second she tried to resist them, wanting to share what she was experiencing with Silas, but he wouldn't let her.

'Let it happen, Verity,' he begged her, his voice shaking with male arousal. 'I want to see it happen for you, feel it happen...'

'Silas,' she protested, but it was already too late.

With a small cry she gave in to the urgency of Silas' plea and her body's own demands.

'Have you thought...?' Silas questioned her later, when they were sitting up in bed eating the smoked salmon sandwiches he had gone down to make for them and drinking the bottle of white wine they had decided would have to stand in lieu of celebratory champagne.

They probably looked more like a couple of naughty children, sitting side by side in the nest they had made of the duvet and pillows, Verity acknowledged, than adults, but she felt almost childlike, full of all the youthful hope and shining joy that she had lost when she had thought she had lost Silas. She felt, she recognised, like a girl again, only this time she was able to appreciate what she had, what they had, with all the maturity of a woman.

'Have I thought what?' she prompted, taking a bite of the sandwich he was proffering her and giggling when he withdrew it so that her teeth grazed his skin, and then teasingly licking at his fingers as though she hadn't known all along that that was just what he'd wanted her to do.

'Mmm...' he retaliated, bending to nibble on her own fingertips. 'Tastes good, but not as good as—'

'Silas,' Verity reproved. 'Have I thought what?'

'Well, I don't know about you,' he told her seriously, 'but I certainly wasn't using any precautions.' He shook his head. 'To be truthful, that was the last thing on my mind, irresponsible though it sounds.'

Verity gave him a concerned look.

'I'm not protected from conceiving,' she admitted,

adding semi-shyly, 'I don't... Well, there's never been any need, not since... Not since, well, not since you and I...'

The sandwiches were pushed to one side as he took her in his arms and groaned.

'Oh, Verity, I never expected... I couldn't, and I love you just the same no matter what... Have you any idea just how much that means to me? It's the same for me, you know,' he told her quietly. 'I haven't...'

'Not even with Myra?' Verity asked him.

'Most especially not with Myra.' Silas grinned.

'She wanted you,' Verity told him.

'Mmm...but she didn't get me. There wasn't anything here for her,' he told her seriously, touching his own heart lightly and then adding, 'and so there couldn't be anything here either...' Verity watched as he touched his sex.

'I thought it didn't work like that for men,' was all she could manage to say.

'For some men, but not for me. Perhaps that's why I'm so hungry for you now,' he told her with a soft groan. 'I've got a lot of lonely nights to make up for...'

'I don't want to get pregnant,' Verity told him, explaining when she saw the look in his eyes, 'I mean, not just yet. Not until Honor has had a chance to...to adjust...to know that she'll always be very special to both of us... We need time together as a unit, a family... We need to bond properly together as a threesome, Silas, before we introduce a new baby into our family. We owe it to Honor to wait until *she's* ready.'

When she looked at him she saw that his eyes were bright with emotion.

'What is it?' she asked him warily. 'Have I...?'

'You're perfect, just perfect, do you know that?' he told her passionately. 'No wonder Honor is so determined to have you as her stepmother. Come here and let me kiss you...'

Smiling at him, Verity complied...

EPILOGUE

'WHAT are you doing?' Catherine asked Honor curiously.

They were both standing in Verity's bedroom, still wearing their bridesmaid's dresses from the afternoon wedding ceremony which had taken place in the garden. Honor was writing something down on a piece of paper, shielding it with her hand as she kept a weather eye on the half-open bedroom door.

Down below them, in the garden, Verity and Silas were mingling with their guests, Silas' arm wrapped protectively around his new wife's waist.

'I'm writing a list of babies' names,' Honor informed her friend loftily.

'Babies names... What for? *You* won't be having a baby for ages yet,' Catherine told her.

'It's not for me, stupid,' Honor told her. 'It's for Verity.'

'Is Verity having a baby?' Catherine asked her, looking confused.

'Maybe not quite yet. But she soon will be now that she and Dad are married,' Honor told her confidently. 'I think, if it's a girl we should call her Mel and if it's a boy...I think Adam...'

'Why Adam?' Catherine asked her.

'It's a nice name for a baby brother.'

Down below them in the garden, happily oblivious to the plans that were being made for their future, Verity leaned a little closer into Silas' body.

'Looking forward to tonight?' he teased her wickedly as he felt the soft warmth of her body.

Laughing ruefully, Verity wrinkled her nose at him.

'You're the one who's supposed not to be able to wait to get *me* into bed, not the other way around,' she reminded him.

'What makes you think I'm not?' Silas challenged her. 'We're going to have to make the most of tonight,' he warned her. 'It's the last night we're going to have to ourselves for quite some time.'

'Mmm... I know,' Verity agreed, closing her eyes as she dwelt blissfully on the thought of the luxurious suite at the hotel where he had once made love to her that Silas had booked in their names for their wedding night. She smiled as she remembered that on their first stay there they had a much smaller room.

'If I ever thought about where I'd spend a honeymoon, it certainly wasn't Disneyland,' he told Verity dryly.

She opened her eyes and laughed.

'No, me neither,' she admitted.

'So how come *you* were the one who insisted that we make the booking?' Silas asked her gently. 'Or can I guess?'

'We couldn't have gone away without her,' she told him quickly.

'Maybe *you* couldn't,' Silas agreed roundly, 'but I certainly could!'

'You don't mean that.'

'Don't I?' He gave her a wide, almost boyish grin that made him look heartachingly young. 'We must be mad. Three *weeks* in Disneyland with Honor in tow...'

'Either that or we must be grateful,' Verity acknowledged, whispering the words into a soft kiss. 'After all, without her...'

'Yes,' he admitted. 'Without her...'

Both of them glanced up towards Verity's open bedroom window where they could hear the sound of raised voices.

'Well, I think Adam is a stupid name for a baby,' Catherine was shouting.

'I don't care what *you* think,' Honor was retaliating in an equally loud voice. 'I like it and he's going to be *my* brother.'

Her what? Verity and Silas looked at one another whilst all around them their guests started to grin.

'Honor,' Silas began sternly.

Verity touched his arm and shook her head.

'Don't say anything to her,' she begged him. 'I think this is probably my fault.'

'Your fault? How can it be?'

'She came into the bathroom this morning whilst I was being sick,' Verity told him quietly.

'You were being *sick*...?' Silas stared at her, his face changing colour and then becoming suffused with tender emotion as he took hold of her gently and asked, 'Are you?'

'I don't know...not yet... But Honor seems to have made up her mind what *she* thinks if it proves to be true,' she told him ruefully. 'She was thrilled—so much for us waiting.'

Silas gave a small sigh.

'You do realise that this baby is going to make her

completely impossible, don't you?' He groaned. 'She'll never let either of us near her or him…'

Glancing towards the upper window and her small stepdaughter, Verity smiled.

'She's going to be the best sister that any baby could have,' she told him softly—and meant it.

Born and raised in Berkshire, **Liz Fielding** started writing at the age of twelve when she won a hymn-writing competition at her convent school. After a gap of more years than she is prepared to admit to, during which she worked as a secretary in Africa and the Middle East, got married and had two children, she was finally able to realise her ambition and turn to full-time writing in 1992.

She now lives with her husband, John, in West Wales, surrounded by mystical countryside and romantic, crumbling castles, content to leave the travelling to her grown-up children and keeping in touch with the rest of the world via the Internet.

Liz Fielding is the winner of the **2001 RITA award** for *The Best Man and the Bridesmaid*. To find out more about the author, visit her website at
www.lizfielding.com

Look out for:
The Engagement Effect – two wonderful novellas by
Betty Neels and Liz Fielding – **available
this month in Tender Romance™!**

The Three-Year Itch

by
Liz Fielding

CHAPTER ONE

ABBIE LOCKWOOD glanced sympathetically at the crowds milling around the luggage carousel as she walked by, but she didn't stop. She didn't have to. Travelling time was too precious a commodity to be wasted queueing for luggage, and she carried no more than the drip-dry, crumple-free essentials, packed along with her precious laptop computer and camera, in a canvas bag small enough to be carried aboard a plane with her.

She moved swiftly, eagerly through the formalities and into the airport arrival hall, glancing about her for Grey, her excitement deflating just a little as she didn't immediately spot the heart-churning smile that told her he was glad she was home. She stretched slightly onto her toes, although at five feet ten in her drip-dry socks, she didn't really need to. Besides, he wasn't the kind of man you could miss. He stood a head clear of the most pressing crowd and she knew that if she hadn't immediately caught sight of his tall, athletic figure it was because he wasn't there.

Abbie's sharp stab of disappointment punctured her brilliant feeling of elation at being home, at a job well done. Grey always came to meet her. Never failed, no matter how busy he was. Then she shook herself severely. It was ridiculous to be so cast down. He might just have been delayed, or a client might have needed him urgently—he might even be in court. She hadn't been able to contact him directly, so he hadn't been able to explain...

He'd probably left a message, she thought, fighting her way through the crowds to the information desk. It was unreasonable to expect him to drop everything and come running just because she had been away for a couple of weeks and was dizzily desperate to hold him in her arms and hug him tight. It was just that he had never failed her before. That was all.

'My name is Abigail Lockwood,' she told the young woman at the desk. 'I was expecting my husband to meet me but he isn't here. I wonder if he left a message for me?'

The girl checked. 'I'm afraid there's nothing here for you, Mrs Lockwood.'

'Oh, well,' she said, trying to hide a sudden tiny tremor of unease, the totally ridiculous feeling that something must be wrong. 'I expect we've got our wires crossed somewhere. I'd better take a taxi.' The girl smiled on automatic; she had clearly heard it all a thousand times before.

All the excitement, the high of returning home had drained from her by the time the taxi set her down outside the elegant mansion block where she and Grey lived, and she just felt tired. But she found a smile for the porter, who gallantly admired her tan and asked her if she'd had a good trip.

'Fine, thanks, Peter,' she replied. 'But I'm glad to be home.' Two fraught weeks touring the sprawling streets of Karachi with a distraught mother in search of her snatched daughter in a tug-of-love case had not been a barrel of laughs.

'That's just what Mr Lockwood said not five minutes ago, when he got back.'

'He's home?' In the middle of the afternoon? Something must be seriously wrong.

'Yes, Mrs Lockwood, and very glad to see *you* back safe and sound, I'm sure. Leave your bag; I'll bring...'

But Abbie, too impatient to wait for the ornate wrought-iron lift to crank her up two floors, was already flying up the stairs, her bag banging against her back, her long legs taking the steps two at a time, all tiredness forgotten in her need for reassurance. Then as she reached the door she felt suddenly quite foolish. If Grey had been ill, or hurt, Peter would certainly have said something.

It was far more likely that, realising that he wouldn't make the airport in time, Grey had come home to surprise her. Well, she thought, her full mouth lifting into a mischievous little smile, she would surprise him instead. She opened the door quietly, put her bag on the hall floor and for a moment just enjoyed the wonderful sensation of being in her own home, surrounded by the accumulated clutter of their lives, instead of confined to the anonymous comfort of a hotel room.

She could hear sounds of activity coming from the small study that they shared and, easing off her shoes, she padded silently across the hall. Grey was propped on the edge of his desk, listening to the messages on the answering machine, pen poised above his notepad to jot down anything that needed a response.

For a moment she stood in the doorway, simply enjoying the secret pleasure of watching him. She never tired of looking at the way his thick, dark hair curled onto his strong neck, at the sculptured shape of his ear, the long, determined set of his jaw. She could see his beloved face reflected in the glass-fronted bookcase, the furrow of concentration as he noted a telephone number. She was reflected beside him but, head bent over the notepad, he had not yet noticed her.

Then, as he reached her message, telling him the arrival time and flight number of her plane, he swore softly, glanced swiftly at his watch and reached for the phone. As he did so he finally caught sight of her reflection and their eyes met through the glass.

'Abbie!' he exclaimed. 'I'm so sorry! I've only just got your message...'

'So I heard,' she said, her soft voice full of mock reproach. 'And since I rang twenty-four hours ago I shall want a detailed itinerary of your movements to cover every last second of that time.' She had been teasing, expecting him to respond in kind, with lurid details of an impossible night of debauchery and an offer to demonstrate... Instead he raked his long fingers distractedly through his hair.

'I had to go away for a couple of days. I've only just got back.'

'Oh?' It was odd, she thought, flinging herself into his arms in the frenetic excitement of the arrivals hall at the airport had always seemed the most natural thing in the world, but here, in their own home, the atmosphere was more constrained, with the answering machine droning on the background and Grey poised on the edge of the desk, pen still in his hand. 'And what exotic paradise have you been gadding off to the minute I turn my back?' she asked.

For the space of a moment, no more, his eyes

blanked. 'Manchester,' he said. 'A case conference.' If it hadn't been so ridiculous, Abbie would have sworn he'd said the first thing that came into his head, but she had no time to think about it before he dropped the pen and closed the space between them, gathering her into his arms. 'Lord, but I've missed you,' he said.

She couldn't answer, couldn't tell him how much she had missed him, because her mouth was entirely occupied with a long and hungry kiss that scorched her in a way that the Karachi sun had quite failed to do. When finally he lifted his head, his warm brown eyes were creased into a smile. 'Welcome home, Mrs Lockwood.'

'Now that,' she said huskily, 'is what I call a welcome.' Abbie lifted her hands to his face, smoothed out the lines that fanned about his eyes with the tips of her fingers. 'You look tired. I suppose you've been working all the hours in the day, and half the night as well, while I've been away?'

'It helps to pass the time,' he agreed. 'But you're absolutely right. I am tired. So tired, in fact, that I think I shall have to go to bed. Immediately.' Abbie squealed as he swiftly bent and caught her behind the knees, swinging her up into his arms. 'And I'm going to have to insist you come with me. You know how very badly I sleep when I'm on my own.'

'Idiot!' she exclaimed, laughing. 'Put me down this minute. I've been travelling all day, and if I don't have a shower...'

'A shower?' Grey came to a sudden halt. Then his mouth curved into a slow smile that was so much more dangerous than his swift grin. 'Now that *is* a good idea.'

'No, Grey!' she warned him.

He took no notice of her protest, or her ineffectual struggles to free herself from his arms, but headed straight into the bathroom and, stopping only to kick off his shoes, stepped with her into the shower stall.

'No!' Her voice rose to a shriek as the jet of water hit them both. Then he was kissing her hungrily as the water ran over their faces, pulling her close as the water drenched her T-shirt, pouring in warm rivulets between her breasts and across the aching desire of her abdomen. Then she gave a whispered, 'Oh, yes,' as he eased her T-shirt over her head, unfastened her bra and tossed them into a dripping pile upon the bathroom floor.

His lips tormented hers as he hooked his finger under the waistband of her jeans, flicking open the button as with shaking fingers she reached up and began to unfasten his shirt. Then he slipped his hands inside her jeans and over her buttocks, easing them down her legs.

She was almost melting with desire by the time he turned her round and began slowly to stroke shower gel across her shoulders and down her back. A long, delicious quiver of pleasure escaped her lips and he laughed softly. 'I thought you said no,' he murmured, his tongue tracing a delicate little line along the curve of her ear as his hands slid round to cradle her breasts and draw her back against him.

'I'll give you twenty-four hours to stop,' she sighed, lying back against him, relishing the intense pleasure of his wet skin against hers, the touch of his hands stroking the soap over her body. She had dreamed of this in the sterile emptiness of her hotel room five thousand miles away and had determined that, no matter what the temptation, how good the story, she had accepted her last foreign assignment.

It would be a wrench. She loved her job. She was a good photo-journalist and knew the feature on tug-of-love children that she was putting together needed the on-the-spot reality of her Karachi trip. The desperate hunt, the endless knocking on the doors, an officialdom that seemed not to care about a woman deprived of her child, the photographs that would show the anguish when she had finally found her daughter, only to have her snatched from her grasp and bundled away once more, would make a heart-breakingly compelling story.

But no more. Every time she went away it seemed that her marriage suffered just a little. Nothing that she could put her finger on. Tiny irritations. But things happened to them while they were apart that they seemed unable to share. She came back impatient at complaints about a leaky washing machine or some other domestic drama when she had spent a week with refugees or the victims of some terrible natural catastrophe. But Grey was the senior partner in a prestigious law firm. He didn't have time to deal with the minor domestic trivialities of life. He had once joked that they could do with someone else—a job-share wife to take care of the details while she was away.

'I think I'd rather have a job-share husband,' she had returned, easily enough, joining in with his laughter, but the warning had not been lost on her.

Grey Lockwood was the kind of man who turned women's heads. And, like most men, he only had to look helpless and they flocked to mother him. Except that mothering wasn't all they had in mind. She worked very hard to ensure that her absences were as painless as possible, but some things couldn't be foreseen. How long would it be before some sympathetic secretary noticed the vulnerable chink in their marriage and began to lever it apart with personal services that extended beyond the use of her washing machine? Certain as she was that he loved her, she knew Grey was not made of wood. He was a warm, flesh-and-blood man—full of life, full of love. And she loved him as much as life itself.

She turned eagerly in his arms and began to soap him, spreading her hands across his broad shoulders, slipping the tips of her fingers through the coarse dark hair that spread across his chest and arrowed down across his flat belly until she heard him gasp.

'I don't know about you, Grey,' she said, tipping her head back to look at him from beneath the heavy lids of her fine grey eyes, 'but I think I'm clean enough.'

He said nothing, simply flipped the shower switch, pulled a towel from the rack to wrap about her shoulders, then, sweeping her up into his arms, he stepped out of the shower stall and carried her to bed.

The first time after she had been away was always special. A slow rediscovery of one another, a reaffirmation of their love. But now Grey seemed seized by an almost desperate urgency to know her, to reclaim her as his. Even as he followed her down onto the bed she saw something in his face, some savage, primeval need that excited her even as a quiver of apprehension rippled through her.

'Grey?' Her almost tentative query was brushed aside as he reared above her, his knee parting her legs, the dominant male driven by the desire to plant his seed.

She cried out as her breath was driven from her, her hands seizing the muscle-packed flesh of his shoulders, her nails digging in as he took her on a roller-coaster ride of meteoric intensity—a ride which she began as a passenger but then, as the pace, almost the fury of his driving passion set alight a hitherto unsuspected chord of wanton sensuality deep within her, she rose to him, matching his ardour thrust for thrust until they came crashing back to earth, satiated, exhausted, drenched with sweat.

As he rolled away from her and lay staring at the ceiling a long shuddering sigh escaped him. 'You've been away too long, Abbie.' Then he turned to her. 'Did I hurt you?'

She shook her head. 'Surprised me a little, that's all.' She touched the score-marks her nails had riven in his shoulders in the heat of passion. 'But I like surprises.' And she reached forward to lay her lips against the slick salty warmth of his skin, sighing contentedly as he gathered her into his arms.

Tomorrow she would ache a little, but it would be a good feeling and she would carry it with her as a secret knowledge, a constant reminder of the fact that she was desired, loved.

Abbie was the first to wake, the weight of Grey's arm across her waist disturbing her as she moved. For a moment she remained perfectly still, soaking in the pleasure of having his face buried against her shoulder, the pleasure of being home. Going away had its miseries, but without separation there would never be these blissful reunions. She lay quietly, her face inches from his, reminding herself of every feature, every tiny line that life had bestowed upon him, very gently touching an old childhood scar above his brow.

She could tell the exact moment when he woke. He didn't move, didn't open his eyes. There was just the faintest change in breathing, the tiniest contraction of the muscles about his eyes. She grinned. It was an old game, this.

How long could he maintain the pretence? She began slowly to trace the outline of his face with the tip of one finger, moving slowly up the darkening shadow of his chin to his lower lip. Did it quiver slightly under the lightest teasing of her nail? She gave him the benefit of the doubt, this was not a game to be hurried. She dipped her head to trail a tiny tattoo of kisses across his throat, his chest, her tongue flickering across flat male nipples that leapt to attention.

Still he did not move, and she continued her teasing quest across the hard, flat plane of his stomach until the tell-tale stirring of his manhood could no longer be ignored. But, before she had quite registered the fact that the game was over and won, he had turned, flipping her over onto her back, his hands on her wrists, holding her arms above her head, pinning her to the bed, utterly at his mercy. 'So, you want to play games, do you, Mrs Lockwood?'

She lowered her lashes seductively. 'Why, sir, I don't know what you mean.'

'Then I'll have to show—' The telephone began to ring. For a moment Grey gazed down at her, then he dropped the briefest kiss on her mouth. 'It appears that you have a reprieve.' He released her, rolling away and rising to his feet in one smooth movement.

She didn't want a reprieve and reached out for him. 'Whoever it is will leave a message, Grey. Don't go.'

'It'll be Robert. I should have phoned him an hour ago.' He raised her hand absently to his lips. 'Why don't you go and see if you can rustle up something for supper?'

'Well, gee, shucks, thanks, mister,' she murmured as he disappeared in the direction of the study. It was the first time she had ever come *third*. To a phone call and food.

'Grey?' He lifted his head from his distant contemplation of the supper Abbie had thrown together from the rather sparse contents of the refrigerator. 'Can we talk?'

'Mmm?' He had been distracted ever since he had talked to Robert; now he seemed to come back from a long way off, but as he looked up he caught her eye, became very still. 'Go ahead, I'm listening.'

I want to have a baby. Your baby. It sounded so emotional, almost desperate put like that. Not a good start. But that heartfelt 'You've been away too long...' gave her the courage to press on.

'I wondered what you thought about starting a family,' she said.

He looked up, momentarily shaken, his eyes dark with something that might almost have been pain. Then he shook his head. 'Leave it, Abbie. This is not a good moment.'

Whatever reaction she had expected, it certainly wasn't that. 'Not a good moment'? What on earth did that mean? 'You did say we were apart too much...' she began, trying to lift an atmosphere that had suddenly become about as light as a lead-filled balloon.

'And a baby would fix that?' Grey sat back in his chair, abandoning any further attempt to eat. 'That's a somewhat drastic solution, isn't it?'

Drastic? The second she had opened her mouth Abbie had realised the moment was all wrong, but it shouldn't ever be *that* wrong, surely? Confused, hurt, she said, 'I...I thought we both wanted children.'

'Eventually,' he agreed coolly. 'But we had an agreement, Abbie. No children until you're ready to give them your full-time care.'

'Yes, but—'

'Do you really think you can have it all?' he demanded, cutting off her protest, and she saw to her astonishment that he was now genuinely angry with her. 'Most of your friends manage it, I know, by cobbling their lives together with nannies and living from one crisis to the next. But they don't disappear into the wide blue yonder for a couple of weeks whenever a tantalising commission is dangled in front of them.'

'Neither do I! I never go anywhere without discussing it with you first.'

'But you still go,' he declared. 'That was the deal we made. God knows I miss you when you're away, Abbie, I've never made any secret of that fact—but it's a choice we both made right at the beginning. You said you'd need five years to establish yourself in your career, then you could take a break.'

'I don't remember carving it on a tablet of stone!' Suddenly the discussion was getting too heated, too emotional, but she couldn't stop. 'I...I want to have a child now, Grey.'

'Why?'

Because I love you and having your baby would be the most wonderful thing that could happen to me.

His detached expression did not invite such a declaration.

In the absence of an immediate answer, he provided one for her. 'Because all your friends are having babies,' he said dismissively.

'Rubbish!'

'Cogently argued,' he replied.

'God, I hate it when you go all *lawyerish* on me,' she declared fervently. 'What would you do if I simply stopped taking the pill?' The words were out. It was too late to call them back.

But his expression betrayed nothing. 'Is that emotional blackmail, Abbie,' he asked, very quietly, 'or a statement of intent?'

Her face darkened in a flush of shame. She had always considered their marriage an equal partnership. Right now it didn't feel that equal, but a child needed two loving parents and it was a decision they had to make together. Slowly, deliberately she shook her head. 'I've been thinking about this for months, Grey,' she told him.

The planes of his face hardened imperceptibly. 'And now you've made up your mind, you've decided to inform me of your unilateral decision?'

'It wasn't like that, Grey. I...I just wanted to be sure.'

'Well, I want to be sure, too,' he declared. Then, as if trying to claw away from the edge of some yawning precipice, he went on, more gently, 'What about your career? You're beginning to make a real name for yourself—'

'I don't intend to stop working, Grey,' she said, interrupting. Lord, if that was his only concern then there was no problem. 'I thought if we had a nanny I could get on with—'

The tight constraint finally snapped. 'Damn it, Abbie, a baby is not an accessory that every professional woman needs to prove that she's some kind of superwoman. I won't have a child of mine dumped at six weeks with a nanny while her mother gets on with her real life.' He flung his napkin on the table, pushed back his chair and rose to his feet.

'You don't understand!' she flung at him. 'Why won't you listen to me?'

'I've listened. Now it's my turn to think. Months you said you'd been thinking about this? How many months? I think I should at least be granted as long as you.'

'Don't walk away from this, Grey,' she warned him. 'I'm serious.'

'So am I.' For a moment they stared at one another across the table as if they were strangers. Then Grey gave an awkward little shrug. 'We'll talk about it again in six months. Now, since I'm really not very hungry, I'll go and deal with the messages that have piled up on the machine.'

Abbie, stunned into silence, remained where she was. She didn't understand what had happened. One moment they had been sitting quietly having their supper and the next they were tearing emotional lumps off one another.

'Well, you really made a mess of that, Abigail Lockwood,' she told herself aloud. More of a mess than she would have thought possible. If she hadn't known better, she would have thought he didn't want her to have his child... But that was ridiculous. Grey loved to be around children. She had been the one who'd wanted to wait a while to give her career a chance. She almost wished she hadn't been so successful...

With a sigh, she gathered the plates, cleared away and collected her bag from the hall. If he had decided to work, then so would she; while he dealt with his calls she could download her laptop onto the PC. But before that she would insist that he listen to her. He might still oppose the idea of starting a family, but at least he would know she had no intention of dumping her longed for baby with a nanny and departing for all corners of the globe at a moment's notice. Hardly any wonder he was angry if he thought that was her intention.

Grey, on the telephone, stopped speaking and looked up as she entered the study, placing his hand over the receiver. 'Give me a minute will you, Abbie?' he asked. 'This is—' She didn't wait to find out what it was, but backed out, closing the door behind her with a sharp snap.

'Abbie?' He found her a few minutes later, loading the washing machine.

'Where's your bag, Grey? You must have some washing if you've been away.'

'In the bedroom. Abbie, about the phone call...'

She didn't want to listen to him explaining why suddenly he had secrets where there had never been secrets before. She knew some of his work was highly confidential, but they had always shared a study; he trusted her discretion... Or maybe it wasn't work at all. The thought leapt unbidden into her head. She straightened, pushed past him and crossed the hall to the bedroom, where she unzipped his bag and began to remove his clothes.

Then she collected the clothes they had so carelessly jettisoned while under the shower. Two pairs of wet jeans? She glanced at the pair she was already holding which had come from his bag. What kind of lawyer took jeans to a case conference, for heaven's sake? Not Grey. He had a wardrobe full of sober, well-cut suits that he kept for the office. And as she scooped up the pair he had been wearing she caught the faintest scent of woodsmoke that clung to the cloth, reminding her of the cottage.

He was still in the kitchen standing in front of the washing machine when she returned, so that she had to ask him to move before she could load the clothes.

'Excuse me, Grey,' she said stiffly.

For a moment she thought he wasn't going to move. Then he shrugged, shifted sideways. 'Abbie, will you stop fussing about and let me explain?' he demanded as she pushed in the clothes, keeping her eyes determinedly upon her task.

'Explain? You wanted to make a private telephone call. What's there to explain about that?' Everything, she thought as she banged the door shut, set the programme, and when she turned away he was standing in front of her, blocking the way.

'I know you're angry with me for not wanting you to have a baby right now—'

'Give the man a coconut,' she interrupted flippantly as she tried to sidestep him. But it wasn't true. She was angry with him for not wanting to talk about it, for not listening. It was so unlike him.

He caught her arm as she brushed past, held her at his side. 'I'm sorry if I seemed as if I didn't care. I do. And I will think about it...it's just that it's been a difficult couple of weeks.'

'Difficult?' She was immediately contrite. 'What's happened? Is it Robert?' she asked, remembering the earlier telephone call.

'Robert?' At her mention of his brother his eyes narrowed.

'You rang him earlier. I just wondered...' She hesitated in the face of his guarded expression. 'I thought perhaps Susan had been causing more trouble.'

'No. It's not Susan...' He gave another of those awkward little shrugs that were so out of character. 'I can't explain right now.'

'No?' She stiffened abruptly. 'Then I can't understand. If you'll excuse me, Grey?' she said with polite formality. 'It's been a very long day, and if I don't lie down right now, I think I might just fall down.'

He stared at her as if he couldn't believe what he was hearing. Well, that was fine with her. That made two of them who were having that kind of trouble today. He stepped back abruptly to let her pass, his jaw tight, a small angry muscle ticking away at the corner of his mouth. 'Then I certainly won't disturb you when I come to bed. Goodnight, Abbie.'

She made it to the bedroom before the tears stung her eyes. What on earth was happening to them? They had been married for three years. Three blissfully happy years. Of course they'd had rows. Loud, throwing-the-china rows on more than one occasion, rows that had lasted for seconds, blowing away the tensions, before the most glorious and lengthy reconciliations. But never a row like this, that you couldn't put your finger on. A tight-lipped, hidden secrets, *polite* kind of row.

Something was wrong. She had sensed it from the moment of her arrival at the airport when he hadn't been there to meet her. He would normally have checked the answering machine from his hotel while he was away. He'd had plenty of time to get her message last night. But he hadn't. Something had happened while she was away. But what? She curbed the instinct to turn back and confront him. Demand to know. Things were bad enough.

True to his word, Grey didn't disturb her when he came to bed. Despite the long hours of travelling, sleep eluded her, but hours later, when Grey finally came to bed, she closed her eyes, and whether he believed it or not he didn't challenge her pretence. He didn't put on the light, but quietly slipped out of his clothes and lowered himself gently into the bed beside her, and after a moment he turned his back.

She opened her eyes in the darkness and lay for hours, listening to his soft breathing and thinking about the plans she had made so eagerly on her journey home. Was it possible, she wondered miserably, that she had left the decision not to accept any more overseas jobs just one assignment too late?

She woke to a room still darkened by the heavy velvet curtains drawn across the window, but the sunlight was spilling in from the hallway and she knew instantly that it was late. She lay for a moment in the silent flat, knowing that she was alone and hating it. She had hoped that the morning would bring some kind of reconciliation. Neither of them had behaved exactly brilliantly, but they had both been tired last night and she was prepared to acknowledge that, while Grey might have been a little more receptive, she might have picked a better moment to suggest a total upheaval to their lives.

Instead he had left while she was asleep. Gone to his office without even saying goodbye. She had intended to stay at home that day, attend to wifely things. Shop, prepare a good meal. Reclaim her surroundings from two weeks of Grey's bachelor housekeeping. Instead she found she had a need to reinforce herself as a person in her own right. And there was no better way of doing that than work.

She flung back the cover and slipped out of bed. But as she reached for her wrap she frowned. On the wall opposite the bed had hung a small Degas. Not a great painting—nothing that would set the galleries of the world at each other's throats—but very pretty and very genuine. It was gone. Had they been burgled while she was away and he hadn't wanted to frighten her? Was that why it had been a difficult week? Abbie flew to her jewellery box, locked in a small drawer in her dressing table, but it was there with all the pieces he had bought her during three happy years. She picked up the phone to call him at his office, then hesitated.

There was probably some perfectly logical explanation. Grey sometimes lent it to galleries for exhibition—maybe he had simply forgotten to mention it to her. They hadn't exactly spent the evening in close conversation. She replaced the receiver. That was probably it, she decided. It would wait until he came home.

Trembling just a little, she went into the kitchen to make some tea. On the centre island, where she couldn't possibly miss it, stood the silver bud-holder that Grey had bought her for their first wedding anniversary. In it was a red rose, a half-opened bud. And there was a note propped against the bud-holder—a plain sheet of paper, folded once. She opened it. 'I thought you needed to sleep. I'll see you this evening. Grey.'

That was all. No apology. But then he had taken the trouble to go out and find a rose for her before he drove into his City office. It wasn't quite like buying a pint of milk from the corner shop. It couldn't have been the easiest thing to find at seven-thirty in the morning. Yet why did she have the disturbing feeling that he might have found it a whole lot easier than waking her up and saying that he was sorry?

CHAPTER TWO

Two hours later Abbie, dressed in a loose-fitting pair of heavy slub silk trousers in her favourite bitter chocolate colour and a soft creamy peach top that glowed against her tanned skin and hair, bleached to a streaked blonde by the sun, was discussing the layout of her feature for the colour supplement of a major newspaper with her commissioning editor. Her photographs had been forwarded by courier and now the two of them were bent over the light box, deciding which ones to use.

'You've done a great job, Abbie. This photograph of the mother getting into that tiny plane to fly up into the hills to start looking all over again—'

'I tried to stop her. If only I could have gone with her...'

'No. That's the right place to end it. A touch of hope, bags of determination and courage. A mother alone, searching for her missing child. You deserve an award for this one.'

'I don't deserve anything, Steve,' she said, suddenly disgusted with herself for being so pleased with the finished result. 'I just hope she's all right. Anything could happen to her up there and no one would ever know.'

Steve Morley gave her a sharp look. 'You sound as if you've got just a little bit too emotionally involved in this one, Abbie. You were there to record what happened, not become responsible for the result.

The woman has made her decision. It's her daughter. And your story will make a difference…'

'Will it? I wish I thought so.'

'Trust me,' he said firmly. 'Come on, I'll take you out to lunch.'

Trust. An emotive word. But without it there was nothing. Was too much time apart eroding that precious commodity between her and Grey? She would trust him with her life, and yet…and yet… There were too many gaps, too many empty spaces yawning dangerously between them. Baby or not, her mind was made up. She wouldn't be going away again.

As they made their way down in the lift Steve distracted her by asking her where she would like to eat, and reluctantly she let go of her thoughts about the future to concentrate on more immediate concerns. 'I've found this really good Indian restaurant,' he continued, 'but after two weeks on the sub-continent, I don't suppose you'd be interested—'

'You suppose right, Mr Morley,' she interrupted, very firmly. Then she grinned. 'Now, how good did you say that feature was?'

Steve groaned. 'L'Escargot?'

'L'Escargot,' she affirmed with a grin. 'Upstairs.'

Lunch was a light-hearted affair, with Steve bringing her up to date on what had been happening during her absence and offering several suggestions for future features.

'How do you feel about a month in the States for us?' He continued hurriedly as he saw she was about to object, 'Human interest stuff in the deep South—Atlanta. It's the sort of thing you're particularly good at. Although since your charming husband got a decent price for his Degas at auction last week I don't suppose you actually need the money,' he added, with an offhand little shrug.

The Degas? Sold? Despite the whirl of conflicting emotions storming through her brain she wasn't fooled by Steve Morley's casual manner. He had hoped to take her unawares, provoke some unguarded response. If he thought the Lockwood family were in any sort of financial trouble he would want to know. It was probably the whole reason for this lunch. 'You don't normally cover the art market, do you, Steve?' she asked, arching her fine brows in apparent surprise. 'I mean, doesn't that take brains…?'

He grinned, aware that he had been caught out, but was unrepentant. 'I cover everything that has the Lockwood name attached to it, and if you're ever seriously in need of funds, Abbie, I'm always deeply interested in brother Robert's doings.'

'I thought we had an agreement? You don't ask me about Robert and I'll continue to work for you.'

He shrugged. 'It doesn't hurt to remind you now and again that I'm always receptive to a change of heart.'

'Forget it. And Atlanta. I'm not in the market for overseas work for a while.'

'The old man getting a bit restive, is he?' He had gone straight to the heart of the matter, and she had known Steve too long to attempt to string him some line.

'Even the best marriage needs to be worked at, Steve.'

'I won't argue with that. I only wish my wife had been quite so dedicated.' He shrugged. 'And if the pretty piece I saw Grey having lunch with last week is anything to go by, I'd say you haven't left it a day too long.'

'Pretty piece?' Abbie felt the smile freeze on her face.

Steve shrugged. 'From what you said, I thought you must at least suspect something was up…'

'Suspect something?' It had been a moment's shock, that was all. On top of everything else that had happened she should have been reeling. But if there was one thing of which she was absolutely certain it was this: if her husband had been lunching with another woman, there had to be some perfectly rational explanation. 'Oh, Steve, really!' she chided, even managing a small laugh to show him how ridiculous such an idea was. But she knew it would need more than that. Taking his hand between her fingers, she regarded him solemnly with large grey eyes. 'Would you like me to tell you something that has just occurred to me?' she asked. 'Something rather amusing?'

Relieved that she was apparently not about to have hysterics, Steve smiled. 'Fire away.'

'It's just that… well, I wondered what Grey would say if someone mentioned to him that they had seen me having lunch upstairs at L'Escargot with one of the best looking men in London.' And she leaned forward and kissed him, very lightly on the lips, before releasing his hand. It was a reproach. A gentle one, but it wasn't lost on her companion.

'Ah,' he said. 'Point taken. I suppose I jumped to the most obvious conclusion because you were away… A bad habit. My only excuse is that I started out on a gossip column.'

'It's a bad habit that will cost you the biggest bowl of strawberries in this house,' she replied sweetly.

'Yes, ma'am,' he said, summoning the waiter, but somehow they didn't taste of anything very much, although she forced herself to eat every one. And when Steve dropped her off outside her home, she didn't go straight inside, but walked across the road to a small park, occupied in the middle of the afternoon by nannies, identifiable only by their youth and the expensive coach-built prams they wheeled before them in the sunshine, and middle-aged ladies walking small, immaculately groomed dogs.

Surely she was right? Grey was straight down the line. If he had found someone else he would tell her. He could never have made love to her like he had yesterday if he was having an affair, could he? Except that he had never before made love to her in that desperate, almost angry way. And then, afterwards, he had left her without a backward glance.

Oh, that was ridiculous, she chided herself. She was feeling bruised by their row, that was all. But even as she sat in the sunshine, convincing herself of the fact that he loved her, she wondered why she felt the need to do so. They were the perfect couple, after all. Teased by their friends because they were always the first to leave a party, envied for the freedom they were able to give one another, the almost transparent trust.

And yet were things quite so perfect? Grey's willingness to co-operate with a career that took her away regularly had always, to her, seemed a demonstration of how much he loved and trusted her. She had always rather pitied friends who hinted they would never leave a man that good-looking on his own for more than five minutes, let alone five days. But now little things that hadn't seemed important suddenly took on a new significance. Grey had had a series of late nights working on a difficult case just before she went to Karachi. Yet he had once said that the need to work late betrayed one of two things: a man incompetent at his job, or a man unwilling to go home to his wife. And Grey was certainly not incompetent.

She caught herself, unable to believe the direction in which her mind was travelling. The fact that Steve had seen him having lunch with another woman meant nothing. She was probably a client, or a colleague. Even if she was nothing whatsoever to do with his work she *trusted* him, for heaven's sake. It was certainly no more sinister than her lunch with Steve. The whole thing was utter nonsense. She was just edgy with him because of that stupid row. And if he had sold the Degas because of financial worries, that would certainly explain his reluctance to start a family, his reluctance for her to give up lucrative assignments. If only he had explained, trusted her. Trust. The word seemed to be everywhere today.

Happier, she was even willing to concede that his reaction to her immediate desire for a baby had been justified. She had been so full of her plans that she had expected him to leap into line without a thought. Well, she could start the necessary reorganisation of her life without making an issue of it. In fact she had already begun. No more overseas assignments.

She would tell him all about it when they were at the cottage. A couple of weeks at Ty Bach would give them a chance to talk when they were more relaxed, time to discuss the future properly. She should have waited until then to broach her plans. And, feeling considerably happier, Abbie stood up, dusted herself off and walked briskly back to the flat.

Yet Grey's key in the lock just after six brought an unexpected nervous catch to her throat.

'Abbie?' He came to the kitchen doorway and leaned against the door, smiling a little as if pleased to see her there. 'Hello.'

'Hello.' A little shy, just a little formal. 'You're early.'

'Mmm,' he agreed. 'I asked the boss if I could leave early so that I could take my wife out.'

'Idiot,' she murmured, laughing softly. 'You *are* the boss.'

'Obviously a very good one...' he said, walking across to her and resting his hands lightly about her waist. There was only the slightest tenseness about his eyes to betray what they both knew. That this was a peace overture. 'I said yes.'

So that was the way he was going to deal with it. Pretend last night had never happened. Love means never having to say that you're sorry? Maybe. She lifted her hands to his shoulders, raised herself a little on her toes and kissed him, very lightly. 'Thank you for the rose.'

'I'm glad you liked it.' His face relaxed into a smile. 'I risked life and limb climbing over the park railings to pick it for you.'

'Grey!' she gasped, her hand flying to her mouth at the idea of a sober-suited solicitor clambering over the park fence at dawn. 'You didn't!' He lifted one brow. 'Idiot!' she exclaimed. 'Suppose someone had seen you?'

'If it made you happy it was worth the risk.' He put one arm about her to draw her closer, and with his other hand he raked back the thick fringe of hair that grew over her brow and dropped a kiss there. 'Besides, I know I could rely on you to bake me a sponge with a file in it and ingeniously smuggle it into jail. Your cakes are so heavy that no one would suspect a thing.'

'Idiot!' she repeated, but this time flinging a punch at his shoulder.

'Possibly,' he agreed. 'And I've got something else.' He produced a pair of theatre tickets from his inside pocket and held them before her eyes. 'You did want to see this?'

'Grey! How on earth did you manage to get hold of them?' she demanded, eagerly reaching for them so that she could see for herself. 'They're like gold-dust.'

He smiled at her reaction. 'You'll have to retract the "idiot" first,' he warned her, holding them tantalisingly out of her reach.

'Unreservedly. Heavens, all this attention will go to my head,' she said happily, leaning her head against his chest.

'Oh? And who else has been spoiling you?'

'Only Steve Morley. He took me out to lunch,' she added, lifting her head to look into his eyes. Was she hoping for some immediate confession about his own lunch date? If so, she was disappointed.

'Lucky Steve,' he said, with just a touch of acid in his voice. It was not lost on Abbie. Grey had never said anything, but Abbie sensed a certain reserve in his enthusiasm for that particular journalist and his newspaper. But then, since they took particular relish in hounding his brother, Robert Lockwood, a politician and the most glamorous member of the government front benches—including the women—that was hardly surprising.

'Did he take you somewhere nice?' She told him and his brows rose to a satisfactory height. 'Spoilt indeed,' he said, releasing her and crossing to the fridge to extract a carton of juice. 'He must have been very pleased with your feature.'

'Very—in fact he immediately offered me a month in America.'

'I'm impressed,' he said, without much enthusiasm, as he tipped the juice into the glass.

'And so you should be,' she declared, and, just a little peeved by the lack of congratulations, didn't bother to tell him that she had turned it down. 'You're apparently married to one hot property. Steve was talking about awards for the tug-of-love story.'

'Just as well I didn't leap at the chance of fatherhood, then.' He sipped the juice. 'So when will you be going?'

'You wouldn't mind?' she asked, heart sinking just a little. 'I've never been away that long before.'

'We made a deal, Abbie. I'm not going to start coming the heavy husband now you're on the brink of something special. You have to be available if you're going to be a star.'

Being a star was becoming less attractive by the day. 'I thought being good meant that you were able to pick and choose your assignments,' she said. 'Besides, what about our holiday? I'm looking forward to having you to myself for a couple of weeks.'

'You'd trade two weeks at an isolated cottage in Wales for a month in the States?' She would trade anything for two weeks alone with him, and it didn't matter where, but he didn't wait for her answer. 'Anyway, there's been a bit of a hitch about the cottage.'

'Oh? I thought it was all arranged.' Before she had gone away he had been full of plans. Most of them involving lying on the beach and doing absolutely nothing except making love for two weeks. He must have seen her disappointment, because he put down the glass and crossed to her.

'I'm sorry, but Robert wants to use the cottage this summer, Abbie. It's the one place the Press don't know about; even if they found out, it's hardly the easiest place to find, and the locals have a way of forgetting how to speak English when anybody starts getting nosy. He needs to spend some time with his family.'

Abbie felt a little stab of guilt. She had a very soft spot for her brother-in-law. Grey's older brother was good-looking, brilliant—the youngest minister in the government. He should have been the happiest man alive. But he had a wife who kept him glued to her side with the threat of a scandal that would wipe out his career should he take one step to end their disastrous marriage. So he continued to play happy families for the benefit of the media, although he spent as much time as possible at his London flat and Jonathan, their son, was now at boarding-school.

'How is Robert? I saw his photograph in the newspaper when I was on the plane. I thought he looked more at ease than I've seen him for a long time. Has there been some kind of reconciliation?' she asked. 'Is Susan going to the cottage with them?'

Grey didn't answer, although his mouth hardened into a straight line. 'Come on, let's go out and enjoy ourselves.' And it was only later, as she drifted off into sleep, that she remembered about the painting.

It was three days later that Abbie saw Grey with his 'pretty piece'. She had been shopping and had decided to drop in and see if he could join her for lunch in a local wine bar they occasionally went to.

Her cab had just dropped her off outside the office when she saw his tall figure heading purposefully along the road and then turning into the small park in the square around the corner from his office. She set off after him. If he'd bought sandwiches to eat in the park she would happily share them.

The good weather had brought out the office workers in droves, and they were sitting on benches and lying on the grass, soaking up the sun. Abbie lifted her hand to shade her eyes and swept the area for Grey. For a moment she didn't see him. Then she did. And in that moment she wished, more than anything in the world, that she hadn't seen him. That she hadn't followed him. That she had decided to stay at home and do some dusting. That she was anywhere but this small green City oasis.

A 'pretty piece' Steve had called her. Steve was right. But then he had a well-tuned eye when it came to a woman. She was small, with a delicate bone structure and the translucent complexion that so often went with very dark hair—hair that hung down her back, straight and shiny as a blackbird's wing. Abbie felt a sharp stab of jealousy as she recognised that special kind of fragility that made men feel protective—the kind of fragility that she had never possessed as a self-consciously gawky teenager, a tall young woman.

Grey was the only man she had ever known who had to bend to kiss her, but never in the way he bent now to tenderly kiss the cheek of his dark beauty. Then he put his arm about her shoulder as he leaned forward over the padded baby buggy she was wheeling, reaching out to touch the tiny starfish fingers of the infant lying there. It was a scene of such touching domesticity that if he had been some unknown man she would have glanced at the pair of them and thought what a perfectly charming picture they made.

Abbie shrank back into the darker shade of the trees, her heart beating painfully, her throat aching with the urgent desire to scream, her hand clamped over her mouth to make sure she didn't. She wanted to leave. Walk away. Run away from that place. The idea of spying on her own husband was so alien, so disgusting that she felt sick. But she remained rooted to the spot, unable to make her feet move, to tear her eyes from the two figures, or the baby lying gazing up at its mother, as they walked almost within touching distance of her on their slow circumnavigation of the path that rimmed the little park.

'If there's anything else you need, Emma, just ring me,' Grey said as they passed, blithely unaware of Abbie standing motionless in the shadow of the trees. The girl murmured something that Abbie couldn't hear and he shook his head. 'At the office unless it's an emergency.' Then the girl looked up at Grey, her dark eyes anxious. 'Yes, she came back a couple of days ago.' There was apparently no need for further explanation. 'I'll take you down to the cottage as soon as...'

As they moved on, turned the corner, his voice no longer reached her. The cottage. He had arranged to take this girl called Emma to Ty Bach. All that talk about Robert had been lies...lies...

No wonder he had wanted her to go to America. He had other plans for his summer vacation. And it was hardly surprising that he didn't want her to have a child. He hadn't wasted much time in arranging for a job-share wife, it seemed. But obviously one family at a time was enough.

No, Abbie. A small voice inside her head issued an urgent warning. You're leaping to conclusions. There might be a rational explanation. Must be. This was some girl from the office who had become pregnant, needed help. Or someone from the law centre. A client. No, not a client. He had kissed her, and kissing clients—even on the cheek—was asking for trouble. But something. Please God, something—anything. Think! But her brain was as responsive as cotton wool.

When the pair reached an unoccupied bench on the far side of the park, Emma sat down and Grey joined her, his arm stretched protectively along the back of the seat. They chatted easily for a while, laughed at some shared joke. Then Grey, glancing at his watch, produced an envelope from inside his jacket pocket. Emma took it, stowed it carefully in her bag without opening it and then, when Grey stood up, got quickly to her feet and hugged him. He held her for a moment, then, disengaging himself, he looked once more at the sleeping child and touched the baby's dark curls before turning to walk briskly back towards the gate.

There had been nothing in their behaviour to excite interest. No passionate kiss, no lingering glances. They had looked for all the world like any happily married couple with a new baby, meeting in the park at lunchtime.

Abbie instinctively took a step further back into the cover of the bushes as Grey approached the gate, but he looked neither to left nor right. Then he crossed the road and stopped at a flower stall to buy a bunch of creamy pink roses, laughing at something the flower-seller said as he paid for them. A moment later he had disappeared from sight, and Abbie finally stepped out into the dazzling sunlight.

For once in her life—her ordered, planned, tidy life—Abbie didn't know what to do. And then quite suddenly she did. It was perfectly clear. She was a journalist. Not the foot-in-the-door investigative kind, but nevertheless a trained observer, with a mind cued to extract information as painlessly as possible from even the most reluctant of interviewees. If this were a story she would go across to where the girl was still sitting on the shady bench and find some way to strike up a conversation.

It shouldn't be difficult, for heaven's sake. Babies and dogs were a gift—guaranteed to make the most reserved people open up. She didn't want to do it, but she had to. And on legs that felt as if they were made of watery jelly, Abbie forced herself to walk towards the girl her husband had put his arm around and called Emma.

She had nothing in her mind. No plan. No idea of what she was going to say. But it wasn't necessary. As she approached the bench the girl looked up and smiled. No, not a girl. Close up, Abbie realised that she must be nearer thirty than twenty. A woman.

'It's really too hot for shopping, isn't it?' she said

as she saw Abbie's bags. Her voice was silvery, light and delicate, like the rest of her.

'Yes, I suppose it is.' Was it hot? She felt so terribly cold inside that she couldn't have said. But it was an opening and she sat down.

'Did you buy anything nice?'

A simple question. Difficult to answer, but she managed it. 'A shirt and a sweater. For my husband,' she added, unable to help herself. *No!* Put the woman at her ease—talk to her, her subconscious prodded her. Forget that this is personal. Treat it like any other story. 'And socks,' she continued. 'Men never seem to have enough socks, do they?' Smile. Make yourself smile. 'I have this theory that there is a conspiracy between the washing machine manufacturers and the sock-makers…'

Apparently the grimace that locked her jaw had been somehow convincing, because Emma laughed. 'You could be right. But I wouldn't care if I could only just go out and buy a pair of socks for my man. Unfortunately he has the kind of wife who would notice.'

'Oh?' Would she? Would she query strange socks in the laundry? Yes, she rather thought she would.

'I can't even keep things for him at my place. It would be so easy to get them muddled up.'

'I suppose so.' Abbie felt herself blushing at such unexpected frankness, yet she was well aware of how easily some people would talk about even their most intimate lives to perfect strangers. Especially if there were constraints on talking to family or friends. But the last thing on earth she wanted to discuss with this woman was her 'man's' wife.

She stared at the buggy. 'A baby is rather more

personal than a pair of socks,' she said, forcing the words from her unwilling lips. But she had to be sure. 'The greatest gift of all.'

The woman's smile was full of secrets as she leaned forward and touched the child's fingers. 'That's what he said. And, while he may leave me one day, I'll always have his child.'

'How old is he?' Abbie asked hoarsely, as jealousy, like bile burning in her throat, swept over her.

'Twelve weeks.' The woman called Emma brushed back the mop of dark hair that decorated his tiny head. 'He was born just after Easter.'

When Abbie had been steeping herself in the miseries of an African refugee camp. Had Grey been with this woman, holding her hand, encouraging her as she went through the pangs of giving birth to his son? No! Her heart rebelled. Surely it was impossible. And yet... She leaned over the buggy, letting her hair swing forward to cover her expression, and as she came face to face with the sleepy child she felt the blood drain from her face.

'He's beautiful,' she said, her voice coming from somewhere miles distant. As beautiful as his father had been as a baby.

Abbie remembered her laughter as they had looked through a pile of old family photograph albums that they had found when they had cleared his father's house last year. Grey had been a bonny, bright-eyed baby, with a mop of black curly hair. The child lying in front of her might have been his twin.

'What's his name?' she asked, wondering that she could sit there and pretend that nothing was happening. Grateful for the numbness that somehow stopped her screaming with pain...

'Matthew.'

'Matthew?' Not Grey. At least he hadn't done that to her. But it was bad enough as with every painful scrap of hard-won fact she became more certain of just what he had done.

Matthew Lockwood. Founder of Lockwood, Gates and Meadows, solicitors. Grey's father, her dear, kind father-in-law, who had been dead for just a year. The child had been named for him.

'It's a lovely name,' she said quickly, as she saw that some response was expected. 'Your...' What? What could she call him? Friend? Lover? Her mouth refused to frame the word. 'He must be very happy.'

The woman leaned forward and touched the child, and his little hand tightened trustingly about her finger. 'Yes. He's thrilled with the baby—sees him whenever he can. But it's difficult for him.' She gave an awkward little shrug. 'His wife would never give him a divorce.'

And that finally broke through the pain and at last made her angry. 'Wouldn't she?' Abbie asked, a little grimly.

Now she knew, was absolutely certain, that Grey had been having an affair, deceiving her for at least the better part of a year. And in a way he was deceiving this woman too, with his lies. What had he said about her? How had he described her? Did the mother of his child know that when he left her bed, when he came home, he made sweet love to her as if...as if she was the only woman in the world?

Except that she wasn't. How could he do that? The man she loved, had thought she knew, was suddenly a stranger. A stranger who could, it seemed, smile as if his heart was all hers, tell her that he loved her, with the taste of this woman's kisses still upon his lips. The very thought was like a knife driving through her heart. How could she not have suspected? Not have seen the deceit in his eyes?

Only anger made her strong enough to sit there and carry on as if her world wasn't disintegrating about her, kept her head high as she turned to Emma, determined to discover just how far his lies extended. 'Has he asked his wife for a divorce?'

The woman gave the tiniest little shrug, the bravest of smiles. 'I wouldn't let him. A messy divorce would cause problems. With his job.' She gave a little shake of the baby's hand, turning her head away to hide the sparkle of tears. 'And we can't let Daddy have that, can we, sweetheart?' And the baby gave a broad, gummy smile.

It was a nightmare. A waking nightmare from which there could never be the escape of knowing that, no matter how dreadful, it had all been nothing but a horrible dream. But still Abbie pushed herself. The greater the betrayal, the more it hurt her, the better. With every thrust of the knife the easier it would be to do what she had once thought impossible and hate him.

'A divorce is no big deal these days, surely?' she insisted, denying herself any avenue of escape. Then she added hopefully, 'Unless he's your doctor?'

'Oh, no!' Emma exclaimed, horrified. 'He's...' She hesitated, as if she shouldn't say what he was. 'He's a lawyer.'

'I see.' And she did see—all too clearly. She had wanted to be sure and now Emma's words rang like the clang of doom, slamming the door closed on any possibility of doubt. His confession written in blood couldn't have been more convincing.

One of Grey's associates had been obliged to resign from the firm a year or so back, after having an affair with one of his clients. Her husband had turned nasty. She looked at the hand linked with the baby's fingers and she could see the telltale mark where a wedding ring had once rested. Was that how she had met Grey? Sobbing out her heartbreak in her husband's office? How impossible to refuse this fragile creature a comfortable shoulder to cry on. How easy to become emotionally entangled when your wife was away for weeks at a time.

'I don't mind, really. I knew all along that he would never leave her and I accepted that. At least I have Matthew.'

'Maybe it will all work out,' Abbie said dully. 'You mustn't give up hope. Things change.'

'Do you think so? I do sometimes dream about it.' Emma gave a little smile. 'Sometimes we can be together for a while and pretend. He has a cottage in the country that he shares with his brother. They're very close, and he's been so good about us using it...' She glanced at her watch and leapt to her feet. 'Is that the time? I must be off—it'll soon be time for Matthew's feed.' She kicked off the buggy's brake, then paused to look down at Abbie, her face creased in concern. 'Are you all right? You look rather pale. Would you like a drink? I've got a can...'

'No!' She made an effort to pull herself together. 'Really, I'm fine. Thank you.'

Civilised behaviour. She should be scratching the woman's eyes out...but what good would that do?

The woman called Emma smiled uncertainly. 'If you're sure?'

'Don't keep Matthew waiting for his lunch,' she said, forcing a smile. For a moment she remained where she was, watching Emma wheel the jaunty little buggy around the bright flowerbeds. Then she too stood up and walked away, leaving her shopping behind her on the bench.

It was just after three when she arrived at the flat. Plenty of time to put the matter beyond all doubt before Grey came home. Not that there was any doubt left in her mind, but the evidence so far was purely circumstantial. She knew enough of the law to know the dangers of convicting on that.

She took the ring binders from the shelf and flicked back through the credit card accounts, meticulously filed month by month and paid on the dot. April. The day after she had flown out to Africa. Petrol purchased at a service station just inside the Welsh border. The same date. A trip to a supermarket in Carmarthen. She and Grey had shopped there the last time they had stayed at the cottage.

May. Where had she been in May? Two days on an oil rig in the north sea. More petrol. Another trip to the supermarket. She wondered what had headed the shopping list. Disposable nappies?

June. Another trip to Wales. Each entry was a knife wound in her heart.

The July account had not yet arrived, but the slips were there to prove his lie. On the day he had told her he was working in Manchester he had filled his petrol tank on the M4 near Cardiff. She remembered that he had been wearing jeans the day she'd come home, the scent of woodsmoke clinging to them. For a moment misery threatened to engulf her as she clung to the desk. Then, taking a deep breath, she forced herself to go on. There was no time for misery. Yet.

She put the file back on the shelf and took down the one containing the statements for Grey's personal account.

He hadn't even bothered to disguise his transactions. Large single payments of exactly the same amount for the last three months. And, remembering the envelope she had seen him pass to Emma, she had presumably witnessed another of those payments today. Tucked into the correspondence pocket of the file was a letter dated two days earlier from the bank, confirming that a trust fund had been set up in the name of Matthew Harper, using the proceeds of the sale of the Degas...

She had asked him what had happened to the painting. He had told her that it had been sold to help Robert out of a financial jam. And she had believed him.

CHAPTER THREE

FOR a long time Abbie sat there considering the possibility of revenge. Why not? She could wreck his career, drag in his brother, throw the kind of mud that, no matter how much you tried to wash it off, stuck like glue. One call to Steve and all the deceit, the lies would be plastered on the front page. Not because anyone would care about Grey or her, but because of Robert. And hurting Robert would hurt Grey. And she wanted to hurt him. She wanted him to know how it felt to be betrayed.

She knew all the right people to call in order to do the maximum amount of damage. She could break apart his life, make him suffer as she was suffering now. She was hunched over the desk, her head resting on tense little fists as she forced herself to believe what a week ago would have been unthinkable: that he had lied to her, deceived her, betrayed her. She had every right to hurt him with any weapon she could lay her hand on...

The shrill ring of the telephone sliced into her misery, startling her upright. She reached automatically for the receiver, then snatched back her hand, staring at it. Suppose it was Grey? How could she possibly speak to him? Behave in a civilised fashion when she felt positively savage?

The answering machine clicked in, and as she found herself listening to his warm voice inviting the caller to leave a message a tear splashed onto the bank statement. There was the long bleep of the tone.

'Grey? Are you listening to me?' Susan Lockwood's petulant voice whined into the machine. 'You'd better be listening!' She drew breath to spit her bile. 'You'd better tell your precious brother that he can't avoid me for ever. If he isn't home this weekend I'm talking to the newspapers. I'll tell them...'

Abbie put her hands over her ears, trying to shut out her sister-in-law's terrible threats. It was horrible, a nightmare, and five minutes ago she had been feeling exactly the same—wanting to lash out, hurt everybody because she was hurting. Eventually the stream of abuse stopped and she slumped over the desk, her head on her arms. Never, never, never, she promised herself, would she allow herself to become like that bitter woman, who was prepared to wreck her own life along with everyone else's in her possessive obsession with a man who could no longer stand even to be in the same room with her.

Abbie loved Grey. Being his wife had been the most perfect, the most beautiful thing in her life. He might have betrayed her, but the three years they had had together were full of precious memories. They were all she had left of him, and she would need those in the dark days ahead to keep her strong.

If it had been a straight fight between the two of them things might have been different. She would have done everything, fought with every weapon at her disposal to keep the man she loved more than life itself. But the memory of a dark-haired woman, the very image of femininity, bent lovingly over her baby kept pushing itself to the forefront of her mind. It wasn't a straight fight. Break her heart as it might, that tiny baby needed his father far more than she needed a husband. And there was more than one way to love someone. Sometimes love meant letting go.

She picked up the telephone and dialled a number. 'Steve? This is Abbie. About that job in America—is it still open?'

Grey arrived home bearing the roses she had seen him buy. It had never occurred to her that he could be so cruel. But then it had never occurred to her that he could look her in the eye and lie to her. And he didn't know that she had seen him. That she had seen him touch his infant son and then cross the street and buy roses for his wife. It almost undid all her careful planning, all the effort that had gone into keeping back the tears.

'No!' she said quickly, drawing her hands back as he moved to hold her. If he touched her she would never be able to keep back the pain and her precious gift to him would be lost. 'Wet nail polish.'

'You can do it again,' he said, with that special little smile that she knew so well—an invitation to love that normally no amount of wet nail polish would ever have stopped her accepting.

'No time,' she said, twisting away to avoid him. She nodded in the direction of her bag standing in the hall and he followed her eyes. 'Steve called an hour ago. I'm booked on the evening flight to Houston. An oil well fire has broken out in Venezuela; I'm going with the team to cover it.'

A muscle tightened in his jaw and he dropped the flowers onto the hall table. 'That's rather short notice, isn't it?' He eyed the suitcase that was standing by her canvas bag. 'And rather more luggage than you normally take.'

She hadn't expected an argument, she'd thought he would be glad to see the back of her, but there wasn't time to think about that now. 'These guys aren't going to hang around while I catch up on my private life,' she said, turning to the mirror, smoothing a wayward strand of hair into place, lifting the collar of her crisp white shirt to a more flattering angle, giving herself time to get herself back in control. 'And the job fits in with the one I told you about. I'm going to stay on and do that afterwards.' He didn't say anything. 'So I'll need more clothes than I normally take...' She rushed to fill the silence.

'You'll be away for six weeks...more...' His face creased in a puzzled frown. 'I thought we were going away for a couple of weeks in August?'

'Away?' She discovered that she couldn't quite meet his eyes. 'You said the cottage wasn't available.'

'There's the rest of the world,' he said. 'Forget your oil men and I'll take you to the Maldives again...' She nearly jumped out of her skin as he put his hands on her shoulders and met her eyes in the mirror. 'You loved it there.'

The place hadn't mattered. She'd loved it because she had been with him. Because he had loved her. 'I c-can't,' she stammered.

'Can't?' He frowned. 'Or won't?'

She turned to face him. 'You're not going to come the heavy husband after all, are you, Grey?' she said, her throat so tight that she could barely get the words out. 'You were the one who said that if I wasn't available they'd never make me a star.'

His hands dropped to his sides. 'You didn't seem bothered at the time.'

'I was tired. Not thinking straight.' He didn't appear to be convinced. She would have to try a little harder. 'Oh, come on, Grey. Another year and I'll be able to pick and choose the jobs I want. I've worked hard to get where I am. It hasn't been easy and I'm not about to throw it away now.'

'I know that better than anyone, but I don't want you to leave like this—in a rush. You can catch up with your oil men later, Abbie. I think we need a little time together before you go. We need to talk.'

'*Later*, darling?' How *dared* he make it so difficult for her when she was trying to make it easy for him? 'Have you any idea what you're asking? If I'm not there to fly out with these guys…' Her gesture to him through the mirror said it all. 'And there isn't time to brief anyone else. If I pull out, there'll be no feature at all.'

'Would that matter?'

'Matter?' She forced a laugh. 'What are you saying?' Her voice very nearly cracked in her attempt to make a joke of it.

Why wouldn't he just take the chance she was giving him? After the torments his brother had suffered she could understand his fear that she would cause trouble, why he would make every attempt to keep her happy—even make love to her as if he meant it. Susan's call had cleared her head, made her understand it all. Well, this way he would know that he was free, but he was making it so much harder than she had anticipated.

She could have taken the easy route. Been packed and long gone by the time he'd come home. How she had longed to do that. Just to disappear, never to have to see him again. Or she could have confronted him with the damning evidence, watched the love-light in his eyes die as he realised he no longer needed to keep up a front, a pretence that they still had a marriage. Even now, as the tension heightened between them, it would be so easy to tip it over into a fight and simply storm out. Except that he had never been a man to leave loose ends and he might just come after her.

'Of course it matters. I'd never get another job again, and what on earth would I do then?' she said, turning back to the mirror, flicking at her fringe—anything rather than face him.

'You could always stay at home. Last week you were desperate to have a baby.'

'You weren't very keen, as I recall.' She caught the touch of bitterness that had crept into her voice, forced a smile.

This was her last gift to him. A gift of love. Not wrapped in fancy paper, but in careless words calculated to wound, to destroy the fragile house of cards that their marriage had become. She was giving him the freedom to walk free without guilt. Guilt would not be a good start for a new life. And that was her only concern. The brand new life that he had created in a careless moment of passion—or of love, it hardly mattered. She had put her career before her marriage and was at least in some part to blame for what had happened, and she would take her share of the responsibility.

'You were right, of course. You always are. It was simply a case of my hormones going into overdrive.' She wouldn't be able to keep this up for much longer.

She glanced at her watch, willing the taxi to arrive. 'I don't think I'm cut out for motherhood at all.'

'I don't believe you.' As she tried to pass him he caught her and held her, his face creased in a frown. 'What's going on, Abbie?'

'Going on?' She tried a careless laugh. It didn't work. 'Grey!' she protested as his fingers bit into her arm. 'You're hurting me!'

'There's something wrong. Tell me!'

'No!' she cried, then, 'No,' she repeated, more carefully. 'I'm just in a hurry. I'm afraid I haven't had time to—'

'Stop it! For heaven's sake look at yourself.' He swung her around so that they were both facing the mirror. Her cheeks were hectic, her eyes overbright from the desperate need to weep that she was keeping at bay by sheer will-power. 'Tell me, Abbie.' He gave her a little shake. 'You're not going anywhere until you tell me what's happening.'

'H-how are you going to stop me?' Her challenge sounded feeble enough to her own ears. Grey simply laughed. It wasn't a pleasant sound.

'You don't need to ask that, Abbie. You know how I'll stop you.' Her arm still grasped firmly in one hand, he raised his hand to her cheek and brushed it lightly with the back of his fingers. She shuddered. 'Catch a later plane, Abbie. It wouldn't be the first time, would it?' he murmured as, without haste, he began to unbutton her shirt. 'Remember?'

Remember? How could she ever forget? They had known one another ten glorious days when he had arrived at her flat just as she was getting ready to fly to Paris. She might even have made it if he hadn't decided to help her get ready...

'Grey, no,' she begged, desperate to stop him while she still had some control over her racketing senses. 'Please. The taxi will be here any minute.'

'It can wait,' he ground out harshly, his hand slipping beneath the flimsy lace of her bra, his long fingers cradling her breast, his thumb teasing its betraying, eager bud.

Her mind, sure of its purpose, screamed a silent protest. Her body refused to listen, cleaving to him as naturally as breathing while his insistent mouth demanded her utter slavery. She was helpless; she had always been helpless in his arms.

The long, insistent peal of the doorbell finally impinged on their consciousness, bringing them both back from some far place. But as they broke apart Grey raised his head to look at her from beneath heavy-lidded eyes. 'I don't want you to go, Abbie.'

And she could almost have believed him, except that when she opened her eyes she saw the faint smear of lipstick on the lapel of his suit and remembered that hours ago another head had rested there as he had briefly held the mother of his child in his arms.

That image brought her crashing back to sanity. 'If you have ever loved me, Grey, let me go. Please!'

'If I've ever…' He looked as if she had struck him, releasing her so abruptly that she staggered back against the hall table. When she put out her hand to save herself it came down heavily on the abandoned roses, the sharp jab of a thorn spearing the pad of her thumb so that as her shaking fingers fumbled with the buttons of her shirt a tiny smear of blood stained the white cloth.

The bell rang again—an impatient tattoo. Grateful for the interruption, she turned from him and stumbled to the door, flinging it open. 'Will you take this bag?' she asked the driver. 'I'll bring the other one.' She picked up the canvas bag and turned unwillingly to face Grey. But he wasn't in the hall, and for a moment she thought she might scream out her agony for everyone to hear. Then suddenly he was there. Taking her hand in his, he fixed a small plaster to her bleeding thumb, and that...that was just so much worse.

He lifted her hand to his mouth, kissed the tip of her thumb. 'Take care of yourself, Abbie,' he said, all emotion clamped down under his masked expression. 'Ring me to let me know you've arrived safely.'

He bent towards her as if to kiss her, but she stepped back before he could touch her. And, because she was on the edge of breaking down, of letting out all the pain, all the heartbreak that she had been keeping under lock and key while she acted out the role of a careless wife, she turned and fled down the stairs without a word.

Abbie was hot. She had arrived in Atlanta expecting her senses to be assaulted by magnolia-scented air and the ante-bellum mansions of the old South, only to find the skyscraper skyline of a modern city that might just as well have been New York—except that it was hotter.

She was wearing nothing but a silk wrapper, but even so her motel room seemed like a steam bath in the summer heat. She continued tapping her first impressions of the city into her laptop nevertheless, determined not to allow herself the luxury of a cold shower until the job was done.

A sharp rap at the door disturbed the flow of her

writing and she paused, irritated at the interruption, to push her damp hair back from her forehead. But then everything was irritating her right now.

'Who is it?' she demanded.

'It's me,' a deep voice replied, and, startled, she crossed swiftly to the door and flung it open.

'Steve!' She stared at him in astonishment. 'What in heaven's name are you doing here?'

'The features editor collapsed trying to prove that he could still play five sets of tennis.' He grinned. 'Someone had to step in and take his place at the last moment...' His shrug was eloquent.

'So nobly, above and beyond the call of duty, you volunteered,' she said, somewhat cynically. 'And who's doing your job?'

'This is the silly season, Abbie. I was going on holiday anyway.'

'How convenient. And how nice of the paper to pick up the tab for you.'

'I'm here to work,' he protested. 'I thought you might be glad to see me. Aren't you going to invite me in?'

Conscious that she was wearing nothing beneath her silk wrapper, she shrugged a little awkwardly, but stepped back. 'Do you want a cold drink?' she asked.

'No, thanks, but I could do with a shower. My room isn't available for another hour and I'm about to melt.'

She glanced at her watch. 'You've got ten minutes,' she said, waving in the direction of the bathroom. 'Then you'll have to find someone else's time to waste. I've got an appointment.'

'Sure.' He didn't seem in the least put out by her

less than enthusiastic welcome. 'I'll just get my bag from the car.'

A few minutes later, with the noise of the shower as a cooling backdrop, she was putting the finishing touches to her piece when there was another rap at the door. Abbie frowned, but this time refused to be diverted from her task, ignoring the sound as she typed in the last few sentences. The knock was repeated— louder, more insistent.

'Just a minute!'

But as she pressed the 'save' button she heard the door open behind her, and spun in her seat to find Grey already inside, the door closed, his tall figure barring the exit.

'Grey,' she said foolishly, rising to her feet. 'I—I didn't expect... H-how did you find me?'

'Were you hiding, Abbie? I was beginning to wonder.'

'I...um...' Not hiding, exactly, but then she hadn't expected him to follow her. She had given him his freedom and she had expected him to take it and run. But he was here, in her motel room, regarding her intently from beneath heavy-lidded eyes. It was a look at once arousing and terrifying, and her breasts responded, peaking beneath the flimsy silk wrapper that clung seductively to her overheated body. Her cheeks suffused with fierce colour and she wanted to clutch the silk about her protectively, but that would only make things worse.

'You didn't phone me,' he said at last.

'The Venezuelan oil fields were a little short on facilities for personal calls—' she began, but he wasn't interested in excuses.

'At first I thought you were just making me suffer

a little because I'd tried to pressure you into staying with me. I mean, what other reason could there possibly be? And I knew that if something was wrong your paper would be in touch fast enough. Dear, kind Steve would phone me himself.'

Steve. She clamped down on her lips, tried not to look towards the bathroom. The shower had stopped running; it was quiet. Surely if he heard Grey's voice he would have the sense to stay put?

'But after a week, I thought you were overreacting just a bit, so I phoned the paper and asked dear, kind Steve's secretary for a contact number. You were on the move, she said, and could she pass on a message? I thought since our holiday had been cancelled we might spend a few days together sipping mint julep under the southern stars. I wanted to check on the best time to come. She said she would ask you to ring me.'

Something like a moan escaped Abbie's lips and he paused, inviting her to speak. But she shook her head. He was angry. It was a chillingly restrained anger that froze her to the core, so that despite the heat she shivered.

'I *imagine* she passed on the message. But you didn't ring me, did you, Abbie? Instead of a phone call from my loving wife, I received this.' He took a letter from his jacket pocket and flung it on the table beside them. 'I would have thought, after three years of marriage, that I might at least rate some kind of explanation. Not just a letter from a stranger informing me that my wife has applied for a divorce on the grounds of irretrievable breakdown of marriage. Would you care to tell me when our marriage broke down, Abbie? I seemed to have missed it.'

She shook her head, unable to speak.

'Talk to me, Abbie!' The cool tone of his voice sharpened and she shrank back against her desk. 'Oh, for heaven's sake, I'm not going to... Just talk to me, Abbie. I'm not that unreasonable, am I? We've never run away from problems.' He took another step towards her, but as she drew back even further he stopped, raked his fingers through his hair.

'If this is about having a baby—' He stopped as he saw that he had hit a nerve. 'So that's all it is.' Relief seemed to swamp him momentarily. 'I'm sorry, Abbie. Truly sorry. I reacted with about as much sensitivity as a concrete mixer, but if it's that important to you I'm sure we can work something out—'

'Work something...?' She closed her eyes as words utterly failed her. He wanted her to come back? He was prepared to let her have a baby and carry on with his double life?

'The last few months have been difficult,' he continued. 'You've been away too much and I've had a lot on my mind...' He was closer. As her eyes flew open his hand slipped about her waist and he touched her cheek with the tips of his fingers. 'Talk to me, Abbie,' he murmured softly, as she shivered helplessly against him. 'Don't shut me out.'

It was unbearable. She would never have thought it was possible to miss anyone so much. They had been apart for longer, but then there had always been the promise that in a few days they would be together. Now, seeing him like this, his eyes lying to her, his gentle hands lying to her, it was almost more than she could bear.

She had thought that once she was away on the other side of the Atlantic, once she had instituted divorce proceedings, he would seize the chance to make a clean break and start a new life with Emma and Matthew. She had never anticipated that he would come after her and demand...explanations.

She stiffened, wrenched herself away from the drugging pleasure of his touch. 'I shouldn't have just left like that.' She held herself so rigid that she thought she might break. 'I'm sorry, Grey, but you're right. I've been away too much. When I came home last time nothing seemed to work for us. I suppose we've just grown apart. I thought it would be easier like this...'

'Easier?' For a moment he didn't seem to understand. 'To run away?'

His hands grasped her shoulders as if he wanted to shake some sense into her. But he restrained himself, biting down hard on his lip, so that the muscles in his jaw knotted with the effort. For a moment it was deathly quiet in the spacious motel room.

'Easier?' he repeated, more quietly, relaxing his grip so that he was no longer hurting her. But he didn't let go. 'I don't believe you, Abbie. You're not that kind of coward. And if you think it was easier for me, I have to tell you that you are mistaken.'

It had been so hard. Every day. Making herself get up, get on with the job, when all she'd wanted to do was turn her face to the wall and die. But it wasn't in her nature to lie down and let life walk all over her. He had accused her of wanting to have it all. Well, she had discovered the hard way that she couldn't. But every day she got up, put on her make-up and her prettiest clothes, and got on with the only life that was left to her. Work. And that would have to be her cover story now.

'I wanted a clean break, Grey,' she said, lifting her head, forcing a hard edge into her voice. 'I'm staying in America. You were right. I can't have a career—not this career—and a marriage. You need more than I can give you.'

'You've decided that, have you?' His eyes, those meltingly warm brown eyes, hardened as she had never seen them harden before. 'All by yourself? Perhaps I should remind you exactly what we've had for the last three years.'

In one swift movement he tugged at the tie of the flimsy silk gown and it slipped treacherously away from her body, leaving her defenceless against his raking glance. Then he reached for her, his hands enfolding her narrow waist and drawing her against him.

Certain now of easy victory, he tipped back her head and stared down into her face. 'What do you say, Abbie?'

Why was he doing this? Why had he come to torture her with his presence when she was trying to make it easy for him? 'Oh, come on, Grey,' she said, her voice as brittle as glass. 'We've had a lot of fun, but I've been spending more and more time away, not less. You need more than that. Deserve more than that...'

Her voice trailed away as she realised how close she was to betraying herself. That wasn't the way. She didn't want his guilt on her conscience; she wanted him to walk away and never look back. It was her final gift to him. A gift of love.

'I...I'm sorry, Grey. I simply don't love you any more.'

His eyes continued to regard her with a puzzled expression. 'You're lying, Abbie.' His hands on her arms might have tightened fractionally, but his voice remained cool, restrained, only the whiteness where his jaw muscles clamped down on his emotions betrayed how close to the edge he was.

'Lying?' From somewhere she conjured up a careless lift of her shoulders. 'What's the matter, Grey, can't your ego take it? I wanted to let you down lightly, but if you must know…the truth of the matter is…' She faltered. The brazen lie did not come easily to her lips. 'The truth is that journalists are a clannish group. They always use the same hotels. It's like a club where you meet old friends, have a few drinks and—well…sometimes rather more than a few drinks…' Her throat hurt so much she didn't know how the hateful words managed to creep out. 'Things happen…'

'Really? And then you run home and tell your husband that you want to have his baby?'

He didn't believe her. She'd told him that she had affairs in hotels with whoever happened to be around and he didn't believe her. He was angry enough to kill, but he didn't believe her. Her heart rejoiced at that, but her head knew that it wouldn't do. She had to make him believe her lies.

But she couldn't meet his eyes and lie, so she turned away as if in shame. 'I thought if I had a child, if I didn't have to go away again, it would be all right.' The silence was awful. She looked up then, and flinched at his face, masked with horror, but there was no turning back. 'But then, as soon as I was back in the office…'

Something died in his eyes. Some light. And as he took a sharp step back she knew she was close to achieving her aim. Close to making him hate her. It would be easy now. She moved after him, the air lifting the light robe away from her glistening skin, and she looped her arms about his neck, pressing her body against his. 'But sex with you was the best, Grey.' Her voice was little more than a husky murmur as she forced it through the pain. 'If you want to give it one last whirl for old times' sake...' And she pressed her lips against his.

Even as she felt him stiffen, felt his hands tighten to push her away, the click of the bathroom door was gunshot-loud in the silent room. Grey's head came up sharply at the sound.

As she swung round she saw Steve, fair hair slicked back from the shower, nothing but a towel wrapped about his waist, standing in the doorway.

Grey's eyes dropped to hers. 'I see. I appear to have been singularly stupid.' He pulled the edges of her gown together and tied it firmly about her waist before stepping clear of her. Then he turned to confront the man standing in the doorway. 'Abbie was trying desperately hard to protect you, bury you in a host of lovers—anything to get rid of me. If you had stayed put for another five seconds she would have succeeded—'

No! Abbie clutched at Grey's arm as his hands bunched into fists, but no sound came from her throat as he brushed her aside, crossing the room in a stride.

Steve did not move. 'Go on, hit me,' he invited. 'I can see the headline now. MINISTER'S BROTHER IN MOTEL BRAWL—' That was when Grey's fist crashed into his chin, sending him flying back into the bathroom.

For a moment he stood over the prone figure. 'Anything to oblige, Morley,' he said. 'Have a nice day.'

Then he swung round and strode out through the door, without so much as a glance at Abbie.

For a moment she remained motionless, unable to do or say anything. When she had made the decision to let her husband go in the most painless way possible, to take to herself the pain of loss and the anguish of guilt as her parting gift to him, she could never, in all her wildest fantasies, have imagined that pure emotion could have such a physical pain, that her heart breaking in two would hurt just as surely as if she had broken a bone.

And as she stared at the open door through which Grey had walked away from her for ever it began to retreat, to grow smaller as the blood pounded louder and louder in her ears. She put out her hand as if to call it back, and it was her hand that hit the floor first.

When she opened her eyes she was staring at the ceiling, and for a moment nothing made sense. Then a cool flannel was placed on her forehead and she turned to see Steve, standing looking down at her.

'You fainted, Abbie. Just lie still for a moment.'

And then everything did make sense, and she groaned, trying to sit up even as Steve pushed her gently back onto the bed. 'Please don't put this in the paper.' There was no answer. 'Steve? For me?'

'Why not?' he demanded. Then added more reasonably, 'I would have thought that after what he's done to you it would give you the most thorough satisfaction to see him sued for assault.'

She groaned. 'Please! I...I couldn't bear it.'

'Most women in your position would give their eye-teeth to embarrass the man who had betrayed them. Embarrassing an entire government into the bargain would surely be the icing on the cake?' She shook her head. 'No? Why should *you* be so damned noble about it?'

'I...I don't expect you to understand.'

He gave a little shrug. 'Perhaps I understand more than you think.' He rubbed his chin, already darkening from its contact with Grey's fist, then sat on the edge of the bed. 'It must have been quite a shock to find me in your bathroom after he had flown all the way to Atlanta to be with you.' He regarded her thoughtfully, his forehead creased in a deep frown. 'It seems an odd thing to do, don't you think, when he has a surrogate wife lined up at home?'

Steve might not be able to work it out—he didn't have all the facts—but she could make a good guess at the reason. Grey was covering himself. He would be able to stand up in court and tell the judge that he had done everything in his power to save his marriage. He had even flown across the Atlantic to plead with his wife to come back to him. Or maybe he really did want to carry on with things just the way they were... No. That hardly bore thinking about. In fact she refused to think about it for another second.

'I'd better do something about that bruise,' she said abruptly, swinging her feet to the floor and fetching some ice from the fridge. 'I'm just sorry you were involved in all this,' she went on, sitting beside him on the bed and applying a makeshift ice-pack to his face.

'Yes, well,' he said, wincing a little. 'Serves me right for helping myself to other people's bathrooms, I suppose.' He searched her eyes. 'Grey's knuckles will be just as sore as my chin, but I've got you to give me first aid. I think I know who I'd rather be at the moment.' He put his arm about her shoulders. 'You know that, Abbie, don't you?'

There was a shocked moment when Abbie realised that Steve was offering considerably more than his broad shoulder to cry on. She could hardly blame him. He was an attractive man, and most women would probably be very happy to accept the easy comfort of his arms. But there had only ever been one man in her life, and she wasn't about to break the habit of a lifetime. She eased herself away from the casual embrace and stood up, putting a safe distance between them before she turned to face him.

'I'm sorry, Steve,' she said. 'But I believe it's time you booked into your own room.'

He rose to his feet and gave a little shrug. 'Of course. You said you had an appointment. If you don't feel up to it, perhaps I could take over?'

'No, thanks. I think you'd be better off lying down quietly in your room, with an ice-pack on that bruise.'

CHAPTER FOUR

'ABBIE? Have they come?' Polly burst through the door, dumping her school bag with a triumphant 'Yes!' as she saw the line of cardboard crates in the study. 'Can I help you unpack?'

Abbie regarded the boxed remnants of her marriage. 'I'd only have to pack it all again when I find a flat of my own,' she said unenthusiastically.

'But that could take months.' Polly, seventeen, had a directness that wasn't any easier to take just because she was so often right.

'Not if I can help it. I'm just…um…housesitting while your parents are away.' *Baby*sitting, was the term Polly's mother had used, but that wouldn't go down too well. 'Your mother may be a dear friend, but she certainly won't want me as a permanent lodger.'

'Well, you'll need your computer,' Polly pointed out. 'You said so.'

'Did I?' The truth was that Abbie had no desire to confront the possessions that Grey, so anxious to be rid of every reminder of her, had put into storage, sending an inventory to her solicitor. The sigh that escaped her was involuntary. It was six months since she had left him. Long enough, surely, for the jagged edges of heartache to have worn smooth?

It wasn't as if she had sat around and moped. She had been inundated with work after the appearance of the tug-of-love story, and on the run from one commission to the next she had been able to keep one step ahead of the pain. But all it had taken to sharpen the heartbreak into agonising focus had been a pile of ordinary cardboard boxes, and finally the urge to weep swept over her.

'Abbie?' Polly's voice had lost its eager certainty. 'Are you all right? I didn't mean to upset you...'

'Upset me?' She blinked back the sting of tears and briskly picked up the contents list that had arrived with the boxes, meticulously written in Grey's clear, bold handwriting. Her books, files, clothes, the collection of fine china figures that had been gifts for birthdays, anniversaries, dull Mondays, happy Wednesdays—any excuse had done when Grey saw something that he thought she would like. Things she loved, things she dreaded facing. Each carefully listed. 'Of course not. And you're right. I do need the computer, and some more winter clothes.'

The decision made, it should have been easy. Her computer was a work tool. Hardly endowed with emotion. And yet when it had been new and terrifying she had constantly turned to Grey for help. He had grinned and leaned over her to press some magic key that made sense of everything. He had always known the magic keys to press. And as she hesitated now over the cables she heard his laughing voice in her head. 'Parallel printer...it goes there, see? It's easy.' She swallowed hard against the lump in her throat and pushed the connection home. Easy.

'Which box are your clothes in?' Polly asked, looking about her.

'That one,' she said, with a silent prayer of thanks to whichever kindly deity had prompted Grey to list everything, sparing her any unexpected confrontation with memories that would jar loose the fragile protective shell she had erected about herself.

But life was never that simple. As Polly scored through the thick tape and folded back the lid of the box Abbie saw the leather-bound album. A photograph album. Deliberate? Or had Emma found it and dumped it there without telling him? It hardly mattered. The shock was just as great.

'I love other people's photographs,' Polly said, idly flipping the pages. 'Wow! You look fabulous in a bikini, Abbie. Where is this?'

'The Maldives,' she said faintly. She didn't have to look. She knew the album. Honeymoon photographs. They had taken silly photographs of one another with silly expressions on their faces because they were so happy.

'Is this your husband?' Polly asked. Her voice seemed to be coming from a long way off. 'He looks just like Jon's father.'

'Jon?'

'A boy I know. At school. His dad's a politician—you must have seen him; he's always on the television...' Her voice dried up as she looked across and saw the tears pouring down Abbie's cheeks. 'Oh, Lord.' She snapped the album shut. 'I'm sorry. I shouldn't have said anything. Can I get you a cup of tea? Or a drink? Brandy? Mum usually dishes that out for cases of shock...'

'It's all right, Polly.' She brushed the tears away with the palm of her hand. 'It just caught me by surprise, that's all.'

She crossed to the box, deliberately opened the album and turned the pages slowly. 'Did you say that your friend was called Jon?' she asked as the painful images flashed by. White-powdered beaches, hibiscus flowers, Grey snorkelling, his powerful body eerily green under water.

'Well, it's Jonathan actually,' Polly answered. 'Jonathan Lockwood. Oh, Lord!' She clapped her hand dramatically over her mouth. 'That was your married name!'

Robert's London flat was not far from Polly's home; it was hardly surprising that she and Jonathan would go to the same school. 'He's my husband's...Grey's nephew—'

'Grey? You mean *Grey* is your husband? But Jon talks about him all the time. There was an enormous row when he ran away from boarding-school at the beginning of the Christmas term, and Grey told his father that it was time he sorted himself out and put his family before his work.'

'Did he? Well, he was right.' She had learned that too late. Abbie looked up. 'What about his mother?'

'She comes up to London sometimes, I think... What's she like?'

'Susan?' A woman who took loyalty and love and used them as weapons. 'I never saw much of her,' she said, turning another page of the album. Grey smiled back at her.

Her hand hovered over the image, briefly touching the dark, straight brows that she so loved, the twist of his mouth as he smiled into the lens, the long, arrow-straight nose. Loving him was a feeling of such intensity that it hurt. Every night she promised herself that the next day would be easier. But every morning she woke up and was forced to face the truth once more. It didn't get easier. Each day was harder to bear. The image began to swim and then Polly was pushing a glass into her hand.

'Sit down. Drink that slowly.'

'I'm supposed to be looking after you, Polly,' she protested feebly as she sank onto a chair. Some babysitter.

'I don't need looking after. Mum thinks I'm a baby, but I'm not.'

'No.' She took a reluctant sip of the brandy. 'But with me here to keep an eye on things she can visit her new grandson without worrying about you.' She looked up at the pretty, bright-eyed girl and tried to remember what it was like to be on the brink of womanhood. Those intense, brittle feelings that one day made you feel on top of the world and the next in the depths of despair. A wonderful age, but a dangerous one too. Perhaps she should be taking her role a little more seriously. 'Are you and Jon...close friends?' she asked.

The girl flushed slightly. 'I won't bring him here if it would bother you.'

'It's all right, Polly. But I wouldn't want to embarrass him... Just warn me and I'll hide upstairs.'

'You still love him, don't you?' She made a gesture towards the album. 'Grey, I mean. Why did you split up?'

Her mother had never asked. Margaret had simply offered open arms and an open door. Seventeen was different. It was an age when you poked at life with a blunt stick, blissfully unaware that there were hornets' nests lying in wait for the unwary. But it was probably better to tell the girl the simple truth than have her inventing some fanciful drama.

'He had an affair, Polly,' she said, matter-of-factly. 'It happens every day.'

'An affair? But—'

'Come on,' Abbie said firmly, cutting off the question. 'I thought you were going to help me unpack these clothes.'

She seized the red cloak with determination, but as she shook out the creases she caught the faintest scent of dry leaves and bonfires and Grey, and without warning the memory of that first crazy Sunday together, when they had walked in St James's Park, rose up and overwhelmed her.

She had been to a party on the Saturday evening but had left early, pleading a headache. But she hadn't slept, haunted by the face of an unknown man who had glanced at her once, capturing her, holding her prisoner with his warm brown eyes for the space of a heartbeat, no more.

He hadn't looked at her again. Why would he have done? He had arrived with a delicate, exotic beauty who barely reached his shoulder, her eyes and hair as dark as night—the kind of woman who always made Abbie feel gawky and every last inch of her five feet ten inches. But her own eyes had strayed in his direction more than once, drawn irresistibly to the impressive black-clad figure who had so easily dominated the room. They had only dropped by on their way to somewhere grander, to leave a present and wish their hostess a happy birthday, and Abbie had felt a sense of something close to relief when they left. But this briefest of encounters had been oddly disturbing, and shortly afterwards she had made her own excuses and gone home.

After a sleepless night, the imperious ring on her

doorbell just as the red autumn sun crept over the horizon had been hardly welcome. Crawling unwillingly from bed, Abbie had pushed the tousled mop of hair from her face, tugged on her dressing gown and pulled open the door, expecting to find a neighbour desperate for milk. But it hadn't been a neighbour. It had been him.

Shock had stilled the complaint poised on her tongue, and this time his eyes had remained on her face as without a word spoken between them he had stepped over the threshold and shut the door behind him.

'You really are that tall,' he said, as if he couldn't quite believe it.

If he'd woken her up to discuss her height… 'Five foot…' Abbie considered taking off an inch. Changed her mind. He wasn't the kind of man you could fool. '…ten.'

His mouth straightened as if he had read her mind. 'Only ten? Not ten and a half?' He was laughing at her, but she didn't mind. Perhaps she was floating. It felt as if she was floating, and that would make her look taller. Whatever the reason, she didn't contradict him. And she didn't move even when he reached out his hand and touched her cheek with the tips of his fingers.

'My name is Grey Lockwood. I'm a lawyer, thirty years old, and I've never been married. Until last night I'd never been in the least bit tempted.' He regarded her steadily. 'But I've spent the entire night thinking about kissing every single inch of you, Abigail Cartwright,' he said, with the utmost seriousness. 'All seventy of them. I couldn't wait any longer.'

She knew she should be indignant, outraged by this dawn raid on her emotions and heaven knew what else. But she wasn't. She didn't ask how he knew her name, or even how he had found her. Instead, equally earnest, she simply said, 'Me too.'

'That's all right, then.' His slow smile was oddly seductive, drawing her to him until his hands were gently cupping her face, his long fingers sliding through her sleep-tousled hair. 'I'll start, shall I? And we'll take it from there.' He seemed to look at her for ever, as if imprinting her upon his memory before he kissed her, slowly, thoughtfully, tenderly. And it was, she decided, a great deal more than all right.

She held the soft wool of the cloak against her cheek now, remembering. Her friends had predicted disaster as she had been spun headlong into a whirlwind of romance. It was too fast, they'd warned her. She wasn't experienced enough to handle a man like Grey. But, for once in her sensible, organised life, she hadn't listened to the voice of reason. It *had* been crazy. She knew that. Crazy and blissful and quite perfect.

Autumn walks in St James's Park with the scent of bonfires in the air followed by afternoon tea at the Ritz. A picnic on a deserted October beach. A stolen Wednesday afternoon at the Victoria and Albert Museum. And roses. He'd given her so many roses. They had wanted it to last for ever and so, six breathless weeks later, they had been married.

With no family of her own, she'd had no desire for a huge church affair. Instead they'd had a beautifully intimate wedding, with just his father and brother and a few close friends to witness their vows to one another. It had all seemed like some glorious fairytale.

For a long time it had seemed that they would make 'happy ever after'.

Abbie wondered what had happened to the exotic, dark-eyed beauty that Grey had been with that first time she saw him. She had been the daughter of some wealthy South American client, passing through London and needing an escort to the ballet. She sighed. Clearly that dark, delicate beauty had made a lasting impression on Grey.

'I think I should get this stuff cleaned before putting it away,' she said flatly to Polly as she dropped the cloak back into the box. That would deal with the treacherously lingering scents that sent her vulnerable memory winging back to happier days.

'I think you should finish your brandy,' Polly said, regarding her with daunting pity. 'It'll do you good.'

'Maybe.' Abbie regarded the half-filled tumbler doubtfully, and without warning her sense of humour bubbled through the painful memories. 'But do you feel capable of carrying me to bed?'

Abbie lay back on the sofa, put her feet up and groaned. 'I wouldn't have believed there were so many awful flats in the world.'

Polly looked up from her textbook. 'I expect, subconsciously, you're looking for somewhere like the lovely flat you shared with Grey,' she said earnestly.

'I'm doing nothing of the kind,' Abbie snapped, aching feet and a wasted day having severely blunted her patience. 'My subconscious is well aware that I couldn't possibly afford it.' Then she lifted her head and looked at the girl. 'How do you know it was lovely?'

Polly blushed fiercely. 'Jon took me there.'

'You persuaded Jon to take you to meet Grey?' Abbie was horrified. She had attempted to curb Polly's romantic hopes that her marriage might be mended, but any opportunity to talk about Grey had been sweet and it had seemed harmless enough...

But even as she sat up, determined once and for all to put a stop to the girl's foolish fantasies, something else occurred to her. What had Polly said to Grey? He believed she was swanning about the world without a thought in her head for anything but her career. If he were to discover that she was living quietly in London, looking after a seventeen-year-old while her mother was away in Australia acquainting herself with her new grandson, he might begin to wonder... And she didn't want him wondering. He was too sharp for that...

'It is *so* lovely,' Polly continued, totally unaware of the alarm she had provoked in Abbie's breast. 'The bedroom is—'

'Polly! That's enough!'

'I'll get you a nice cup of tea, shall I?' she asked soothingly.

Abbie refused to be soothed. 'I do not want a "nice cup of tea"!' she returned, but was immediately remorseful. It wasn't Polly's fault. She had simply come too close to the truth for comfort. Traipsing about from one dreary flat to the next had forcefully reminded her of all she had lost. No, not lost. Thrown away.

She had been so certain of his love she had been careless of her marriage, taking it for granted, not recognising the danger until it was too late. She had lost not just her beautiful home, she had lost the company, the shared pleasures, the physical presence of

Grey in her bed. She suffered the pain of her physical need of him as well as the mental agony of separation.

Abbie dragged her mind back to present reality; dwelling on the past would only make matters worse. 'What am I saying?' she demanded, trying on a smile that didn't feel very convincing. 'Of course I want a cup of tea. But I'll make it. You must have some project work you should be getting on with.'

'Can I use the computer?'

Abbie grinned at the ease with which the young exploited any sign of weakness. Then, halfway to the kitchen, something occurred to her. If Polly had been to the flat, why hadn't she said anything about Grey, or Emma or the baby? Tact? That wasn't exactly her style. 'Actually, I bought some teacakes yesterday,' she said. 'Perhaps you'd like one before you start work?'

'Oh, great. I'll toast them while you make the tea.'

'So, tell me,' Abbie said as she filled the kettle, 'now you've met him, what did you think of Grey?' she asked.

'Oh, I didn't meet him. He was away all last week.'

'Really?' Relief was short-lived. 'But if Grey was away, why would Jon take you to the flat?'

'Oh, he told me about the Degas, and as his father has a spare key—'

'Degas?' A jolt like a thousand volts of electricity, shot through her.

'The one with the girl bathing... I'm doing art history for A-levels.'

'I didn't think Degas figured too prominently in the syllabus, Polly.' She thought of Jon, tall and handsome like his father. Like his uncle. She hated what she was thinking. 'Besides, it was sold months ago.'

She turned. 'So, what was the real reason for going to the flat?'

'But the picture was there,' Polly declared. 'I saw it.'

'Did you? Or was it a copy that Jon used to tempt you with?'

'Of course it wasn't a copy. Besides, I didn't need tempting, I wanted to—' Then she realised what Abbie was implying. 'Oh, Abbie, I wouldn't!' Abbie let out a breath of sheer relief that she hadn't even been aware of holding. Too soon. 'Not sneaking around in someone else's flat while they were away. It would have to be a bit more special than that.'

'It rarely is,' Abbie warned her. But her body taunted her, remembering. With Grey the first time had been special. Every time had been special. Even when he was deceiving you? The voice in her head was scornful. Making love to Emma, then coming home to your bed? How special was that? How could he do that? She turned abruptly from her pale reflection in the dark kitchen window. 'Just make sure you don't find somewhere *special* until your mother comes home,' she said.

'Well, actually, Jon did ask me to go away with him next week. It's half-term.'

'Oh?' Abbie chose not to rise to the bait, fairly certain that this was just in the nature of a wind-up— Polly's retaliation for her leap to the wrong conclusion. 'Where did he have in mind? Paris is always romantic...but cold in February. Rome, perhaps? That would fit in with the art history. Or somewhere warmer? That's probably best if you've only got a week. You won't have to waste so much time taking off your clothes.'

A satisfactory blush darkened Polly's cheeks, but she pressed on. 'What would you do if I said I wanted to go?'

'Call your mother to see if she minded?' Abbie offered.

'In that case there's no point in asking.'

The answer was somehow disingenuous. 'If you were thinking of going without permission, Polly, I warn you that I would be forced to call Jon's father and have you both hauled back. The newspapers would greatly enjoy the spectacle. I doubt if you would find it so much fun to have your photograph plastered all over the front pages, and Jon would be back at boarding-school before his feet could touch the ground. I'll leave your mother's reaction to your imagination.'

'Jon's father is away next week,' Polly informed her, with an infuriatingly innocent expression.

'Are those teacakes burning?' The cups rattled against the saucers as Abbie began to lay a tray.

'So you'd have to call Grey instead.'

Abbie lifted her head from her task and met Polly's eye. 'Another word on the subject, Polly, and I promise you will spend your entire half-term chained to my wrist.'

The trouble was, Abbie thought, as she struggled with Margaret's ancient Mini in the driving rain, that interlaced with Polly's madcap romanticism was a steely strand of common sense. And that had completely fooled her into believing that she would never actually do anything so thoughtless, so irresponsible, so downright stupid as taking Jon up on his offer.

Abbie could have kicked herself. If Polly hadn't

mentioned Grey she might have probed a little deeper into the girl's intentions, and she might then have been able to persuade her that it would be wiser to keep her passion on hold until after her A-levels.

It was just luck that Abbie had been able to work out where the wretched pair had gone. Young Romeo wasn't taking his Juliet somewhere sophisticated. And they would need more than love to keep them warm. But it was secret. And it was special. She knew, because she had been there often enough herself. With Grey.

And the day had started with such promise. Details of the perfect flat had arrived in the post, and also a note from Steve Morley, asking her to call at the office to discuss a commission.

Polly, curled up in an armchair by the fire, her revision text at her elbow, had virtuously declined an outing even when offered lunch out, barely lifting her head from Thomas Hardy to wish her luck with the flat. Abbie had left her without a qualm.

The flat had been the first disappointment. It *could* have been perfect. But it had needed far more than the coat of paint the agent had suggested to make it habitable and she didn't have the money to put it right. Although Steve Morley was doing his best to give it to her.

He was offering money, a lot of it, for an exposé on her brother-in-law and his phoney marriage. He seemed to think that now Abbie had split with Grey her loyalty was no longer an issue. When she had made it clear that he was mistaken he had suggested that work might not be so forthcoming as it had been in the past. It hadn't been very subtle, but when she had told him what she thought of him she hadn't been particularly subtle either.

When finally, soaked to the skin and thoroughly miserable, she had arrived home, it had been to find a letter from her solicitor enclosing papers to be signed to end her marriage. She'd stuffed them in her bag, not wanting Polly to see. It was then that she had realised Polly hadn't come bounding out of the living room to ask her about the flat.

'Polly,' she'd called, going through into the kitchen. Polly hadn't been there, but had thoughtfully left her a message on the small chalkboard.

> Decided that Jon's week of passion sounded more fun than revising. Don't worry about a thing, Abbie. I promise we'll be back in time for school on Monday. Love, Polly.

Don't worry! 'Oh, Polly! How could you do this to me?' she'd demanded out loud, but the empty house had offered no answer. Only the blinking light on the answering machine had held out any hope.

She'd pressed the playback button, half expecting it to be some teenage rag and that Polly's familiar laughing voice would shout 'Got you!' down the line.

The voice was familiar. The warm, rich tones were achingly, heart-searingly familiar. But it hadn't been Polly.

'My name is Grey Lockwood. My nephew Jon left this number as a contact for half-term. Could you ask him to call me? It's quite urgent as he seems to have taken the keys to my holiday cottage…'

As shock had buckled her legs Abbie had swayed and clutched at the newel post, kept herself upright, although she could hardly have said how. The holiday cottage. Ty Bach. That was where they had gone.

CHAPTER FIVE

ABBIE had stopped only to pack an overnight bag before backing Margaret's car out of the garage and switching on the radio to get the traffic and weather reports. The radio had hissed uncooperatively at her, and it had quickly become obvious that the little Mini, used mostly for shopping trips, was in no condition for a two-hundred-and-fifty mile dash down a busy motorway. But it was all she had, so she had gritted her teeth in the face of the weather and rush hour traffic, drastically revising her estimate of the time the journey would take.

A dark Mercedes cruised past her now, in the centre lane. A superbly crafted, highly tuned Mercedes 500 SL, exactly like the one that Grey drove, although the colour was impossible to make out in the dark. In *Grey's* car the journey took four hours, she thought grimly. If she had taken Polly's advice and rung him, she might even now be cruising along the motorway in comfort at a steady seventy miles an hour. But comfort would have been a high price to pay for asking for his help. Too high. And this way, with luck, they would all be back home by lunchtime tomorrow without him ever knowing of her involvement.

Beyond the Severn Bridge the rain turned sleety, sticking to the windscreen, and she thought then that it was as bad as it could get. But just after she left the motorway it began to snow.

Despite her aching muscles and the weirdly hypnotic quality of the snowflakes whirling towards her, thicker and thicker in the headlights, Abbie kept her foot firmly on the accelerator until she turned off the dual carriageway to run down beside the Afon Tywi to the coast. Squinting into a darkness so dense that it could almost be cut with a knife, she only just saw the left fork in time, and the squishy noise of the tyres on the road suddenly quietened as she turned onto a narrow and undulating lane that hadn't borne traffic since the snow had begun to fall.

She was moving slowly now, second gear slow, looking for the stunted oak that marked the almost hidden turning, but her headlights, reflected blindingly by the snow, reached only a few feet in front of her.

Afraid that she had missed it, Abbie gave an audible cry of relief when she saw the tree, its branches and trunk plastered with driving snow so that the stark outline was blurred. She jammed her foot on the brake and locked the wheels.

The lane sloped steeply, terminating on the rock-strewn beach a few hundred feet from the turning, and the car continued to slide towards it, completely unresponsive to the wheel, for what seemed like a lifetime. But it couldn't last, and as the lane took a sudden sidestep to the left the car continued straight on towards the hedge.

Abbie's relief that there was something to stop her before she slid, unchecked, into the freezing waters of Carmarthen Bay was rudely shattered as the offside front wheel hit the ditch and the car was caught and spun by its impetus until it was facing in the opposite direction. Then the rear wheel followed its partner and the car slipped sideways, tipping over with a rending of metal and glass that seemed wholly alien in that white and silent world.

For a moment Abbie remained very still, hanging in her seat belt against the door and feeling oddly elated that she had survived without so much as a scratch. Then the lights went out, and it took all her self-control to bite back a scream. Forcing her trembling fingers to unhook the seat belt, she clambered on equally shaky legs over the passenger seat and out of the car.

She stood for a moment, shivering with more than cold in the driving snow, although her short thick coat did little enough to protect legs inadequately covered by a flirty little skirt that lifted eagerly to the wind. Suitable for a London creeping towards spring. Hardly appropriate for a blizzard. And her boots— fine, supple black leather that rose elegantly to her knees—had been made for city streets. She had come rushing into Wales hot on the heels of a pair of amorous teenagers; she hadn't had time to listen to the weather forecast.

She grabbed her bag and, pulling her collar up around her neck, turned her face to the wind, her leather soles slipping on the steep surface as she began the hard trek to the cottage. The biting wind that howled under her skirt mocked the flimsy protection of her tights and found every inch of bare skin at wrists and neck. Snowflakes slammed into her face, and the steep, slippery track that led to the cottage rapidly drained every ounce of adrenalin-charged energy from her legs.

Head down, she dug her feet in and kept going, step after wrenching step, until she felt as if she had been walking for hours. If only she'd had some kind of beacon to guide her it would have been easier to judge her progress, take encouragement as she neared her goal. She raised her weary head and strained to see through the blizzard, and just for a moment she imagined that she saw a light flickering ahead of her.

She blinked the snow from her lashes and it disappeared. Had she imagined it? Or had it just been some distant headlight, twisting and dipping on a road miles away? She wrapped her collar tighter round her neck in an effort to keep out the insinuating snowflakes, but then, tempted to look again, she caught another glimmer that seemed tantalisingly closer.

'Jon?' Her voice made no impact against the wind, barely escaping from her mouth. 'Jon!' Suddenly she panicked and, dropping her bag, she tried to run. Tried to reach that elusive little light before it disappeared again. That was when she missed the path and stepped into a drift that seemed to open up and swallow her.

The snow crept in everywhere. Inside her coat, filling her skirt and moulding about her thighs—not that she could feel them any more. It filled her mouth too, and her ears and her nose. Oddly, it wasn't cold, just unbelievably peaceful, lying there wrapped in a snowy blanket after the nightmare of battling against the wind. Too peaceful. Abbie knew that if she didn't get up she would go to sleep where she lay. The kind of sleep from which she would never wake up. And she mustn't let that happen. It was vital that she get up and carry on. For Polly.

'I should have phoned Grey,' she murmured. 'He would have known what to do. He always knows what to do.' And then she closed her eyes.

'Wake up!' Someone was shaking her. 'Wake up,

damn you!' Although her lids were heavy as lead, and lifting them took more effort than she would have believed possible, the voice was imperative, insistent, so she obeyed. 'Abbie?' She saw the word form on his lips, but the wind whipped the sound away.

'Grey?' Her own lips were too numb to move, let alone make a sound. Not that it mattered, because it couldn't be him. She must be dreaming. Or dead. Maybe that was it. Because the apparition's hair was white, not black, and he was wearing some strange white garment. She was dead, she decided, and in her own special hell where the angels all had Grey's face. And that really was too cruel. She might have been careless of his love, but she wasn't the one who had cheated, and she didn't deserve that kind of hell.

So she shut her eyes again, because it was, on the whole, easier than making a formal complaint. She did wonder briefly if angels were allowed to use that kind of language. Then she remembered—he was an angel from hell. A hell's angel. It was encouraging that she was still able to make a joke and she tried to smile, but her face refused to co-operate. Anyway, it really was too much effort.

Her angel, however, had other ideas. He picked her up bodily and dumped her on her feet before giving her a thorough shaking, so that she was forced to put up her arms and defend herself. This show of resistance apparently pleased him.

'That's better,' he said, if a little grimly. 'Now, you're going to have to make some effort to help yourself, Abbie. There's no way I can carry you up the lane.'

She was too big even for angels? 'I've lost weight,' she protested. 'I may be tall, but I'm skinny.' Then, puzzled, 'Can't you fly?' she asked, her frozen lips stumbling over the words. He swore again, but apparently thought better of a repeat shaking, for which she was grateful.

Her gratitude did not last long as he looped his arm around her waist and began to drag her unceremoniously up the hill, slipping and cursing with every step. He fell once with her, pitching headlong into the snow, and she was quite happy to lie there since it was infinitely preferable to the painful jolting. But despite her complaint he refused to leave her there, hauling her back onto her feet, forcing her to continue.

Once she was inside the cottage, she had to admit that it had been worth it. The cottage was warm. At least, it was warm in contrast to the blizzard howling outside, and the glow of the lamplight from the table added to the illusion. But there was no fire in the hearth, and as he dumped her unceremoniously in the centre of the room she began to shiver uncontrollably.

'You'd better get out of those wet clothes while I light the fire,' Grey instructed her, his voice hard and unwelcoming, and Abbie realised that any idea of her rescuer being an angel was an illusion. No angel had ever had that thick dark hair, plastered wet against his head as he shook off the confusing white pelt of snow and pulled off his snow-covered jacket. No angel had those dark eyes, that angry expression.

'I haven't got anything to change into,' she said helplessly, wondering why she was mumbling. Then, because she wasn't helpless, she turned back to the door. 'I dropped my bag. I must get it.'

He moved swiftly across the room to block the way and, catching her arms, steered her back towards the huge black-leaded range that filled the hearth. The fire was already laid, ready for a match, with screws of paper and kindling and a heap of dry logs. There were more logs, logs with snowflakes still clinging to them, lying where they had been dropped untidily by the hearth. Grey struck a match and put a flame to the paper, watching until he was certain that it had properly caught before turning back to her, his face hard and bitter in the dark shadows thrown by the leaping flames.

'For heaven's sake, couldn't you have made some effort?' he demanded.

Then, looking at her more closely, he swore viciously and began to unfasten the buttons of her coat. Without warning her teeth began to chatter uncontrollably, not just from the bitter weather, but from the deep abiding chill that emanated from the man she had renounced so that he could have his heart's desire. Not that she expected him to be grateful, because he didn't know that.

He pulled off her coat and snow scattered everywhere, and he swore once more. It was odd, she thought, he never used to swear at all. Maybe it was the mess she was making on the carpet that was making him so angry. She'd clean up later, if only he'd hurry so that she could feel the warmth of the fire. Sweater, skirt... The fiddly buttons of her blouse seemed to cause him problems, but when she tried to help he simply took her hands and put them back by her sides. 'Leave it, I'll be quicker,' he said harshly.

So she stood, shivering in the firelight, trying not to remember the times without number that he had undressed her in the happier past. Slowly sometimes, tormentingly slowly, his hands brushing against her skin, touching her briefly, as if by accident, so that when he had finished she would be almost collapsing with desire. Never with this dreadful, unseeing expression, as if she were a dress shop dummy that he particularly disliked, snatching his hand back from her skin as if it might contaminate him.

As her sodden bra dropped onto the growing pile of her discarded clothing, she instinctively lifted her arms to cover herself, and his mouth twisted in what once might have been a smile but was now a humourless grimace.

'I'm hardly likely to be impressed with false modesty, Abbie,' he said. 'Not after Atlanta.' And he seized her tights and pants and in one movement stripped them down, waiting impatiently for her to lift her feet so that he could pull off her boots and remove this last vestige of covering. 'Can you walk upstairs to bed, or do I have to carry you?' he enquired distantly as he stood up.

She couldn't see his face, or his expression in the shadowy light. 'Just bring me a blanket. I...I'll be all right here,' she said shivering pitifully.

'You always were a difficult patient,' he said, but he didn't bother to argue, simply bending down and scooping her up in his arms.

She opened her eyes wide. 'I'm n-n-not s-sick,' she stammered.

'Just very nearly dead,' he said, with a grimness that convinced. And, satisfied that he had made his point, he carried her up the wide open-tread staircase to the gallery bedroom that cantilevered over the single room of the old Welsh longhouse, pulling back the thick down-filled quilt before dumping her onto the bed and wrapping her up in it.

'C-c-could I have a hot water bottle?' Abbie managed to stammer the words through her chattering teeth.

'The fire's only just lit,' he said harshly. 'It'll be a while before there's enough heat to boil a kettle.'

She was shaking pitifully—frozen, she was certain, to her very bones. But she was not about to get any sympathy from Grey. Stupid to expect any. He had pulled her out of the snow when, from the look of him, he would rather have left her there to die. She should be grateful for that. So she clung to the quilt, curling herself up as small as she could, turning her back on him.

But he had already moved away. She heard his footsteps move from the rug and onto the wooden floor. Well, what had she expected? That he would lie beside her, hold her in his arms and warm her? When he had Emma? She jabbed herself with the thought. How stupid could you get?

It was darker in the gallery, the flickering firelight and the small glow from the oil lamp downstairs throwing the raftered roof into deep shadows.

She had only been to the cottage once before in winter, not long after they were married, and now it was full of memories, ghosts of the people they had been then, with their lives stretching in front of them. Suddenly, without warning she began to cry. Not noisily—no sob escaped her lips—but with silent tears that poured down her face, scalding hot against her frozen skin.

Then the jar of the bed as Grey sat down beside her warned her that he had not gone far. As she half turned to demand what he was doing, he draped a towel around her head and began to dry her hair.

'I can do that,' she said quickly, lifting her hand from beneath the quilt, but as it collided with his she dropped it rapidly. 'I can do it,' she repeated stubbornly.

'Just stay under the quilt, Abbie, for goodness' sake, and leave it to me.' He didn't sound particularly happy about having to dry her hair, and she supposed that made it all right. Except that his strong hands working at her scalp made her want to weep even more. 'That'll do,' he said abruptly. 'Lie down.'

He tucked the quilt up around her head, but she was facing him now, watching as he briskly rubbed his own hair before tossing the towel back into the tiny bathroom and pulling his sweater and shirt over his head in one single movement. She'd used to get so cross that he didn't undo his buttons before dumping his shirts in the wash. Now the familiar action seemed stupidly endearing. He eased off his shoes and socks and then he stood up, and as she watched from the cocoon of the quilt he shucked off his trousers and briefs and turned to face her.

'Wh-what are y-you doing?' she demanded as he lifted the quilt and eased himself beneath it.

'You're cold, Abbie. It'll be hours before there's enough hot water to do the job, so I'm very much afraid I'm going to have to warm you myself.'

'No!' A moment ago she had been mentally berating him for not doing just that, but now the word was a long, anguished cry, wrenched from her throat.

'You weren't so reluctant when we last met,' he said, his voice like ice. But his skin was unbelievably warm as he looped his arm beneath her and pulled her hard against his body, lifting her still damp hair from her neck. 'What was it you offered? One last whirl for old times' sake...? Now might be a good time.'

She tried to jerk free of his arm, but his grip was painfully strong. 'Let go of me!' she demanded. How dared he touch her? How dared he presume...? But with his free hand he was already rubbing fiercely at her calves, heating her frozen flesh until the feeling began to come back with an agonising rush of pins and needles. As she groaned his hand moved higher, along her thighs, all the time massaging life into her body.

He turned her over onto her stomach and kneeling over her in the cave he made of the quilt, he began briskly to knead her shoulders, working over her arms, down the smooth indentations of her spine to her buttocks. There was nothing loving, nothing gentle about his attentions, and several times she cried out as his pinching fingers hurt her.

'Stop complaining,' he muttered fiercely. 'My God, woman, have you any idea how lucky you are to be alive? That I happened to be here? Not that it would have made any difference if I hadn't just gone outside to fetch some more logs when your car slid into the ditch. It did slide into the ditch, didn't it?' He seemed to gather some satisfaction from that.

'I...d-didn't see the t-tree until the last moment.'

'So you jammed on your brakes. If I hadn't heard the crash...'

He paused briefly in his painful ministrations and she turned over to stare up at him, as with a sudden rush of concern, she remembered what she was doing in this nightmare. He stared down at her, lying naked between his legs, her body flushed where it had been pushed into the mattress as he had pummelled the life back into her. She had turned without thinking, but now his eyes, gleaming in the soft glow of the lamp, warned her that she had made a mistake.

'Why *are* you here, Grey?' she demanded quickly, and her words seemed to jolt him out of his ransacking contemplation of her body.

'I have every right to be here,' he said harshly. 'And as it's a family matter I really don't think it's any of your business, do you? Right now, I'm more interested in finding out *your* reasons for snooping around the cottage. Did your boyfriend send you on a scouting mission?'

'Boyfriend?' She repeated the word faintly, as if she had never heard it before and it had no meaning for her. What on earth did he mean by that?

'Or did you simply sell out to the highest bidder?' She flinched away from him as he began to stroke, more gently now, more dangerously, at her neck, then across her shoulders, his thumbs finding every delicate hollow. But there was no escape from his touch as he straddled her, heating her body with his own. 'What does thirty pieces of silver buy these days?' he demanded.

Oh, she could tell him that. A new kitchen and bathroom, curtains, fitted carpets and gallons of paint... 'I wouldn't take it,' she said.

'You expect me to believe that?' he demanded.

'It's the truth.'

'You wouldn't recognise the truth if it hit you with a ten foot pole,' he said. 'You lie with your mouth and you lie with your body.'

'No,' she protested.

'You're lying now. Cringing away from me, pretending that you don't want me to touch you. But you do, Abbie.' He cradled a breast in the palm of his hand and the nipple leapt to painful attention. 'You're like a junkie in need of a fix, longing for me to touch you—'

'No!'

'Tell the truth, Abbie,' he taunted her. 'How long has it been? Hours? Days?'

Oh, God. Too long. And feeling the heat of his body so close was doing terrible things to her, sapping her will, draining her of everything except the desire to hold him, feel his skin against hers.

'Touch me, Abbie,' he urged. 'If you touch me I won't be able to deny you.'

His voice was breaking up. It was true that he wanted her. In some way that she could not hope to understand he wanted her, with a desperation that reached out to her through the black desire in his eyes. And as his lips touched her throat and the rough, dark hairs of his chest grazed her breasts some primitive response was fired deep within her, and she did as she was told and reached out hungrily for him.

It was as if she had set off a volcanic eruption, not just in Grey, releasing all her own pent-up desires, the battened-down needs that had been smouldering for months beneath the ultra cool exterior she'd maintained for the outside world. She opened up to him, her frozen body melting under the heat of his passion, the blood racing feverishly through her veins as she met his hunger head-on.

Fierce, direct, without any minor key explorations of each other's desires, it was too intense a conflagration to be long sustained. They crash-dived to oblivion and, exhausted, slept.

* * *

Abbie woke, deliciously warm and comfortable, a hot water bottle at her back. Turning over, she clutched it to her stomach and buried herself deeper under the quilt. She felt good. Happy. It was a forgotten, almost alien sensation, this happiness, and her eyes flickered open on the day as she tried to work out what she was so happy about.

The light was strange, bouncing off the rafters with a brilliance that wasn't accompanied by sunlight. Her eyes opened wider. Rafters? And then the happiness, that intense feeling of well-being evaporated as the night, the snow, the cold, all came flooding back. And worse, far worse than that—the memory of what she had done with Grey. She knew then that the glorious sense of well-being was a transitory thing, a feeling that would have to be paid for in remorse and self-loathing, and a groan escaped her lips.

At least she was alone in the bed. She had not woken up to his sleeping figure beside her. But he would have to be faced because there were more urgent concerns to be confronted than her shame over her loss of control. Jon and Polly were out there somewhere. They might be lost, frightened. Or worse, she thought, remembering how she had fallen into the snow and lain there, too weary to make the effort to get up. She gave a little shiver that had nothing to do with the temperature. She would be there still, frozen to death in the snow, if Grey had not been there when she'd needed him.

She sat up and, wrapping the quilt about her, rose to her knees and peered down into the main room. Grey, fully dressed and with a blanket wrapped about him, was stretched out in a chair, asleep in front of the range. Her initial relief that he had not been beside her in the bed evaporated as she realised that he hadn't simply got up to go about the business of clearing snow, or finding her bag, or arranging for her car to be pulled from the ditch.

The fire had burned low enough to betray the fact that he had been there for many hours, that he had chosen to sleep uncomfortably in a chair rather than lie alongside her. Fury bubbled through her veins. She hadn't asked him to make love to her, for heaven's sake! She certainly hadn't wanted him to. Her face flamed as she realised that wasn't entirely true. He had invited her participation, not forced it upon her.

She threw back the quilt and strode into the bathroom. The water was just warm enough, and she scrubbed her body clean of the scent of him, reminding herself forcibly that she had done nothing to be ashamed of. She was the one who had been betrayed.

Her husband had brought Emma to this cottage, shared this shower with her, slept with her in the same bed, given her a child. Then last night... The rat! How could he have made love to *her*? In the same bed? No, not love. It was sex, lust—nothing more. *How could he?* Wasn't one woman at a time enough for him any more? Had it ever been?

She flung open the cupboard door, hoping that the clothes she had left on her last visit would still be there. But her clothes had gone—cleared out to make room for the new occupants in his life. Room for the folding cot, the packs of disposable nappies and all the other paraphernalia that went with child-rearing. All the evidence of his betrayal.

Angry tears stung at her lids as she picked up a thick checked work-shirt that she had bought for him at the market the last time they had come to the cottage. The musky scent of him clung to the cloth, assailing her senses, weakening her fury as she remembered him cutting logs for the fire. She had watched him, admiring the economy of effort with which he had worked, the strength of his shoulders. Painful thoughts, dangerous thoughts and she pushed them away—furiously away. Lust was no substitute for love.

She dressed quickly, clambering into the over-large clothes, cinching in the waist of a pair of Grey's jeans with a belt, rolling up the legs. She found a pair of white woollen socks normally worn inside wellington boots. Well, that was fine. There were always heaps of wellingtons in the scullery and she would be needing a pair, because she certainly wasn't staying at Ty Bach a moment longer than necessary.

She made her way down the stairs to discover that Grey was still asleep. Her lips tightened, but she told herself that she didn't care one way or another as she braved the chill of the scullery to find some outdoor clothes. Five minutes later, warmly covered in a padded gilet, scarf, a heavy waxed jacket and wellington boots, she stomped back into the main room.

Grey had moved, shifted in the chair, and now his head was propped on his hand. He had always been able to sleep on a clothesline, but his relaxed and peaceful posture when so much needed to be done added insult to injury.

Angrily she swept away the arm propping up his head and he shot forward in the chair, waking a fraction before cracking his head on the wooden arm. 'What the...?'

'Your early-morning alarm call, sir,' Abbie said,

with a syrupy sweetness that belied the look in her eyes.

Grey regarded her sourly. 'Has anyone ever told you that your technique could do with a little work?' he said.

'My technique, Grey Lockwood, is none of your business. We're all but divorced. But, since you've brought it up, I've got one or two complaints of my own. When you force yourself into somebody's bed and have sex with them, the very least you can do is stick around until they wake up so that you can apologise!'

CHAPTER SIX

'APOLOGISE!' He was wide awake now and on his feet, towering over her. 'Apologise?' he repeated, in utter disbelief. 'For what? Saving your life?'

She blushed but remained defiant. 'You might have saved my life when you dragged me in from the snow,' she declared. 'The rest was...unnecessary.'

'You think so? Have you never heard of hypothermia?'

She bridled. 'Of course I have. You're supposed to wrap the victims in aluminium foil and blankets, give them warm drinks—'

'Oh, *are* you? Well, since I had neither, I did the best I could. I didn't realise I was expected to stick around in case you felt the need of a second application of the treatment.'

She shrank back, her face scarlet, her whole body blushing. Was that what last night had been about? First aid? Her mind suddenly cleared and she remembered with horrifyingly vivid recall just what it was he had said to her. 'If you touch me, I won't be able to deny you...' Had it been that difficult to make himself do what he'd thought necessary?

'I can assure you, Grey, that I haven't the slightest wish to put you to so much trouble.'

'Then, fetching as you look, swaddled up like a home counties mummy, I suggest you take off those outdoor clothes and think about making some breakfast.'

She glared at him. 'Make your own damned breakfast,' she said. 'I've got more important things to do.' She moved across to the door but he beat her to it, cutting off her escape.

'Like what? Rescuing your bag from the snow?'

She refused even to answer such a stupid question, but glared up at him, her eyes huge and dark in her pale face. His fingers brushed against her cheek. A touch so familiar, so longed for, that even now, in this appalling situation, she felt a tremor of some dark longing jar into life.

'I admit you could certainly do with some lipstick, but since you've already indicated a disinclination for my home-made treatment for hypothermia,' he said bitterly, 'you're going to have to put it off for a while.'

His voice jerked her back to reality. 'I...I'm walking down to the village to arrange for some transport out of here. You might not be worried about what has happened to Jon and Polly...' Although his apparent lack of concern did surprise her. 'Well, Jon's a boy. And boys are expected to be boys, so I can't really expect you to work up much of a sweat about it, but Polly is my responsibility and I can't just forget it because of a minor snowfall.'

His eyes gleamed dangerously, but his voice was cool enough. 'Who,' he demanded, 'is Polly?'

'She's Jon's girlfriend. Didn't you know? I expected to find them here. That's why I came—'

'So.' A long breath escaped him. 'That's what you're doing here.' His voice hadn't changed much, just enough to warn her that she had said something to anger him. 'You journalists don't miss a trick, do you? I didn't think even Morley would stoop to putting a trail on young Jon as well.' As well? 'But why not? And who else would he send to ferret out such a juicy story? Because you know all the family secrets, don't you? Well, Miss Feature Writer of the Year, as you can see, the birds have flown. No story. No fee.'

Grey's insults flew over her head. She hadn't wanted the stupid award; she hadn't even bothered to fly back from the States to pick it up at the special dinner.

'For goodness' sake, Grey, can't you forget about me for a moment?'

His eyes were cold. 'I've tried, Abbie. God knows I've tried. But you get under a man's skin.'

She pulled back, stunned by the bitterness in his voice. 'I didn't mean...' No. She had to keep it impersonal. If he and his new love were not as happy as he thought they should be it was none of her business. None. 'We should be getting on to the police, the hospitals,' she urged. 'They might have had an accident.'

'I very much doubt it. Jon at least has been here, but whether he had company I couldn't say—although the fridge is stocked, the freezer too. And, fortunately for you, the bed was made. Domestic touches that Jon would normally overlook.'

'Did they...?'

'No, Abbie, they didn't stop to use it.'

She felt the colour heat her cheeks, but refused to be drawn back down that track. 'Then where are they?' she demanded.

He shrugged. 'I have no idea. They lit a fire but the ashes were cold. They were gone long before I arrived.'

'I've got to try and find them,' she said, moving towards the door.

'Isn't that a bit like shutting the stable door after the filly has bolted?' he asked.

She refused to rise to his somewhat trenchant wit. 'Maybe, but Polly should be revising for her A levels—and I'll have to face her mother when she comes home.'

'That should be an interesting conversation.'

'You're very welcome to come along. Margaret still thinks of Polly as her baby. Jon might just need your protection.'

'Oh, for heaven's sake,' he said, losing patience. 'Aren't you getting this out of proportion? If she's on the brink of her A-levels she must be eighteen, or as near as damn it. And eighteen-year-old virgins are about as rare as hen's teeth.'

'I bow to your wider experience in these matters, although I don't much appreciate being compared to a hen's tooth,' she said, and had the grim pleasure of seeing a dark flush sear his cheekbones. 'However, I can assure you that Polly also falls into that unusual category, so, if you'll let me by, I'd like to try and make certain that what undoubtedly began as a dream for her does not degenerate into a nightmare.'

'Since they have planned this escapade with such care, I imagine that particular aspect of it has not been left to chance,' Grey remarked, with what Abbie considered under the circumstances to be an unforgivably casual attitude to the situation.

'And that makes it all right?'

'No, and Jon will have to answer for his behaviour to his father, but in the meantime—'

'In the meantime?' Abbie interrupted in sheer disbelief, angrier than she would have thought possible. The Grey Lockwood she'd known and loved would never just have sat back and ignored the situation. 'In the meantime I'm supposed to forget it? What on earth has happened to you, Grey?'

Grey stared at her for a moment, and then continued as if she had not spoken. 'In the meantime,' he repeated, 'since there's absolutely nothing you can do about the situation, I suggest you take off your coat and make yourself comfortable. You're not going anywhere, Abbie.'

'You're planning to stop me?' Abbie flared up at him. 'I don't think so.'

As she moved to push past him the left corner of his mouth lifted his face into a sardonic smile, and he raised his hands in a gesture of surrender. 'I wouldn't dream of trying.' And he finally stood aside, offering her the door. 'Help yourself.'

She hesitated for a moment, surprised at this sudden capitulation. Then she shrugged, walking by him with all the dignity her bundled, booted body could manage, and lifted the latch. It was immediately wrenched from her fingers as the door was flung aside and she was enveloped in a white maelstrom of snowflakes that plastered themselves to her face, her boots, the front of her coat. She could see nothing. The world was wiped out, obliterated by a blizzard that sucked the very breath from her body. A white-out.

Grey caught her arm, hauling her back into the safety of the cottage, and by putting his shoulder to the door managed to shut it against the fierce blast. Then, with his back still pressed hard against it, he dropped the latch, and as he looked down at her his mouth finally twisted into a full-blooded grin.

'What's the matter, Abbie?' he asked as she fought to regain her breath. 'Changed your mind?'

'It's never been like this before,' she finally gasped.

'You've never seen it like this before,' he corrected her, as he reached down to brush away the snowflakes that clung to her eyelids with the pads of his thumbs. 'I have.'

'But—'

He removed her hat with a distracted frown and pushed the damp fringe gently back from her forehead. His hands were warm and smelled of woodsmoke. 'You shouldn't get cold again. Come over by the fire.'

'I'm all right, really,' she protested. 'The cottage is warm now.' Too warm, she thought as, ignoring her protest, he propelled her insistently towards the fire.

He unwound the scarf from her neck, shook off the snow and hung it with the hat behind the door. She pulled at the fasteners that held the front of the coat and they popped open. Not quickly enough. Grey had returned and now reached for the ring at the top of the zip. 'I can manage,' she said quickly, and tugged hurriedly at it. It jammed. Why did zips always do that when you were in hurry? she thought furiously as she wrestled with it.

'You'd better leave that to me,' Grey said, and she was forced to stand before him while he untangled a loose thread from the zipper teeth.

'Tell me about the snow,' she said—anything to distract her from the urgent desire to slide her fingers through the dark tousled head just beneath her chin. To be safe, she closed her eyes as well.

'When Robert and I were kids,' he said, concentrating on the zip, 'Mum decided we should all get away from television and the tawdry commercialism of the season and have a genuine, old-fashioned country Christmas.' He paused, apparently expecting some response.

'That sounds...nice.'

'Oh, it was.'

'What did you do?' she asked.

'Do?' He stopped fiddling with the zip and she knew he had looked up. Feeling foolish at being caught with her eyes screwed up tight, she opened them. His face was so close that she could see the tiny gold flecks that gave his eyes that special depth, that special warmth. All illusion, of course. A trick of nature. It meant nothing.

'Without the television,' she said quickly. 'I mean, there isn't a piano to stand around. Isn't that what people always say they used to do in the good old days before television?' Her pathetic attempt at a laugh sounded hollow even in her own ears. 'Stand around the piano and sing?'

'Oh, right. No piano. We had to make do with the wind-up gramophone. You do remember the wind-up gramophone, Abbie?'

She swallowed. Oh, yes, she remembered. Invented in the days when young men had come courting their sweethearts in the front parlour. The playing of gramophone records had been the perfect way for parents to be certain that propriety was being observed, since the machine had to be constantly wound up. One wet afternoon they had found it in the cupboard, and Grey had most memorably demonstrated how a bright youth could buck the system with a little co-operation from his girl.

'Yes, I remember,' she said bleakly, wondering if he had demonstrated the same technique for Emma.

Apparently satisfied with having made her thoroughly miserable, he returned to the zip and continued with his story. 'We spent the first day cutting up logs and collecting a tree from a nearby farm while Mother got to grips with baking on the range. We visited all the local farmers, saw the first new lambs, went to chapel on Christmas morning. We even played cricket on the beach on Boxing Day...' His voice died away as he dwelt on the memory.

'It sounds wonderful,' Abbie prompted dully.

'It was. I always planned to do it again when—' He stopped, ran the freed zipper down. Then, as he straightened, he forced a careless shrug. 'Well, some day.'

When he had a family of his own? She reached out as if to touch his arm, pulled back. 'But what about the snow?' she said quickly.

'Snow?' He seemed to have forgotten the point of his story. 'Oh, yes.' He dropped his eyes from the hand that had so nearly touched him. 'The snow.' He turned to the fire, raking it through, throwing on some logs so that it burst into flaming life, before placing the kettle on the hob. 'That was the only tiny disappointment,' he said as he worked. 'The lack of snow.

'Then, the day before we were due to come home, we had a flurry. Not much, just enough to be fun. We spent our last day making snowmen, eating mince pies, finishing up the milk with mugs of hot chocolate to go with the dripping toast for supper. The perfect end to a perfect holiday.' He straightened, smiled briefly at a distant memory full of warmth and love.

'Then overnight the wind shifted to the north-east and the flurry turned to a blizzard. We were stuck here for three days, eking out the remains of the Christmas feast and with nothing but dried milk powder for the tea. After the second day we ran out of paraffin for the lamps and were reduced to candles. Mother refused ever to come down here again at Christmas, no matter how much Robert and I begged her. After that experience, she said, television and tawdry would suit her just fine.'

'I wish I'd known her.'

'I think I would have spared her that particular pain.' His eyes hardened as the colour drained from her face. 'She was the sort of woman who believed that vows were meant to be kept, that marriage was for ever.'

'Then she was singularly unlucky with both of her sons,' Abbie retaliated, and then clapped her hand over her mouth. She wasn't supposed to know that he had been unfaithful.

The gesture did not go unnoticed. 'Yes, Abbie, a little restraint on that eager tongue of yours might be no bad thing, since we're imprisoned here together for the duration.'

'It would be so much easier if we were strangers,' she said bleakly.

'Infinitely,' he agreed, with feeling. 'We could be very British about the whole thing, very stiff-upper-lip, never straying into the personal...' The idea appeared to offer him some wry amusement. 'Perhaps we should try it? Pretend we've never met. What do you say?' He held out his hand. 'Pax?' he offered. 'For the duration.'

His hands were beautiful. Large, square, with long,

fine fingers that knew every secret of her responsive body...

No! No. She mustn't think about it. She must take his hand as if she had never seen it before. Slowly, reluctantly, she raised her own and he closed his fingers about hers. 'Pax,' she agreed, her voice barely audible. Then, because suddenly the air was so thick with tension that you could have bounced a breeze block off it, she said, 'But I do hope there's a decent supply of paraffin this time. And food.'

'I'll have to check the can next time I battle my way across to the barn. At least there's a good supply of fuel. That at least hasn't changed.'

'Oh, Grey!' she said, because so many other things *had* changed. And then, because that wasn't a good start to their resolution, she straightened her shoulders. 'And since there's no hope of getting to my bag, I suppose I'll just have to try and keep my upper lip stiff without the aid of lipstick.'

'Tough,' Grey said, but he had recognised the spirit that allowed her to poke a little fun at herself, and there was a tinge of humour in his voice that robbed the word of its sting. 'So. We'd better be businesslike about this and check to see what we've got to live on for the next few days. I don't know which of the runaways we've got to thank for the provisions—Jon or... What did you say her name was?'

'Polly,' she said. It hadn't occurred to her that Grey might never have heard of her. Presumably he didn't know that they had been making themselves at home in his flat while he was away either. She glanced up, and as she met the sudden angry glitter in Grey's eyes decided it might be as well to keep that bit of information to herself. 'What is it?'

He shook his head. 'I just find it hard to believe that you actually went out of your way to get to know an innocent teenage girl in order to get a story. Has Steve Morley really dragged you down that far?'

She sighed. So much for being strangers. 'Grey, although I have to admit that right at this minute I could cheerfully throttle Jon, he is your problem—but Polly happens to be the daughter of a friend. I'm supposed to be looking after her for a couple of months. Obviously I have a lot to learn about the deviousness of teenage girls. Now, do you think you could stop parading your prejudices and give some thought as to how we are going to find them and get the pair of them home?' Then she frowned. 'That *is* why you're here, isn't it?'

Grey regarded her with considerable suspicion, but she refused to back down from that watchful scrutiny and eventually he lifted his shoulders in the smallest shrug.

'Yes, that's why I'm here. Robert's in America and I thought I'd bring Jon down here for half-term. But first I discovered the cottage keys were missing. Then I couldn't get an answer from the number Jon left...and Robert's housekeeper had a rather odd phone call from someone who said she was a journalist asking if it was true that Jon had taken a girl down to the family cottage... I thought perhaps I'd better get them out of the way before they made the front page...'

Abbie frowned. 'Journalists don't advertise themselves when they're after that kind of story, Grey.'

'Don't they? Well, I suppose you would know. Whatever. They certainly didn't cover their tracks very well.'

'No.' Like his uncle, she thought, as a lump rose unbidden to her throat. 'Actually I did hear your telephone message. That's why I guessed they had come here. How did you get in, if Jon had the keys?'

'He very kindly left them under the mat. If you heard my message, why didn't you phone me, Abbie?'

And risk Emma answering? 'I...I thought I could handle it. Unfortunately I didn't hear the weather forecast before I set out, and the car radio wasn't working...' She gave an involuntary little sniff as her attempt to be cool wobbled a little, and Grey thrust a handkerchief into her hand. 'I think I must have caught a cold last night.'

'You don't catch a cold from lying in the snow, Abbie. You get pneumonia.'

'Do you? You always did know things like that. Didn't you do a first-aid course once?'

'I went to a session on emergency procedures after I had a witness collapse in court,' he corrected her.

'I expect that's how you learned the best way to treat hypothermia. Did the instructor demonstrate the technique...?' His face drained of colour. How could she have said that? How *could* she?

'I never said it was the best way. I just read something once...I can't remember where...'

'Forget it!'

'Easier said than done,' he replied. 'I have a retentive memory. In fact, last night—'

'As I was saying,' Abbie said sharply, firmly slamming the door on the subject of last night, 'I thought I could handle it. As you said, it wasn't difficult to work out where they were heading.'

'No. Not difficult. But she's young. With you looking after her I'm sure she'll soon learn to manage things better,' he remarked bitterly.

'That's unfair!' She blazed at him, the words out before she could recall them. Of course it was fair, she reminded herself, quickly retreating from the challenge, dropping her eyes. He only thought what she had wanted him to think. It was ridiculous to get angry because she had done her job so well.

She managed a shrug, as if after all it didn't matter. 'The trouble is, I thought that Polly was winding me up—teasing me. She's pretty good at that. But when I got back from seeing Steve last night...' She faltered as his eyes narrowed dangerously at Steve's name, but he did not pursue it. 'When I got back from my meeting,' she continued, more carefully, 'I was confronted with a message informing me that she and Jon intended to pursue a week of passion in order to break up the monotony of A-level revision—'

'She actually wrote that?' he demanded, shocked out of his scornful posture.

'Polly is somewhat direct. She also promised they would be back in time for school on Monday. I'm sure she meant it, but I find it very difficult to believe that she thought I would just leave it at that—'

'Tell me about Polly,' he interrupted.

'She's bright, bubbly and great company. I'm not surprised Jon fell for her.'

'I wasn't asking for a reference. I meant your connection. What is your connection with her?' The hard lines of his face suggested that he was still not entirely convinced that she wasn't simply out on a story.

'I told you, I'm keeping an eye on her for a friend. No one you've ever met.'

'I can believe that,' he said, his voice heavy with meaning.

'Polly's *mother*,' Abbie said. 'Margaret was a mature student when I was at college. Her husband is a botanist and she wanted to take photographs for him. They spent the last few years in Australia...' His expression told her that he wasn't interested in the occupation of Polly's father or her mother's desire to help him. 'We lost touch. They were moving about a lot and I was busy. It's so easy to let things slip away from you...' She snapped herself back to the matter in hand. 'They came home about a year ago, and Margaret wrote to me at the paper when I received the award.'

'How very touching.'

She ignored his sarcasm, telling herself that it didn't hurt—at least no more than a splinter under a nail. 'Her older daughter married an Australian and still lives out there. She...she's just had a baby. Margaret gave me a roof over my head when I came home, and keeping an eye on Polly while she visited her new grandson seemed the least I could do—' His exclamation of disgust cut her short. 'What's that supposed to mean?' she demanded, at last snapping under his barrage of abuse.

But, having driven her to lose control, Grey finally relaxed, rewarding himself with the faintest of smiles. 'It means, my dear, that anyone who leaves a teenage girl in your care deserves everything they get.' The sudden whine of the kettle as it began to boil cut off her furious reply. 'I think that's your cue to make some breakfast,' he said.

'And what are you going to do? Sit there and watch me?' she threw at him.

'How could any man resist an invitation couched in such tender terms?'

'Try,' she instructed. 'Very hard.'

'Well, you always did say I got under your feet,' he said. 'But then, you do have very large feet.'

'Long,' she corrected automatically. She had long, narrow feet. Too late she saw the glint in his eye.

'Some things never change. The vanity of women is as unfailing as the tides. Although why you should be so sensitive about your feet beats me,' he said, retreating into the scullery. 'I mean, you're tall—you need them for balance...'

It was an old taunt with a time-honoured response. But Abbie caught herself as she cast about her for something to throw. That kind of row only had one possible ending. Surely Grey, with his retentive memory, knew that as well as she did?

'All right! I admit it, they're large,' she called after him. 'Huge. Positively flipper-sized feet. Does that make you happy...?' The words died on her lips as he reappeared, clad in a jacket and boots. 'You're not going out in this weather?' she demanded, shocked out of her couldn't-care-less response.

'I have to. We need more logs,' he said. 'But don't fret. If I don't make it, you'll be a rich widow instead of a penniless divorcee.'

'What a perfectly beastly thing to say,' she retaliated. 'Do you think I would take a penny from you? Emma and Matthew—'

His face registered blank shock. 'You *know* about Emma?'

She should take her large feet and stick them in her large mouth, but it was too late to call the words back, to pretend any more. 'Yes,' she admitted. 'I know.'

'And Matthew? I suppose Morley told you?'

Anything was better than confessing to witnessing that scene in the park. And it was near enough to the truth. 'Yes,' she said. 'He saw you having lunch with her.'

He frowned. 'But that was months ago. Before—before you left.' He regarded her with sharp, penetrating eyes that sought out her secrets. 'Have you known that long?' She nodded. 'Morley too?' She nodded again. 'Then why didn't he use it? I mean, once I'd hit him he had the perfect opportunity to bring the whole messy business out into the open.'

'I asked him not to, Grey.'

His head flew back as if she had struck him and pain, real pain, creased his eyes. 'He did that for you?' His reaction was unexpected. He should have been pleased, for heaven's sake, but he looked angry. 'I didn't think the man capable of...of loving anyone enough to suppress a story that big. And I was blindly taking you for granted, so wrapped up in my own problems that I couldn't see. I suppose I got what any careless lover deserves.'

'You were never that, Grey.'

'No?' He raised his hand and very briefly touched her cheek. 'I must have been doing something wrong.' He reached for the latch, but turned back to her. 'When I walked out of that motel room in Atlanta, Abbie, I really wanted to believe your lies. It was so much easier to think that you had changed overnight from the girl I took to my bed, when I discovered to my joy that I was her first lover. It was so much easier than acknowledging that you had fallen in love with someone else, that you would have done anything to get me out of that room, said anything to protect Steve Morley. I should have known better.'

And with that he opened the door and disappeared into the blizzard driving across the yard.

CHAPTER SEVEN

ABBIE struggled to close the door behind him, battling against the fierceness of the wind. Finally it was done, the wild elements shut out along with Grey. Leaning weakly against it, she lifted her hand to where the touch of his fingers still burned against her cheek, wet from the snow and the warmer touch of tears.

She didn't know how she was going to bear it. Being stranded at the cottage with Grey was like something from her worst nightmare—a nightmare in which she was forced to relive every moment they had ever spent there together.

She had surrendered her own happiness so that he could begin again with his new love. But something had gone wrong. Badly wrong. Because he wasn't happy. It didn't take any kind of a genius to see that. She wanted to hold him, to cradle him in her arms and tell him that it didn't matter. But it did. He had betrayed her, and last night he had betrayed Emma too. There was no way back for either of them.

But life continued, and when he returned he would be cold and hungry. If she couldn't tell him that she loved him, she could at least provide him with more substantial succour.

When he burst in through the door, arms full of logs, she was bending over a pan of bacon. He dropped the wood beside the hearth with a clatter that made her jump. 'This is quite like old times,' he said, straightening. 'Apart from the snow.'

She flinched. Too much like. But as she turned and handed him a mug of tea she managed to meet his eyes. 'Apart from a lot of things. I thought we had an agreement, Grey, that this would be a lot easier if we pretended to be strangers.'

'The trouble is, Abbie, I don't want it to be easy for you. I want you to hurt as much as me.'

'Hurt! You've got some kind of nerve, Grey Lockwood,' she declared hotly. 'After what you've done...'

He looked at her as if she was crazy. 'And what precisely have I done?'

Something snapped inside her. 'You've lied to me, cheated, betrayed me...' He was going to deny it, she could see it by the look of stunned disbelief that crossed his features. 'I offer in evidence a non-existent case conference in Manchester,' she threw at him, 'when in fact you were here all the time. With Emma.' That stopped him in his tracks.

'I was protecting you—' he began.

'By lying to me?'

He tilted his head back, looked somewhere over her head. 'Yes. By lying to you. At the time I thought it was for the best.' He turned away. 'But clearly you didn't want to be protected. At least, not by me.' He shrugged out of his coat and hung it behind the door. 'My mistake.' When he turned back to face her, his eyes had hardened to stone. 'You're right, Abbie. We are strangers. The girl I married would never have hurt anyone.'

'I trusted you, Grey. I would have trusted you with my life.'

'Would have?' His jaw tightened ominously. 'Your

memory seems to have short-circuited. I thought you just did.'

And with that exchange they might indeed have become total strangers, because breakfast passed without another word between them, and as Abbie rose to clear the plates Grey took himself off to the far side of the room to attend to the fire. The sharp scent of the woodsmoke caught in her throat as she cleared away, making her eyes sting. What other reason could there possibly be for the tears that washed her eyes? Stupid, ridiculous tears.

Oh, Polly, how could you do this to me? she silently demanded of the absent girl as she watched Grey sink to his haunches to riddle through the ash. Superbly muscled thighs packed the workmanlike denim of his jeans as he jabbed at the fire, his shoulders stretching the thick flannel shirt. And as the heavy, painful ache of her longing for him sucked the strength from her limbs she fled to the safer discomfort of the freezing scullery and the washing up.

'Have you checked the freezer?' Grey's voice so close behind her made her jump, and the cup she had been about to place on the draining board slithered from her cold fingers and smashed on the stone floor. She quickly bent to pick up the pieces, and in her haste jagged her hand on the sharp edge of the china.

'Still accident-prone,' Grey said as he saw the blood oozing from her finger, and, taking her hand, drew her back to her feet. 'Everything changes, everything stays the same.' He turned and reached for the first aid box, kept on the shelf above the sink, deftly cleaned the wound and applied a plaster. Then, as he always had, he raised the finger to his lips to kiss it better.

'Don't!' He stepped back sharply at her panic-stricken exclamation and the china crunched beneath his shoe. Stupid! A stupid overreaction to a purely automatic gesture.

'You'd better put something on your feet before you cut something else,' he said, staring at her for a long moment before turning away, fishing a pair of trainers from the pile in the corner. 'Here.'

They were hers, apparently overlooked in the general eradication of her presence from his life. 'Yes. Yes, of course,' she agreed quickly, taking them from him. Anything to stop him looking at her like that. While he swept up the mess she slipped her feet into the shoes and bent to tie the laces.

When she straightened he was bending over the freezer. Come on, Abbie, she urged herself. You can do this. She had to, it was imperative that she keep a grip on her emotions. 'Well, are we going to starve?' she asked, with a cool attempt at humour.

The cottage had no electricity supply and the refrigerator and the large chest freezer were both run on bottled gas. Grey was still leaning over the freezer, regarding its contents with a slightly puzzled expression. 'They've left us pretty well supplied. Is Polly taking domestic science for her A-levels?'

'Polly!' she exclaimed, startled out of her pretence. 'Good grief, no. I've never seen her cook anything but pizzas and bean burgers.'

'Well, it looks as if she was going to play the good little housewife to the hilt for Jon's benefit. Not a convenience package in sight.'

'I don't believe it!' she exclaimed. He stepped aside so that she could see for herself. 'There are even some frozen vegetables,' she said. Polly would do anything rather than eat vegetables. A fact Abbie had always considered rather odd, since she was going through the almost mandatory vegetarian stage of adolescence. 'Does Jon like broccoli? There seems to be rather a lot of it.'

'The only person I know who actually likes frozen broccoli, Abbie, is you.'

'Spinach?' she asked hopefully.

'Likewise.'

'Well. That's me taken care of. And there's cauliflower for you.'

'Only if you make a cheese sauce.'

She opened the fridge door. 'You appear to be in luck. There's no shortage of the stuff.'

'Right, well, what do you fancy for lunch? There's steak and lamb. I don't suppose there's any—'

'Mint?' As she produced a jar from the refrigerator a puzzled frown plucked at her brow. 'It seems you're right. Polly had planned a week of total domesticity. I do hope she had the foresight to provide herself with a cookery book.' She closed the fridge door a touch thoughtfully. The vegetarian phase hadn't lasted for long, it seemed. 'Can you get a loaf out of the freezer while you're there?'

'There isn't one.'

'Oh, great! Trust them to forget the simple things.'

Grey had transferred his attention to the cupboards. 'I don't think they forgot. I think they were planning to do-it-yourself.' He indicated several packs of bread flour and some dried yeast.

It was if someone had struck a bell in her head. She and Polly had been toasting muffins in front of the fire one day, and Polly had been digging away as usual about Grey. To distract her, she had told Polly about the cottage, where everything had to be done on the range—even baking bread if you missed the *barra* man on his rounds. She had extolled the pleasures of breadmaking, she remembered, the rich smell of the dough rising in front of the fire... Anything to stop herself from thinking about Grey...

He turned to her now. 'Are you sure they planned a week of passion?' he asked. 'Because frankly I don't think they were likely to have much time for—'

'How long did you say this weather is likely to keep up?' she interrupted shortly.

'I didn't.'

'What about the radio? Can we get a forecast?'

He shook his head. 'The batteries are dead. If I can coincide my next dash across the yard for logs with the news, I'll try the car radio. But that rather depends upon the weather.'

She looked at the flour, took it reluctantly from the cupboard. 'Right. Well, since I've no choice, I suppose I'd better get baking.'

Grey watched as she laid out her ingredients on the table. 'Can I do anything to help?'

'I don't know, Grey. You tell me,' she demanded, looking up at him.

She was angry, but not with him, with herself. She had allowed her longing for Grey to spill over into her new life, talking too much about the past under Polly's eager prompting. She hadn't even realised she was doing it until now, when it kept coming back to haunt her, because dear, sweet, romantic Polly had thought it would be 'special' to experience that same enclosed intensity of experience that came when you were totally alone with someone you loved.

'If you were really stranded alone with a strange woman,' she asked, 'what would you be doing?'

His mouth twisted in a wry smile. 'That rather depends on the woman.' She supposed she had asked for that, but again it reminded her too forcibly of the kind of remark he would have made in happier days, when they had been certain enough of each other's love to make such jokes. Everything reminded her—every word, every gesture—of a love carelessly lost. He shrugged as she continued to stare wordlessly at him. 'No? Probably not. I'd probably stay as far out of her way as possible.'

She snapped back to reality. 'Then feel free to do just that,' she invited. 'I won't be offended.'

His eyes taunted her. 'But you're not a stranger, Abbie.'

'Pretend, Grey. It was your idea.' She didn't want him anywhere near her. Nearness hurt. 'And while you're working on that,' she added, 'you might consider the sleeping arrangements for tonight.'

'There's only one bed. And one night in a chair is enough.'

He hadn't spent the entire night in a chair, but she wasn't about to remind him of that. 'You've forgotten that I'm a stranger.' She saw the protest form on his lips and forestalled it. 'A very prim and proper maiden lady who will not expect to share her bed with a man.'

'Oh, yes? And I'm the Archbishop of Canterbury.'

'Not even His Grace,' Abbie returned, doing her best to ignore this attempt to wound.

'In that case she's very welcome to the chair,' he replied, turning away. 'Although I'd advise her to miss out on the wake-up call.' Then he settled himself by the fire, apparently fascinated by an old paperback.

Abbie let out a long, heartfelt breath, and began the slow, soothing process of breadmaking. She heeled the dough, turned it and repeated the action with the same smooth, repetitive movements that had been handed down the centuries. It was quite possible, she thought, as she worked out her tensions on the dough, that if bread were still made by hand in every kitchen, there would be rather less need for tranquillisers.

She put the dough in a clean bowl and, after covering it with a damp cloth, set it to rise near the fire. Grey did not lift his head from the book but moved his feet sideways to give her more room.

'Thank you,' she said stiffly.

'It's no trouble at all.' There was nothing wrong with the words, but she still wanted to hit him.

'Would you like some coffee?' she asked, considering that on the whole it would be wiser to be polite.

'What kind of coffee?'

'You're perfectly safe, Grey, it's not instant.' He finally lifted his eyes from the book, apparently unable to hide his amusement.

'Polly really was trying to impress Jon with her domesticity, wasn't she?' She refused to be drawn on what Polly had been trying to do and he shrugged. 'Coffee will be most acceptable. You'll find the cafetière in the scullery. And since you've got your baker's hat on why don't you make a few Welsh cakes to go with it? It'll help you to pass the time.'

She looked at him in stunned disbelief. 'Make your own damned Welsh cakes,' she flung at him. 'And your own damned coffee too.' And with that she took herself into the scullery to peel potatoes in water that froze the ends of her fingers, although the scalding tears that fell unchecked into the bowl should have made a difference.

'I'm sorry, Abbie. I shouldn't have...' She twitched her shoulder away from his hand. 'It was seeing you kneading the bread, that special smell... It was as if the clock had been turned back a year... As if everything was as it had always been.'

'Well, it isn't the same!' She turned abruptly to confront him and saw, to her astonishment, that the pain that ate at her was echoed all too plainly in his face, deepening the lines etched into his cheeks.

He reached out, touched her cheek, using his thumb to wipe away the tears. His hands moved, slowly, surely, up to her temples, his fingers splaying out through her hair to cradle her face, lift it to his. 'Don't cry, Abbie,' he murmured softly. And his lips brushed her forehead. 'Please, don't cry.' For a moment they remained perfectly still in the ice box of the scullery, and the silence ran dangerous as a lit fuse between them. Then Grey reached over her and picked up the cafetière. 'I'll make some coffee,' he said. 'You're cold.'

'I'll survive,' she said hoarsely.

'You don't have to act tough with me, Abbie. I know you too well.'

'Do you?' Her challenge died on her lips as she remembered the way he had driven her beyond control the night before. Yes. He knew her far too well for safety. Her scalp still tingled where his fingers had rested moments before. 'If you want something sweet with your coffee why don't you see if the young lovers left us some biscuits,' she said, shakily changing the subject.

She turned back to the sink, aware that for long moments he continued to stare down at her. Then she heard him lift down the biscuit tin and open the lid. 'They thought of everything. Bourbons and...' She heard him bite into something crisp. 'Mmm. Almond Crunch. I wonder which of our lovebirds did the shopping?'

'Jon, probably,' she said, looking round. 'Polly didn't have the time. Why?'

'Nothing. It's just that whoever went to the supermarket seems to have thoughtfully provided us both with our favourite biscuits. That's all.'

Abbie wandered over to the window and rubbed at the glass. 'I think it's easing a bit out there. I can actually see the barn.'

Grey, half asleep in the chair by the fire after lunch, looked up. 'Can you? In that case I'd better go and fetch some more logs while I can.' He stretched and heaved himself to his feet.

'I'll give you a hand,' she offered.

'I can manage.'

'It'll be dark soon. The quicker we work, the better.'

He hesitated for just a second and then shrugged. 'Come on, then. Just make sure you're well wrapped up.'

A few minutes later they were floundering across the yard, up to their knees in soft powdered snow, gasping breathlessly as they reached the shelter of the barn.

'Why don't you try and get the weather on the radio?' she suggested.

Grey glanced at his watch. 'It's too early. Anyway,

we know what the weather's doing. Stocking up with fuel while we can is more important.'

She could hardly argue with that, and the two of them staggered back to the cottage with their arms full. They repeated the journey half a dozen more times. 'Stay here, Abbie,' Grey ordered as he turned back for another trip. 'You've done enough.'

'I can keep going as long as you can,' she declared breathlessly.

'Humour me,' he said, and not waiting for her answer he went back out into the snow.

Three more trips and he was beginning to look waxen with the cold. 'Grey, that's enough, surely?' she protested as he dropped the logs in the doorway for her to stack and turned away once more, not bothering to waste his breath on a reply.

By the time she had stacked the logs neatly along the wall by the hearth he still hadn't returned. She opened the door and peered anxiously into the gathering gloom. It was oddly quiet, and she suddenly realised that the wind had dropped considerably in the last half-hour. But there was something—the faintest distressed cry that raised gooseflesh on her skin. 'Grey?' She strained her ears for his answering call.

This time there was no mistake. But the sound came not from the barn but from the field beyond it. What on earth was he doing there? She had only removed her topcoat and boots and she quickly pulled them back on over the gilet and two pairs of socks. Outside she stopped to listen. Silence. Absolute silence. Away from the lamplight of the cottage, she realised just how dark it had become outside, and a quiver of anxiety feathered her spine.

'Grey?' She heard the sound again, and without

stopping to consider the wisdom of her action she plunged into the knee-deep snow and headed in the direction it had come from.

She couldn't open the gate into the field and didn't waste time trying, but climbed over it, plunging into snow up to her thighs and pitching forward as she landed, knocking the wind from her body. But she scrambled quickly to her feet. The sound was nearer, louder—an eerie, wavering cry. And, suddenly realising what it was, she began to dig in the snow with her bare hands.

'Grey!' She raised her voice to heaven, wondering why on earth he didn't answer her. 'There's a ewe buried here. Where are you?' She continued to shout, cursing him with every breath even as she clawed frantically at the snow.

'Abbie!' Relief flooded through her as she finally heard his voice from the yard.

'Over here, in the field.' She saw the jerky movements of the torch as he approached the gate. 'Watch out, it's deeper—' Too late. The torch described a crazy arc as he tumbled, rolled and cursed as he righted himself.

'What the hell...?' And then he saw for himself as the beam of his torch picked up the head of the ewe. 'Is she alive?'

'Just about. Can you open the gate? We'll never get her over it from this side.'

He didn't stop to discuss the matter but began to work at the frozen metal hoop that held the gate fast, banging at it with his torch until it shifted and he could prise it off the post. Then he handed the battered torch to Abbie, lifted the poor frozen creature from the snow cave made by her body and carried her into the barn.

'What can we do for her?' Abbie asked.

'Rub her with straw. Dry her off.'

'Poor thing,' she said, grabbing a handful of straw and working over the ewe's back.

'It gets worse,' Grey said. 'She's about to drop her lamb.'

Abbie looked up at him in astonishment. 'How can you tell?'

'She's sort of hunched at the rear and she's dropped her head.' He fumbled in his pocket for his car keys and handed them to her. 'Put on the headlights so that I can see properly.'

'What are you going to do?' she asked as he began to strip off his coat and sweater, roll up the sleeves of his shirt.

He looked up into the thin torchlight, his face thrown into dark, chiselled shadows. 'With any luck she'll do it all herself.'

The light from the headlamps bounced off the stone walls, throwing their figures into long, distorted shadows as they hunched over the poor creature, their breath smoking in the freezing air as they watched and waited.

The lamb came surprisingly easily, the delivery over in moments, with just a little help from Grey.

'How do you know about sheep?' Abbie asked as he rubbed the little body with straw, cleaned its mouth and made certain that it was breathing properly.

He looked up briefly. 'There was a time you couldn't keep Robert out of the lambing sheds. He wanted to be a farmer. And at that age, wherever Robert went,' he said, glancing up at her, 'I followed.'

'Robert! A farmer?' The idea of the suave politician bent over the straw, helping a ewe in distress, was even more extraordinary than the sight of Grey now running his hands confidently over the ewe's belly.

His face was thrown into shadows as he looked up. 'There's another one. She's going to need some help.'

'What are you going to do?'

'Deliver it, if I can,' he said, his voice grim as he wrapped the first lamb in his sweater.

'Just tell me what to do—'

'No. I want you to take this one into the warm.' As if sensing the protest forming on her lips, he looked up. 'Now, Abbie, please.' There was no arguing with the determined set of his jaw.

'Right.' She took the tiny creature and, tucking it beneath her coat, hurried through the still, cold night into the warmth of the cottage. He was close behind her, and he put the second lamb with its sibling on the sweater, before heading back to the door. 'Grey? Where's the ewe? Won't she want her lambs?'

'The ewe is dead. Exhaustion.'

He had known it would happen. That was why he had sent her inside. 'Oh, Grey. I'm sorry.'

'It could have been you,' he said angrily. 'Wandering off into the night by yourself like that—I thought you would have learned your lesson...' He caught himself.

'I heard a noise. I—I thought it was you. That you'd fallen...' Her voice died away under a pair of clear, dark eyes that seemed to be able to read her thoughts—nightmare thoughts in which he lay hurt... 'Where were you anyway?' she demanded, with an angry little gesture that betrayed the concern that had driven her out into the dark more clearly than any words. 'I called and called…'

'I was in the barn,' he said, more gently. 'Trying to get the weather forecast on the radio. Apparently the storm has blown itself out. A warm front is moving in from the west.' He opened the door, then turned back. 'If you still want to do something, Abbie, you could make me a very large drink. You'll find some brandy in the cupboard.'

Her hands were shaking as she broke the seal on the bottle and poured a generous measure into a glass. It wasn't long before he returned, crossing quickly to the scullery to wash his hands. When he returned, he took the glass she offered, covering her hands with his cold fingers to steady her.

'You should have one too, Abbie. You don't look so good.' He bent down and took another glass from the cupboard, poured a drop into it and pressed it into her hand.

'There's some quite good wine in there,' she said, over-brightly, trying not to show how his fingers wrapped about hers were sending dangerous messages racing through her body. She took a quick sip of the brandy, hoping it would steady her racketing pulse. 'Did Jon buy that too?' she asked. 'You never used to leave alcohol here.'

'He must have done. Although, looking at it, I think it probably came from his father's cellar.' He was sipping thoughtfully at the drink she had poured for him. 'It's not supermarket plonk. What with that, and a whole bottle of brandy, it suggests that he thought he might have to get the poor girl plastered. But your Polly doesn't sound like the unwilling victim of Jon's youthful lust.'

'She's not *my* Polly,' Abbie protested. 'She's her very *own* Polly.' She gave a little shrug. 'In fact I'm rather afraid that the brandy might have been her idea. She seems to think it should be dished out in tumblers full for shock.'

'Does she?' His lips twitched into a smile. 'I wonder how many of her patients actually survive the treatment?'

She gave a little shrug to cover her own amusement. 'I think I was probably her first. Perhaps it's fortunate that I don't much care for brandy.'

'Treatment for shock, is it?' Grey continued to stare into his glass, apparently giving this piece of information considerable thought. Then he raised his eyes to hers. 'And...er...which of them do you suppose she thought would need it the most?' One dark brow kicked sharply upward in sardonic query.

Abbie gasped, caught herself in an attempt to stifle a wayward giggle. This was not a laughing matter. It was all terribly serious. But the giggle refused to be stifled. In fact the harder she tried to keep the corners of her mouth under control the worse it got, until without warning a bubble of soft, irresistible laughter burst into the quiet room.

She clapped a hand over her mouth in an attempt to stem the tide, but it was too late. It was so long since she had laughed, really laughed, that it was as if the floodgates had been breached.

'D-don't!' she warned, as Grey turned away a second too late to hide the fact that his face too had creased in a broad grin. 'Oh, don't, Grey!' But it was too late. His shoulders were shaking, and a sudden guffaw of laughter ripped from his chest, filling the room.

'Shock!' He shouted with laughter. 'I'll give him shock when I get hold of him.' But the words were drowned in his laughter. 'I'm s-sorry. It's really not in the least bit f-funny,' he said, trying unsuccessfully to get a grip on himself.

She shook her head, quite unable to answer as she was shaken by another uncontrollable fit of giggles, and collapsed against his shoulder. It seemed the most natural thing in the world for him to gather her close, and they clung on to one another and finally gave up the struggle to stop laughing, allowing the sheer, tension-relieving bliss of it to sweep over them.

It was the tiny piping of the lambs that finally brought them crashing back to earth. 'Oh, look,' Abbie said, brushing the tears from her cheeks as the stronger of the two struggled up onto wobbly legs. 'Poor little things.' She lifted her head from Grey's shoulder to discover her face inches from his own, her mouth a second away from bliss.

'It's so long since I've laughed, Abbie, that I thought I had forgotten how,' he said, his voice ragged.

'Me too,' she murmured. She hadn't realised until that moment just how desperately unhappy she was. No wonder she had spilled out her heart to Polly's eager ears. And now she was in Grey's arms and his eyes tempted her; the sharp, clean outdoor scent of the wind that enveloped him tempted her.

Horrified at how easy it would be simply to surrender, she pulled back, disentangling herself self-consciously from his arms, and turned purposefully to the lambs. 'H-how are we going to feed them?' she asked quickly. 'Will they take cow's milk?'

There was a long, dangerous pause. Then Grey

sank to his haunches and stretched out his hand to the lambs' eager nuzzling. 'I don't know. Hugh uses a special formula for orphan lambs.' He looked up. 'You know—like baby milk.'

She knew. 'Then we'll have to get them to the farm. If we carry one each inside our coats—'

He didn't argue, but said, 'It's too far for you to walk in this. I'll take them. You stay here.'

'And worry myself to death about you?'

His eyes gleamed darkly as he looked up at her. 'Why on earth would you do that, Abbie?'

'I—I'd worry about anyone out in this weather. It'll be much safer with two of us.' Anything would be safer than staying in the dangerous atmosphere of the cottage, where every word, every gesture reminded her so forcibly of the past, rekindling emotions and feelings best left buried.

'I don't think you should risk it,' he asserted, rising to his feet. 'You've been half-frozen once.'

'Well, you've a ready-made cure if I should succumb again,' she declared boldly. 'If you can bring yourself to apply it.' His face tightened so that every feature seemed to leap into focus, sharper, leaner. He had lost weight, she realised with dismay. 'I found that ewe, Grey,' she rushed on, shutting out the treacherous thoughts that tormented her. 'I'm not about to let her lambs die because I might get cold feet.'

'Even if they're going to end up as lamb chops on someone's plate?' he demanded harshly. Abbie stared down at the tiny creatures and one of them, the first-born, lifted its little head and bleated at her. She clapped her hand over her mouth as lunch came vividly back to haunt her.

'Oh, Polly,' she murmured as the blood drained from her face. 'How could you?'

'What?'

'Buy lamb. She's going through a vegetarian phase. Or she was until yesterday... Her mother said it would wear off...'

He frowned. 'But if... Damn!' As she swayed on her feet he grabbed the brandy glass from the nearby table and thrust it to her lips. 'Just a sip. No more.'

She obeyed, because it was easier than fighting him, and she gasped as the spirit burned down her throat, spreading its warmth across her stomach. 'I'm sorry. A tendency to faint at the drop of a hat seems to be getting to be something of a habit.'

'Does it?' His arm was round her shoulders, grasping her tightly so that she had no choice but to face him. 'Why?' he demanded. 'What's the matter with you?' He seemed genuinely concerned.

'Nothing. Let me go,' she insisted, keeping her eyes cast down. 'I'm fine.'

'You don't look fine. You've lost weight. Your cheeks are hollow...' He caught himself. Then he very carefully put down the glass. 'How very stupid of me,' he said. 'I should have realised. It's what you wanted after all...'

'Wanted?'

'You're pregnant, aren't you?'

CHAPTER EIGHT

PREGNANT. If only she were. If only she could have had his child... A part of him that no one could ever take away. That must have been what Emma had wanted. And now Emma had everything, while she was alone—would always be alone.

In that bleak moment Abbie wanted to hurt him, to bare her pain and let him see what he had done to her in depriving her for ever of the special fulfilment of motherhood, but as she raised lids heavy with the pain of her loss and met his eyes she saw with a shock that his expression was too intent, her answer was too important to him.

In that moment she knew that she was balancing on the edge of a bottomless chasm into which it would be all too easy to fall. A chasm into which some deep part of her wanted to fall. One touch, one look, would ignite a spark that might give her what she desired, but she would have to live with herself ever afterwards. She had made her decision. There was no way back. Last night had meant nothing...if it happened again...

'I...I thought you said I'd lost weight,' she said stupidly. She had to say something—break the tension that stretched the air between them somehow.

But he didn't back off. 'In the early weeks women sometimes lose weight.'

He knew that? Was he a 'new' man, who'd read all the books, studied natural childbirth? Oh, yes.

Grey Lockwood had never done anything by halves. He would want to be involved in everything to do with his child. Anger snapped her back from the abyss, and the heady surge of adrenalin sent her heart pounding into overdrive, finally provoking her beyond the steely control that had kept her emotions under wraps for so long.

'Emma lost weight, did she?' Her flaring reaction startled him and that pleased her; it pleased her so much that she went on. 'Tell me, did you take her to the antenatal clinic every week? Natural childbirth classes?' He made a gesture that dismissed the idea as ridiculous, but she wasn't put off by that. 'How did you account for your time in your appointments diary, Grey? Was that covered neatly by the phrase "case conference" too?' His head jerked back as if she had hit him.

'I should have told you,' he said. It was an appeal for her to understand, but she was beyond understanding.

'Too damn right you should!'

He shook his head. 'I should never have let Robert persuade me... Did it really matter that much to you?'

'Matter?' She stared at him. 'You were deceiving me...how do you think I felt? I sensed something was wrong. That you were hiding something from me. But never in my wildest nightmares...' She couldn't go on.

'And Steve Morley offered you a sympathetic shoulder to cry on.' He was angry too now. 'Why didn't you come to me? You didn't even give me a chance to explain.'

'Because I didn't—' She stopped herself just in time. She had been through six months of hell to give him something important. The chance to begin again. If she blurted out the truth now, in a rush of anger, it would all have been for nothing. She drew back a little, managed a shrug, although she couldn't have said how. 'Because I didn't want to,' she said, concealing her anger now, under the painful mask of indifference. 'Steve offered something new.' True enough. He had offered, she just hadn't taken him up on it. 'Maybe I was just ready for that.'

'In a pig's eye! You were hurt and angry and he took advantage of that. Oh, God, what a mess! I'm sorry, Abbie.' He seized her hands. 'So sorry. It seemed the best thing to do at the time. I never meant to hurt you. Hindsight is so clear—it's so easy to see now the way that secrets create an atmosphere that distorts everything, even love...'

She was rigid with shock as he poured out his remorse, unable to speak, unable even to take back her hands. Grey shook his head as if unable to go on. To see him hurting, to be unable to help him, was almost more than flesh and blood could stand. But she had to stand it. He had made his choice and he would have to live with it—as she did.

He gathered himself. 'You should look after yourself, Abbie. Rest—'

'Keep your antenatal advice for those who need it,' she told him, finally finding the strength to snatch back her hands from his warm grasp. 'I'm not expecting a baby—not that it would be any of your business if I were.'

For a moment she thought relief touched his eyes, but it was so fleeting, so unlikely that it actually mattered to him, that she dismissed it. 'We are still married, Abbie. Everything you do concerns me.'

'For a few more days. That's all.'

His head came up sharply. 'Have you signed the papers?'

'I only received them yesterday. They're in my bag. Out there in the snow.'

'You brought them with you in case you passed a convenient postbox? Were you in that much of a hurry to end our marriage?'

'I'm sure you couldn't wait to put your name to the papers,' she retaliated defensively.

'I've had other things on my mind.' He looked at her. 'Look, Abbie, just in case...if there's any possibility that you might be pregnant...you shouldn't be around pregnant sheep.'

'Well, there isn't and I'm not,' she snapped. Never have been and never likely to be, she thought bitterly. *Unless*... The word popped unbidden into her head and her eyes flickered back to Grey. Unless last night produced some kind of miracle. The timing was right...

She caught her breath and his eyes narrowed. 'What is it?'

She shook her head. 'Nothing.' The second lamb lying nearest her butted at her leg, then struggled to its feet and with a tiny wavering bleat demanded to be fed. She reached down, touched its head. 'Not lamb chops,' she promised it. 'Not if I have to rent a field and keep you for the next ten years.' And when she glanced up, she surprised such a look of tenderness on Grey's face that she smiled. 'Come on,' she said. 'We'd better get going. This little chap's hungry.'

His mouth straightened in a wry smile. 'If you're seriously planning to keep livestock, Abbie, you've one or two things to learn. Your little chap is a ewe. They both are.'

The blizzard had blown itself out. The evening sky was brilliant with stars and, once out of the sheltered hollow where the cottage lay, the snow was not so deep. It crunched and squeaked beneath their feet as they made their way up the narrow path towards the farm that nestled on the far side of the hill.

'All right?' Grey's hand shot out and caught Abbie's arm to steady her as she slipped a little on the frosted snow.

'Fine. I'm fine,' she said breathlessly, pulling free of his supporting grasp and stopping to stamp the snow out of the tread of her boots. Any excuse to rest for a moment, because she wasn't feeling fine at all. She was horribly aware that despite the fact she was forcing her legs to go through the motions, Grey was reining in his stride to match hers. The still, sharp cold bit painfully at her cheeks, fingers and toes, and as she dragged air into her lungs it hurt.

'We're nearly there,' he said encouragingly.

'Don't baby me, Grey,' she gasped. 'I know exactly how far we have to go.'

'Then be quiet and save your breath.' And before she could protest, or stop him, he had removed the scarf from about his neck and had wrapped it around her face, covering her nose and mouth so that the sharp air was warmed before it hit her lungs.

'Grey, don't be silly...' she mumbled, but he raised a warning finger, linking his arm firmly under hers, and somehow his strength seemed to transmit itself to her and she found a second wind, so that ten minutes later they breasted the hill, saw the lights of the farm beneath them, heard the anxious voices of the ewes in the lambing shed.

They paused for a moment to catch breath, and as they stood there the moon appeared from behind a scudding cloud, turning the sea below them to gleaming pewter, illuminating the glistening virgin snow.

'It should be Christmas,' Abbie whispered, and she looked down at the barn below them, heard the bleating of the sheep on the still air. 'There should be bells.'

Grey turned to her. 'And if it was,' he asked, 'what present would you want to find under your Christmas tree?'

She gave a quick shrug, but whether he saw it under her heavy layers of clothing she couldn't tell. She knew what she wanted most in the entire world, but that was her own deep secret. 'Come on,' she said. 'Let's go.'

Hugh looked up as they appeared in the doorway. 'Well, well,' he said, with a nod. 'Nice night for a walk if you've nothing better to do.' His weather-hardened face split into a broad grin at his own dry wit.

'We've brought you a couple of orphans,' Grey said. 'I'm afraid the ewe didn't make it.'

'Well, well.' Hugh said again, and straightened. 'I went out with the dog looking for her, but the weather was so bad we had to turn back.' His glance fell on Abbie, pinched and white with the cold. 'Better take them indoors, *bach*. Nancy will look after them.'

'You're on your own?' Grey asked, looking around. 'I'll come back and give you a hand if you like.'

Nancy handed Grey a flask of tea to take back out

with him and then turned to the lambs. 'I'm not sure which of you looks the worst for wear, Abbie, you or these little ones,' she said.

'I'm fine.' But as she held her hands out to the fire her teeth began to chatter audibly. 'J-just a b-bit cold.' She tried a reassuring smile but her mouth, juddering idiotically, refused to co-operate.

'A *bit* cold, is it?' she scolded cheerfully. 'Your jeans are soaking wet and you're shivering like a sick child. Straight upstairs with you and into the bath. I'll find you something warm now to put on.'

'But the lambs,' Abbie protested. 'Shouldn't we be doing something for them?'

'Not you, *bach*, me. And indeed the sooner you do as you're told, the sooner they'll be seen to,' she said. 'Upstairs with you now.' The farmhouse only had two bedrooms, the third little boxroom having been converted to a bathroom by Hugh's father years before. 'Out of those wet things now, there's a bathrobe behind the door.'

And, assuming total obedience, Nancy bustled off to the airing cupboard to fetch fresh towels. She reappeared a few minutes later with a nightdress and a thick dressing gown and thrust them at Abbie. 'You might as well put these on,' she said, picking up the damp clothes that Abbie had discarded. 'You won't be going out again tonight. Supper will be ready when you come down.'

'But, Nancy—' she began. There was no way that they could stay the night.

'I don't suppose they're quite what you're used to,' the older woman said with a laugh as she retreated in the direction of the kitchen, taking Abbie's wet clothes with her. 'But they're warm.'

'Thanks,' she called, somewhat belatedly, as she looked helplessly at the garments. It would be wonderful to feel warm.

The bath brought a glow back to her cheeks, and feeling decidedly more human she dressed in the soft flannel nightdress that buttoned up to the neck with a frill. Nancy was right, she hadn't had anything like it since she was about ten. The dressing gown had the same comforting nursery feel—thick and fleecy in a cheerful red. It was supposed to reach the floor, but Abbie was a head taller than Nancy and, like the nightdress, it stopped just below her knees, looking decidedly odd. She tied it about her, and, in the absence of a comb, raked her fingers through her hair a couple of times and went downstairs.

Hugh and Grey looked up from the table as she entered the kitchen, feeling somewhat self-conscious in her unconventional attire. 'There now, *bach*, you look better than you did half an hour ago,' Hugh said, evidently very pleased with life. 'Have some *cawl* and Nancy's good bread, and you'll be fit for anything.'

Grey was regarding her appearance with considerable amusement, a fact that she discovered irritated her. Ignoring him, she turned to Nancy. 'How are the lambs?' she asked.

'They're sucking well enough. I've tucked them up by the Aga. If they make it through the night, they'll probably survive.'

'Until they go to market,' Grey reminded her provokingly.

Abbie glared at him. 'If they survive, Hugh,' she said, 'I'd like to buy them.'

Hugh merely patted her hand reassuringly. 'Grey is

teasing you, *cariad*. Since they're ewes I'll be keeping them in the flock.'

'Unless, of course, you have plans to take them back to London to keep as pets?' Grey said, refusing to leave it.

'And what on earth will you do with them in London?' Nancy demanded, with a laugh. 'Keep them in your lovely flat?' Nancy and Hugh had stayed with them once, when they'd come up for the Smithfield Show. 'You leave them here, Abbie,' she advised. 'They'll be a lot happier in the fields.'

But Abbie was tired of being teased. 'Perhaps Matthew would like them as pets,' she said, picking up her spoon and dipping it into the steaming meat and vegetable broth. For a moment an awkward silence descended on the table. Then Hugh turned to Grey to ask after his brother and Nancy began to chatter about the weather and the moment passed.

But it was not forgotten. When Nancy had borne the plates away to the scullery, refusing any help, and Hugh had gone off to look for a drop of something warming left over from Christmas, Grey turned on her. 'Why on earth did you have to bring up Matthew? Nancy's been kindness itself, but she hardly approves. There's no need to flaunt the situation.'

'Me?' He had brought his lover to the cottage with their child and he accused *her* of flaunting the situation?

He caught at her wrist as Hugh returned. 'And since they don't know that we've split up, I'd rather you kept it that way,' he hissed. 'You've embarrassed them enough for one evening.'

Didn't know? What on earth did they think had

been going on, for heaven's sake? But she was prevented from demanding to know exactly what the neighbours thought of his indiscretions by the return of Hugh, holding an unopened bottle of single malt that looked suspiciously like the one they had given him the Christmas before last.

Grey was right about one thing: Nancy was strict chapel, and as Hugh caught his wife's disapproving eye he said, 'Why don't you come through to the parlour, Grey. Leave the women to their gossip.'

'Shouldn't we go back out to the shed?'

'Nothing doing for half an hour or so. Might as well put our feet up by the fire.'

Grey hesitated, apparently unwilling to leave her to gossip with Nancy. 'Well, now, here we are.' Nancy bustled back with a tray. 'I made a few Welsh cakes yesterday. We'll have them with a cup of tea, Abbie, while you tell me all about your travels. I read your piece about that poor woman who had her little girl snatched. Terrible thing. Did she ever get her back?'

Abbie turned away from Grey's insistent gaze. 'Yes, she did eventually. She spent months in the mountains, travelling from village to village. She had a terrible time, but I think her dogged refusal to give up finally won her a kind of respect. To see someone endure so much for pure love touches the heart...' The door clicked shut behind her.

'Well, well,' Nancy said. 'You must be very pleased. You're away such a lot these days, but if what you do helps...'

Nancy was easy to talk to, she did most of the work. She rattled on about what had been happening in the village, about the farm, and all Abbie had to do was drop in the occasional word to prompt her onto the next saga. Then a yawn caught her by surprise and Nancy tutted.

'There's me rattling on about nothing when you should be in bed. Come along, now, I've put in a bottle to air the bed.'

'No, really, Nancy, we can't put you to all this trouble.'

Nancy put her hands on her hips in a stance that brooked no argument. 'It wasn't any trouble coming all this way in the snow with two lambs, I suppose?'

'But I don't think we locked the cottage door...' she protested.

'And who do you think is going to tour the neighbourhood in this weather, trying doors on the off chance that there's something worth stealing?'

Nancy was right, the whole idea was ridiculous. But she didn't want to go upstairs and lie in that big double bed waiting for Grey to come in. 'Then can I help with the lambs? They'll need feeding through the night and you've got enough to do.'

'Don't you bother your head about it. You've done enough.'

But Abbie had a stubborn streak too. 'I can take a turn, at least. I won't go to bed unless you promise to wake me.' She glanced at her watch, and saw to her chagrin that it was only nine-thirty. 'Call me at twelve. Promise?'

Nancy gave her a little push in the direction of the stairs. 'All right,' she said. 'I promise.'

She woke with a start in a strange room and a strange bed, and for a moment panic swept over her. Then she remembered. She groped for the bedside light and peered at her watch. It was past one o'clock and

Nancy hadn't called her. She swung her feet out of bed but as they hit the rug she saw Grey, slumped in the chair in the corner. For just a second she thought he was asleep and she froze, unwilling to risk waking him.

'There's no need to get up, Abbie.'

His voice rumbling from the dim recesses of the room startled her and she sank back onto the bed. 'Didn't the lambs survive?'

'They're going to be fine. One of the other ewes lost her lamb and Hugh convinced her that our orphans were hers.'

'How——?' Then she shuddered as she remembered. 'No, don't tell me.'

'I didn't intend to.'

The farmhouse did not have central heating, and her breath smoked out towards him in the cold air. 'Why are you sitting there?' she asked, shivering.

'It's called keeping up appearances, Abbie. I would have stayed out in the lambing shed, but Hugh caught me yawning and turned me out. And since he and Nancy don't actually seem to go to bed at all during the lambing season, I had no choice but to come up here.'

She slipped on the thick robe and crossed to him. 'You must be freezing.' She stretched out her fingers to his hand, but he pulled back. 'You can't sit there all night.'

'I'll be fine, Abbie. Go back to bed.'

She saw how he was huddled into the chair and knew that he wasn't fine. He was far from fine. He had been out in the lambing sheds for hours and she had no idea how long he had been sitting there. Her own concern about sharing the bed with him seemed petty in the extreme. 'For heaven's sake, Grey, we can be adult about this, surely?'

'Adult?' His voice mocked the word. 'Why, Abbie, whatever do you mean?'

'You know what I mean,' she said crossly. 'We can surely share a bed without...well, without...'

He rescued her. 'You've changed your tune since this morning.'

'This morning you weren't half frozen to death. Come to bed.'

'I can't, Abbie.'

She knelt in front of him, took his cold hands in hers and pressed them against her cheek to warm them. 'Then I'll have to sit up with you.'

'Please! Please, don't do this!'

She looked up at him, shocked by the pain in his voice. 'What is it?'

His eyes glittered in the lamplight as their breath condensed and mingled. 'I can't get into bed with you, Abbie. Just leave it at that.'

'This is silly. I'll stuff a bolster between us if that'll make you happy—'

'No!' he shouted. Until that moment she hadn't realised they had been whispering. 'You don't understand,' he said, his voice lower, but still insistent.

'Then you'd better do your best to make me understand, Grey,' she replied, with equal vehemence, 'because I'm staying here until you do.'

'Abbie!' He pleaded with her, but she took no notice of him, curling up against his leg, laying her cheek along his hard, denim-clad thigh. He touched her sleek, dark blonde head. 'Abbie, look at me.' She lifted her face to his and he cradled it between his hands, so that her warm cheeks lay against his freezing fingers. That must be why she was shivering despite the thick dressing gown.

'While I stay here I can continue to pretend that last night was the result of the cold. If I get into bed with you I'm going to have to admit that I've been lying to myself.' She tried to interrupt but he laid a finger over her lips. 'I'm going to have to admit that last night had nothing to do with hypothermia or first aid or even plain, unadorned lust. It had everything to do with desire. I'm going to have to admit to myself that I was capable of desiring you to the point where it blotted out everything else. And if I lied to myself, I lied to you.'

His fingers slipped from her face and he slumped back in the chair. 'So, if it's all the same to you, I'd rather sit here in the cold and keep my self-respect.'

This morning she'd thought she wanted to hear that. She'd thought she'd give anything to wake in his arms and hear him say those words. But now she knew that she had been wrong. To believe he loved someone else was a nightmare. If she allowed herself to believe that he loved her, allowed herself to hold him and tell him that she had wanted it too, it would destroy them both. What she had to do now, in this freezing cold room, was make him hate her enough not to care.

'Well, that's very noble of you,' she said, rising to her feet, turning away. She shrugged out of the dressing gown and with what she hoped sounded like careless indifference said, 'I'm sure Steve will find it highly amusing when I tell him that you still want me so much that you'd rather freeze to death than risk getting into bed with me.' She lifted the covers and eased herself back into bed.

'When you what?' He was on his feet and across the room in a stride. 'You're going to run back to your lover and tell him—'

It was working, but she had to be careful not to overplay her hand. 'You didn't think I'd keep it a secret from him? That's *your* way of handling unpalatable truths. But I don't believe in keeping secrets, Grey. Not from someone you're supposed to love.'

'Well, we might as well give him something to have a real laugh about,' he declared, angry enough to kill.

He pulled his shirt and sweater over his head, not bothering to turn away as he stripped off his remaining clothes and tugged back the covers. She rocketed across to the cold part of the bed, but the mattress sagged, and as he hit the mattress his weight brought her crashing back against his body and his arm shot out and pinned her there.

'Now,' he said grimly, 'what do you think would most *amuse* Mr Morley?' His eyes were inches from hers, gold lights sparking angrily in the warm autumn depths. 'It's been a while, but I'm sure I can remember—'

'I'm sure you can, Grey,' she said quickly, shaking from the impact of his aroused body so close. She swallowed. She hadn't expected quite such a dangerously instant reaction to her taunts. 'But I know you'll understand if I tell you that I've...um...got a headache.'

'A headache?' For a moment he held her crushed hard against his ribcage, and there was no indication that he had any intention of understanding. For a moment everything was silent, the air taut as elastic, until, with a slow, deliberate expulsion of breath, he reached out and switched off the bedside light.

Abbie held her breath, still fastened by his hard, sinewy arm against his chest, very much afraid that she had misjudged him, driven him beyond the point of no return. Then he turned back to her.

'Turn round, Abbie,' he said, and she obeyed instantly, seizing her freedom as he moved his arm, but congratulating herself too soon as he scooped her flannel-wrapped body back against him. 'It's all right,' he murmured as she stiffened, his sweet breath on her cheek as his lips brushed her hair. 'You're perfectly safe. But I wouldn't try that trick with anyone who doesn't know you as well as I do. They might not understand. Go to sleep, now. We'll talk about it in the morning.'

Sleep? With his body curved about her? With her back against his chest, her hips pressed into his groin? She was just grateful for the thick flannelette nightdress, which muffled the urgent peaking of her breasts in its deep folds, as his arm, draped protectively over her, provoked a yearning ache for him deep within her.

Abbie woke, and turned in the warm bed to discover that she was alone. She was always alone. She ached for a different time, when Grey would have been there, when he would have reached for her in that early-morning quiet.

Yesterday she had been angry with him for leaving her to go and sleep in a chair. But it hadn't been that simple. His desire for her had driven him away, and she understood that now. Even in her fitful sleep she had been painfully conscious of him lying alongside her all the long night, and she understood why he hadn't waited for her to wake up. To wake against a warm, enticing body was to be utterly defenceless—at the mercy of the moment. He knew that as well as she did—he was fighting it too.

She rose, washed and scrambled into yesterday's clothes—dried and left on the chair for her—then walked, with an odd reluctance to face the day, to face him, down the stairs.

In the doorway she stopped. Unaware of her presence, and singing softly to himself, Grey turned bacon in the pan. The kettle began to boil and he lifted it from the hob, pouring water onto the tea. His movements were so spare, so effortless. He was a man who fitted his environment. In the City he wore a suit, commanded instant respect from his peers, stood head and shoulders above the crowd. In the country he looked as if he had never seen a City desk.

There was a tray on the table, laid for one. He was going to bring her breakfast in bed. He had only ever done that when she was ill, or when he'd wanted to say that he was sorry. Rare enough. The small choking noise in her throat must have reached him over the sound of his own voice orchestrating some appallingly cheerful overture. He stopped, turned and smiled. Oh, God, he smiled. Not one of those tight, restrained smiles which had punctuated the past twenty-four hours, but the kind of smile that came straight from the heart.

But she couldn't allow herself the luxury of smiling back. His body against hers was too recent, too bittersweet an experience. She had to keep her distance, pretend that it had never happened. So she didn't smile. Although it broke her heart, she didn't smile.

Instead she forced a brightness into her voice. 'You should have woken me,' she said.

Grey's smile faded. 'I shook you for half an hour. You didn't stir, so I thought I'd better bring you up a tray.'

'Liar,' she said, fielding the joke with a carelessness that hurt.

'Well, perhaps twenty minutes.'

'That's more like it. How are the lambs?'

'They're fine.'

'Really? You wouldn't just say that...'

'I'm not about to lie over the fate of a couple of lambs.' Why? Weren't they important enough to lie about? Unaware of the fury he had provoked in her breast, he lifted the bacon onto a plate and cracked a couple of eggs into the pan. 'Since you're up, you might as well make yourself useful and get on with the toast.'

She had no intention of making herself useful. She certainly didn't want any breakfast. 'Where's Nancy?' she asked.

'She's still in the milking parlour. She and Hugh had breakfast some time ago.'

'I'll take them out some tea and I can say goodbye at the same time,' she said.

He looked up. 'They'll have tea when they come in. And you're not going anywhere until you've had something to eat.' She opened her mouth to protest. 'I mean it, Abbie, so don't even bother to argue.' She didn't. She recognised the look and closed her mouth, picked up the bread-knife and hacked a couple of pieces off the loaf before dumping them in the toaster. Apparently satisfied with this demonstration of obedience, he turned back to the pan. 'Abbie, about last night...' he began.

'Forget it.'

He swivelled back to her. 'You keep telling me to forget things. Good things. Why?'

'Because...' She trailed off. Challenged, she was unable to offer an answer. She picked up the teapot and began to pour out two huge mugs of the stuff so that she wouldn't have to meet his eyes. 'I couldn't leave you sitting in the cold,' she said stiffly. 'I mean...I wouldn't have the first idea how to go about dealing with a *genuine* case of hypothermia.'

'Ah.' He turned to face her. 'You're sore that I lied about that.' He regarded her steadily. 'Then I suppose, after last night, you could say honour is about even. I mean, you're not about to rush back to Steve Morley and tell him your midnight secrets, are you, Abbie?'

'Honour?' She grasped at the word in order to evade answering him. 'You have the nerve to use that word?'

He wasn't fooled. 'You're avoiding my question. Are you and Morley still together?' He didn't wait for her reply. 'I warn you, don't lie to me, Abbie, because I'll find out.'

'It's none of your business.'

He deftly slipped the eggs onto the plates and looked up at her. 'I'm making it my business,' he informed her. 'And, unwittingly or not, you've already answered my question. Is the toast ready yet?'

It burst from the toaster, making her jump. She turned quickly to butter it, keep her hands busy. Her head wasn't so easily distracted. It was all going wrong. Stupidly wrong.

She just couldn't understand why he was determined to find out what she was doing. It didn't matter what she was doing or who she was doing it with. At least, it shouldn't matter. She flickered a glance in his direction. But somehow it did.

CHAPTER NINE

Grey put a plate in front of her. She stared at the food. Perfectly plain, good food. After a moment he said, 'You might as well eat it hot, Abbie. Because you're going to eat it before you leave here. One way or another.'

She shook her head. 'I was just thinking about Polly.' Anything was better than thinking about the mess she and Grey had made of their lives.

He was unimpressed. 'You can eat and think at the same time.'

'Did I tell you that she was going through a vegetarian phase?'

'I think you mentioned it. Why?'

'I cooked some bacon one day and she left the room. She couldn't bear to watch me eat it, she said. She kept seeing little pink piglets...'

'It's quite common, you know, for young girls to go through that sort of thing—'

'You don't understand,' she interrupted, a little impatiently.

'If you're trying to make a specific point, Abbie, then you'll have to try harder.'

'It was on Sunday. The day before she and Jon took off.' She shook her head. 'It might just be a phase she's going through, Grey, but somehow I just can't believe she would change back into a ravening carnivore overnight. There was *nothing* at the cottage for her...'

He stared into the mug of tea. 'But if Jon did the shopping?'

'You're not suggesting he didn't know? She'd been trying to convert him for weeks... Besides, Polly has a somewhat managing disposition—I'm sure she would have given him a list. Even at seventeen she's perfectly well aware that no man is to be trusted alone in a supermarket.'

For a moment he regarded the bacon on her plate before raising his eyes to hers. 'Tell me, Abbie,' he said at last, 'just how difficult did little Polly Flinders make it for you to work out where she had gone?'

'Difficult?' She gave a little shrug. 'It wasn't difficult at all. I mean, you telephoned and practically told me... Did Jon know you were thinking of taking him to Wales?'

'I mentioned it.'

'So he'd know you would look for the keys?' She lifted her head and met his eyes head on. 'And, just in case, Polly telephoned Robert's housekeeper pretending to be a journalist.'

'Why didn't she phone me?'

'Because you would have seen through her. I think the answer to your question, Grey, is that she and Jon didn't make it very difficult at all. In fact they laid a trail.' Abbie raised her hands to her face and, elbows on the table, propped her head on her hands. 'Oh, good grief, I can't believe that I've been so slow-witted. Lying in the snow must have frozen my brain.'

'But why? Why have they lured us down here, supplied us with a selection of our favourite food and disappeared?' He swore. 'They've backtracked. While they've been jerking our strings, stranding us here, they could be anywhere. They knew we wouldn't just wait for them to come back on Monday. That we'd come after them—'

'They couldn't know that we'd be snowbound, Grey,' she pointed out.

He considered this, a frown furrowing his brow. 'Then what on earth are they up to?'

Abbie was very afraid that she knew what they were up to, but admitting it wasn't going to be easy. She took a deep breath. 'I think I'd better tell you some more about Polly.'

'She's bright, pretty, clever and managing. Are you telling me there's more?' he demanded.

'Would you like some more toast?' she asked, slicing into the loaf. He made an impatient gesture which she took as an affirmative. 'Tea?'

'Abbie!'

She looked up. 'Promise not to be angry with them. They clearly didn't understand what they were doing.'

'I'm promising nothing,' he thundered. She picked up her knife and fork and began to eat. For a moment he watched her and fumed. Then he reached across the table and caught her wrist. 'I promise,' he said impatiently. She lifted her eyes, her glance challenging him. 'I promise,' he repeated, more gently this time. 'Obviously they're somewhere safe, or you would be bouncing off the ceiling by now.'

'I haven't the faintest idea where they are. Unless...' She gave a little gasp, raising her hand to her mouth. 'Oh, no, they wouldn't be that cheeky.'

'Since this has been a very one-sided conversation, I haven't any idea. But, taking the situation so far, I wouldn't count on it. Now, are you going to let me in on the joke?' he demanded.

'It's not funny.'

'Then why are you grinning like a Cheshire cat?'

'I'm sorry.' She rapidly straightened her face and, pushing her plate to one side, she tried to think how on earth she was going to explain what Jon and Polly were up to without betraying herself. 'The trouble is that Polly is a romantic.'

'I think I've grasped that already. But she's seventeen. At that age it's to be expected.'

'Perhaps. But I'm afraid she took it into her head that I was…' there was no easy way to say it '…well, that I was still in love with you.' She stared at a knot in the table, waiting for the exclamation of disgust. There was nothing but the sudden collapse of fuel in the grate to make her jump.

'Why would she think that, Abbie?' His voice was deceptively gentle. She had heard that tone before, leading people on until they were deep in some quagmire from which it was impossible to extricate themselves.

'Oh, that was your fault,' she declared brightly.

'*My* fault?' The words had a dangerous edge to them.

'Well, yes. It was the photograph album. It wasn't on your beautifully efficient list, you see. Polly opened the carton and there it was right on top. Being young and thoughtless, she opened it. It was a bit of shock…' Like a kick in the stomach from a mule. She was still bruised.

'The kind of shock you needed a tumbler full of brandy for?'

She sidestepped the shock, concentrated on the brandy. 'Enough to put me under the table for a week if I'd drunk it all,' she said, with a wry little lift of her lips. 'When she realised who you were, that you were Jon's uncle, she just went on and on. There were some pictures of the cottage and she wanted to know all about that too.'

'Why didn't she ask Jon? He's been there often enough.'

'Oh, I'm sure she did. In fact, on reflection, I think he must have been priming her,' she said thoughtfully. 'She once asked me what a slurry pit was.' She raised her eyes to Grey's.

'So you told her all about the time one of Hugh's cows knocked me into one, I suppose. I've no doubt the two of you howled with laughter.'

'I'm afraid so.' She bit her lower lip, trying not to laugh now. It had been dangerous, horribly dangerous.

'If you'd been on the other end of the hosepipe, you wouldn't have thought it was so funny, I can tell you.' She shook her head, unable to speak. 'Damn it, you had to break the ice off the damned thing before you could even unravel it.'

'If I'd let you into the cottage we would never have got rid of the smell,' she gasped.

'And as if it wasn't bad enough being stripped to the buff while you hosed me down with ice water...' a bubble of laughter finally escaped Abbie's lips '...some wretched woman chose that moment to come into the yard shaking her collecting box for suffering animals.'

'It wasn't *personal*, Grey,' she gasped. 'The cow didn't mean you any harm, and the poor woman didn't come *very* close. The smell...'

Grey finally succumbed to a grin. 'No, well, she could see I didn't have any pockets for loose change.

I always promised myself that one day I'd turn the hose on you…' He walked to the far side of the room, as far away as he could go. For a moment—just for a moment—it had been as if nothing had changed. 'So,' he said abruptly. 'I think I've got the general idea. Polly thought if we were stranded together overnight nature could be left to take its course.' He propped his elbow on the mantle. 'She's clever, I think you said. In the circumstances I'd have to agree.'

'I don't imagine she had your somewhat drastic cure for hypothermia in mind.'

'She seems to have overlooked Steve Morley as well. Or didn't you bother to fill her in on all the sordid details?'

She had hoped he would miss the gaping holes in her tale, but he was too quick for that. 'I didn't fill her in on *any* details. Do you think if I'd told her the real reason for our break-up she would have gone to all this trouble?'

'No. In fact I find it hard to believe that a seventeen-year-old would go to so much trouble without a great deal of encouragement. It seems far more likely that after trailing around a lot of dreary flats you decided that my nest was infinitely more comfortable. Was that why you went to see Morley before you came down here? To tell him it was over?'

'I certainly told him to get lost, but not quite in the way you mean,' she said. 'He wanted—'

But Grey cut her off, not interested in listening to her explanations. 'Once you realised that Polly and Jon were friends it must have seemed so simple to manipulate the pair of them.'

'And am I supposed to have manipulated a blizzard, a car accident and my near demise in the snow?' she demanded.

He shrugged. 'They were just good luck.' Her explosion of rage bounced off him. 'I imagine you thought once you had me here I would be a push-over.'

'Why on earth would I think that?' she demanded, then flushed deeply as she realised, as he must do, that he had indeed been a push-over. 'And whatever was Jon thinking of?' she went on quickly. 'He must know what the situation is.'

'When your wife walks out on you for another man, Abbie, you don't exactly bellow it from the hilltops. You certainly don't discuss the details with an eighteen-year-old boy.'

'I would have thought you were finding the details just a little difficult to keep secret!' Or could it be that he was doing just that? Maybe Emma hadn't moved in with him. Maybe he felt that discretion was vital until after the decree absolute was granted. She shrugged. 'Well, I don't suppose it matters. Did you say the weather was clearing today? Maybe I can get back to London—'

He shook his head. 'The sun is out now, but the snow froze solid last night, and according to the local radio the road is still blocked halfway to Carmarthen—so I'm afraid you're stuck with your plot for another day or two. And, since you clearly know where Polly and Jon are, you can cut out the concerned babysitter routine.' He glowered at her. 'Where exactly are they, by the way?'

'I can't be sure, but I think they've probably helped themselves to your flat.' She regarded him levelly. 'Jon took her there once before, on the pretext of showing her the Degas. The one you sold for a great deal of money to set up a trust fund for Matthew. Tell me, Grey, doesn't Jon know that the picture apparently hanging in its place is simply a very good copy? Or is he as devious as you? Did he take his own?'

He stared at her. 'The Degas is genuine. I'm not sure which of your questions that answers. Take your pick.'

'Steve told me about the sale, Grey. It was in the paper, for heaven's sake. And it might have slipped your memory, but you told me yourself that you sold it to help Robert out of some financial difficulty—'

'I did.'

'And now you have it back?'

'Robert's difficulty was not a lack of funds, it was simply moving them without attracting attention—' He stopped abruptly as the door behind her opened. 'Ah, Nancy, we were just saying that we should be getting back to the cottage. The fire will have gone out and everything will be freezing.'

'Have you had enough to eat—?'

'Yes, thank you,' Abbie broke in, standing up. 'I'll just clear up. Can I make you a fresh pot of tea?'

'No. Not just now. And leave the dishes, *bach*.' She lowered herself heavily into a seat in front of the fire.

'It's no trouble,' Abbie said.

But Grey reached for her coat and began to feed her arms into the sleeves. 'Time to go. We don't want to outstay our welcome.'

'You'll never do that, Grey,' Nancy said, with a laugh, but Abbie could see that she was already half asleep.

They grabbed their boots and put them on in the

porch. 'She just wanted to doze off for an hour. I told you, they don't seem to go to bed during the lambing season, but if we'd stayed she'd have felt obliged to keep awake.'

They looked in on Hugh on the way out of the yard and Abbie saw that her lambs had truly settled with their foster mother. Then they set off back to the cottage.

The walk was less daunting in the daylight, and with the sun sparkling on the snow, and the sea reflecting the pale blue of the winter sky in the distance, it seemed picture-postcard perfect. The curl of smoke drifting straight up from the cottage chimney in the still air seemed to bring a final touch to the glistening landscape. A promise of warmth. Abbie stopped suddenly and Grey turned to her.

'What's the matter?'

'There's someone in the cottage,' she said. 'The fire's lit. It can't possibly still be burning from last night.'

'Jon and Polly?'

They exchanged a look and broke into a slithering run. Grey was first through the door, shedding snow from his boots over the floor, and Abbie was close on his heels. They both came to an abrupt halt as the man bending over, prodding at the fire, looked up and smiled.

'Well, well, well,' he said, straightening. 'Mr and Mrs Lockwood, together again. How very charming.'

'What the hell—?'

'Steve?' Abbie could hardly believe her eyes. 'How on earth did you get here? Are the roads open?'

'I'm afraid not. I came down on Monday afternoon, my dear, not long after our somewhat heated discussion. I had a report from the man who was tailing him that young Master Jonathan Lockwood came here over the weekend and stocked the place up with groceries before beating it back to London. I knew it wouldn't be long before someone more interesting came along and I was right. Unfortunately the snow kept me in the village until this morning.'

He turned back to the fire and threw on another log. 'You really shouldn't go out and leave the place unlocked, you know. Anybody might come in and help themselves to your brandy. Or is it your brother's?' He picked up a glass and tipped it back. 'He has excellent taste.'

'I'm glad it meets with your approval. Now you are most welcome to leave and to take my wife with you. Presumably that is why you're here?'

Before Abbie could utter a word Steve Morley smiled. 'Sorry, old man. Quick thinking, I grant you. But you've blown it. Not that I ever really believed in this little broken-hearted charade of yours, Abbie.'

'Charade?' Abbie looked from Steve's self-satisfied face to Grey's angry mask and felt like slapping them both. 'What are you talking about?'

'It's all right, my dear, no need to keep up the pretence. I don't blame *you*. Your husband would do anything for his brother and you would do anything for him. In a perfect world, that's how it should be.'

'But—' she began, but Grey's fingers fastened around her wrist warningly.

'I doubt if I would have fallen for it in the first place if you hadn't seemed so genuinely shocked when I told you I had seen your loving husband lunching with a beautiful young woman.'

Abbie knew he was going to say something that

would destroy everything, and she had to stop him. 'Steve—' she said, taking half a step towards him, but Grey's hand held her fast.

'I think we should listen to the man, Abbie. Clearly he thinks he has a tale to tell. Since he's been kind enough to light the fire for us, why don't we take off our coats and join him in a glass of Robert's excellent brandy.'

Steve looked at Grey uncertainly. He knew what to expect when he was angry, but this calm, self-controlled mood clearly disturbed him far more. He shifted awkwardly as Grey finally released Abbie's wrist and helped her out of her coat.

'Fetch a couple of glasses, Abbie,' he said, with every appearance of good humour as he hung up their coats and stood their boots on the mat. Then he took the poker from an unresisting Steve Morley, riddled through the grate and made it up with the logs they had brought in the night before. 'Please, Mr Morley, do sit down and make yourself at home.'

It was extraordinary, Abbie thought, how a few seconds earlier Steve Morley had been in leering control of the situation, but, having too quickly accepted the invitation to make himself comfortable, he was now at a total disadvantage as Grey remained on his feet, leaning one elbow against the mantle, the poker swinging freely from his fingers. She handed Grey a glass an inch deep in the glowing amber spirit, and did not think twice about pouring another for herself. She was certain she was going to need it.

'So, Mr Morley. You saw me lunching with a beautiful young woman. I don't imagine that was just coincidence?'

'Hardly. Although I have to confess it was your brother I was expecting to see.'

'Then that answers my next question. Clearly it was Mrs Harper you were having followed, not me. So you thought you'd mention my little assignation to Abbie, hoping to pry loose some indiscretion…'

'Unfortunately it didn't work.' Abbie sank into the other chair as Steve replied, remembering the casual way that he had dropped it into the conversation that day at L'Escargot. Something about a 'pretty piece'. The man had an unbelievably vulgar turn of phrase. 'I mean, she'd been telling me that she wasn't going to take any more overseas jobs because she thought her marriage needed a little work, so I thought it was worth a chance. She was so shocked that I actually believed it…'

Abbie refused to look up, to face him, but she knew that Grey's eyes were on her. She could feel them burning into her brain. 'She's quite an actress, isn't she? I'm really very proud of her.'

Actress!

'You should be. When she told me that she had discovered her loving husband had been having an affair for months, that he had a child by another woman, well, I have to say that it isn't an award for photo-journalism she should have received, but an Academy Award.'

'Was she very convincing?'

'She convinced me.'

'Will you two stop talking about me as if I'm not here?'

Grey's hand rested lightly on her shoulder. 'Hush, love. Mr Morley has come a long way on a fool's errand, the least we can do is let him tell us just how big a fool he has been.'

'I'm not that much of a fool.' Steve regarded them both malevolently, all pretence of politeness wiped from his face. 'The minute you booked a seat on a flight to Atlanta I twigged. I mean, if my old lady had decided to walk away without any hassle, leaving me free and clear to get on with a new woman and a new baby, I sure as hell wouldn't have gone chasing after her.'

'Quite.'

'You should have seen your face. There you were, with your arms all wrapped nice and neat around each other, and I popped out of the bathroom.'

'It was quite an entrance.'

'Got carried away, did you, Abbie? Forgot I was there?' Steve shook his head. 'I have to admit that you put on the injured husband routine a treat, Mr Lockwood. I mean, I've seen the real thing and you still come top of the list.' He rubbed his jaw. 'I have the feeling you put everything you had into that punch you threw.'

Grey smiled slightly. 'If I convinced you, Mr Morley, the bruised knuckles were worth it.'

'But then there she was, weeping all over me, begging me not to put it in the papers.' Steve looked at Abbie. 'That's when she let you down, Mr Lockwood.'

Grey's fingers tightened on her shoulder. 'Let me down?'

'Well, there I was with a big broad shoulder, all ready to cry on, and under the circumstances you would have thought she would be grateful...'

'I'm afraid that there are some things that, even to protect my brother, I would not ask Abbie to bear.'

'Pity, that. Because when I got back from Atlanta I put the tail back on Mrs Harper. And guess what?'

'What?' Abbie was half out of her seat, the word uttered before her brain had engaged. She forced herself to relax back into the comfortable, baggy cushions. 'What happened then?'

'Well, to be sure Mr Grey Lockwood frequently drove Mrs Emma Harper to some quiet country house. In fact I have hundreds of photographs of them arriving at all kinds of interesting places.' He paused as Abbie drew in a long, shuddering breath. 'Try a drop of that brandy, my dear, it's really very good.'

'I think you should get on, Mr Morley.' There was hardly any change to that urbane tone, yet Abbie knew that Grey was very near the edge of losing his temper. 'You're taking too long to come to your point.'

'Oh, right. Where was I?' He turned to Abbie. 'Oh, yes, your supposedly estranged husband arriving at some discreet retreat with Mrs Harper. His car staying there all night for the world to see.'

Her hand was trembling on the heavy glass and she put it down before she dropped it.

'It's quite striking—not the sort of car you would mistake... But apparently only the car remained. I don't suppose I would ever have realised what was happening if I hadn't seen Mr Grey Lockwood, live on the ten o'clock news, discussing some benchmark case he'd won on behalf of his neighbourhood law centre, when his car was parked outside a house in St John's Wood.

But he must have realised his mistake, because by

the time I got to the house and rang the bell, with a photographer staking out every exit, well, there was Mr Grey Lockwood—a trifle short of breath, it's true, but wearing nothing more than a silk dressing gown—to open the door and invite us in for a nightcap. Since then Mrs Harper has been living quietly in a cottage on the river at Henley. And neither Mr Grey Lockwood or his brother have been near the house—not even in frogman's flippers.'

'That's all very illuminating, Mr Morley. What do you want me to say? That you've been a very clever boy?' Grey didn't wait for him to answer. 'Not quite clever enough, if you expected to find my brother *in flagrante* with Mrs Harper at Ty Bach.'

'Clever enough to have taken photographs of a cupboard full of baby equipment. Clever enough to have matched dates and times when *you* were supposed to be with Mrs Harper, but, oddly, your *brother* was also not available. And now I *know* that you two have been playing me for a fool—well, I have enough to make life extremely difficult for the Right Honourable Robert Lockwood, MP.'

'Why?' Abbie never had been able to understand why Steve Morley was so obsessed with hurting Robert.

'Why not? People like him set themselves above everyone else. It makes them a target.'

'No, they don't. Robert is a decent human being, trying to do a job.'

'He's a politician, with his sights set firmly on number ten. All holier than thou on the outside and cheating on his wife on the inside. And with you so close to the throne, so to speak, it was too good an opportunity to miss.' He drained his glass. 'You know, you were slow, Abbie. You should have taken the money I offered you to spill the beans. I mean, no one is as unselfish, as generous as you seemed to be. And a wronged woman would never have allowed her husband to get off scot-free. Human nature just isn't like that, is it?'

'Well, this has all been very illuminating, Mr Morley,' Grey said, moving towards the door. 'Don't let us keep you.'

Steve stood up a little uncertainly. 'Aren't you going to frisk me for the film?'

'Certainly not. That would be a gross infringement of your rights.'

'His rights!' Abbie exploded. 'What about our rights? He snooped, spied, took photographs…'

'He was only doing his job, Abbie. He didn't break in. The door was open. And you seem to forget that he very kindly lit the fire for us.'

'Oh, right… Perhaps we should invite him to stay for lunch?'

'There's no need to go that far. Besides, I'm sure he's absolutely dying to get to the nearest telephone. We shouldn't delay him.'

Steve Morley regarded Grey suspiciously. 'If you think the telephone lines being down will stop me, you're wrong. I have a portable telephone.'

'Of course you do. But I'm afraid it's not going to do you much good. Robert informed the Prime Minister that he would not be standing at the next election some time ago.'

'You think people won't still want to know—'

'But they do know. Or at least, they will. There will be a statement in the evening papers to the effect that he has resigned to spend more time with his family.' Steve Morley's snort of disgust made no impression upon Grey. 'His new family. Emma and Matthew. Jon, incidentally, is delighted with the arrangement. And I don't think the private life of an ex-politician will provide a great deal of news value. Not with the blizzard. And today's announcement that Mrs Susan Lockwood will be his party's candidate at the by-election.'

'What?' Steve Morley went white. He fumbled in his pocket for his portable telephone, but Grey plucked it from his hand before he could use it and removed the batteries, dropping them in his pocket before returning it to him.

'I'm afraid I really can't permit you to conduct your business under my roof. I'm fussy that way.' Grey glanced at his watch. 'But if you get a move on, you might catch the announcement on the one o'clock news.'

Steve did not need encouragement, he was already scrambling into his coat.

'It's such a pity,' Grey went on. 'You've been in the wrong place chasing the wrong story for the past couple of days, Mr Morley. You should have stayed in London; no doubt your paper's proprietor will want to know why you weren't at your desk.'

He took his coat from behind the door and stepped into his boots before opening the door. 'Now, I'll walk you down to the road. The lane can be treacherous in this weather, and I wouldn't want anything bad to happen to you.' He looked back at Abbie. 'I won't be long,' he said.

But as the door banged shut behind them she didn't find that promise particularly reassuring.

CHAPTER TEN

ABBIE waited. For a long time she sat beside the fire and waited for him to come back, to tell her that he understood what she had done, why she had done it. She waited for him to say that everything was going to be all right. But he didn't come back.

When an hour had passed, she got up, cleared away the glasses, put the kettle on the range and searched the freezer for something to eat. They would still have to eat. Ordinary everyday things, to keep her mind occupied. To keep her thoughts from dwelling on the nightmare of what she had done.

Pan-fried steak, jacket potatoes, tomato salad. She ticked them off on her fingers as she laid out the ingredients, looked for peppercorns and, to her astonishment, found that even those had been thought of by Polly. She turned with the tub in her hand and he was there, his silent figure filling the doorway. The peppers rattled betrayingly against the plastic container.

'I didn't hear you come in,' she said. She hadn't been hearing anything except the silent scream of her heart... 'You were gone a long time. Wh-what did you do to Steve?'

'Does it matter?' He glanced at the food. 'If we're having steak, there's a claret to go with it. I'll open it now if you'll pass me the corkscrew.'

'Corkscrew?' Why were they talking about corkscrews?

'In the drawer behind you.'

'Did you hurt him?' she asked, head down, hunting through the muddle of the drawer. If he had lost his temper it would have been better than this cold indifference.

'Should I have done? He was just doing his job, no matter how distasteful. I would have thought having to justify the cost of pursuing Robert for the last twelve months and coming up empty-handed to a stony-faced newspaper proprietor would be far more sobering than anything I could dish out.' He had moved up behind her, and he looked over her shoulder and fished out the corkscrew from a tangle of string, taking great care not to touch her. 'Besides, he has a hard chin.' He flexed his hand, as if remembering the pain.

She turned against the sink unit to face him. 'I'm sorry, Grey. I should have trusted you...' He shrugged and began to move away. 'Grey?' She put her hand on his sleeve. 'It was all a misunderstanding, don't you see?' His eyes remained blank of expression, cutting her off, freezing her out. 'Please, speak to me.'

'What do you want me to say, Abbie? I thought you were having an affair. You did go to some trouble to convince me of that, as I recall. You even managed to produce a naked man from your bathroom to prove the point.'

'I wanted you to be free—'

'Now I have to deal with the fact that when this creep who spies on decent people for a living told you that he saw me having *lunch* with another woman you decided that I was cheating on you. Three years of respect and trust and love get dumped and I don't even get a chance to defend myself? Can you have any idea what that feels like?'

He removed her fingers from his arm, walked out of the scullery, leaned his forehead against the heavy beam over the fire and stared down into the flames. He was hurting. She could see that, understand that, but while he had been playing games to keep Robert's indiscretions out of the newspapers she had been hurt too.

'Is that what you really think, Grey?' she asked from the doorway. 'Do you really believe that I thought for one moment that you were being unfaithful to me just because of what Steve said? I admit it was a jolt, but then I thought, Oh, *come on*, Abbie. This is Grey we're talking about. He might have been a bit distracted lately, not exactly willing to listen when you asked him to discuss the rest of your life, but he's a straight-down-the-line kind of a guy. If he'd found someone else he would tell you. He would *never* deceive you...'

He turned his head to look at her. 'Then why?'

'Because I saw you. With my own two eyes. I dropped by your office to take you out to lunch and as I got out of the taxi I saw you walking down the road. You were too far away for me to shout, but I could see you were going into the park so I followed you. Not to spy on you, simply to catch up with you so that I could be with you.

'And do you know what I saw then?' His face drained of colour but she didn't spare him. 'I saw you put your arm around a beautiful woman and then bend over and touch...' The words caught in her throat. 'I saw you touch her baby. So tenderly. So lovingly. You'd made it perfectly clear that you didn't want me to have your child and suddenly it all began to make sense—'

'No!' He straightened. 'Good grief, didn't I make it clear why I thought we should wait?'

'Matthew is the image of you when you were a baby.'

'He's the image of Robert too.' Then his eyes narrowed. 'How do you know what he looks like? Did you actually go across and look in his pram?'

'Women do that all the time. Look in prams, chat on park benches, tell total strangers all their problems. She never knew who I was.'

'You talked to Emma?'

'Yes, I talked to Emma.' It still hurt so much to remember that day. 'After you had gone I wanted to run away, pretend I hadn't seen anything. It was all so horrible.'

'But you couldn't?'

'Emma was so sweet, so open. And, considering her situation, very careless. I suppose she thought that she was safe because I was just another woman—a perfect stranger. Or maybe it was that she'd had to keep everything bottled up for too long and I just pushed the right buttons.' She gave a little shrug. 'Whatever. It all came pouring out. How her lover was a lawyer and a divorce would destroy his career—'

'Good grief, Abbie, divorced lawyers are ten a penny these days—like every other profession.'

'I know. And Robert is a lawyer too,' she said, with a little sigh. 'But it's so long since he practised that it never even occurred to me. All I could think of was poor Henry.'

'Henry? But that was different—he got involved with a client. He *caused* the divorce, for heaven's sake...' His head went back. 'You thought that Emma had been my client?'

'There was a mark where she had worn a ring. It seemed...possible.'

'I sometimes forget that you're a journalist as well as a photographer, Abbie.'

'Not often enough, it seems. That's why you didn't tell me, isn't it? Did you think I'd put my career before my family?'

'No, of course not,' he said impatiently. Then he crossed to her, took her hands. 'I was simply trying to protect you, Abbie.'

His hands had been by the fire and were warm against her cold fingers. She looked up into his eyes. 'Protect me?' He'd said that before, and suddenly it made sense.

'From the likes of Steve Morley, who is just as good as you are at pressing the right buttons. And a great deal more ruthless about it.'

'I see.' And she did see. 'The trouble is, my love, that while you were busy convincing the rest of the world that it was *you* having an affair with Emma Harper, you convinced me as well.'

'It never crossed my mind that you would jump to conclusions and walk out without even giving me an opportunity to explain the situation. Besides, you were away so much—'

'That it didn't matter?'

'Of course it mattered,' he said bleakly. 'But you saw the lengths Steve Morley was prepared to go to. If he'd thought you'd had any idea what was going on he wouldn't have given you a moment's peace. I suppose he told you about the trust fund for Matthew too?'

'No, he never mentioned it. He told me that he'd seen you, and that you'd sold the Degas, that was all.'

'Then how did you find out about it?'

'Even after I'd talked to Emma, seen Matthew, I tried to tell myself that it couldn't be true. That there had to be some explanation. But I had to know, Grey. So I came home and checked the credit card statements—and there it was, in black and white. All those trips to Wales when I was away. And for the day you told me you'd driven back from Manchester there was a voucher from a petrol station on the M4. It's odd, but I knew you weren't telling me the truth about that, but I couldn't think why. Lying is so alien to you that I just let it go.'

'It's the only direct lie I ever told you.'

'It must have been extremely inconvenient to have me arrive home unexpectedly. I don't suppose I'd have even known you'd been away but for that.' His silence answered her question. 'Indirect lies are just as bad, Grey,' she said.

'Yes, I suppose they are. I was trying to do the best I could for everyone.'

She pulled her hands away from his, shivered and walked across to the fire. She held out her hands to it, rubbed her arms. 'I saw the letter from the bank,' she said. 'Considering the circumstances, I thought it was rather careless of you to leave it lying around.'

'It was meant to be indiscreet. I'd had a copy leaked to Morley and I thought that would put an end to the matter until Robert could settle his affairs and leave the government without a scandal.'

'Well, lucky old Robert.'

'He only ever wanted to be a farmer, Abbie. But he knew that Dad expected him to follow him into the firm, and then Susan came along and she had much bigger plans for him. Robert was to be Prime Minister by the time he was fifty.'

'What about Susan? She's not really going to sit back and let Robert quietly resign from his post and then divorce her?'

'Well, yes, actually, she is. She comes from a family where the men do things and the women make the tea. She thought that was the way it had to be. But I convinced her that it isn't. She really is going to stand for his seat in the by-election. Politics was *her* ambition, Abbie. It was the frustration of seeing Robert do the things that she knew she could do as well—better, perhaps—that drove her crazy with jealousy. She's a changed woman.'

'I'm glad. Very glad it's all worked out so well for everyone.' She turned abruptly away from him. 'Now, if you'll excuse me, I have to get on with lunch.'

'Lunch can wait, Abbie.' His hands were on her shoulders and her shoulders were shaking. 'Oh, look, you're crying.' He turned her round to face him. 'You shouldn't be crying.' He pulled her rigid body close, so that her tears flooded onto his sweater. He tucked his fingers under her chin and lifted her face to his. It was serious, deadly serious. 'It's all over, Abbie. You know that, don't you?'

Over. She had thought it was over six months ago. She'd thought she had lost him, but she hadn't lost him—she had thrown him away. 'I didn't trust you enough. I've hurt you—' She tried to pull free, but he wasn't letting her go. Instead he stroked away the tears from her cheeks with his fingers.

'Hurt?' he murmured softly. 'I didn't think it was possible to suffer so much and still live.'

'Do you think I don't know.' She knew that pain only too well, and she closed her eyes to blot out the agony of it. 'I'm sorry, Grey. I don't know what else to say.'

'Words won't do it, Abbie.' The tiny bud of hope that had begun to unfurl in her heart shrank back. 'Of course,' he continued, 'you could always try kissing me better.'

She lifted tear-jewelled lashes, saw the gold sparks heating the depths of his eyes. 'There's an awful lot of you to kiss, Grey. I—I really wouldn't know where to begin.'

'Then let me show you.' He dropped a kiss on the top of her head and it somehow fluttered down onto her forehead. 'You see? You start at the top and just...work down.'

His mouth brushed her temple, the high, blushing cheekbone, the delicate hollow beneath her jaw, and suddenly it was not a game any more, and as his lips lightly crossed hers the glorious weakness in her legs left her clinging to him. For a moment they were suspended there, lips a millimetre apart.

'I love you so much, Abbie,' Grey murmured huskily. 'So very much.' And then his lips were on hers, sweet, demanding, loving, telling her that the nightmare was over. After a long while he lifted his head. 'Do you think you've got the hang of it so far, my love?'

She was *his* love. His *love*. Was it possible that she could ever show him how much he was hers? Steadying herself with her hands on his shoulders, she stood up on her toes, determined to try. 'I can't reach the top,' she said.

'No?' His smile was teasing as he stood there, straight as a ramrod, making no attempt to help her by bending, even a little bit.

'I'm afraid...' she began and he waited, not making any effort to ease her difficulty. 'I'm afraid that I'm going to have to ask you to lie down.'

He regarded her with the slow, teasing smile that seemed to go on and on for ever. 'Abbie?'

'What is it?'

'You will be gentle with me?'

Her own mouth straightened into the widest smile. 'Don't count on it, Grey Lockwood—' But the threat disintegrated into a scream as he picked her up and carried her up the stairs.

'Abbie?' She turned sleepily in his arms and nestled against his shoulder. 'I love you. I don't know how to tell you how much I love you.'

She opened her eyes, wide awake now. 'You punched Steve Morley on the chin. That says it all. I should have known. I mean, if a louse like Steve could work it out, why couldn't I?'

'I still don't understand why you didn't say anything. Most women would have screamed, raged, smashed the china. Keeping you in the dark about what was really happening was bad enough...but what you thought was going on has driven less balanced women to murder.' He drew her closer into the curve of his arm. 'But then you always were cool under pressure.'

'Oh, not that cool. I wanted to hurt you, Grey. I was going to plaster your family in headlines a foot high across the tabloids. And then Susan rang and it was like hearing an echo of the words in my head. Horrible words. Hateful words.' Grey turned to her, held her comfortingly in his arms. 'I know that some of it was my fault, you see. I was never there. I was always away chasing the perfect story, the one that would make my name. And I thought you had found someone to fill the gap. A delicate, beautiful, *little* part-time wife.'

He swore softly. 'I didn't mean it, idiot. I love every inch of you.'

'Do you?'

'All seventy-one of them,' he assured her seriously.

'Seventy!' She flung a fist at his shoulder and he laughed. 'Rat,' she murmured, but, as he proceeded to kiss every inch to prove his point, it was a while before she could continue.

'I thought if I went away for good, made you think it didn't matter, you could get on with your new life. No complications, no guilt.'

'You really did that for me?' He rocked her gently. 'Oh, Abbie, sweetheart, is it any wonder that Steve Morley didn't believe it? Self-sacrifice is the purest of all the emotions. I doubt he's ever encountered it before.'

Abbie was cooking breakfast when there was a sharp rap at the door. 'Come in,' she called, expecting to see Hugh. But it was the postman who put his head around the door.

'Is this yours?' he asked, holding out her bag. 'I found it down the lane, sticking out of the snow.'

'Oh, yes. Thank you so much for bringing it all the way up here.'

'I had to come anyway. I've a letter for you. Sorry for the delay—it should have been here Tuesday, but the roads have only just opened up.' It was postmarked with Monday's date and addressed to Mr and Mrs Lockwood.

'How is it out there?' she asked, turning it over.

'Passable. Although I see someone ended up in the ditch.'

'Oh, that was me, I'm afraid. No damage done, except to the car. If you're going into the village can you get someone to tow it down to the garage for me?' The postman, quite used to unusual requests from the more isolated dwellings on his round, assured her that it would be done.

'What's that?'

Abbie looked up as Grey walked down the stairs. 'A letter. From Polly and Jon, I think.'

'Oh, Lord, the runaway lovers. I'd forgotten all about them. What do they have to say for themselves?'

She opened it and began to read. '"Dear Abbie and Grey (I hope you don't mind me calling you that, but Dear Abbie and Mr Lockwood sounded silly)..."'

Abbie looked up and met Grey's eyes. 'Do you mind?' she asked.

He leaned forward, dropped a kiss on her waiting mouth and grinned. 'What do you think?'

'"Jon and I decided that since neither of you are in the least bit happy living apart we would have to do something to get you together so that you could sort out your problems. I know you think that Grey was having an affair, Abbie, but Jon says he wasn't—"'

'And how would Jon know?' Grey wondered idly,

his arms sliding around her waist, pulling her back against him so that he could nuzzle her neck.

'Shh. "Anyway, you seem to have had such good times at Ty Bach that I thought that was the best place for you to be. Jon agreed."'

'He had a choice?'

Abbie giggled. '"Talk to one another, take all the time you need. I'm staying with Jennie Blake and Jon has gone to stay with his mother for half-term, so sadly no passion *this time*, and you needn't worry about either of us. Much love, Polly and Jon."'

'"Talk to one another..." You were right, Abbie. She's a clever little minx,' Grey said.

'Mmm. She'll need to be when she tries to explain to her mother just how I came to write off her car.'

'I'll sort out the insurance for her.'

'The sooner the better. The postman says the roads are passable.'

'In a hurry to leave, are you? Some assignment that just won't wait?' There was just the faintest tension in his voice, and she turned and slipped her arms about his neck.

'No, love. Nothing in the whole wide world that won't wait.'

'Then I don't think we should take any chances. Leave it a day or two...' But as he began to kiss her it was her turn to tense.

'Grey! The bacon's burning.'

Without pausing in what he was doing, he reached behind her and pulled the pan from the hob.

Margaret, deeply sun-tanned and equally flustered, whispered, 'Why on earth didn't you let me know, Abbie? I would have come back earlier.' She smiled at Grey as he closed the boot. 'He is gorgeous! And you look wonderful too. How did it happen?'

'Ask Polly,' she said, laughing. 'She's got a lot to tell you.'

Margaret turned to her daughter, frowning a little as she noticed the antique gold locket that hung at her throat—her reward from Grey for playing cupid. 'Has she been a nuisance?' she asked anxiously.

'No, she's been quite wonderful. She can come and stay any time she likes.' She hugged Polly and they exchanged a conspiratorial grin. 'And...er...I'll leave her to explain why you've got a new car.'

'What?' And, while Margaret was busy opening the garage door and exclaiming over the shiny up-to-date model lodged within, Abbie slipped into the passenger seat of the Mercedes beside Grey.

'Ready to go home?' he asked.

'I can't wait. I've got a new job lined up.'

'So soon? I thought...' He gave a little shrug, then leaned forward and started the engine. Then he turned it off again. 'No, damn it! I will *not* be quiet. I don't want you to go rushing off all over the world. I want you at home. With me.'

Abbie slotted in her seat belt and then looked up at him through her long dark lashes. 'Grey Lockwood, are you planning to be terribly masterful and forbid me to work?' she enquired softly.

'Why don't you try me?' he growled.

'I'm almost tempted,' she replied, then, as his eyes gleamed dangerously, she held up her hands in mock surrender. 'Only kidding, my love. I promise. Actually, I'm going to be working from home—that's why I'm so eager to get back into a routine. Secret lunchtime trysts are a lot of fun, but this new project needs my full attention.'

'I see.' Slightly mollified, he restarted the engine. 'When were you planning to start this new project?'

'Mmm? Oh, it's already under way.'

'Already? When did this—?' He stopped himself. 'Look, can't you put it on hold? I wanted to take you away. Somewhere warm, just the two of us.'

'Oh, I'd like that.'

'You're sure it won't interfere with your new *project*?' he asked, just a little tetchily.

'Oh, no, it'll be quite perfect. I can arrange for the decorator to be in while we're away.'

'Decorator!' He threw a startled glance at her.

'Yes. I'm going to need a special room, you see. I thought the study would be best, since it's next door to the bathroom. It will be easiest for the plumbing.' He didn't answer, and she leaned forward to look into his face. 'You don't seem very interested in my new venture. It's really very exciting.'

'I'm capable of providing all the excitement you can handle.' Then he added, with a lift of one shoulder, 'You should have discussed it with me first. We always used to discuss things.'

'I had intended to, but this just sort of cropped up...quite unexpectedly.'

'I see. Do you want me to do anything? Apart from evacuate the study, that is?'

Abbie smiled serenely. 'I think you've done everything you can for now, love, but I will need your help from time to time during the next few months—on a fairly regular basis. Don't worry, I'll give you plenty of notice. Then it's just a question of holding my hand, giving me some support during the crucial period. I don't want you disappearing on some... um...case conference at the vital moment.'

Her mischievous smile robbed the words of their sting, but nevertheless his dark brows drew into the slightest frown. 'I imagine you're going to need some finance. Plumbing can be expensive. And the kind of equipment you'll need for a darkroom.'

'Darkroom?' Her grey eyes danced. 'Whatever gave you the idea I was going to build a darkroom?'

'You're a photographer—what else...?' He pulled into the kerb and turned to her. 'Tell me, Abbie, does this project of yours have any particular time-scale?'

She dropped her lashes demurely. 'Well, the initial production period is about nine months. After that it's...well, I suppose it's a lifetime.'

There was a moment's silence, then he reached across and took her hands. He was trembling and she clasped his fingers to steady them. 'You're having my baby?' he breathed. 'Are you certain? I mean... Oh, dear God, I don't know what I mean.'

'You don't mind? Last time we talked about it you weren't exactly enthusiastic. In fact, you were really rather angry about the whole thing.'

'Oh, my love. When you said that you wanted to start a family I had one moment of utter joy and then agony, as I realised that it couldn't happen—not then. That was why I was so angry. I was angry with Robert and Susan and Emma. Most of all I was angry with myself, for getting involved in all their stupid deceptions.'

He stared down at their interlocked fingers. 'And then, when you seemed to be treating the whole thing as something to be got over with so that you could carry on with your career...I was angry with you.' He looked up. 'I was wrong, wasn't I? Completely wrong.' He released his seat belt and hers and put his hand very gently on her waist. 'He's there. A life we've made together. Abbie and Grey Lockwood made into a new person.'

'You're sure it's going to be a boy?' she teased.

'It doesn't matter.' He took her into his arms and held her. 'Abbie, I don't know what to say—how to tell you how much I love you. You are so beautiful, so good, so generous in your love that I can hardly believe that you're mine. I'll always be there for you,' he said, suddenly fierce. 'Always.'

She took his face in her hands and kissed him, very gently. 'I think we should continue this conversation at home. We seem to have an audience.'

He looked around, saw three small boys staring at them from across the road and turned back to her with a grin. 'They're not interested in us, love. They're just looking at the car.'

'Are you sure?'

'Trust me,' he said. Then, as the darkness in his eyes intensified, Abbie sensed that he was no longer talking about the small boys. He was asking her to trust him for the rest of their lives.

'With all my heart, Grey,' Abbie murmured softly. 'With my life itself.'

Then, with a soft groan, Grey Lockwood took his wife into his arms and, mindless of their small audience, he kissed her.

Jessica Hart had a haphazard career before she began writing to finance a degree in history. Her experience ranged from waitress, theatre production assistant and outback cook to newsdesk secretary, expedition PA and English teacher, and she has worked in countries as different as France and Indonesia, Australia and Cameroon. She now lives in the north of England, where her hobbies are limited to eating and drinking and travelling when she can, preferably to places where she'll find good food or desert or tropical rain.

To find out more about Jessica Hart, visit her website at www.jessicahart.co.uk
And if you're looking for a story with extra fizz and sparkle, Jessica's fresh, feel-good writing style shines wonderfully in her next book . . .

Don't miss:
The Honeymoon Prize **by Jessica Hart
in Tender Romance™, July 2002**

WORKING GIRL

by
Jessica Hart

For Ali and Fully

CHAPTER ONE

IT WAS like running into a rock.

'Ouf!' Head down, struggling with her heavy suitcase, Phyllida didn't notice the man heading for the same terminal door until she cannoned into him. She hadn't known that a man's body could feel so solid.

The force of the impact drove the breath from her lungs, and she staggered back and would have tripped over her suitcase if a hand hadn't shot out to catch her and set her back on her feet.

'Careful!' The iron grip on her arm relaxed as Phyllida recovered her balance and looked up to find a man regarding her frowningly.

He was deeply tanned, with brown hair and a cool, watchful face, and her first thought was that he was not as big as he had seemed when she had run into the powerful body. Its strength was unmistakable, but kept compact and very controlled. Her second was that he looked distinctly unfriendly.

'Don't you think it would be an idea to look where you're going with that thing?' he said, nodding down at the huge suitcase, which had toppled over onto its side. His voice managed to be deep and cool at the same time.

Phyllida, who had opened her mouth to apologise, felt unaccountably ruffled. She was still jarred and breathless from the collision, and she rubbed her arm where he had gripped her.

'I'm in a hurry,' she said, rather more sharply than she

had intended. But, after all, *he* hadn't apologised for running into *her* had he? 'I didn't see you.'

'Obviously not.'

The sardonic note in his voice made her glance up from her arm, and her heart jerked strangely as she found herself looking into his eyes. They were a dark, guarded green, almost grey, and disconcertingly observant.

Phyllida was suddenly conscious of how she must look. She had been travelling for over thirty-seven hours, and was sure that she looked as tired and crumpled as she felt. Her cream and white suit, which had looked so smart in London, was irretrievably creased, and the gold shoes which matched her belt were pinching painfully at her swollen feet.

Phyllida wasn't a tall girl, but usually there was a dynamism about her that more than made up for her lack of inches. Unfortunately, this man with his faintly contemptuous gaze would be hard put to it to spot any dynamism at the moment. All he would see was that she was short and flustered, and that her face was bright red after the race between the terminals.

He could probably see that the backs of her tights were badly laddered, too. He had that sort of look about him.

'My plane from London only landed a few minutes ago,' she found herself explaining. 'We were hours late, but someone said I might be just in time to catch the last flight to Port Lincoln if I hurried. I've just run all the way from the international terminal...' She tailed off. Why was she telling him all this? He wasn't interested in her nightmare journey.

She glanced distractedly at her watch. Eight-forty. The flight was due to leave in five minutes.

'In that case, how inconsiderate of me to get in your way,' said the man.

There was something in his voice, an undercurrent of derision, that made Phyllida's hackles rise. Typical man—superior, patronising, determined to make a woman feel unreasonable, whatever she did! She had had enough of men like that recently. It was just her luck that the first man she came across in Australia had to conform to type!

Lips tightening, she bent to set her case back on its wheels. She was supposed to be able to pull it along behind her, but it kept slewing sideways, scraping itself down the back of her legs as it did so. Her tights were ruined and her ankles would be black and blue tomorrow.

Phyllida had learned to hate the wheels with a deep and passionate loathing since she had left her flat. Unfortunately, the case was too heavy for her to carry any other way.

The man was watching her struggle to right it. Leaning down with a muttered exclamation, he made to lift the case, but Phyllida had heard the irritable click of the tongue, and it only seemed to confirm her opinion of him. He was just like all the rest—convinced that a woman couldn't do anything for herself.

'I can manage!' she snapped, glaring at him.

'You don't look as if you're managing very well,' he pointed out, with that same hatefully sardonic edge. 'Wouldn't it make life easier if you travelled with a case that wasn't almost as big as you are?'

Phyllida's chin came up at his sarcasm. 'I may be small, but it doesn't mean my brain is!' she said defiantly. 'Why do men always think women are incapable of looking after themselves? I've managed to get myself to the other side of the world without some patronising man telling me how I ought to travel or how much I need to pack.'

As if to prove her point, she managed to haul the case up with a grunt of effort. She shot him a look of triumph. 'See? I can cope quite well by myself!'

The man was unimpressed. 'It looks more like struggling than coping to me,' he said. 'Personally, I'd have preferred to have had a chance of catching my plane than to try and prove a point. But if you think you can get that case to the check-in desk just as quickly by yourself, you'd better carry on—and if you want to catch the Port Lincoln flight, I should forget about your principles and hurry!'

'That's precisely what I was doing,' said Phyllida frostily. Still breathing hard, she took hold of the lead. In theory, the case was supposed to glide along behind you, like a particularly well-behaved dog, but it never seemed to work like that in practice.

'Now, if you'll excuse me?' she added, with awful politeness. But her grand manner didn't really fit the small, slight figure in the crumpled suit, and a disturbing gleam of amusement sprang into the grey-green eyes.

'Of course,' he said, with equally insincere politeness.

Humiliatingly certain that he found her ridiculous, Phyllida stuck her chin in the air and tried to stalk off towards the row of check-in desks, but her dignified departure was ruined by the fact that she had only taken two steps before the case promptly toppled over again.

Betrayed into an extremely unladylike word, Phyllida wrestled it upright again, very conscious of the man's cool, amused eyes on her back. Her cheeks burned with mortification, and an obscure conviction that it was somehow all his fault.

The case fell over twice before she reached the check-in desks, and by then, of course, it was too late anyway. The young official behind the counter was sympathetic, but positive. The flight had gone, and there wouldn't be another to Port Lincoln until the following day.

Phyllida had known she was too late, but she had been hoping against hope that this flight would be delayed—like every other one on her marathon journey from London—and the knowledge that she had missed it by minutes only made things worse.

She slumped against the check-in desk in despair. She was beginning to wish that she'd never decided to come to Australia. Her rushed departure, the long delays and missed connections, the cramped conditions and ghastly food, the two-year-old across the aisle who had screamed for hours on end... She had gritted her teeth and endured them all, promising herself that it would all be worth it when she got to Port Lincoln.

Chris and Mike would be there, and they would welcome her in, and she could throw her hateful suitcase to the back of a wardrobe and forget about it for three months. Phyllida had set her heart on being there that night, and the news that her arrival would have to be delayed yet again brought her close to tears of exhaustion and sheer frustration.

Out of the corner of her eye, she could see the man she had bumped into at the terminal door. She wouldn't have been able to catch the flight anyway, so it was quite illogical to blame him for the fact that she had missed it, but Phyllida still eyed him with resentment.

He was chatting to an airline official a few yards away, looking infuriatingly cool and assured. Phyllida wished she felt like that. She wondered where he was going. He was wearing beautifully cut trousers and a short-sleeved shirt and tie, so understated they had to be expensive. His only luggage was an equally discreet leather briefcase, so he couldn't be going far.

Was he going back to a home, a family? There was something self-contained about him that made it hard to imagine him surrounded by wife and children, she decided, then abruptly changed her mind as he smiled at something his companion had said.

The effect was totally unexpected, dissolving the guarded expression into warmth and humour and softening the rather hard lines of his face. Even from some distance away Phyllida could see how white his teeth were against his tan, and she felt as if she had run into him all over again. Why hadn't she seen what an attractive man he was before?

Stunned by the transformation, Phyllida had momentarily forgotten her own situation, but as she stared he looked over unexpectedly, and across the empty terminal their eyes met with a jolting sensation. His expression was unnervingly keen, and Phyllida stiffened, only too aware of how she must appear, slumped wearily against the counter. She was sure she could read mockery in those grey-green eyes. He was probably remembering her proud boast that she could manage perfectly well by herself.

And so she could. Phyllida straightened. She had decided to arrive in Port Lincoln tonight, and she would get there if it killed her—if only to prove that she could to the stranger with the unsettling eyes and the unexpected smile. The fact that he would never know if she succeeded was forgotten. All that mattered was showing him that she wouldn't let herself be beaten by anything!

She smiled appealingly at the young man behind the desk. In spite of her tiredness, there was still some bounce in the glossy nut-brown hair that was cut in a short bob to frame a gamine face with a pert nose and a pair of wide, expressive brown eyes.

'Isn't there *any* way I can get to Port Lincoln tonight?' she pleaded, and let him see the shimmer of tears in her eyes.

Few men were proof against Phyllida's wide brown gaze. 'I really am sorry,' he said regretfully. 'But unless—' He broke off as he caught sight of someone over her shoulder.

'You might be in luck after all!' He grinned. 'That's Jake Tregowan. He flies his own plane, and it looks as if he's heading back to Port Lincoln now. If you asked him, I'm sure he'd give you a lift.' He waved an arm. 'Jake! Have you got a moment?'

Even before she turned, something told Phyllida who Jake Tregowan would be.

It was him. Of course it was him. He was walking towards them with a deliberate, unhurried tread, the disconcerting eyes alight with mockery as they rested on her face.

Phyllida's heart sank. Why did it have to be him? The one person who could help her; the one person she couldn't ask. She winced as she remembered how she had scorned his help with her case, had boasted about the fact that she didn't need a man to get from A to B.

Jake was exchanging greetings with the young man behind the desk. He seemed to be on first-name terms with everyone here, she thought sourly. He must spend his whole time at the airport. He was standing a couple of feet away, but she could sense the coiled power of his body as if it were pressed against her.

The thought made her shiver. Jake glanced towards her, one brow raised enquiringly.

'This lady's plane from England was delayed, and she's missed her connection,' her champion explained.

'She's very anxious to get to Port Lincoln tonight. Are you on your way back there now?'

'Yes,' said Jake, deliberately ignoring his cue to offer her a lift.

Phyllida bit her lip. She couldn't really blame him, not after all she had had to say before. Tiredness washed over her. She didn't want to swallow her pride and beg him for a lift; she didn't want to go anywhere with him. What she really wanted to do was sit down and cry, but she couldn't do that—not with him watching her with that sardonic expression of his.

And she *did* want to get to Port Lincoln. If she could just get to Chris and Mike, everything would be all right. She had reached the point where that was all that mattered.

Clenching her jaw, Phyllida pressed the betraying waver of her lips fiercely together and looked Jake straight in the eye. 'My name's Phyllida Grant,' she said with some difficulty. 'If you're flying to Port Lincoln, I'd be very grateful if you'd take me with you.'

'Surely you don't mean you want some help after all?' he mocked. 'I thought you were quite capable of getting yourself to Port Lincoln without any patronising male assistance?'

Phyllida gritted her teeth. 'I would have been if I hadn't missed the last flight,' she said.

'And that was presumably my fault, for letting myself be run into?'

'No,' she admitted honestly. 'I was too late anyway.' She pushed her fringe off her forehead, leaving the shiny brown hair sticking out at different angles like a small child's.

She was wondering if she should try to explain that the collision in the doors had just been the culmination of a series of small disasters that had begun six weeks ago, when she had lost her job and thrown Rupert's ring back in his face. Nothing had gone right since then, but Phyllida had carried on doggedly, refusing to let herself be beaten by circumstance.

Looking at Jake Tregowan's cool, guarded features, she didn't think he would understand. Things would never dare go wrong for him. In the end, she simply passed her hand over her face in an age-old gesture of weariness. 'It's been a long trip,' was all she said.

Jake looked at her, a small, tense figure standing by her huge suitcase. She wasn't a beautiful girl, but the wide brown eyes, tilted nose and curving mouth had a charm and piquancy of their own, and there was something gallant in the stubborn way she was keeping the tears at bay. She looked defiant, determined...and very tired.

He sighed. 'You'd better come with me,' he said resignedly.

'Thank you,' said Phyllida, a little wary of his sudden change in attitude, but too relieved at the prospect of getting to Port Lincoln to ask why.

'I'm leaving right now,' he warned, as if regretting his decision already.

'That's all right.' She reached down for her suitcase. 'I'm ready.'

'Let's go, then.' Jake strode off without another word, leaving Phyllida to thank the young official behind the counter for his help and hurry after him.

She was hampered as usual by her wretched case, which lurched from side to side no matter how carefully she pulled it. She was very aware of Jake, who had halted impatiently and was watching her awkward progress with an expression of barely disguised exasperation. He hadn't offered to carry her case, and there was no way she was going to ask him, Phyllida told herself. Swallowing her pride over the lift had been bad enough.

'Ouch!' She hadn't been concentrating, and the case had keeled over, raking one corner down the back of her legs before falling with a heavy thud that echoed down the empty corridor.

'You appear to be having some difficulty,' said Jake. 'Or is this another example of you coping by yourself?'

Phyllida had been rubbing her calf, but now she aimed a childish kick at the case. 'It's supposed to run along on wheels,' she complained, with a venomous look at it. 'But they keep swivelling round so that it can savage the back of my legs.' She twisted her leg round so that he could see the full extent of the damage. 'Look, my tights are ruined!'

Jake wasn't interested in her laddered tights. 'There's no point in blaming the case,' he said astringently. 'It's not designed to take that kind of weight. If you'd packed less, it might work better.'

'I had to leave half my clothes behind as it was,' Phyllida grumbled. 'What's the point in having a case if you can't fill it?'

'What's the point in having a case you can't carry?' he retorted as she struggled to lift it up from the floor.

'I *can*—' Phyllida began to protest, jaw clenched with effort as she heaved at the case. But she was interrupted by Jake's exclamation of impatience.

Putting her aside with hard hands, he took the case from her. 'You can't carry it, can you?'

Phyllida looked at the floor. 'No,' she muttered.

'Pardon?'

'No, I can't carry it!' she shouted, provoked just as he had intended. 'It's too heavy and I wish I had brought a smaller one.' She glared at him. 'There! Satisfied now, or would you like me to write it out fifty times and sign every page in triplicate?'

Jake looked down at her. He wasn't exactly smiling, but the cool eyes were gleaming with humour, and the crease at the corner of his mouth had deepened almost imperceptibly. 'Haven't you ever heard of giving in graciously?'

'I don't like giving in.' Phyllida's chin was set at a stubborn angle, and Jake eyed her with amusement as he bent to pick up the case.

'You might have to learn to get used to it,' he said.

Phyllida watched resentfully as he carried her case with perfect ease. It might as well have been empty for all the strain it showed in the muscles of his arms, and she found herself remembering again how strong and solid his body had been when she had bumped against him. The memory was uncomfortably vivid.

Jake kicked open a swing-door and held it open for her with his foot. Outside, a row of small planes was parked on the tarmac, and Phyllida trailed past after him to where a tiny plane with a propeller on its nose stood at the end of the line. Jake pulled open the door in its side, threw in her case, and then swung himself easily up after it.

Phyllida stopped dead, appalled at the sight of the flimsy little plane. 'We're not going in *that*?'

'What were you expecting? Concorde?'

'I thought you'd have your own jet,' she said, confused. It was the only kind of private plane she had ever come across before.

'A private jet would be very nice, but a touch ostentatious for flying between Port Lincoln and Adelaide,' said Jake drily. 'This is more than adequate.'

She looked doubtfully at the propeller. 'It's not very...*big*, is it?'

'It can take four people if necessary, so it should be quite big enough for you, me and even your suitcase. Of course,' he added, 'you can stay behind and catch a flight tomorrow morning if you prefer. It won't make any difference to me.'

'No,' said Phyllida quickly. She wasn't going to turn back when she was this close to Port Lincoln. 'I mean, I'd like to come, thank you.'

Jake reached a hand down from the doorway. 'Well, if you're going to come, come on!'

Phyllida looked up at him. The doorway was about level with her shoulder. 'Haven't you got any steps?'

'No,' he said bluntly. 'There are some steps back in the terminal, but if you think I'm going to go back and get them for you, you've got another think coming!'

'How am I supposed to get in, then?'

'You've got arms and legs, haven't you? Just take my hand and climb up!'

'Climb? I'd need a pole vault to get up there!'

'Don't be ridiculous,' said Jake, his patience rapidly running out. 'It's perfectly easy. Here, take my hand.'

He reached down, and Phyllida took his hand reluctantly, conscious of a strange jolt of reaction all the way down her spine as his fingers closed firmly around hers. They were warm and strong and infinitely reassuring, and she looked at their linked hands in surprise that she could feel so much from a simple clasp.

Jake sighed. 'I don't know about you, Phyllida, but I've got better things to do than stand here all night holding hands. Now, if you want to stay here in Adelaide, that's fine by me. But if you want to come to Port Lincoln, then hurry up and get on with it!'

Phyllida did try. She managed to get one arm and a shoulder onto the floor of the plane, while Jake hauled on the other one, but her legs flailed around hopelessly, hampered by her short skirt, and in the end she fell back, panting with humiliation.

'I told you I couldn't get up there,' she gasped. 'I'm not Superwoman!'

'That's not the impression you were giving earlier on,' Jake pointed out with some acidity. 'Although if you were as capable as you claimed, you wouldn't even have considered travelling in a skirt like that.'

'Had I known that I was going to be taking part in an obstacle course, I would have worn my tracksuit!' snapped Phyllida, forgetting for a moment that she was quite dependent on Jake Tregowan's good nature if she wanted to get to Port Lincoln tonight. She brushed at the sleeve of her jacket, where she had clung to the floor of the plane. 'As it is, this suit will never be the same again!'

Muttering under his breath, Jake jumped out of the plane and landed lightly beside her. 'Frankly, your suit is the least of my worries at the moment,' he said. He glanced from Phyllida to the plane, as if judging the distance, then put his hands to her waist and hoisted her bodily up towards the door.

Phyllida squeaked in surprise at finding herself suddenly grabbed, but managed to clutch at the opening. She was very aware of the hard hands at her waist, hands that slid impersonally down her legs as he pushed her up until she could collapse in an inelegant heap inside the plane.

For a long moment she just lay there, gasping like a landed fish and wondering what on earth she was doing sprawled on the floor of some tinpot aeroplane with a disagreeable stranger stepping over her as if she was of no more importance than a sack of potatoes—which was exactly what she felt like.

'Welcome aboard,' said Jake, with an unmistakable edge of dry amusement.

Phyllida struggled wearily into a sitting position and looked down at her filthy hands. 'British Airways was never like this,' she sighed, and Jake's mouth twitched into a smile—the same devastating smile that she had noticed across the terminal. His teeth gleamed in the dim light as he reached down and helped her to her feet with what she was sure was mock gallantry.

'Service is everything,' he said.

Phyllida took her hand from his rather quickly, alarmed by the way all the nerves down her spine seemed to shiver whenever he touched her. His smile made her edgy. It wasn't at all the sort of smile she would have expected him to have. He should have a cool, contained smile to go with his cool, contained image. Not a smile with this warmth that tugged at her own mouth in response even as it dried the breath in her throat.

She dragged her eyes away from it with an effort. Desperate for a distraction, she looked around her with spurious interest, but his smile still danced tantalisingly in front of her eyes. She had to shake her head to banish it. 'Where's the pilot?' she asked, once she could see properly again.

'You seem to have very strange ideas of my grandeur, Phyllida,' said Jake drily, pointing her towards the co-pilot's seat. 'I hate to disappoint you, but not only do I not have a private jet, I don't have a pilot waiting on my convenience either.'

'You mean, you fly yourself?'

'Why not?'

'I just assumed...' She trailed off, feeling foolish.

'Assumed what? That I was incapable of flying a plane?'

'No!' Jake Tregowan didn't look incapable of *any-thing*. 'I suppose I thought you looked successful enough to have someone to fly it for you.'

He watched critically as she strapped herself in, then settled into the pilot's seat beside her. 'What made you think that?'

It was the way he walked, the way he turned his head—even the way he stood, looking cool and decisive. Phyllida didn't think she could tell Jake any of that. 'Just the clothes you were wearing,' she said lamely.

'That's a big assumption to base on a pair of trousers and a shirt,' he commented, with one of his sardonic looks. 'Do you always leap to conclusions like that?'

'I wasn't that far wrong, was I?' she challenged him. 'You're obviously successful enough to have your own plane, anyway.'

'Australia's a big country.' He shrugged as the propeller coughed and started to turn, slowly at first and then with increasing speed, but she noticed that he didn't deny it. 'Flying is often the best way to get around.'

He began checking his instrument panel while Phyllida watched the propeller rather nervously. She had never been in anything smaller than a jumbo before, and she was beginning to regret asking Jake for a lift. Really, she would have done much better to have stayed in Adelaide, where she would have been able to have a good night's sleep. She could have showered and changed into clean clothes, and arrived in Port Lincoln refreshed.

As it was, she was going to turn up on Chris's doorstep looking a total wreck. Why hadn't she thought of that before?

Phyllida looked down at her smudged and rumpled

suit, and repressed a sigh as she remembered what Jake had said about leaping to conclusions. She liked to think of herself as businesslike and professional, but the truth was that she had always been too impetuous, with a tendency towards snap decisions and making a bee-line for what she wanted without stopping to think about what was involved.

She glanced across at Jake, absorbed in his instruments. She couldn't imagine *him* ever acting without thinking. He was too deliberate, too controlled. Her eyes fell on his hands, reaching up to the panel above his head, moving competently over the switches with the minimum of fuss, and an unidentifiable feeling gripped the base of her spine.

Rupert would have flourished his arms about, impressing her with his knowledge, Phyllida thought wryly. He wouldn't have just sat there ignoring her, as Jake was doing, working steadily through his routine.

She frowned slightly as she realised that she couldn't quite visualise Rupert's face. She had been engaged to him until that disastrous afternoon six weeks ago. Surely she couldn't have forgotten him in that time? Closing her eyes, she made an effort to conjure up his image. But all she could see was Jake's watchful eyes and Jake's cool mouth and Jake's disturbing smile.

'Right.' His voice broke into her thoughts. 'Ready?'

Phyllida looked at the propeller again and swallowed. 'I suppose so.' It was too late to change her mind now, but next time she really *would* think before she rushed into a decision.

They waited while a jet landed with a roar at the international terminal, and then they were speeding down the runway. Phyllida kept her eyes squeezed shut and clutched her hands together as the pressure forced her back into her seat.

The lurch of her stomach told her that the plane had left the ground, but she kept her eyes firmly closed until the plane's steep climb into the air had levelled off. When she opened them, Jake was watching her with a mixture of amusement and exasperation.

'Wishing you'd waited for tomorrow morning's flight after all?'

Phyllida's chin went up at the mockery in his voice. 'No,' she lied, and a smile touched the corners of his mouth.

'Stubborn little thing, aren't you?'

She thought of the determination she had needed to succeed in her advertising career, and how little it had counted when set against the fact that she was female. She would show them, though! 'Sometimes you have to be,' she said.

'What's made you so stubborn about getting to Port Lincoln?' Jake asked, guiding the plane round in a wide arc.

Phyllida looked down at the lights of Adelaide spread out below her and swallowed. 'I just wanted to get there tonight.'

'And what you want, you get—regardless of inconvenience to other people?'

She glanced at him curiously, wondering what had provoked the bitterness in his voice. 'No,' she said slowly, thinking of the day her world had fallen apart and she had lost her job and her fiancé in the course of a single afternoon. 'Not always.'

'Oh?' Jake's eyes flicked towards her in disbelief. 'I had you down as a real career girl in your smart suit.'

His voice was edged with sudden contempt, and

Phyllida stiffened. 'I thought it was dangerous to base assumptions on what people were wearing?' she reminded him.

'I was going by the way you behaved, not by what you were wearing—typically unsuitable though it is,' he retorted. 'All fragile and feminine when it suits you, but hard as nails underneath.'

'What do you mean?' said Phyllida, offended.

'Oh, come on, I saw the way you were making up to that poor unsuspecting boy at the check-in desk! Opening those big brown eyes of yours at him, bravely choking back a few tears...it was quite a performance! Unfortunately, I've seen it all before, and I know that the performance only ever lasts as long as it takes to get your own way. You're full of fine words about not needing men, but you don't mind using them when it suits you, do you?'

Phyllida's face was white with anger. 'And what about the men who use women?' she demanded. 'It's all right for them to make the most of our talents and abilities, but as soon as we start asking for some acknowledgement, that's another matter!

'We're only supposed to be there to support men, to fill in time before we run back to our proper place as housekeepers and mothers. Do you have any idea how hard it is for a woman to get to the top of her career?' she asked him furiously.

'You have to work twice as hard as any man to get taken seriously. Instead of getting on with the job, you have to prove that you can be just as ruthless as your male colleagues, and when you are, they turn round and accuse you of being hard and unfeminine! But of course we're not allowed to be feminine either, because that's unfair to men!' Phyllida paused for breath, brown eyes bright with indignation.

'The only way you can succeed is by being utterly determined to beat all the odds, but it shouldn't be that hard. Women are just as capable as men. Why shouldn't we have the same opportunities to be successful and show what we can do?'

'Very vehement,' said Jake, with an ironic sidelong glance. 'I was obviously right about you being a career girl, anyway.'

'Yes, I am,' she said defiantly. 'And proud of it!'

'What do you do?'

'I'm in advertising.'

'How can you be proud of being in advertising?' he asked nastily.

'Easily,' said Phyllida, determinedly dignified. 'Our advertising affects the way people think about almost everything, and we take our responsibility very seriously. It's a very professional business.'

She would have gone on, but at that moment Jake took his hands off the joystick and settled himself back in his seat. To her horror, he proceeded to shift himself into a more comfortable position and calmly propped his legs up against the instrument panel.

'What are you doing?' she asked, her voice rising to an extremely unprofessional squeak.

Jake gave an irritable sigh. 'We're on autopilot. There's no need to panic.'

'I wasn't panicking,' said Phyllida coldly. She hated the way Jake Tregowan made her feel stupid. 'I was just...concerned.'

'I should keep your concern for a society subjected to a barrage of pointless advertising, if I were you,' said

Jake, and forestalled her protest by reaching behind his seat to pull out a Thermos flask.

As he unscrewed the top a tantalising aroma of fresh coffee drifted out into the cockpit, distracting Phyllida from her dignified and well-reasoned arguments in favour of advertising. Her nose twitched. She had last eaten at thirty thousand feet, somewhere between Singapore and Adelaide, and it seemed a very long time ago.

'Want some?' he asked, filling the top which doubled as a mug.

The smell was irresistible. 'I'd love some,' she admitted, abandoning her dignity along with her arguments. Her swollen feet were killing her, and she grimaced with relief as she eased off her shoes.

Jake handed her the mug. Her fingers brushed against his as she took it from him, and her grateful smile faltered slightly at the electric effect of his touch.

Clasping her hands around the mug, she tried to concentrate fiercely on the coffee, but her eyes kept sliding sideways to study him from under her lashes. They rested on his profile, on the strong features lit from below by the dim lights of the instruments, caught on the set of his jaw and the peculiarly exciting line of his mouth, and something stirred strangely inside her.

She must be even more tired than she'd thought, Phyllida decided. There was something vaguely surreal about sitting here in the darkness, high above the ground, drinking coffee with a perfect stranger while the propeller droned mesmerisingly in the background. Only Jake seemed real. Real and solid and somehow *immediate*.

Even in the dim light, everything about him was distinct. She could sense the muscles in the legs bent so casually against the instrument panel, the strength in the lean, compact body, could almost feel the texture of his skin. So vivid was the sensation that Phyllida had to look down at her fingers, to make sure that they weren't in fact exploring the angle of his cheek and jaw.

She wished she couldn't remember every time he had touched her. The steely grip on her arm, setting her back on her feet, his hand clasping hers to haul her into the plane, the hard hold at her waist... Her body throbbed as if every touch had seared into her skin. If a brief, impersonal contact could feel like this, what would it be like if he touched her lovingly, running his hands over her skin, exploring her softness...?

Phyllida's throat dried at the thought, and she gulped at the last of the coffee. What on earth was the matter with her? She hardly knew Jake Tregowan, and what she did know she didn't like. Why could she picture him making love to her with such alarming clarity?

Jet lag, she told herself firmly. Her mind was confused and disorientated by the long flight, just as her body was. Phyllida grasped at the explanation with something akin to desperation. It meant that there was a perfectly logical reason for the sudden, heart-stopping rush of desire, and that it had nothing—absolutely nothing!—to do with Jake Tregowan.

CHAPTER TWO

SHE handed him back the mug, careful not to touch him this time. 'Thank you.'

Jake raised his brows at the strained formality of her tone, but to Phyllida's relief he didn't comment. Instead he poured himself some coffee from the Thermos. 'What are you doing in Port Lincoln?' he asked, with that undercurrent of mockery that so riled her. 'I wouldn't have thought it was exactly the mecca of the advertising world. Or have you got some brief to jazz up our international image?'

'I'm on a three-month sabbatical,' said Phyllida. She had no intention of telling Jake Tregowan that the job she had loved so much was no longer hers.

'Sabbatical? Isn't that what the rest of us would call a holiday?'

'I'm taking a long break from work to give me a chance to reassess my career,' she said grandly. It was almost the truth, anyway.

'Port Lincoln seems a funny place to choose to do that,' Jake commented, watching her over the rim of the mug. 'I thought you career girls only ever did things that looked good on your CVs?'

Phyllida eyed him with some hostility. 'You seem to know a lot about career girls.'

'I've learnt from bitter experience,' he said flatly.

'Your experience can't be that wide if it hasn't taught you that we're not all the same,' she pointed out in a tart voice. 'For your information, I'm going to visit my cousin, not add to my CV.'

'Aha! So you *are* on holiday!'

'Partly,' she admitted through clenched teeth. 'Of course I want to see Chris again, but I wouldn't be here now unless it was a good time as far as my firm was concerned.'

'If they can spare you for three months, they probably don't need you at all,' said Jake with disagreeable logic. 'Are you sure you're going to have a job when you get back?'

She lifted her chin. 'Not only will I have a job, I'm going to be promoted,' she said proudly.

And she would. Liedermann, Marshall & Jones would regret giving her job to someone who was less experienced and less qualified, but who operated under the enormous advantage of being male. Phyllida had vowed that day to make them come crawling back on their knees and beg her to accept promotion, and she had dreamt of it so often that it had come to seem almost an established fact.

'And in the meantime you're going to spend three months in Port Lincoln thinking about things?' Jake's voice was edged with disbelief.

'Yes,' said Phyllida firmly. She had a nasty suspicion that Jake was less than convinced about her impressive career. 'I'll go and see other parts of Australia, but I'll be quite happy to spend most of my time with Chris,' she went on, anxious to prevent him asking any more awkward questions about her career and just why it was that she could take three months off right now.

To her relief, Jake allowed himself to be diverted. 'That's your cousin?'

She nodded. 'Her father—my mother's brother—emigrated to Australia years ago and married an Australian. I'd only ever heard about Chris through letters until she and her husband came to England on a working holiday. They stayed with me in London and we hit it off immediately.' She smiled reminiscently.

'It was wonderful to discover a friend instead of just a relative. We've kept in touch ever since, although I haven't seen them for five years now. It's such a long way that I've never thought about coming out before.'

'What made you change your mind?'

'Chris sent me a photograph.' Phyllida dug in her bag for it. She had carried it around like a talisman ever since Chris's letter had dropped through the door along with a pile of Christmas cards.

Her fingers found the picture tucked into the back of her passport, and she pulled it out to look down at it again in the dim light. It showed Chris and Mike on a boat, sharply outlined in the bright Australia light. They both looked relaxed and happy, with the wind lifting their hair and the sun making them screw up their eyes. It was hard to tell now, but behind them the sea was an unreal shade of turquoise, the sky a deep, bright blue.

She passed the photograph across to Jake, who glanced at it and stiffened suddenly. Phyllida didn't notice. She was remembering how miserable she had been feeling when she had first seen it. 'I know it's just an ordinary snapshot, but it arrived on a horrible December day. It was drizzling, and everything looked wet and grey and... I don't know...*dreary*.'

'I can see that this would have looked more appealing,' said Jake. There was an odd note in his voice as he handed her back the photograph.

'Maybe if it had arrived on a bright, frosty day, it wouldn't have meant so much,' Phyllida said reflectively.

The snapshot had seemed so vivid. She had practically been able to feel the sunshine on her back, and smell the fresh, sharp tang of the sea.

'I've always been a real city girl, but when I looked at it, I suddenly wanted to be there with them.' She had wanted to leave the greyness behind and forget about her job, forget about Rupert, forget about everything but the bright light and the sea spray on her face.

'And you just happened to have a three-month sabbatical coming up, is that it?' Jake didn't even bother to hide his sarcasm, and Phyllida flushed, glad that the light wasn't good enough for him to tell.

'More or less,' she said stiffly. 'I hadn't really decided what I was going to do.' Until then, she hadn't thought beyond a single-minded determination to prove both LMJ and Rupert wrong, but Chris's letter with its usual warm invitation to visit had changed that.

There was no reason why she shouldn't go to Australia, she had realised. She had been earning a good salary, and had worked so hard that she had never had the time to spend much of it. She had no commitments— no ties since she had stormed out of Rupert's flat. Instead of plodding through a grim, grey January, she could lie in the sun and come home tanned and refreshed and ready to prove herself again.

'I could have gone anywhere, but the photograph made me realise what a perfect opportunity it was to see Chris and Mike again.'

'They look fairly cheerful types,' he commented lightly.

Phyllida's face changed. 'They were *then*. Whether they will be now is another matter.'

'Oh?' He shot her a swift glance. 'Why's that?'

'Mike's always been a restless type, but he and Chris

had finally settled down to what they really wanted to do, which was run a marine charter company, hiring out their two yachts. It was only a small business, but at least it was theirs—until some rival company comes along and decides it can't tolerate a little fair competition!'

Phyllida sat straighter, remembering her indignation as she had read Chris's letter telling her about the takeover.

'Chris and Mike wouldn't have been a threat to anybody, but that didn't make any difference to the man who took them over. All *he* cares about is profit. He doesn't care that they've put all their effort, not to mention all their savings into making their business a success. People don't matter to men like that,' she said bitterly. 'They just brush aside anyone who stands in their way!'

'I had no idea there was such a ruthless operator in Port Lincoln,' said Jake. 'Did your cousin tell you his name, so I can take care to avoid him in future?' His face was quite grave, but Phyllida had the distinct impression that he was amused by something.

She glared at him. It might be a joke to him, but it wasn't a very funny one as far as Chris and Mike were concerned. 'She just said they'd been taken over by a bigger company,' she admitted. 'But she didn't need to give me the details. Believe me, I know what happens when smaller companies get taken over by bigger ones, and I don't suppose it's any different here.'

'Oh, I think you'll find it is,' said Jake, with that infuriating undercurrent of amusement. 'Port Lincoln is a different place from London.' He glared at her, and she could see the smile just deepening the intriguing dent at the corner of his mouth. 'Very different.'

The airport at Port Lincoln seemed to be a long way from the town. Phyllida eyed the distant glow of its lights in dismay as the little plane sank lower and lower towards a suspiciously empty-looking collection of buildings set alone in the darkness.

'Will your cousin have waited?' Jake asked as the plane taxied slowly to a halt. 'I presume she was expecting you on the eight forty-five flight?'

'No, she doesn't know I'm coming,' said Phyllida, her heart sinking as she realised that her journey wasn't over yet. She still had to get from the airport to Chris's house. 'At least, she *does* know I'm coming,' she added hurriedly as Jake opened his mouth, no doubt to make some caustic comment, 'but she doesn't know when.

'All the flights to Australia were completely full for December and January, so I had to go on a wait-list. A seat came up at the very last minute—I only just had time to pack! I did try ringing Chris, to let her know that I was on my way, but I couldn't get a reply. I didn't want to miss the flight, so in the end I just came…'

Phyllida found herself trailing to a halt, as if she were confessing to some idiocy instead of a perfectly reasonable decision. She had wanted to come, an opportunity had arisen and she had taken it. What was wrong with that?

Jake glanced at her, his brows raised. 'You just upped and left at a moment's notice? Seems a funny way to organise a sabbatical.'

'I'd made all the arrangements,' said Phyllida defensively, even as she wondered why she was bothering to explain herself to Jake Tregowan. 'It wasn't a spur-of-the-moment decision.'

Well, it *had* been originally, but in the end it had taken over three weeks before the travel agent had had enough of her badgering and had in desperation found her a wait-listed seat on a flight out of London. It had involved changing planes four times at various Asian airports, but at the time Phyllida had been so desperate to get away that she would have accepted anything.

The engine died, and the blur of the propellers slowed until she could see the individual blades turning slowly, as if exhausted by all their effort. Jake unclipped his seat-belt and climbed into the back to open the door and heave her suitcase out onto the tarmac.

Phyllida winced as she heard the loud thump, remembering how many shampoos, cleansers and moisturisers were tucked away in every available inch, pushed down shoes or wrapped in underwear. If every baggage handler since London had treated her case like Jake, she dreaded to think of what a mess there would be when she opened it.

Sighing, she retrieved her shoes from the floor by her seat and tried to put them on, but her feet were so swollen that it was an agonising squeeze. In the end she decided that she would have to go barefoot, and to hell with elegance.

Getting into the plane had been bad enough; getting out looked as if it was going to be even more daunting. Phyllida clutched her bag to her chest with one hand and held onto her shoes with the other as she peered down at Jake, who was looking up at her with an expression of irritated resignation.

'You can get out of your door onto the wing and climb down from there if you'd rather,' he said impatiently. 'But whatever you decide to do, do it quickly!'

Phyllida eyed the wing dubiously. It looked just as bad a drop as this one, and would involve yet more awkward clambering in her tight skirt. No, she would just have to jump down from here.

With an inward sigh, she dropped her bag and shoes

down to Jake, and wriggled up her skirt so that she could sit down in the doorway and dangle her legs over the edge. It wasn't that big a drop, but the very thought of landing heavily on her poor feet made her flinch.

Jake muttered something under his breath and stepped forward to hold up his arms. 'I thought you were in a hurry to get to Port Lincoln?'

'I am.'

'Then will you please stop dithering around and just *jump*?'

There was no way she was going to jump, but his peremptory command was enough to get Phyllida moving. Edging forward, she eased herself off the edge, and suddenly Jake's arms were there, holding her firmly around the waist and lifting her gently to the ground.

Phyllida's hands found his shoulders, and tightened there to steady herself. She could feel the reassuring strength of his muscles through the fine cotton shirt, the hardness of his hands against her body, and then wished she hadn't noticed.

Glancing up to thank him, she found him looking down into her face with an unreadable expression, and the words dried in her throat as she was shaken by a sudden, terrifying gust of awareness. His hands seemed to be burning through her suit onto her body, and her fingers itched with the desire to slide over his shoulders, to drift down his arms and smooth along his skin, over the short dark hairs and back up to the rock-like security of his chest.

Appalled by the treacherous drift of her thoughts, Phyllida jerked herself out of his hold, passionately grateful for the darkness that hid the burning colour in her cheeks. 'I don't know why you can't get yourself a proper set of steps,' she muttered, instead of thanking him as she had originally intended.

'I can usually rely on my passengers to wear a proper set of travelling clothes,' he pointed out, unperturbed.

There was something unsettling about the way his eyes gleamed through the darkness. Phyllida was sure that he was secretly laughing at her. What if he had guessed how she had wanted to run her hands over him, to touch him and feel him? Oh, God, what if he had? She bent to pick up her bag and shoes.

'Yes, well…' She cleared her throat awkwardly, desperate to get away from his disturbing presence. 'Thank you for the lift. I appreciate it.' Tilting her case back on its wheels, she swung her bag over her shoulder, shifted her shoes to her spare hand and wished Jake a stiff goodbye.

'Where are you going?' he asked, and this time the amusement was obvious.

'I won't impose on your kindness any longer,' she said, very much on her dignity. 'I'll take a taxi to my cousin's house.'

'You'd be lucky to find a taxi out here at this time of night!' he said. 'This isn't Heathrow.'

'I'll find something,' she said, with a stubborn tilt of her chin.

Jake looked resigned. 'Still trying to prove that you can look after yourself, Phyllida?'

'I *can* look after myself!' Phyllida readjusted her grip on her suitcase with a defiant look. 'Goodbye,' she said tightly, and set off towards the terminal without waiting for him to reply.

She felt like stalking, but her bare, swollen feet ached so much that she was reduced to a less than dignified hobble. At least going so slowly meant that her case behaved with more restraint. It only fell over once. Stooping wearily to pick it up, Phyllida glanced back at the plane, irrationally piqued to discover that, far from staring after her in consternation, Jake was unconcernedly setting blocks behind the wheels.

Determined not to look back again, she carried doggedly on to the terminal building. It was certainly the smallest airport she had ever been in, but the terminal itself—barely bigger than her sitting-room at home—was clean and modern—and completely empty. Phyllida pulled open the glass door and, in spite of her best intentions, glanced over her shoulder. But Jake was nowhere in sight.

Good. He was the most disagreeable, obnoxious man she had ever met, and she was happy to think that she would never have to see him again. Very happy.

Pushing her way through the doors leading to the front of the terminal, she found herself in what was obviously a pick-up area. Any taxis would certainly be waiting here, but of course there weren't any. Jake had been right. There were no taxis, no buses, no nothing.

She was stuck.

If Phyllida had been thinking clearly, she would have realised that Jake would have a vehicle, that there would be a phone somewhere she could use to ring Chris, or call a taxi out to pick her up. But she was tired and disorientated by the long flight, and thinking clearly was the last thing she was capable of. All she knew was that this ghastly journey seemed as if it was never going to end, and as she looked around her hopelessly it was impossible to imagine a time when this would all be over.

Phyllida was overwhelmed by a sudden, desperate conviction that she was doomed to spend the rest of her life waiting here in front of this deserted airport.

She slumped wearily down onto her suitcase. Somehow this last blow was the worst. She hadn't cried once after she lost her job, or after that terrible argument with Rupert. Instead, she had let her unhappiness crystallise into a hard, burning anger and a fierce determination to show them all just how wrong they were. She wouldn't have given them the satisfaction of crying then—or when everything else had leapt on the bandwagon of disaster and gone wrong too.

Her car had been broken into, the washing machine had leaked all over the kitchen floor, she had lost one of a favourite pair of earrings... Trivial problems, easily dealt with normally, but all had accumulated into a great weight on her spirits that made coping with even the most minor of crises an insuperable task.

Phyllida hadn't given in, though. She had gritted her teeth, thought of the sun and the sea in Chris's photograph, and refused to cry. She had always despised girls who burst into tears at the most minor provocation, but now, as she sat on her hated suitcase, the problem of how to get the last few miles to Port Lincoln assumed the proportions of a major disaster. Putting her hands abruptly to her face, she succumbed at last to the shamefully weak tears of exhaustion and frustration.

Behind her, the doors were pushed open and footsteps approached.

Jake.

Phyllida's face was buried in her hands, and she couldn't see anything, but the tingling of her spine told her who it was more clearly than words. She stiffened, hastily brushing the tears from her cheeks and turning her face into the shadows.

'What's the matter?' asked Jake, and Phyllida's precarious hold on her control shattered completely.

'What do you think the matter is?' she demanded furiously. 'I've just had the worst month of my life, followed by the worst journey of my life, and now I'm stuck in the middle of nowhere, when all I want to do is get to Chris's house. And you were right, there aren't any taxis, and I'll probably have to spend all night here, and I'm tired and cold and hungry, and my feet hurt and I want to go home!'

Burying her face back into her hands, she burst into fresh tears. 'I never cry,' she wept. 'It's just that I'm tired...'

'It's hard work looking after yourself, isn't it?' said Jake.

Phyllida hated the way laughter warred with irritation in his voice. Here she was, reduced to this pitiful state, and he found it funny!

'Go away!' she sobbed, rather muffled.

There was no reply other than an exasperated sigh, and when she peeked through her fingers she saw with incredulity that he had taken her at her word and was walking away. He was just going to leave her here, she realised, aghast. How heartless could you get?

Phyllida would have died rather than run after him, but his desertion was the final straw, and the knowledge that she had sent away her one chance of help didn't help. Unable to think of anything better to do, she dropped her head into her arms and abandoned herself to her misery.

She was crying so bitterly that she didn't hear the sound of an engine starting in the car park, or even realise that it was coming towards her until the dazzle of headlights swept over her. She lifted her head to see a big four-wheel drive turn in to where she sat, a miserably huddled figure in the unforgiving light of the neon strip over her head.

A door slammed, and she squinted into the lights as Jake came striding round the bonnet towards her. 'Leave me alone!' she muttered, but surreptitiously wiped the mascara that had run down from her eyes with her knuckle.

Jake ignored her anyway, hauling her to her feet without a word and reaching down for her suitcase.

'What are you doing?'

'What do you think I'm doing?' He mimicked her earlier outburst. 'It's only fair to tell you that I too have had a long, frustrating day, topped off by having a strange woman thrust into my plane. And I do *not* feel like dealing sympathetically with hysterics at this time of night, so get in!'

'I am not hysterical!' said Phyllida, with more than a touch of hysteria. 'I'm just tired—'

'I know, and your feet hurt,' Jake interrupted her unsympathetically. 'If you stopped thinking about them, they wouldn't hurt nearly so much.'

'And if you knew how much they hurt, you wouldn't even suggest thinking about anything else,' she retorted sullenly as he threw the case into the back of the car. At least his reappearance had stopped her crying, which, as she was uncomfortably aware, had only too clearly been verging on the hysterical.

Conscious of what a mess she must be looking, she wiped at the tearstains on her cheeks with the backs of her hands and tucked her hair behind her ears.

The gesture made her look curiously vulnerable in her bare feet and her smart suit, grubby now after her struggles to get into the plane. Her brown eyes were enormous in her pale face, and the bright, vivid look that usually characterised her was muted by tiredness.

'Nothing could take my mind off my feet at the moment,' she added, lifting one so that she could inspect it gingerly and wondering if she would ever be able to walk normally again.

'You must be able to think of something that'll stop you feeling so sorry for yourself,' he said, reluctant amusement creeping back into his voice.

'You suggest something, if you're so clever,' snapped Phyllida, changing feet and grimacing at the angry red marks where her shoes had dug into her toes. 'And I'll think about it!'

'All right,' said Jake equably, and calmly took her in his arms. 'How about this?'

Phyllida, still balancing on one tender foot, was taken completely unawares and toppled against him, clutching automatically at his chest as he bent his head and kissed her.

His mouth was cool and firm, the effect of his touch electrifying. Phyllida clung to the front of his shirt, so shaken by the strange, jolting excitement that she was afraid her legs would simply give way beneath her if she let go. Jake's kiss was deliberately tantalising, deliciously persuasive, and she was quite unprepared for her own leap of response.

It was as if she had lost all control over her own body, which had succumbed with barely a protest to the enticing beat of a sudden, shocking desire that was drumming along her senses. Her mind might shriek at her to pull away, but her lips parted beneath his regardless, and her treacherous hands slid slowly down his chest and around his waist to savour the taut power of his body. He was lean and reassuringly hard, all compact strength, like tempered steel.

Phyllida had lost all sense of time and place. She had forgotten her tiredness, forgotten the fact that Jake

Tregowan was to all effects and purposes a perfect stranger. All that mattered was the wash of sensation that had engulfed her the moment his mouth had touched hers, swirling her around and leaving her giddy with a new and totally unexpected pleasure.

She had no idea how long the kiss lasted—it might have been seconds, it might have been hours—and when Jake released her she could only blink up at him dazedly.

He grinned at her expression. 'How are your feet now?'

'Feet?' She stared at him blankly.

'I *thought* that might work,' said Jake with satisfaction, calmly walking over to open the passenger door for her. 'All you needed was a little distraction.'

'A...a *distraction*?' Phyllida didn't seem to be able to do anything more than echo him stupidly. She shook her head, as if to clear it, and reality hit her like a slap in the face.

Jake had kissed her in the most casual way possible, and she had responded with humiliating eagerness. She had *never* reacted like that before. What must he think of her?

Shock had made her face even paler than before, but now a rush of colour surged up her throat and stained her cheeks with embarrassment. Jake didn't seem to notice anything amiss. He was still too busy congratulating himself on the success of his tactics.

'You've got to admit that it was effective,' he said. 'I must remember it as a cure for imminent hysteria in the future.'

Phyllida opened her mouth to deny vehemently any suggestion of hysteria in her behaviour, then remembered that she could hardly claim to have been in full possession of her senses when he kissed her, and shut it again.

The last thing she wanted was for Jake to think that she had known exactly what she was doing.

Phyllida chose not to remember how easily she could have pushed him away. The fact that she hadn't reacted with justifiable outrage just proved that she wasn't herself!

She should have been angry... She *was* angry, now she came to think about it. Phyllida's eyes snapped as she remembered how he had taken advantage of her, how he had captured her lips with the same casual competence with which he did everything else. And then he had dared to laugh at her!

'Are you coming?' said Jake, still holding open the door.

'I'm not getting into a car with a man who...who *grabs* me like that!'

'I was grabbing you in a good cause,' he pointed out, assuming an expression of hurt indignation that made Phyllida want to hit him. 'I was merely giving you something else to think about. It was your suggestion, after all.'

'A kiss wasn't exactly what I had in mind!'

'It worked, didn't it? You could still be grizzling about your feet, but you're complaining about me kissing you instead.'

'What do you expect me to do?' she demanded. 'Kiss your feet?'

'Well, I think you might be a little more grateful.'

'I don't feel very grateful,' said Phyllida sullenly.

'You might not be feeling grateful, but at least you're feeling better,' said Jake. 'You must be if you're refusing a lift into town. I suppose that means you're planning to walk? It's about twenty minutes in a car, so you should be there by morning.' He watched Phyllida's expression as she assimilated this.

'There isn't a lot of traffic out here at this time of night,' he went on, 'but if you're prepared to walk, that won't bother you, will it? You could set off right now...or you could stop being silly and get in the car!'

Phyllida hesitated, biting her lip, then gave in. Without looking at Jake, she climbed into the passenger seat, and he shut the door behind her with deliberately mock gallantry.

He drove with the same sureness and competence with which he had flown the plane. It occurred to Phyllida that it was odd to feel so safe with someone she knew absolutely nothing about. She didn't know who he was, where he lived or what he did, but somehow he didn't feel like a stranger.

It was as if she had always known that reassuringly capable air, the understated but unmistakable toughness, the warm strength of his hands and the way his smile curled the corner of that cool, firm mouth.

His mouth... Something stirred inside Phyllida as she remembered how it had felt against hers. Something disturbing that uncurled itself and shivered up and down her spine. His lips had been as sure as his hands, surprisingly warm, dangerously persuasive, his kiss terrifyingly exciting. Phyllida began to wish she was still thinking about her feet.

They seemed to have been driving for hours through the darkness, along an interminably straight road. Preoccupied by her own thoughts, Phyllida had hardly noticed her surroundings—or what there was to see of them—but at last the lights of Port Lincoln appeared spread out before them, curving around the bay with its long pier jutting out from the huge grain silos and the dark bulk of Boston Island looming in the distance.

Acutely aware that she had been less than gracious about accepting a lift, Phyllida told Jake Chris's address rather awkwardly. He nodded without comment, but she was left with the peculiar conviction that he hadn't needed to be told—a suspicion that strengthened when, only a couple of minutes later, he drew up outside a neat bungalow.

'Here we are—number forty-three.' He hadn't even had to look at the number, and Phyllida looked at him accusingly.

'You knew where you were going all along, didn't you?'

Jake grinned as he got out of the car and retrieved her suitcase from the back, carrying it up to the door. 'I have to admit that I've been here before,' he said unrepentantly.

'You know Chris and Mike?'

'Very well. I recognised them as soon as I saw that photograph.'

'You might have told me!' protested Phyllida.

'I might have done,' he agreed. 'But then, I thought you'd find out anyway, sooner or later.'

Phyllida regarded him angrily. 'You mean I'm likely to see you again?' It was bad enough him having kissed her, without knowing that she would have to face him again with the memory of her own response between them!

'I'm afraid so,' said Jake, with that disconcerting laugh in his voice. 'Never mind, Phyllida, at least you've arrived at last—and the light's on, so Chris is home. Aren't you going to go in?'

Phyllida's face was a study in frustration. She was

longing to tell Jake exactly what she thought of his duplicity, but she could hardly do that now that she knew he was a friend of Chris. Besides, if it hadn't been for him, she wouldn't be here at all. It was all very annoying.

Jake was watching her with amusement, obviously having no trouble interpreting her expression. Phyllida took a deep breath and gathered the tattered remnants of her dignity about her.

'Yes... Well, I'll go in, then.' She cleared her throat and held out her hand, so that he didn't get any ideas about kissing her again. 'Er, thank you for everything.'

'Everything?' he queried mockingly, taking her hand. His fingers closed around hers, and Phyllida's nerves jolted in reaction.

She snatched her hand away. 'Not quite everything,' she said coldly, knowing quite well that he was referring to that awful kiss.

Jake grinned. 'Enjoy your stay in Port Lincoln,' was all he said. He got back into his car and drove off, leaving Phyllida with a perverse sense of disappointment that he hadn't even tried to kiss her again. Her hand felt very odd, too.

She looked down at it with a peculiar expression, as if expecting it to be glowing in the dark. It felt uncomfortably sensitive, as if every line of his palm had imprinted itself on hers, and she flexed her fingers experimentally before realising how ridiculously she was behaving.

Shaking her hand irritably, to rid herself of the feeling, she took a firm grip of herself, along with her bag and shoes, pushed open the gate, and limped the last few feet to Chris's door.

CHAPTER THREE

HALF an hour later, Phyllida was curled up in an armchair with a glass of champagne in her hand. The warmth of Chris's welcome had made the whole ghastly trip worthwhile, and she smiled affectionately across at her cousin.

Chris was tall, blonde and serenely pretty, with none of Phyllida's dark, quicksilver quality. The two girls could hardly have been more different—in temperament as well as looks.

Completely lacking in vanity, Chris always wore plain, sensible clothes, while Phyllida was famous for her jazzy earrings and unsuitable shoes. Chris was an outdoor girl; Phyllida belonged in a city—rushing from gym to office, office to wine bar, wine bar to party, in a hectic whirl of activity—and yet, in spite of all the differences between them, the cousins shared a closeness that was quite unaffected by the distance that was normally between them. They might have last seen each other a week ago, instead of the five years it had been.

Phyllida was fond of Mike too, but she wasn't sorry to have Chris to herself. Mike, it appeared, had taken the car up to Queensland to see if there might be better opportunities to start a marine charter company in the Whitsunday Islands.

'It must have been awful for you,' Phyllida sympathised, when Chris told her about losing the business they had built up in Port Lincoln to a company called Sailaway.

'It could have been worse,' said Chris, cheerfully philosophical as always. 'We got a good price for our boats, and it wasn't as if we suddenly found ourselves out of a job. Mike carried on skippering inexperienced parties, and when his help took off without warning, Jake took me on in her place.'

Phyllida's heart gave a sickening lurch and her hand jerked, slopping champagne over her skirt. 'Jake?'

'Jake Tregowan. He owns Sailaway.' Chris glanced curiously at her cousin's appalled expression. 'What's the matter?'

'Nothing,' said Phyllida in a hollow voice. Oh, God, why did it have to be *him*? 'Nothing at all.'

'He's been absolutely fantastic,' Chris went on enthusiastically. 'He didn't *have* to buy us out. It would have made much more sense for him to wait for us to go bust, but he stepped in just in time before we lost everything. He didn't have to take Mike on as a skipper either. There are plenty of other experienced sailors who'd be delighted to work for him.' She smiled. 'He's got quite a reputation as a skipper himself—he's won the Sydney-Hobart twice.'

'What's that?' asked Phyllida, still frantically trying to remember what she had said to Jake about the company that had taken over Chris and Mike's business.

It was bad enough discovering that he knew them, without her having held forth about his supposedly callous treatment of them. Why, why, *why* hadn't she kept her mouth shut? Chris hadn't complained in her letter, but, still smarting from the effects of a takeover herself, she had simply assumed that Chris's experience would have been as bitter as hers. No wonder Jake had seemed amused!

He could have told her, though, Phyllida reasoned resentfully. Instead he had chosen to let her make a fool of herself, knowing that she would be bound to find out the truth from Chris.

Her cousin was still talking about the Sydney-Hobart. 'It's one of the toughest ocean races in the world. The conditions on the Bass Strait can be horrific. I love sailing, but you wouldn't catch me out there! Jake seems to love it, though. He's a real yachtsman—only really at home on a boat.

'You'd never guess he came from such a wealthy background,' she went on confidentially. 'Tregowan's is one of the biggest companies in New South Wales. Jake even ran it for a while, but he opted out of the rat race and now he just keeps an eye on their interests in Adelaide. He says he doesn't want to waste his life sitting behind a desk when he could be on a boat.'

Well, that explained the private plane and the intangible aura of wealth and confidence, Phyllida thought, still chagrined. But how was she to have guessed that he ran a marine charter company when he dressed like the successful executive he had obviously once been?

'He sounds quite a paragon,' she said lightly. She longed to ask more, but she didn't want Chris to wonder why she was showing such interest in a man she had never met.

Her cousin had exclaimed at the state of her suit, and demanded to know how she had managed to appear out of nowhere, but, with her hand still tingling from his touch, Phyllida had given a vague answer, curiously reluctant to talk about Jake. Now it seemed too late to explain.

'Oh, he is!' said Chris cheerfully. 'If I didn't love Mike so much, I'm sure I'd be in love with Jake! And, talking of love, what's happened to this Rupert you wrote to me about? I thought you were engaged? Couldn't he come with you?'

'He wasn't invited,' said Phyllida with a wry smile.

'Oh, dear. What happened? All you said on the phone was that you were planning to come out for three months and would get a flight as soon as possible.'

'I didn't tell you that I was sacked?'

'No!' Chris sat bolt-upright and stared at Phyllida. 'I don't believe it! You loved that job!'

'I know, but Pritchard Price was only a small agency, and when Liedermann, Marshall & Jones took it over they decided that a mere woman couldn't be a group account director. They gave my job to one of their own executives—male, of course!

'The fact that I'd been a very successful group account director for the last two years didn't count, apparently,' she remembered bitterly. 'They said it was all part of the reorganisation involved in merging two agencies, but if I'd been a man there would have been no question about keeping me on.'

Chris frowned. She knew how much her job had meant to Phyllida. 'Rupert doesn't work for the firm that sacked you, does he?'

'Rupert? No, he's a wine merchant. Very successful, but very traditional—old school tie, and that kind of thing. That should have been a warning,' Phyllida added bleakly.

'Why, what did he do?'

'I was so angry when I heard about my job that I stormed round to see Rupert. I thought he understood how much I cared about my work, but he had the nerve to tell me that he thought it would all work out for the best!' Phyllida's face was flushed with the memory of her blazing indignation at Rupert's patronising reaction.

'We hadn't been engaged very long, and we hadn't really talked about when the wedding would be or what would happen after we were married. I'd assumed that things would go on as before, but it turned out that Rupert thought that wives should be kept firmly at home. Losing my job meant that I could give up my "career nonsense" and settle down to looking after him!'

She shook her head, still outraged whenever she thought about Rupert's attitude. 'I can see now that we just didn't know each other well enough to get married, and that it would have been a disaster if we had, but at the time it all blew up into the most terrible argument.' Her careful smile went a little awry. 'I ended up throwing his ring in his face and walking out.'

'Oh, Phyl, I'm so sorry,' said Chris sympathetically. 'Two blows in one day!'

'The awful thing is that when I'd calmed down a bit, I realised that losing my job hurt far more than losing Rupert,' Phyllida confessed. 'Oh, I know I thought he was perfect—handsome, successful, sophisticated—but I couldn't marry anyone who thought of me as just another decorative item.'

'He sounded ideal for you,' sighed Chris. 'But then, perhaps you're like me, and need someone completely different?'

For some reason, Jake Tregowan's image wavered in front of Phyllida's eyes.

She could picture him far too clearly for her own comfort: the cool, distinctive angles of his face, the decisive line of his jaw, the quiet, curling mouth and those disconcerting eyes with their smile lurking behind the exasperated expression...

They were all unaccountably familiar, and she

frowned. 'All I need at the moment is to get away from it all for a bit.'

'Well, you've come to the right place for that,' said Chris cheerfully. 'Unfortunately this is a very busy time at the marina, so I'll have to work, but you can come along too if you like. It's hard work, but fun—and you'll like Jake.'

Now, if ever, was the time to tell Chris that she had already met Jake, and hadn't liked him at all, but the words stuck in Phyllida's throat. For some reason, Chris obviously thought that he was wonderful, and Phyllida didn't want to spoil their first evening by disillusioning her. The complicated explanations could wait until tomorrow.

But Phyllida never had the chance to explain just why she had unaccountably forgotten to mention her meeting with Jake Tregowan. She fell into an exhausted sleep as soon as her head hit the pillow, and didn't wake until the sun came streaming into her room.

A phone was ringing somewhere. That must have been what had woken her, she realised, but it stopped abruptly when the receiver was picked up. Chris must still be at home.

Phyllida lay for a while trying to remember the last time she had seen hot, bright sunshine, but her thoughts began to drift to the previous night. In the clear light of day, the trip from Adelaide had acquired an even more surreal quality in retrospect. Had she really flown through the darkness in that tiny plane? Had that been *her* sobbing on her suitcase? Had Jake Tregowan really kissed her, and had she really kissed him back?

Phyllida sat up abruptly. It would have been nice to dismiss it all as a bad dream, but Jake's memory was much too vivid for that. Her palm still tingled where he had clasped her hand. He was real, all right. Much too real.

Swinging her legs out of bed, she pulled on a towelling dressing-gown rather crossly. She would have liked to have stayed in bed, but Jake Tregowan had ruined that. She had no intention of lying there thinking about *him*. Now that she was awake, she might as well get up.

Yawning, she tied the robe round her as she wandered along to the kitchen. Chris was there, talking on the phone with her back to the door, but as Phyllida hesitated in the doorway she put down the receiver and turned.

The look on her face drove all thoughts of Jake Tregowan from Phyllida's mind. 'Chris! What on earth's the matter? You look terrible!'

'It's Mike,' said Chris, her expression blank with shock. 'That was the hospital in Brisbane. He's been in an accident. Oh, Phyl, what am I going to do?'

Phyllida paid off the taxi and turned to look at the marina. In front of her steps led down to a long jetty, branching out into wooden pontoons which were lined with an impressive array of yachts. They rocked gently in the swell, their masts tall and straight against the vast, glaring blueness of the sky and their pennants slapping in the breeze that sighed and sang through the rigging.

At the end of the jetty was a small wooden building. Phyllida could see the sign painted over its door: SAIL-AWAY. She swallowed, and wiped her hands surreptitiously on her trousers. It had all sounded so easy when she had assured Chris that she would sort everything out with Jake Tregowan, but the prospect of seeing him again made her heart thud painfully against her ribs.

Phyllida squared her shoulders. This was ridiculous! She had coped with far more difficult situations, soothed angry clients and sorted out seemingly intractable problems, so she ought to be more than capable of dealing with Jake Tregowan. She had promised Chris.

A tiny frown creased her forehead. Chris—sturdy, reliable Chris—had gone to pieces when she had heard about Mike's accident, and it had been Phyllida who had arranged a flight to Brisbane, organised a taxi and packed a case. And now she was here to keep the promise she had made as she hugged her goodbye at the airport.

Taking a deep breath, Phyllida walked down the steps and along the jetty to the Sailaway office. The door was standing open to the sunlight. It was stupid to be so nervous, she told herself as she hesitated outside. She had been in such a confused state last night that she had probably built Jake up out of all proportion. She told herself that in the clear light of day he would turn out to be a perfectly ordinary, inoffensive man.

But when she stepped through the door and saw Jake standing by a filing cabinet she knew that she hadn't imagined any of it. He had turned as she knocked lightly on the door, and his brows shot up in surprise.

He was dressed very casually today, in jeans and a plain white T-shirt, but if anything he looked even tougher and more assured than she remembered—the planes of his face more distinct, the impression of controlled competence more striking than ever. His eyes seemed greener, too, flecked with grey, but just as unnervingly sharp as they had been last night.

He dropped the file he had been holding onto the top of the cabinet and pushed the drawer shut with the flat of his hand. 'Well, well,' he said. 'What an unexpected surprise! Don't tell me you need another lift somewhere?'

'No.' It wasn't fair the way the air whooshed from her lungs whenever she saw him, leaving her breathless and flustered. She was supposed to be the cool, capable career girl, not the dithering idiot she became as soon as Jake looked at her with those unsettling, ironic eyes of his. She cleared her throat. 'I came to talk to you.'

'I'm flattered.' He swept a pile of brochures off a chair and gestured her towards it with what Phyllida was sure was mock courtesy. 'You'd better sit down.'

Unsure of where to begin, Phyllida looked around her. Windows on three sides gave a good view of the marina, and through a door at the back she could see a storeroom stacked with piles of towels, linen and cleaning materials. A marine radio stood on the desk, crackling out a weather report, and Jake leant across to turn it down.

'I suppose Chris told you where to find me,' he said, swinging the desk chair round and sitting down. 'I wasn't expecting to see you so soon. When I left you last night, I was under the distinct impression that you'd be happy if you never saw me again!'

Faint colour tinged her cheeks as she remembered how flustered and ungracious she had been. 'That was last night,' she said. 'I'm here for Chris, not for myself. She's had to go to Brisbane. Mike's had an accident.'

His face changed to instant concern. 'That's terrible news,' he said, shocked. 'Is he badly hurt?'

'We don't really know yet. When the hospital rang this morning, they said he hadn't regained consciousness.'

Jake frowned. 'Do they know what happened?'

'He was driving down to Brisbane on his way home,' said Phyllida. 'A witness told the police that he swerved to avoid an overtaking truck and his car turned over as it went off the road.' Her voice wavered slightly and she drew a steadying breath. 'Poor Chris was in a terrible state. I put her on a flight up to Brisbane about an hour ago. She's going to ring me tonight and let me know how he is.'

'Is there anything I can do?' asked Jake, getting to his feet and pacing the office as he assimilated the news.

'Yes,' said Phyllida evenly, glad that he had given her an opening. 'There is. You can take me on in Chris's place while she's away.'

He swung round. '*What*?'

'Chris is worried about her job,' she explained hastily. The last thing she wanted was for Jake to think that *she* wanted to come and work for him! 'With Mike out of action, that's the only income they've got, and she's afraid that if she has to be away for a while, you might have to give her job to someone else. Apparently this is your busiest time?'

'It is, but there's no question of Chris losing her job,' said Jake angrily. 'Quite apart from my responsibilities as an employer, I wouldn't do that to Chris.' He glowered accusingly at Phyllida. 'She and Mike are friends of mine.'

'There's no need to bite my head off!' she snapped. 'It wasn't *my* idea. I told Chris you'd have to be a monster to treat her like that, but she wasn't thinking rationally. She was in such a panic about Mike that she couldn't deal calmly with anything. When something like that happens, you lose all sense of proportion. Trivial things suddenly become major disasters…'

Phyllida faltered as she felt Jake's sardonic eyes on her. She knew he was remembering how she had sat and wept on her suitcase last night, and she shifted uncomfortably in her seat. How trivial her problems had been compared to Chris's!

'Chris was frantic,' she went on, trying to sound calm and reasonable, and not at all like a girl who would burst into tears just because she was tired and her feet hurt. 'She was desperate to go to Mike, but she was worried about letting you down.

'I wanted to go with her to Brisbane, but in the end the only way I could reassure her was to offer to work for you in her place. She said that way she'd know that she could come back whenever she was ready, without letting anybody else get their hopes up about it turning into a permanent job.'

Jake put his hands in his pockets and stood frowning out of the window. A motor boat cruised past, leaving the moored yachts rocking in its curved wake.

'You'll just have to reassure Chris that there's no need for her to worry. I'll have to get someone else in to help out over the next few weeks, but it'll only be a temporary measure, and I'll carry on paying her as normal so that money isn't a problem. She can have her job back whenever she wants it—and Mike too, of course. Though if he's badly hurt it may be some time before he's fit to sail again.'

Phyllida twisted round in her seat to watch him. 'You don't want me to come and work for you, do you?'

'Frankly, no. I'd much rather get someone more suitable in.'

'What do you mean, "more suitable"?' she asked, offended. 'What's wrong with me?'

'You're English, for a start.'

'What difference does that make?'

Jake turned from the window and came back to his seat. 'I took on an English girl for the summer last November. She seemed to have all the right experience, and I thought I'd give international relations a chance, but she was a sloppy worker and she only lasted a couple of weeks before deciding that it was too much like hard work and heading off to Adelaide. If it hadn't been for Chris, I would have been stuck. English girls aren't top of my popularity list at the moment.'

'So?' said Phyllida defiantly. 'I'm not asking you to like me.'

'It's just as well,' said Jake, with a distinct edge to his voice, and they glared at each other. He sighed abruptly. 'I wonder if you realise quite what's involved?'

'Chris didn't have time to tell me much, but I gathered it was some cooking and a bit of cleaning.'

'It's rather more than that,' said Jake, raking his fingers through his hair in exasperation. 'I operate fifteen boats from here. Some are chartered by experienced sailors, other parties need a skipper like Mike to go with them. Occasionally a party will bring everything with them, but most people ask us to do the provisioning for them.

'It's very flexible. They can either take the food we've provided and do the cooking themselves, or Chris prepares as many meals as possible in advance so they just need to be heated up.' He swivelled round to face Phyllida again. 'Can you cook?'

'Of course,' she said loftily. 'My dinner parties are famous.'

'I'm talking about good, plain food, not pretentious dinner party fare,' said Jake with a repressive look. 'Sailing parties aren't interested in nouvelle cuisine.'

'Well, I expect I can manage to cook something boring, if that's what you really want!' snapped Phyllida, provoked. 'It can't be that difficult.'

'You'd be surprised,' he warned her. 'Chris not only plans the menus for each boat, but does the shopping, stocks the fridge and the lockers and prepares meals for those who've ordered them. On top of that she cleans the boats as they come in, so they're ready for the change-over. That means changing the linen in the cabins, checking the inventory and replacing anything not up to standard. Everything has to be spotless. She also helps out in the office—answering the phone, typing, that kind of thing.'

'That's not a job, that's slave labour!' said Phyllida, appalled.

'I didn't think you'd like it,' said Jake. 'Chris makes it look easy, but you're not used to working.'

'Yes, I am!' When she *thought* of the hours she'd spent in the office, working late over a report or a special presentation! Phyllida's brown eyes snapped. 'It may interest you to know that I'm used to working extremely hard!'

'You're used to sitting behind a desk and being clever,' he said, unimpressed. 'That's not work. I need someone who's not afraid to roll up her sleeves and get her hands dirty—not someone with a fancy title whose greatest physical exertion is picking up the phone!'

'I may not get my hands dirty, but I still need to be tough to survive,' Phyllida pointed out. 'I have to be able to manage people, take responsibility, and organise work so that it gets done in the most efficient way possible. Instead of sneering, you could be thinking about how to make the most of my executive skills.'

'You don't need to be able to run a committee meeting or dictate memos to clean a boat!' Jake leant forward suddenly and took her hands, turning them up to run his thumbs over her palms. 'Look at these hands! They're not tough enough to cope with weeks on end of scrubbing and polishing and scouring.'

Phyllida's mouth was dry. It was as if her whole body was focused on the light stroke of his thumbs. She was excruciatingly aware of every millimetre of his skin touching hers as the fire flickered up from palm to wrist, wrist to shoulder, and on to burn right through her, melting her bones and setting her spine aquiver.

'They'll get used to it.' Her tongue felt thick and unwieldy, and it was a real effort to get the words out.

'Ah, but will you?' Jake released her hands and sat back in his chair, studying her as if she was a rather awkward bit of furniture he had to decide what to do with.

'I'm tougher than I look.' She was sitting bolt-upright, chin lifted stubbornly, although the brown eyes were wide and indignant.

Conscious of the ridiculously pathetic impression she must have made last night, she had made an effort to look crisp and practical, in blue and white striped trousers and a white top, but she was convinced that Jake still saw her as she had been then, weeping on her suitcase in her crumpled suit.

The light through the window caught the nut-coloured tints in the shining bob that framed her small, determined face, and, unsettled by his inspection, she lifted a hand and smoothed the hair behind one ear in an unconsciously nervous gesture.

'I don't think you're nearly as tough as you'd like to think you are,' sighed Jake, and her face flamed at the challenge.

'Try me!'

An irritable expression crossed his face. 'Last night you were full of what a high-powered executive you were and how important your career was. Are you really asking me to believe you'd be happy chopping onions and scrubbing decks for the next few weeks?'

'I would if it put Chris's mind at rest,' said Phyllida, looking him straight in the eye. 'Look, I don't *want* to spend my time in Australia working for you, any more than you want to have me, but I promised Chris that I would, so that's what I'm going to do.

'I don't know why you're objecting,' she went on crossly. 'You said you wanted to help Chris, and this would reassure her more than anything. Hasn't she got enough problems at the moment without worrying about what's happening here? Maybe I'm not the most suitable person you could have, but I'm saving you the trouble of finding someone else, and you might at least give me a chance before you decide that I can't cope!'

She stuck her chin up proudly and stared at him with bright, challenging eyes. 'You never know, you might even find that I'm tougher than you think!'

There was a tiny silence. Jake looked at her curiously, the grey-green eyes narrowed, a gleam of what might have been admiration in their depths. 'I might,' he agreed slowly, and the air was suddenly strumming with tension. It was as if someone had flicked a switch, sending an electric charge between them, and Phyllida's heart began a slow, painful thud.

'Why are you doing this, Phyllida?' he asked. 'You don't have to. I could get someone else in and we could just tell Chris that you were working here. She wouldn't be any the wiser.'

She shook her head. 'I couldn't lie to Chris.'

'And what about your holiday?' He clicked his fingers in mock apology. 'Sorry! Your *sabbatical*. Aren't you supposed to be spending the next few weeks planning your next career moves and preparing for your great promotion?'

Phyllida's eyes slid from his. She had forgotten about that particular lie. If Jake hadn't been so sarcastic about the whole idea of her having a career, she might have been tempted to tell him the truth. As it was, she was damned if she would give him the satisfaction!

'I came out to get a change of perspective,' she said. 'All I really need is time to think, and I presume I'll be allowed to do that while I'm scrubbing the decks. Or is that too executive for you?' she added acidly.

'No, thinking's allowed,' said Jake with some amusement. 'Arguing isn't. You can leave your career at home every day. I don't want to hear about how important you are, or how different things could be if only I wasn't so unreasonable and prejudiced. A lot of the work is boring and menial, so don't say you weren't warned and don't complain!'

'You mean you'll take me on?' said Phyllida, sitting up, and he sighed.

'Only for Chris's sake. If it means so much to her, then I'm prepared to put up with you. But only if you're prepared to work as hard as she does.'

'I will,' she promised eagerly. She had begun to think that he was going to refuse to take her after all, and now she was too relieved at being able to reassure Chris to object to his tone.

'Let's hope it's not for too long,' said Jake, resigned to his fate. 'When Chris and Mike come back I'm sure we'll both welcome them with open arms, but until then it looks as if we're stuck with each other!'

CHAPTER FOUR

DECISION made, Jake immediately became brisk and businesslike. 'Have you got a driving licence?'

'Not with me,' said Phyllida guiltily. 'Packing was such a rush when a seat came up at the last minute. I never even thought about my driving licence.'

'Judging by the size of that case, you seemed to have had time to think about bringing everything else,' he commented with some acidity. 'I'd have thought a high-powered executive like you would have been a little more organised about everything.'

'I remembered everything else,' she said, stung. 'How was I to know I'd need a driving licence?'

'I suppose you were expecting Chris and Mike to act as unpaid chauffeurs?'

Phyllida ground her teeth. 'I didn't know *what* to expect! I certainly didn't expect to be cross-examined just because I forgot one piece of paper! What does it matter anyway?'

'I was going to give you the van so that you could go shopping, but now it looks as if I'm going to have to ferry you around everywhere. It's beginning to become something of a habit!'

'Well, it's not one of my choosing, I can assure you!'

'Oh, I forgot—you're the girl who's so good at looking after yourself, aren't you?' said Jake nastily. 'Funny how it always seems to involve someone else doing all the work!'

'We're only talking about the occasional trip to the

shops,' Phyllida snapped. 'If it's such an appalling prospect for you, I'll find some other way to get there!'

'Like you did last night?'

'Last night was different,' she said sullenly. 'I wasn't myself, and you know it! Anybody would have given up after the journey I'd had—and you didn't help, being so...so...'

'So what?' he asked, amusement gleaming suddenly in his eyes.

'So disagreeable!' said Phyllida, provoked into an undiplomatic retort.

Jake wasn't going to let her get away with that. 'Disagreeable?' he echoed in mock astonishment. 'I carried your case, I flew you all the way to Port Lincoln, I drove you to Chris's door... What did I do that was so disagreeable?'

Phyllida felt as if she was being driven into a corner, and searched her mind frantically for some instance of his ungallant behaviour. It wasn't so much what he had done, it was the mockery in his eyes and the ironic note in his voice and the disturbing way he had made her feel, but she couldn't tell him that.

'You kissed me,' she said sulkily at last. It was the only thing she could think of that she could reasonably hold against him.

'You didn't think it was that disagreeable at the time,' said Jake unfairly, not in the least put out at being reminded of the embarrassing incident.

'You took advantage of me,' she accused him, but he only looked back at her blandly.

'In that case we're quits, aren't we?'

It was Phyllida who dropped her eyes first. Why had she brought up that wretched kiss? Its memory seemed to shimmer in the air between them, tingling on her lips and shivering down her spine. She could still feel the hardness of his body beneath her hands, the jolting excitement of his mouth on hers.

'There must be some way I can get myself around, anyway,' she said, struggling to bring the conversation back to less dangerous ground. 'Aren't there any buses?'

'This isn't London,' said Jake. 'You might be able to get to the shops all right, but even if you did you wouldn't be able to carry everything back.'

'I could get a taxi,' she said defiantly.

'You could,' he agreed, 'if you were prepared to pay for it. Because I'm not going to when I've got a perfectly good van standing empty! Were you proposing to get a taxi from Chris and Mike's house every morning, too?'

'I hadn't thought about it.'

'Well, think about it now. The marina's a long way from their house, and you certainly won't find a convenient bus waiting at the end of the road.'

Phyllida pressed her lips together. 'I've managed to hold down a tough job and live on my own in London for several years,' she reminded him coldly. 'I expect I'll be able to survive in Port Lincoln.'

'That's a matter of opinion,' said Jake astringently. He pointed out of the window. 'I live on that headland on the other side of the marina. It's close enough for you to walk if necessary.' He sounded unflatteringly resigned. 'You'd better come and stay with me, I suppose.'

'Stay with *you*?' echoed Phyllida, horrified. 'I'd rather sleep on the beach!'

Jake clicked his tongue in exasperation. 'However you got to the top of your supposedly high-flying career, it obviously wasn't by tact!'

'And you didn't get where you are by charm!' she snapped back. 'It wasn't exactly the warmest of invitations! Anyway, there's no question of my moving in with you!'

'This isn't some ruse to get my hands on your body, if that's what you're worried about, so there's really no need to react like some outraged spinster,' sighed Jake. 'Quite frankly, I can think of more congenial companions myself. I don't particularly fancy spending the next few weeks with a little spitfire, but I don't see any alternative.'

'The alternative is that I stay at Chris and Mike's house!'

'And how are you going to get here every morning?'

'I'll think of something!'

'The house is quite big enough for two of us, you know. You could treat it just like a flat.'

'I'd rather stay where I am,' said Phyllida firmly. The thought of spending her days near Jake was disturbing enough, but living with him as well...! She felt twitchy at the very idea.

Jake regarded the small, stubborn figure sitting opposite him with frustration. 'Why do you always insist on learning things the hard way, Phyllida?'

'Why do *you* refuse to accept that I can look after myself?' she retorted, and held up a hand before he could answer. 'And if you mention last night again, I shall scream! I *know* I was pathetic, but believe me, it won't happen again.' She met his sceptical gaze defiantly. 'I'm good at what I do, and I'll be good at this too. You just wait and see!'

'Well, if you're so determined to prove yourself, you can begin right now,' said Jake, resigned. He got to his feet. 'I'll show you round, then you can get straight to work. We've got a lot to do this week.'

He showed her the storeroom and the filing system,

and explained how the radio worked. 'We keep a twenty-four-hour listening watch for our boats,' he said. 'So if you hear someone calling up and I'm not around, you'll have to come and answer. It should be mostly straightforward, but you may be asked for some advice. Have you got any experience of sailing?'

'Does a day-trip to Boulogne count?'

Jake sighed. 'Oh, that's a great help! You must have done *some* sailing?'

'I don't see why,' Phyllida objected. 'Sailing at home always sounds cold and wet and uncomfortable. Chris and Mike love that sort of thing, but my idea of outdoor activity is sitting on a terrace in the sun!'

Jake glanced down at her vivid face. 'You're not very like Chris, are you?'

Phyllida's expression softened. 'No, it's hard to believe that we're related, isn't it? I think we get on so well just because we *are* so different. I wish I could be more like Chris sometimes,' she admitted, wondering how best she could describe her cousin. 'She's so...restful.'

'It's certainly not a word I'd use to describe *you*,' Jake agreed, and she met his eyes challengingly.

'Oh? What *would* you use?'

He grinned unexpectedly. 'That would be telling.'

His smile took Phyllida unawares. Just when she had decided that he was even more insufferable than she had remembered, he had to go and do that to her! It had been disturbing enough in the dim light of the plane, but now her heart missed a beat.

She could see the way laughter starred lines beneath his eyes, and creased his cheeks with humour. His teeth were heartstoppingly white against his brown skin. Phyllida felt something twist alarmingly inside her. She even forgot to breathe until the sharpening look in Jake's eyes reminded her of where she was and what she was supposed to be doing.

Breathe in, breathe out. It was easy when you tried.

Outside, the sky was a blazing blue, the sun high and glaring. Phyllida had to screw up her eyes as Jake led her out to the boats. A stiff breeze from the sea blew her neat, shining brown hair about her face, and she had to hold it back with one hand as she looked down the jetty, Jake's smile still burning at the back of her mind.

The water looked almost colourless in the fierce glitter of the sun, but Phyllida could hear it slapping against the sides of the jetty and effortlessly lifting the boats up and down. She watched their gently hypnotic rise and fall as if she had never seen a yacht before, never noticed how the curve of the hull contrasted with the lance-like straightness of the mast and the geometric lines of the rigging.

It must be something to do with the diamond-bright air, she decided, so unlike the soft light of England. Everything seemed almost unnaturally distinct, every boat uniquely outlined against its neighbour. Each one was different—graceful yachts were moored next to huge motor cruisers bristling with antennae, sleek speedboats next to sturdy fishing smacks—but as they rocked together in the water it seemed to Phyllida that they all evoked the same tantalising promise of the sea, with its exhilarating freedom and freshness.

Closing her eyes, she turned her face up to the sun and sniffed at the sharp tang of the sea carried in by the breeze, smiling at the sound of the gulls squabbling on the water, the creak of the ropes and the chink and rattle of the halyards against a hundred masts.

It was all very different from the sounds she was used

to: phones ringing, the chatter of computer printers, voices raised in argument or laughter, the subdued roar of traffic outside the window and the distant wail of a siren. The sounds of the marina were at once alien and strangely familiar.

In spite of everything, Phyllida was suddenly, fiercely glad that she had come, and as she opened her eyes and turned to Jake she was still smiling.

He was watching her with an odd expression in his eyes. 'I thought you'd fallen asleep,' he said, as if making an effort to sound his usual acid self.

Phyllida shook her head, and her mock-diamond earrings, shaped in a square like a battery of floodlights, flashed in the sunlight. 'I was just...thinking.'

'That makes a change, anyway,' said Jake drily, turning away to lead her along the jetty. The pontoon rose and fell beneath their feet as he told her the names of the boats, pointing out each one affectionately.

'Most of the boats are out at the moment, but this is *Persephone*. That's *Dora Dee* next to her—she's a beauty, isn't she?—and this one here is *Calypso*. She only came in yesterday, so she needs cleaning. So does *Valli*.' He pointed to a boat tied up to *Calypso*, her name proudly proclaimed on the blue cover tied neatly over the folded mainsail.

The name sounded familiar to Phyllida. 'That's one of Chris and Mike's boats, isn't it?'

'She was, until I so callously bought her from them in my ruthless takeover of their company.'

Phyllida had the grace to blush. 'I'm sorry about that,' she said awkwardly, cringing as she remembered how she had held forth about her cousin's misfortune. 'Chris told me what really happened. She's very grateful to you. I just jumped to the wrong conclusions from her letter—takeovers were rather a sore point with me at the time.'

'Does that mean that you've now jumped to the right conclusions about me?' Jake asked.

There was a teasing look in his grey-green eyes, and the long, cool mouth twitched as he tried not to smile at her determinedly humble expression. His hands were thrust casually into the pockets of his jeans, and the wind riffled his brown hair, fluttering the cotton T-shirt against the hard outline of his body.

For one dismaying moment, Phyllida felt her insides melt as she looked at him. It wasn't fair the way he could do that to her just by standing there, with his eyes half screwed up against the bright light and the smile tugging at his mouth. Resentment made her sound colder than she had intended. 'I think I'll suspend judgement on that until I know you better.'

'It's not like you to be so cautious, is it, Phyllida?'

'How do you know what I'm like?' she demanded suspiciously, following him on down the jetty.

'Observation,' said Jake. He stepped from the pontoon into the cockpit of a boat with *Ariadne* painted on her side and held out a hand to help Phyllida across. 'You told me yourself that you were impulsive, and everything I've seen of you so far suggests that you're far too prone to leap before you look!'

Dithering on the edge of the pontoon, Phyllida came to the reluctant conclusion that, unless she accepted his hand, there was no way to get down into the boat without making a complete and utter fool of herself. Grudgingly, she gave him her hand and let him steady her as she clambered awkwardly over the guard rails. A sudden gust of wind made the boat rock abruptly, sending her staggering against the rock-steady hardness of his body.

Cheeks aflame, she jerked herself away, only to stumble over some ropes lying coiled in the cockpit. 'It's a constant surprise to me how someone who looks so fragile and delicate can be so clumsy,' said Jake acidly, picking her up.

'I am not clumsy! Anyone would trip over with all these stupid ropes lying around!'

'I didn't notice any ropes around when you were dealing with your suitcase last night,' said Jake unfairly. 'And, for the record, these are not ropes. They're known as sheets on a boat.'

'They look like ropes to me,' Phyllida muttered under her breath, but she followed Jake down some wooden steps into a surprisingly light and airy saloon, high enough for Jake to stand up with ease. There were two comfortably padded seats on either side of a table, and a neat area with a small oven set on gimbals and a lid with a metal handle set into the worktop.

Phyllida lifted it and peered down into a sloping compartment with an element fixed to one side. 'What's this?'

'A battery-operated fridge,' said Jake. 'We put in a block of ice as well, and it'll keep food fresh for a week. You'll need to bear that in mind when drawing up your menus.'

'This is the kitchen, then?' said Phyllida, looking about her with interest, and sliding open locker doors to reveal neatly stacked plates and glasses.

'No, it's the galley,' he said repressively, and she rolled her eyes.

'Oh, all right—the *galley*.'

She was soon lost in a welter of nautical terminology as Jake showed her over the boat. She peered into the three immaculately fitted out cabins and the tiny cramped space allotted for a shower, basin and loo—or head, as she was supposed to call it now. Jake's face was alight with enthusiasm, and he ran his hand lovingly over the wooden fittings, pointing out radios, charts and compasses and a baffling array of instruments that Phyllida could only stare at blankly, until Jake accused her of not paying attention.

'I am,' she protested. 'It's just all a bit confusing if you've never been on a boat before.' She didn't tell him that it would have been a lot easier to concentrate if she hadn't kept bumping into him. There wasn't all that much room to move below deck, and whenever she stepped back from looking at something she would find herself brushing against Jake.

She was disturbingly aware of the taut solidity of his body and the feel of his steadying hand, and, infuriatingly, she kept remembering last night's kiss in vivid detail—how he had held her against him, how tantalisingly persuasive his lips had been, how the treacherous excitement had shivered along her senses. That was all far, far more confusing than bilge pumps, depth sounders or dials showing wind speed in knots.

She was immensely relieved when Jake made his way back on deck. 'Well, what do you think?' he asked, patting the fibreglass with unashamed affection.

Phyllida looked at the fibreglass and wondered if *it* tingled when he touched it. 'I think you obviously like boats more than women,' she said a little tartly. 'It's interesting that all yours have girls' names.'

'Nothing unusual in that,' said Jake with a glimmering smile. 'But since you mention it, Phyllida, you're quite right. I *do* prefer boats to women. They're just as expensive to run, but no woman ever gave the pleasure of being out at sea, with the boat singing through the waves, just you and the boat and the elements, and nobody there to nag or argue or demand to be taken home as soon as the wind gets stiff enough to mess up her hair!'

His tone was suddenly acid, and Phyllida couldn't help wondering if he was remembering anyone in particular. She wondered what it would be like to be the girl Jake loved, the girl he took sailing. It was hard to imagine the kind of girl who would worry about her hair when she had Jake.

'So there's no room for women in your life?' she asked as he helped her back onto the pontoon.

Jake glanced down at her, the grey-flecked eyes unreadable. 'I didn't say that.'

'But you haven't yet met anyone who can compete with a good sail?' Phyllida had meant to sound sarcastic, but instead succeeded in merely sounding rather put out as she pointedly drew her hand from his.

He considered her, his gaze resting on her vivid elfin face, with the wide brown eyes catching the sunlight and the hair which had been so smooth and neat tangling in the breeze. She looked small and vibrant, and somehow defiant.

'Not yet,' he said slowly.

Phyllida felt herself grow incalculably hot as his eyes slid down the line of her throat to her open collar, and on over the slender, deceptively delicate figure. 'Do you have a boat of your own, or do you charter them all?' she asked quickly.

'No, that's mine, moored at the end there.' Jake's tone changed as he pointed to a particularly elegant yacht with a gleaming wooden deck, its brass fittings glittering in the sun. 'The *Ali B*. Isn't she beautiful?'

'Gorgeous,' said Phyllida, but there was a suspicious undercurrent of jealousy to her sarcasm.

Jake laughed, unperturbed. 'I think so, anyway. Do you want to see her?'

'I thought I was here to work?' said Phyllida, who had no desire to see Jake drooling over a stupid boat. 'What shall I do first?' she asked, looking around.

'You can start by cleaning *Calypso*,' Jake told her. He took her back to the office and found her an aluminium bucket stuffed full of cleaning materials. 'You'll find water at points along the jetty,' he said, handing it to her.

Phyllida took the bucket, inspecting its contents rather dubiously. 'Is that it?' she asked as he turned back to his desk without further instructions.

'What more do you want?'

'Well...aren't you going to tell me what I should do?'

'You're the great career woman, Phyllida. Use those much-vaunted executive skills of yours to work it out for yourself. You seemed very sure you could do the job just as well as anyone else; now's your chance to prove it. I'll check things over when you've finished, and let you know if you're up to standard.'

The idea of her work being checked by Jake Tregowan brought Phyllida's chin up. So he was waiting for her to make a mess of things, was he? She would show him!

Marching down the jetty, she encountered her first problem—getting onto *Calypso* by herself. It wasn't that it was such a big jump, but the boat kept riding up and away from the pontoon, just as Phyllida was about to step off, and when she did finally manage to get one leg over the guard rail another wave caught her spreadeagled between boat and pontoon, and only an extremely undignified scramble got her onto the deck with her bucket in one piece. Phyllida brushed herself down and hoped that no one had been watching.

'Would you like me to get some water for you,

Phyllida?' Jake's voice from the pontoon behind her made her swing around. 'You seemed to be having a little trouble getting aboard there.'

Of course, he *would* have been watching! Phyllida glared at him, about to tell him what he could do with his water when it occurred to her that it would be even more difficult making the jump with a full bucket of water. 'Thank you,' she said in a frosty voice, emptying the contents of the bucket onto the cockpit seat and swinging it back across the gap.

'I'm sure a professional like you will be able to master the tricky business of getting on and off a boat in no time,' said Jake with a mocking smile as he passed the full bucket back to her.

Some of the water slopped out of the bucket, and Phyllida was sorely tempted to chuck the rest of it back into Jake Tregowan's smugly smiling face. She contented herself with a freezing look and an implacable determination to clean the boat to such a pitch of perfection that even Jake wouldn't be able to find fault with it.

It proved to be much harder work than she had anticipated. The sun beat down on the fibreglass above her head, and without the cooling breeze Phyllida was soon very hot. Her shirt and trousers were sticking to her uncomfortably, and she could feel the sweat trickling down her back.

Calypso was showing all the signs of having been lived in by six people for a week—six people who had spent most of their time on the beach, judging by the amount of sand Phyllida swept up. They had also spent a lot of time eating and drinking. She had to rescrub most of the pots, and the barbecue that had been fixed to the back of the boat was so disgusting that she put it aside to clean properly when she had hot water and a decent pair of rubber gloves.

She gathered up dirty bedlinen, wiped down sinks and shelves, contorted herself into impossible positions to clean out every nook and cranny she could find, scrubbed the stove until it gleamed and swept every inch of the floor. When it go so hot that she couldn't bear it any more, she climbed up the companionway to dump a pile of bedding in the cockpit and feel the blessedly cool breeze against her skin for a moment.

Her face was bright red, her hair sticking unpleasantly to the back of her neck. She felt as limp as a wrung rag, and the sight of Jake looking relaxed on the neighbouring boat did nothing to improve her temper. He was sitting on the raised edge of the cockpit, his feet on the lockers, polishing some metal parts with a grubby rag. The sun was dancing on the water around him, the boat rocking gently in the breeze. He looked cool and comfortable and completely at home.

'I see you believe in setting an example of hard work to your staff,' she said acidly, dropping the bedding onto the lockers.

Jake eyed her dishevelled appearance with some amusement. She was hardly recognisable as the girl in the smart suit who had stood at the check-in desk at Adelaide airport. Instead she looked hot and tired and decidedly cross.

'I need to be able to hear the radio and the phone,' he explained, laying down his rag. 'I could sit in the office, but I might as well be out here doing something useful.'

'You could hear them down there,' said Phyllida, pointing down into the hot cabin. 'And then *I* could have a nice time sitting on deck in the sun!'

'Do you know how to put a winch back together

again?' said Jake in a deceptively pleasant tone, gesturing at the bits of metal around his feet.

'No.'

'That's why you're down there and I'm up here.' Picking up his rag, he calmly resumed his polishing. 'If you want a cushier job, Phyllida, you're going to have to learn a bit more about boats.'

'I'm learning quite enough about boats down here, thank you,' she grumbled, disappearing back down the companionway.

At last she had finished. Struggling wearily up the steps with her bucket, Phyllida tipped the dirty water over the side, and stashed all her materials back inside before sarcastically inviting Jake over for an inspection.

He came, moving with the ease and unselfconscious grace of a cat between the two boats. Phyllida thought of her own clumsy boarding and hated him. She watched, simmering, as Jake methodically checked the cabins.

'You haven't cleaned the fridge—it's still full of water. And the lockers beneath the seats are a mess, but otherwise...not bad.'

Not bad! Phyllida blew her damp fringe off her forehead and glowered at him. She had never worked so hard before in her life, and all he could say was 'not bad'!

'That's just below deck,' he added, climbing up to where she sat limply in the cockpit. 'There's still the decks and the cockpit up here to be scrubbed, and the inventory will have to be checked as well.'

Phyllida stared at him, aghast. 'What, now?' She didn't feel as if she could stand up, let alone contemplate another cleaning marathon.

Jake frowned. 'Tomorrow. You look as if you've been hit by a ten-ton truck. Are you all right?'

'I do feel a bit odd, now you mention it,' said Phyllida.

She had felt fine until she'd sat down, but a wave of exhaustion had suddenly engulfed her, leaving her feeling quite light-headed.

'Jet lag,' said Jake tersely. 'That's all we need!'

'I'll be perfectly all right if I just sit down for five minutes,' she said, determined not to give him any excuse for accusing her of being weak and pathetic, but Jake simply ignored her and lifted her bodily to her feet.

'Come on, I'd better get you home.'

'To Chris's house,' she reminded him. She wouldn't put it past Jake to take advantage of her state to get his own way.

Jake sighed. 'Oh, all right. To Chris's house, if you must.' He glanced at her. 'Are you always this stubborn?'

'I'm not some slave you've just acquired,' she told him. 'I've got a mind of my own.'

'Pity you don't use it, then,' said Jake acidly. 'I'll take you back to Chris's now, but this is the last time. You'll have to get yourself in to the marina tomorrow—and if you expect me to subsidise you for taxis, you've got another think coming.'

'I won't need a taxi,' Phyllida told him loftily as he pulled up outside Chris's house. She couldn't wait to get to bed, but after she'd got out and closed the door behind her she leant back through the open window. The brown eyes were clouded with tiredness, but there was no mistaking the challenge in their gaze. 'I'm going to walk.'

CHAPTER FIVE

'YOU'RE late!'

Phyllida collapsed against the door of the office and eyed Jake with acute hostility. It hadn't taken her long that morning to regret her proud boast about walking in. Deep sleep had left her feeling woozy and sluggish, and she had been reaching for the phone to call a taxi when she had remembered that in her rush to get from Adelaide to Port Lincoln she hadn't had time to change any money.

Chris had given her what she could, but it had only just been enough for yesterday's taxi to the marina as it was. It looked as if she was going to have to walk after all.

Now she pushed her fringe wearily out of her eyes and wondered if she looked as hot and bothered as she felt. 'I'm sorry, but it's taken me over an hour to get here,' she told Jake.

It had seemed twice as long as she toiled along the wide, empty streets, wincing as her shoes rubbed against feet that were still tender from the other night. At least she had remembered to wear a hat. She fanned herself with it in an effort to cool her pink face.

Jake was predictably unsympathetic. 'You should have taken that into account before you insisted on walking,' he said. 'You'll just have to leave an hour earlier tomorrow morning. I've got people coming in to charter three of those boats the day after tomorrow, and they won't be ready if you swan in at this time every day.'

'I've said I'm sorry,' said Phyllida through gritted

teeth, pulling off her shoes to rub her sore feet. 'I won't be late tomorrow.'

'You'd better not be,' said Jake in a steel-edged voice. 'If you want to keep this job for Chris, you're going to have to do better than you've done so far. Now, you can start by finishing off *Calypso*, and then move on to *Valli* and *Dora Dee*.'

Phyllida's face was bright with anger as she snatched up the cleaning bucket and stalked down the jetty. She longed to tell Jake what he could do with his job, but Chris had rung last night, and had sounded so tired and anxious about Mike that not for the world would Phyllida add to her worries.

She was just going to have to learn to put up with Jake—although she had been furious to learn that Chris had already spoken to him and had been enthusiastic about the idea of Phyllida moving into his house.

'I'd feel so much better to know that you were with Jake instead of stuck out there on your own,' she had said. 'It's a lovely house, and he's promised to look after you for me.'

Oh, he had, had he? Phyllida had told Chris that she would see, but she had vowed to show Jake once and for all that she didn't need to be looked after—least of all by him!

Now, fury carried her over the guard rails without her stopping to think about falling into the water. She found scrubbing the decks a useful therapy too, and finished cleaning *Calypso* in double-quick time before refilling her water bucket and clambering across onto *Valli*. It wasn't the most elegant of manoeuvres, but at least she did it by herself.

Phyllida scoured and swept and polished with a sort of concentrated fury, imagining Jake's face beneath her scrubbing brush and wishing she could as easily scrub away the memory of that wretched kiss. The feel of his lips, the touch of his hands, the dark throb of excitement...

The memories lurked annoyingly, ready to drift across Phyllida's mind when she least suspected it, and making her falter in what she was doing. That only made her crosser than ever, and she would scrub even harder, but the time passed more quickly than she would have believed possible.

She could hardly believe it when Jake hailed her from the jetty and she sat back on her heels to see that it was one o'clock. 'Come and have some lunch,' he said. 'It's time you had a break.'

Phyllida wiped her forehead with the back of her arm. She had successfully scrubbed out her anger, and could see now that she had been really rather silly in blaming everything on Jake. After all, she was the one who had been over an hour late.

'I haven't got any money,' she said, getting to her feet a little stiffly. 'Is there a bank nearby where I can change some?'

'You can do that when we go and buy the provisions tomorrow,' said Jake. 'I'll buy you lunch today. You look as if you could do with a good square meal. When was the last time you ate?'

'I had some fruit for breakfast, but I wasn't very hungry last night.' Phyllida was almost getting used to climbing on and off boats by now, and she stepped down beside Jake without mishap. 'I suppose I haven't had a proper meal since the plane.'

'You can hardly call airline food a proper meal,' Jake grunted. 'We'll go up to the marina restaurant.'

'I can't go to a restaurant dressed like this!' Phyllida

protested, gesturing down at the shorts and T-shirt she had put on because they were the only things she didn't mind getting dirty. Just as well, too, as they were already splashed and stained and more than a little grimy.

'This isn't exactly a five-star restaurant,' said Jake sardonically. 'There's no need to panic. You look fine.' He paused, watching Phyllida tie the laces of her canvas shoes.

In spite of the damp patches, the yellow T-shirt and white shorts looked fresh and summery, somehow emphasising her gamine quality. She hadn't bothered to blowdry her hair into its usual sleek bob, and instead it fell in a shiny, rather tangled mop around her face.

'In fact,' he went on slowly as she straightened, 'you look very nice—much better than you did in that ridiculous suit. That smart, sophisticated image obviously wasn't the real you.'

'Yes, it was!' She ruffled up instantly, obscurely piqued by that tepid 'very nice'. Hardly the most effusive of compliments! 'You may not think much of dressing smartly, but in my job what you look like is important.'

'Then perhaps your job isn't the real you either?'

'It is,' she insisted. Working at Pritchard Price had been all-absorbing. It had been stimulating, challenging, fun...everything a job should have been, and she had loved it. 'It's the most important thing about me.'

Jake looked at her. 'I'd have said that the most important thing about you was the fact that you're prepared to get down on your hands and knees and tackle a hard, dirty job to help your cousin out,' he said, and headed up the steps leading up from the jetty.

Puzzled, Phyllida stared after him. She found Jake very confusing. It was typical of him to disagree with her so absolutely, but surely that had been a genuine note of respect in his voice?

Rupert had always had a smooth line in compliments, she remembered. In fact, once or twice she had suspected that he flattered her automatically, without actually seeing what she was wearing or tasting what she had cooked. It would be much harder to win a compliment from a man like Jake. Perhaps she hadn't done so badly with 'very nice' after all!

As Jake had promised, the restaurant was far from formal, but the food was delicious. They sat outside, on a terrace overlooking the marina, and Phyllida thought she had rarely enjoyed a meal more. When a platter of local seafood arrived with a crisp salad, she suddenly discovered that she was ravenous.

Jake watched her apply herself to her food with amusement. 'Do you do everything with such fierce determination?' He grinned.

Guiltily, Phyllida realised that she had been bolting her food in a most undignified way. 'I didn't realise I was so hungry,' she apologised.

'Oh, it's not just the way you eat. I've noticed it in the way you set about cleaning as well. You were a small fury on the boats this morning—I thought you were going to scrub through the fibreglass!'

'That was because—' Phyllida stopped. She could hardly tell Jake that she had spent the entire morning thinking about him. 'I've always been a believer in the "do a job, do it properly" philosophy,' she improvised. It was true, anyway. She had always hated not being good at things, and would far rather not do anything at all than be bad at it.

'It's all or nothing for you, isn't it, Phyllida?'

'I suppose you could say that,' she said, returning her

attention to her plate. 'I'm certainly prepared to give everything to whatever job I'm doing.'

'And what about love? Do you throw yourself as wholeheartedly into that, or are you too busy pursuing your precious career?'

Jake's voice held the same bitter edge she had heard in it once or twice before, and she glanced at him curiously. His knuckles were tight around his glass, and the green eyes had darkened to grey, but the contemptuous expression vanished when he saw that she was watching him.

'What's it to you?' she asked suspiciously.

'Just wondering whether you conform to type, that's all.'

'What type?'

'A type of obsessive career woman, determined to succeed whatever it costs.'

'That's absolute rubbish!' said Phyllida scornfully. 'What do you know about career women, anyway?'

'Quite a lot. I was married to one for five years.'

Married? Phyllida put down her knife and fork, shaken by the depth of her own reaction at the idea of Jake living with another woman, loving her, laughing with her. 'I didn't know you'd been married,' she said unsteadily.

'It wasn't an experience I'm anxious to repeat,' said Jake. 'My wife was far more in love with her career than she was with me.'

Phyllida remembered her own discovery that losing her job meant more to her than losing Rupert, and she shifted a little uneasily in her chair. 'Perhaps she wanted a fulfilling career as well as you?' she said, justifying her own position as much as Jake's unknown wife's—although it was hard to imagine feeling like that about Jake.

His wife must have been very dedicated to have put

her career before him. Or was that just Jake being a typical man and resenting a woman's success? 'Men are allowed to have a career and a marriage. Why can't it be the same for women? It ought to be possible to have both.'

'Of course,' he said. 'But that only works as long as the career doesn't develop into an obsession that denies a place to the other things that matter in life.'

'That's good, coming from a man who prefers boats to women!'

Jake laughed suddenly. 'Don't worry, Phyllida. I allow myself plenty of time to devote to other interests—including women!'

'What you do in your spare time is hardly likely to be a source of concern to me,' said Phyllida frigidly and not entirely truthfully.

'Of course not,' said Jake, but his eyes seemed to dance with a laughter that tugged at Phyllida's heart.

Dropping her gaze, she concentrated fiercely on her plate, but the look in his eyes continued to shimmer in her mind. She felt edgy, confused. One minute she could swear that he despised her, the next she was sure that he was coming to like her in spite of herself. The fact that she felt exactly the same about him was somehow not reassuring.

She didn't despise him, exactly, but she had always loathed chauvinistic men who were full of good reasons for women not pursuing a career just as vigorously as men. The fact that Rupert had so unexpectedly turned out to be one of them only made things worse. And Jake had none of Rupert's other advantages to compensate; he wasted no time on charm or flattery, he was disagreeable and deliberately provocative at times, he made no secret of the fact that he found her alternately exasperating and faintly ridiculous...

And yet...

There *was* something intriguing about him, Phyllida admitted to herself reluctantly. He made no effort to impress. She was even beginning to wonder if she had imagined the wealthy executive she had first met at Adelaide airport, with his briefcase and subtly expensive clothes. Now he seemed quite at home in jeans and a casual shirt, and seemed happy to spend his day greasing winches or taking an engine to bits.

It didn't fit at all with Phyllida's idea of how a man who owned a fleet of yachts—not to mention a plane and an enormous four-wheel drive—ought to behave. From what Chris had told her money wasn't a problem, and he must have a shrewd sense of business if he ran his own company as well as the vast Tregowan interests in South Australia.

Why didn't he pay someone else to mend the engine, or do the paperwork? And if he wouldn't have a secretary, why didn't he at least buy himself a mobile phone so that he didn't have to run down the jetty whenever the phone rang in the office? Not that Phyllida had ever seen him run. If the phone did ring, he would wipe his hands on a rag, step off the boat and walk in that infuriatingly unhurried way of his down to the office.

Phyllida had watched him on at least three occasions that morning, and had longed for the phone to stop ringing just as he reached it, but of course it never did. If it had been her, she would have leapt off the boat and belted to the phone only to find the caller had hung up when she got there, but they went on ringing patiently for Jake. It was very unfair.

Phyllida was stiff and weary by the time she had finished cleaning that afternoon. She found Jake sitting in the office for once, checking through some booking forms, but when she asked if there was anything else he wanted her to do he shook his head and told her that she'd done enough for the day.

'You go on home,' he said absently, half his mind still on the forms.

Phyllida hesitated. If she could have been transported by magic carpet back to Chris's home, she would have been delighted to take him up on his offer. As it was, she still didn't have any money, and as Jake obviously wasn't going to offer her a lift it looked as if she would have to embark on the long trek back on her sore feet. It was not an inviting prospect.

Still, she had better get on with it, or she would never get back at all. Silently cursing the stubbornness that had made her insist on staying at Chris's house, Phyllida wished Jake a frosty goodbye, squared her shoulders and set off across the marina.

The morning's breeze had died out, and it was hot and still. She limped out to the main road and stood looking down to where it curved off in a faint haze of heat. There seemed to be very little traffic around, only a van, which sped past her in the opposite direction with a brief blast of its horn—although whether it was in warning or tribute, Phyllida couldn't tell.

She looked helplessly up and down the road. From what she had seen so far, the streets seemed to be permanently empty. Didn't the Australians ever go out in their cars? Or were there just not enough of them to fill up the available space? Whatever, it didn't look as if she was even going to get a lift into town.

Phyllida sighed, and began to walk down the road. Then she stopped abruptly. 'This is ridiculous!' she said out loud, and, turning on her heel, she trudged back into the marina, along the jetty, back to the little wooden office and Jake.

He was leaning back in his chair, long legs propped up on the desk, but he put down the list he was studying as Phyllida slunk in the door. 'Forgotten something?'

'No.' Having got this far, she couldn't quite think what she was going to say next.

'In that case, what can I do for you?' Jake knew why she was here, Phyllida was certain. His face might be deadpan, not even the slightest curl to his mouth, but the grey-green eyes were alight with the ironically amused expression that always made her prickle with an unsettling mixture of confusion and hostility and deep, shameful longing to see him smile properly—at her. At her alone.

As usual, Phyllida let the hostility win. It was easier that way. 'You can stop being hateful and disagreeable for a start!' she snapped, dropping into a chair. 'You must know perfectly well why I've come back. And before you start, I'll say it all for you!'

She looked him straight in the eye, holding up her hand as he opened his mouth to speak, and all at once her anger faded.

'I've already refused your offer to have me to stay in no uncertain terms, and I have absolutely no right to ask you to invite me again. I've been stubborn and unreasonable and rude ever since we first met, and I quite agree that it's entirely my own fault if I'm so tired now that I can't walk another step.

'But if we could take all that as read, will you believe me if I say that I really am very sorry I've been so stupid and ungracious, and could I please take you up on your very generous offer to let me stay with you after all?'

Jake swung his legs down to the floor, the mocking look in his eyes replaced by one much harder to read. 'Your feet *must* be hurting!' he teased, but there was a warmer note in his voice, and instead of ruffling up as she usually did, Phyllida found herself remembering suddenly what had happened the last time her feet had hurt.

'They are,' she said unsteadily.

'I suspect I owe you an apology too,' said Jake unexpectedly. 'Being handed a bucket of cleaning materials and being told to get on with it probably wasn't the welcome to Australia you imagined.'

'Nothing's been as I imagined,' Phyllida admitted a little ruefully. 'If it had been, maybe I wouldn't have been behaving so out of character. I'm not usually this touchy.' She hesitated. 'I'm not proud of the way I behaved the other night either. I never cry and carry on like that. Do you think you could forget it and pretend that we've just met?'

'I'm not sure that I can forget *quite* everything,' said Jake slowly, his eyes resting on her mouth. He made no move to touch her, but suddenly it was as if the memory of that kiss was a tangible thing again, strumming in the air between them. 'Can you?'

Phyllida could feel a trembling start deep inside her, and she was very glad that she was sitting down. This is ridiculous, she told herself desperately. He's only looking at you; he isn't even touching you. There's absolutely no reason for your bones to melt and your skin to tingle and your heart to start booming in your ears. It was just a silly kiss to snap you out of hysterics. It didn't mean anything.

She really must get a hold of herself.

'I'm prepared to try if you are,' she said, appalled at how husky her voice sounded. She cleared her throat awkwardly. Honestly, anyone would think she'd never been kissed before!

'Let's agree on a fresh start, then,' said Jake, leaning forward and holding out his hand. 'Shall we shake on it?'

He was doing this deliberately! Didn't he know how much the touch of his fingers disturbed her? Couldn't he feel her shiver of response? Phyllida steeled herself and took his hand, but when she would have withdrawn it he tightened his hold and drew her to her feet. For one crazy, exhilarating, terrifying moment she thought he was going to kiss her, but he only looked down at their linked hands.

'You're right about one thing, though, Phyllida.'

'What's that?' she croaked.

'You're a lot tougher than you look. It takes guts to admit that you've been wrong, as you did just now, but if it's any consolation, I'm beginning to think I might have been wrong about you too.'

Phyllida sat on the veranda and twisted the wine glass around in her hand as she gazed unseeingly down at the lights of the marina, shimmering reflections over the dark water.

She was glad she had apologised to Jake, but, instead of clearing the air, it had served only to tighten the atmosphere between them during the course of the evening.

Phyllida was excruciatingly aware of Jake, of his fingers around the wine bottle, of the easy, unhurried way he lifted his arm or turned his head, of the whole warm, solid strength of him. She tried not to look at him—whenever she did she felt as if the air was being squeezed slowly but surely out of her lungs. And if it carried on this way, she soon wouldn't be able to breathe at all.

It wasn't supposed to be like this. She had thought that starting afresh would give her the opportunity to prove to Jake just how poised and professional she really was. Instead, she had ended up as tongue-tied and awkward as a schoolgirl on her first date.

Jake had driven her out to Chris's to pick up her case, and then back to this lovely airy house set on the hill, looking down to the marina on one side and out to Boston Island and the distant sea on the other. Phyllida had liked it as soon as she'd walked into its cool, uncluttered rooms, with their polished wooden floors and the long windows opening out onto the wide, shaded veranda.

Jake was as competent in the kitchen as anywhere else. He'd thrown together a salad and barbecued some fish outside on the veranda, reminding Phyllida that he was a man used to looking after himself. She'd watched his face, lit from beneath by a lantern which stood on the wall by the barbecue, and tried to imagine him in a life of happy domesticity.

He must have been happy at some time with his wife, but there was such a detached, independent quality in him now that it was impossible to picture him giving up his freedom again for the dubious prospect of matrimony. Unthinkingly, Phyllida had sighed.

Now she searched her mind for something to say. Jake seemed quite unbothered by the long, sticky silences, but for Phyllida they were agony. The marina lights danced in front of her eyes, but she couldn't mention them again. She had already commented on the view, on the temperature, on the wine, and was convinced that he must think her irredeemably boring and superficial.

The phone ringing in the room behind her was an enormous relief. Jake got up to answer it, and she could tell from what he was saying that he was talking to Chris. Well, that at least would be something else to talk about.

'Yes, I'll tell her,' she heard him say just before he

put the phone down. 'That was Chris,' he confirmed as he came back out onto the veranda. No surprise, no sudden movement, but still Phyllida felt the same tightening of breath at his reappearance. 'I told her you had moved in and she sounded very relieved. She sends her love.'

'How's Mike?'

'Still in Intensive Care, but he's recovered consciousness, so that's a good sign. Chris is sounding a lot more cheerful.'

'Does she have any idea how long he'll have to stay in hospital?'

Jake sat down beside her and looked thoughtfully across at the marina. 'Not yet.' He glanced at her. 'I'm afraid you may have to resign yourself to quite a long stay here.'

'Oh, dear.'

'It's not much of a holiday for you, is it?'

'It's not that,' said Phyllida hesitantly, acutely conscious of him sitting so close beside her.

Her hand was resting on the arm of the wicker chair. She would only have to lift her hand, move it three inches and she could touch his. Her fingers were tingling at the thought, and she pulled her hands down into her lap and linked them together, as if afraid that they might start drifting towards him of their own accord.

'I was thinking about you. You probably didn't bank on having me to stay for such a long time when you offered.'

Jake turned to look at her, his mouth just curling into something that was almost, but not quite a smile. 'No, I must admit that I didn't bank on you...'

There was an odd pause, and Phyllida felt her eyes dragged unwillingly to meet his. She didn't want to look at him, didn't want the trembling inside to build into an insistent, booming rhythm, didn't want him to see that beneath her proud boasts of toughness and independence she was just as vulnerable as anyone else. She couldn't breathe, couldn't move, could only stare back at him, helplessly entangled in a tightening web of awareness.

'There's no problem, though,' Jake continued softly. 'As you can see, there's plenty of room here, so you're welcome to make yourself at home for as long as you want.'

'Thank you,' said Phyllida with a sort of gasp, expelling the last air from her lungs.

With a superhuman effort she lunged to her feet, seriously alarmed by her own bizarre behaviour and desperate in case she succumbed to the terrible temptation of reaching out and touching him. She didn't understand what was happening to her, but she knew that if she didn't get away right now she would do something she would regret.

To her horror, Jake rose to his feet with her. 'Where are you going?'

'I...I thought I'd—er—go and write some letters home,' stammered Phyllida.

'To your fiancé?' His voice was suddenly hard.

Surprise stopped Phyllida in her tracks. 'My fiancé?'

'Chris talks about you a lot. I've heard all about her famous English cousin. How important your job is, how smartly your flat is decorated...how you've got yourself engaged to some smooth charmer who's got everything going for him.'

If she hadn't known better, Phyllida would have suspected that the sneering, almost hostile tone was a cover for jealousy.

'You've had plenty to say about your job, but you've

kept very quiet about your engagement. Why's that, Phyllida?'

'The subject hasn't come up,' she said uneasily. She could have told Jake that she had no intention of marrying Rupert, but some instinct told her that she would be much safer pretending that the engagement was still on.

'We were talking about love only this lunchtime—or don't you associate love with your fiancé?'

'Of course I do,' she said coldly, grateful to him for the hostility that had sprung back into the atmosphere. It was much, much easier to argue with him than to notice the way the light caught his cheek and the line of his jaw. 'Rupert's very special to me, and I didn't feel like discussing him with *you*, that's all.'

'*Rupert*?' Jake jeered, mimicking her English accent. 'Is that really his name?'

'What's wrong with Rupert?' she demanded in a frigid voice.

'It's very...English.'

'I realise that that may place him at a terrible disadvantage in your eyes, but it doesn't in mine. It may have escaped your notice, but I am English too.'

'I could hardly avoid noticing,' said Jake. 'Even before you open your mouth it's obvious—in the way you lift that stubborn little chin of yours and look down your nose!'

'In that case you'll probably agree that Rupert and I suit each other perfectly!'

'I don't know about that. I'd have said you needed a man with a stronger will than yours—and there can't be many of those about!'

Only a minute ago, Phyllida had been desperate with

nerves; now she was blazing with temper. 'What makes you think you know what Rupert's like?'

'Well, if you were my fiancé, I wouldn't let you go gallivanting off to Australia without me. I'd want you right where I could keep an eye on you!'

'Perhaps Rupert trusts me?' Phyllida suggested sweetly. 'Perhaps he admires and encourages my independence—which is more than you obviously did for your wife!'

It was an unfair shot, and Jake's eyes narrowed, but he didn't rise to the bait. 'So Rupert trusts you, does he? Would he still trust you, I wonder, if he knew you were staying here alone with me?'

Phyllida strongly suspected that if they had still been engaged, Rupert would have been intensely suspicious of the whole set-up, but she had no intention of telling Jake *that*. 'Naturally,' she said. 'I'm just about to write and tell him where I am, and what you're like, and that ought to be quite enough to reassure him that he has absolutely no cause for concern!'

She should have known better, of course. If she hadn't been so alarmed by the reactions which had left her stammering and stuttering like a schoolgirl, she wouldn't have been nearly so angry. And if she hadn't been angry she wouldn't have let slip a comment that was bound to goad Jake, who for some reason was nearly as angry as she was.

'It sounds like a very dull letter,' he sneered, moving purposefully towards her.

Phyllida tried to sidestep round the table, but the chair got in her way and she ended up pinned against the veranda rail, her eyes huge and dark and defiant.

'We don't want Rupert to think you're not having a good time in Australia.' He took her face in his hands, feathering his thumbs along the line of her cheekbones and studying her features almost impersonally, like a connoisseur. Quite suddenly, he smiled. 'I think we should find something more exciting for you to write home about, don't you?'

Phyllida never had the chance to reply. His hands tightened and then his mouth was on hers and he was kissing her, long and hard, with a sort of suppressed fury that dissolved almost instantly into intense, unmistakable and utterly unexpected passion. It shook them both off balance.

Jake lifted his head and looked down into Phyllida's face as if he had never seen her before. She stared dazedly back up at him, as confused as he was about the explosion of feeling that had thrilled through her at the first touch of his lips. Her body was glowing, afire with new and dangerous sensations, and her mind was spinning, half frightened by the depth of her reaction, half frantic because Jake had stopped just as she had yielded.

For a long, long moment, they just stared at each other, then Jake's hold slackened. Certain that he was going to step away, Phyllida was conscious of an alarming stab of disappointment before he seemed to change his mind, letting his hands fall from her face only to jerk her abruptly back into his arms.

With a tiny sigh of release, she melted against him, all anger and frustration forgotten. Her lips were soft and sweet beneath his, savouring the same poignant rush of intoxicating pleasure, sharing the same breathless urgency as his arms tightened around her.

She had been clutching him just above the elbow—at first with some vague notion of pulling his hands down from her face, then as her one solid anchor in the turbulent whirl of emotions. Now she let them slide luxuriously down his sides.

His body was so hard, so strong. She could feel the taut muscles flexing through the thin cotton of his shirt as she ran her hands over him, down to his waist and around him to spread over his back, pulling him closer, desperate to feel the solidity and the strength and the sheer power of him.

Heedless of the veranda rail digging into the small of her back, Phyllida murmured deep in her throat with delight and a half conscious disbelief at her own lack of control. Somewhere at the back of her mind a voice was urging her to pull away, before it was too late, but she was lost, tumbling and turning helplessly in a swirling tide of sensation as Jake's lips plundered hers, and Jake's hands slid in insistent exploration over her slenderness, and Jake's body pressed hard and demanding against her.

His mouth was drifting down her throat, his fingers brushing aside the soft material of her skirt to spread over the smooth length of her thigh, his warm hand sliding possessively upwards, until Phyllida gasped at the excruciating twist of desire.

Very slowly, Jake lifted his head, letting his lips travel in final salute along the proud, pure jawline before his hand dropped reluctantly and he smoothed her skirt back into place. In the dim light his eyes gleamed as he put her carefully away from him.

'Give my regards to Rupert when you write,' he said, a little unevenly. 'He's either a very brave man or a very stupid one to let a girl like you out on her own!' And, turning, he walked away into the house without another word.

CHAPTER SIX

THE kiss was never referred to by either of them over the next three weeks. Shaken, bewildered, appalled by her own behaviour, Phyllida lay awake long into the night. How could she have let him kiss her like that? How could she have kissed him back?

She burned with humiliation as the kiss replayed itself over and over again in her mind. She could still feel the sharp thrill of excitement when Jake had pulled her into his arms, the warm persuasion of his lips and the searing pleasure of his hand smoothing up her thigh.

If it had just been that, she could have channelled her shock into anger against Jake. It would have been easy to have blamed him... But it was impossible to forget how she had revelled in the feel of his body beneath her hands, how she had explored his lips with her own and gasped with delight at his touch. Jake wasn't responsible for that, was he?

Phyllida had many faults, but self-deception wasn't one of them. She was just as much to blame as Jake, and she knew it. The fact made her angrier than ever, but much as she would have liked a blazing argument with him, a night's reflection told her that it would be much more dignified to ignore the whole incident. She would be cool and quellingly polite, and with any luck Jake would begin to wonder whether he had imagined the warm, passionate girl he had held in his arms.

It was unfortunate that the weeks that followed were extremely busy ones. Phyllida wrote out long lists of ingredients, sorted out piles of provisions for each boat, and spent long hours simmering fragrant stews in Jake's kitchen. Jake rarely disturbed her there, and it was easy to tell herself that she had succeeded in putting the kiss firmly behind her.

It was a little more difficult when she was down at the marina. There were boats to be cleaned, brochures to be posted, queries to be answered and stores to be sorted, but, no matter how much she had to do, she never quite managed to ignore Jake the way she wanted to be able to.

He was always around, always as busy as she was, but somehow managing to move with the same deliberate, unhurried competence. Phyllida couldn't help feeling brittle and frazzled in comparison.

She didn't know whether to feel relieved or outraged the morning after the kiss, when Jake behaved as if precisely nothing had happened. He continued to treat her with a blend of amusement and faint exasperation, and if his heart stuck in his throat every time she walked into the room—as hers did whenever he appeared—he gave not the slightest sign of it.

Phyllida bitterly resented the effortless way he seemed able to carry on exactly as before. She was finding it much harder. True, she was quite proud of her cool manner, but Jake didn't appear in the slightest bit quelled, and she doubted whether he even noticed. Frustrated by her own inability to impress on him how completely she had forgotten the kiss, Phyllida threw herself into the task of preparing the boats.

As the days passed, and it became obvious that Jake wasn't going to allude to the kiss any more than she was, her embarrassment faded, and with it her frosty manner. Sometimes she forgot about the kiss altogether, and would talk and laugh with him quite easily until her unwary eyes would fall upon his hands or his mouth, and memory would come rushing back.

She grew to love the casual life down at the marina—the jostling boats and the sound of the wind in the rigging and the clear, sharp light. She liked the easy camaraderie of the yachtsmen who stopped to talk to Jake, and envied the confident way they jumped into their boats and pulled up flapping sails as they headed out to sea.

Phyllida found them friendly and fun, and felt increasingly conscious of the fact that she didn't belong. She couldn't talk about luffing or gybing or flogging sails, and stories about mizzens, genoas, spinnakers and storm jibs were frankly baffling. She was constantly getting into trouble from Jake for talking about the beds instead of the bunks, ropes instead of sheets, cupboards instead of lockers, and when she overheard him telling someone that she wouldn't know a reef-knot from a rudder, she decided it was high time she improved her knowledge.

The next time Jake took her into town to stock up on provisions, she slipped off and bought herself a book on sailing for beginners, determined to show Jake that she wasn't as stupid as he thought her. She took to studying it in secret, but it didn't make a lot of sense without a boat to practise on. She spent her day surrounded by yachts, but was much too busy ever to learn more than just how dirty a boat could get in a week.

'Ah, Phyllida, just the girl I want!' said Jake one day as she walked into the office, her arms full of dirty linen. He held up the radio microphone. 'I've got *Valli* on the radio. They've discovered a Tupperware box full of bits of dill and want to know what it's for.'

Phyllida put her bundle down on a chair. 'It's for garnish,' she said, surprised at the question.

'Garnish?' said Jake, dropping his head into his hand. 'Now, why didn't I think of that?'

His sarcasm went over Phyllida's head. 'Well, I must say, I'd have thought it was obvious.'

'Not to four men who are out for a couple of days' fishing,' said Jake sardonically. 'I thought I told you just to make sure they had plenty of beer, some bread and a few potatoes?'

'I did all that, but as you said they'd just be eating fish I thought it would be nice if they had some dill with it—you know, a bit of greenery.'

'Phyllida, this lot aren't interested in the artistic combinations on their plate! You're not catering for a five-star restaurant. If you're out on a sailing trip, you want good, nourishing food and lots of it, not to be poncing around with garnishes! Have you been giving these extras to everyone?'

'Yes,' said Phyllida defensively. 'Dill's very nice with fish. They don't have to use it as a garnish, if that's too subtle for them. They can stuff the fish with it, or chop it up and mix it with mayonnaise...'

'Spare me the recipes,' said Jake holding up a hand. 'I don't think I want to know!' He turned back to the radio. '*Valli*, this is Sailaway. I'm reliably informed that you are indeed supposed to have the box of dill. Phyllida tells me that you can mix it with mayonnaise, or alternatively use it as a garnish. Over.'

There was a baffled silence, and then a voice crackled back, evidently much amused. 'We'll give it a go. And if your Phyllida made the stew we had last night, tell her it was fantastic! We wished we'd asked for one for both nights. This is *Valli*, over and out.'

'Sailaway out, and standing by.' Jake put the microphone down and shook his head at Phyllida. 'Garnishes! What next? Cocktails and canapés?'

Phyllida brightened. 'That's a good idea. We could—'

'No, we couldn't,' Jake interrupted her with a flat note of finality, but his eyes held a lurking smile. 'My reputation might just be able to stand rumours of garnish, but I draw the line at canapés. Do you want to make me a laughing stock of the yachting world?'

She sighed. 'I don't seem to be able to get anything right, do I?'

'That doesn't sound like you, Phyllida.' Pushing back his chair, Jake got to his feet. 'What happened to all that confident defiance? You swore you'd prove you were tougher than you looked, and you have.' He paused, the smile fading from his expression as he looked down into her wary face.

'You've worked really hard over the last three weeks, Phyllida. You heard what *Valli* said just now, and it's not the first time I've been told how good the food is. I didn't think you'd stick at it,' he went on slowly, 'but I was wrong.'

His eyes were very green. Phyllida stood quite still, but a quiver was spreading out from her heart, shivering down to her fingertips and toes, until her whole body vibrated with it.

The atmosphere was taut with a new and unspoken tension. Jake took a deliberate step towards her, and the silence tightened, only to snap abruptly as a huge, bearded figure appeared in the doorway.

'Jake, you didn't tell me you'd got a new assistant!'

'Rod.' Jake seemed to recover himself with an effort, and shook the stranger's hand. 'I wasn't expecting you so soon.'

'I got an earlier flight,' said the man, regarding

Phyllida with undisguised interest. 'I didn't think you'd mind me turning up early, and now I'm glad I did. Aren't you going to introduce us?'

It seemed to Phyllida that Jake performed the introductions with some reserve. 'Phyllida, this is Rod Franklin. He's going to skipper *Persephone* for the party arriving tomorrow. Rod, Phyllida Grant.' He told Rod about Mike's accident and how Phyllida was standing in for Chris.

'That's bad luck on Mike,' said Rod, enveloping Phyllida's hand in a massive paw. He had a jovial face and merry blue eyes. 'But good luck for the rest of us! Have you done much sailing before?'

'Phyllida's still learning the difference between the bow and the stern,' said Jake unfairly, glowering at Phyllida, who found herself snatching her hand out of Rod's.

Cross with herself for reacting so quickly to his look, Phyllida turned a brilliant smile on Rod. 'I'd like to learn, though.'

'Of course you would,' said Rod, delighted. 'My party don't arrive until tomorrow afternoon. I could take you out tomorrow morning if you like?'

Phyllida opened her mouth to reply, but Jake, who was suddenly looking boot-faced, got in first. 'She's got too much to do tomorrow,' he said flatly.

'Oh, well...' Rod looked from one to the other in puzzlement. 'Another time, then?'

'I'll look forward to it,' said Phyllida sweetly, before Jake could answer for her again.

'You've never told me that you wanted to learn to sail,' he accused her when Rod had disappeared up to the house with his bags.

'You've never asked me,' she retorted, picking up the

linen from the chair and dumping it in the laundry bag. The warmth that had shimmered between them before Rod's appearance had vanished, submerged by the more familiar antagonism. Jake might have admitted that he had been wrong about her, but it obviously didn't stop him treating her like some slave! 'You don't need to worry,' she reassured him acidly. 'I haven't forgotten that I'm here to work, not to enjoy myself!'

It had been arranged that Rod was to spend the night at Jake's house, and he was patently delighted to discover that Phyllida was staying there as well. She found him good company, with an endless fund of stories, and although many of them were about sailing, even she could appreciate most of them. It should have been an entertaining evening, but Jake was out of humour.

He did insist on taking them both out to dinner, decreeing that Phyllida had done enough cooking, but her enjoyment was soured when she discovered that he had invited a friend of his to join them for dinner.

It curdled completely when she met the friend, a tall, statuesque blonde called Val, who might have been chosen expressly to provide a contrast to Phyllida. Val had a fresh prettiness and a totally natural look that was like Chris's, but which somehow lacked her cousin's warmth and humour.

Val, Phyllida soon discovered, was an expert sailor, and had been one of an all-female crew on the Sydney-Hobart that had just taken place. It didn't take long to realise that the other girl also had a distinct interest in Jake, although whether he was aware of it or not wasn't nearly as obvious.

It wouldn't be surprising, Phyllida decided glumly. Val was far more his type than a dark, slender career girl who didn't know the first thing about sailing. She found the thought oddly depressing.

Edged deliberately out of the conversation by Val, Phyllida watched Jake surreptitiously. He was listening to Val telling them about the conditions in the Bass Strait, his head slightly bent as he swirled the wine in his glass, his expression absorbed. Phyllida's eyes drifted over his face, noting the rough, tantalising texture of his skin, and the way the brown hair grew at his temple. Her fingers tingled as she imagined how it would feel if she traced the line of his jaw, and she winced at the sudden, sharp ache of desire.

As if catching her expression, Jake lifted his eyes and looked across at Phyllida, with dark green eyes that seemed to reach right inside her and squeeze her heart. It was a physical effort to look away, but she managed it somehow, only to find Val—who had realised that she had lost Jake's attention—regarding her with hostility. Phyllida smiled blandly at her and, turning deliberately to Rod, monopolised his attention for the rest of the evening.

Rod, it appeared, was the only one who enjoyed himself. He made no secret of his admiration for Phyllida, and the more he flattered her the more she responded, and the more thunderous Jake looked. Val tossed her blonde hair and tried to turn the conversation back to sailing, but Rod was riveted by Phyllida, and in the end she and Jake had to resort to a low-voiced conversation together. Phyllida told herself that that was exactly what she had wanted.

Rod left with his party the following afternoon, and by tacit agreement Phyllida and Jake spent the next few days avoiding each other as much as possible. Jake went out in the evenings. He never said where he went, but

Phyllida imagined him with Val, telling each other interminable sailing stories and laughing at silly little Phyllida, who didn't know one end of a boat from another and couldn't even tie a knot.

She felt unaccountably depressed on these evenings alone, and even the news from Chris that Mike was on the mend failed to cheer her up. Chris thought they would be home in about a fortnight, when Phyllida could start her holiday. No more cooking, Chris assured her. No more cleaning. Her time would be her own again.

Phyllida tried to sound enthusiastic, but when she had put the receiver down, she stood and stared bleakly at the phone. No more cleaning meant no more days down at the marina.

No more Jake.

For want of anything better to do, she had taken to spending her evenings in the kitchen, preparing extra quantities of casseroles to put in the freezer ready for the next rush. At least it stopped her sitting on the veranda, wondering where Jake was and trying to forget the way he had kissed her. While she waited for the casseroles to cook she would sit at the kitchen table with her sailing book in front of her and practise knots by tying a piece of kitchen string to the back of another chair.

She was tackling a slip-hitch one evening when Jake walked into the kitchen. He had spent the day in Adelaide and was still wearing his city clothes, with their impeccable cut and restrained good taste, reminding Phyllida of their first meeting. She had got used to seeing him in the faded shirts he wore at the marina, and it was a shock to remember that he was still a wealthy and sophisticated businessman.

Hastily Phyllida shoved the sailing book below a magazine of recipes and got up to stir the casseroles. 'You're back early,' she said a little breathlessly, wishing she could get used to the way the air squeezed from her lungs whenever she saw him. Surely she ought to be getting used to him by now? 'I wasn't expecting you until later.'

'I didn't have any English girls with enormous cases to deal with this time,' said Jake. 'It made the whole trip much easier!'

Phyllida's chin lifted instinctively. 'It sounds very dull.'

'Funnily enough, the plane *did* seem quite empty without you,' said Jake, almost reluctantly. Pulling out a chair, he loosened his tie as he sat down. He looked at Phyllida, still in her apron, and frowned. 'You shouldn't be spending all your evenings working as well, Phyllida. Things aren't so busy now.'

'I don't mind,' she said quickly, wondering if she had heard right. Had Jake actually *missed* her? 'I'm cooking some things for the freezer, so that Chris doesn't have so much to do when she comes back.'

'I see.' He hesitated. 'Does she have any idea when Mike will be able to leave hospital?'

'A couple of weeks, she hopes. She rang tonight.'

'Two weeks?' Jake seemed to hear the flat note in his voice, for he made an effort to sound more positive. 'That's excellent news.'

'Yes,' said Phyllida bleakly.

'You'll be looking forward to starting your holiday.'

'Yes,' she said again.

There was an awkward pause. Jake looked as if he was about to say something, then changed his mind. He lifted the piece of string hanging off the back of the chair instead. 'What's this?'

'Oh, nothing,' said Phyllida, coming back to the table to remove the sailing book before he saw it. But she was too late. Jake had lifted the magazine incuriously and discovered the book beneath it. He pulled it out and studied the front cover, the corner of his mouth twitching as he looked up.

'Doing your homework?'

'I just thought I'd try and master a few knots,' she said a shade sulkily.

Jake looked at the string again. 'What's this supposed to be?'

'A slip-hitch.'

The twitch became a grin, and Phyllida felt her stomach turn over at his smile. 'Don't tell me this tangle's supposed to be a slip-hitch?'

'I get confused,' Phyllida complained. 'The instructions are so complicated, I can't make head or tail of them.'

'Obviously not,' said Jake, with another pained look at the piece of string. 'A slip-hitch is simplicity itself. Come here, I'll show you.' He began disentangling the string. 'Come on,' he said again, as Phyllida hesitated.

She sat down next to him rather nervously, moving her chair so that her knee didn't touch his, and watched as he demonstrated. 'Look...round, under and through here,' he said, but Phyllida wasn't concentrating. She was looking at his fingers, so deft and sure, and remembering how they had felt against her face, against her thigh, sliding over her silken skin. 'There. Easy, isn't it?'

Phyllida swallowed and nodded.

'You have a go.' He handed her the string and she took it helplessly. Her mind was a blank, wiped clean by a terrible wash of desire that left her incapable of thinking about anything other than the strong brown hands on the table next to hers. She fumbled with the string, but got in such a muddle that Jake clicked his tongue in exasperation and pulled it away from her.

'What a mess!' he said, untying the hopelessly complicated knot she had made. 'Here, start again.'

This time he guided her fingers with his own. Phyllida felt them brush against her hands like a series of tiny electric shocks, and fought to control her breathing. It took an immense effort to focus on the string, but his hands danced before her eyes in unnatural detail. She could see every line, every hair, every pore on the tanned skin.

'I see,' she gasped when he had patiently led her through every step.

To her relief, Jake sat back. 'Knots won't mean much until you're on a boat and can practise using them. It's time I took you for a sail. How would you like to go out on the *Ali B* for a couple of days?'

'I thought you were too busy?' said Phyllida, remembering how he had poured cold water on Rod's suggestion.

'That was last week,' said Jake, not quite meeting her eyes. 'There are no boats due in or out for the next few days, and I can just as easily do the radio sched from the *Ali B*, so it seems a good opportunity. After all, I did promise Chris when I spoke to her on the phone that I'd look after you.' He glanced at her, a disturbing smile glimmering at the back of his eyes. 'Not that you need looking after, of course,' he remembered.

'No,' she said, but she didn't sound quite as definite as she had before. Appalled at the suspiciously wistful note in her voice, Phyllida caught herself up firmly. 'But I would love to go for a sail...as long as you don't think I'll get in the way.'

'Not if you do as you're told,' said Jake, getting to his feet. 'And that shouldn't be too hard—even for you!'

Phyllida stood on the jetty and hugged her jacket about her. The sky was so blue and bright that it hurt her eyes, but the wind was whipping her hair around her face, and rattling the rigging as Jake loaded the eskies onto the boat. Out on the water, yachts in full sail were heeling over at what seemed to Phyllida an alarming angle. Suddenly she wasn't so keen on the idea.

'Why don't I stay here and man the office?' she suggested as Jake emerged up the companionway.

'I thought you wanted to learn to sail?'

Phyllida cast another look at the heeling boats. 'I've just remembered that I'm not an outdoor girl,' she said. 'Are you sure it's going to be safe? It looks awfully windy.'

'Windy? Nonsense.' Jake held out an imperative hand and she climbed reluctantly on board. 'It's a nice stiff breeze—perfect sailing conditions, in fact.'

'What if I'm seasick?' asked Phyllida, perching nervously in the cockpit.

Jake was predictably unsympathetic at the prospect. 'If you're going to be sick, make sure you do it over the right side of the boat,' he said briskly, and started the engine.

He manoeuvred the *Ali B* away from its moorings with a characteristic lack of fuss, and Phyllida sat feeling hopelessly inadequate as he coiled ropes, unlashed sails and released the boom—all without appearing to be distracted from the business of steering out through windsurfers and waterskiers and fishing dinghies, not to mention small sailing boats and motor cruisers and other yachts. Phyllida kept squeezing her eyes shut and waiting for the collision, but Jake just steered calmly on, completely in control of his craft.

Once out of the sheltered waters, the wind was even stronger. Jake told Phyllida how to raise the mainsail and the jib, which she managed with much grumbling and puffing after Jake held the end of the sheet steady in one strong hand. 'I'm not strong enough,' she complained, collapsing back down next to him and clutching onto the guard rail as the wind caught the sails and sent the boat creaming through the water.

Jake glanced down at her. The shiny nut-brown hair was tangling in the breeze, and her face was pink with exertion, but her eyes were bright and wide. 'You'll get used to it,' he assured her slowly.

The next lesson was less successful. Phyllida was ordered to let out the jib sheet.

'Why?' she asked.

'Because I want to go about.'

She looked at the empty water ahead of them. 'Go about what?'

Jake sighed. 'I want to turn and tack in the opposite direction.'

'What's wrong with the way we're going?' said Phyllida.

'This is a boat, Phyllida, not a committee meeting,' snapped Jake, exasperated. 'On a boat the skipper makes the decisions and the crew—that's you—obeys his commands without question.'

'That's doesn't seem very fair! How come the crew don't get any say in what's going on?'

'Because by the time everyone's had their say, the boat's usually on the rocks! In an emergency, I don't have time to ask how you'd feel about the boom swinging towards you and knocking you off the boat, or if you'd mind terribly going about because we're about to run into a tanker, so if you want to sail you'd better learn to react quickly to orders.'

'I'd have joined the army if I'd wanted to be bossed about,' Phyllida grumbled, but she let off the jib sheet as he said.

The jib flapped frantically in the wind as Jake swung the boat round, then shouted at her to pull it in the other side. Phyllida blundered around the cockpit, dropping the hand-winch in her haste and straining frantically to pull in the sheet, but after they had repeated the manoeuvre a few times she began to get used to it, and even to feel quite proud of herself—although Jake was unimpressed.

'It's like having a baby elephant on board!' he complained as she stumbled and fell against him yet again, managing to tread on his foot this time as she hauled herself upright.

'I'm not used to operating at a forty-five-degree angle,' Phyllida pointed out, wriggling back into her position beside him, with one arm hooked around the winch and a hand clutching the guard rail for support. Jake's legs were long enough to brace himself against the other side of the cockpit, but hers could only dangle uselessly into the gap.

They had left Boston Island behind them and had settled into a long reach. The *Ali B* slid effortlessly through the waves, her bow rising and falling with the swell, and sending curves of white foam shushing and dazzling over the water in her wake. The wind filled out the sails to an arc, slicing through the blue sky, and heeled the boat over so that Phyllida could sit next to Jake and look down into the heaving, inky blueness of the sea.

Her earlier nervousness had disappeared, and, far from being seasick, she felt giddy with exhilaration. Jake's relaxed, capable presence was infinitely reassuring. In the bright light he was solid, sure, overwhelmingly distinct.

The top half of his face was shaded by a cap, but Phyllida's eye kept catching the set of his jaw and the cool, curling mouth. She had been conscious of the same sense of competence in the way he drove a car or flew a plane, but here, with his eyes screwed up against the glare, one hand controlling the yacht as she sliced through the water and the free breeze in his face, he was in his element.

He looked happy, Phyllida realised with something of a shock, as if this was where he belonged, with the sea and the sky and the bright, bright air.

Where did she belong? Doubt touched Phyllida like a cloud passing over the sun. She was a city girl, wasn't she? She belonged in the bustle of the streets, in wine bars and galleries and welcoming sitting-rooms, securely protected from the elements.

Why, then, did she feel as if she had never been so completely happy before? Ever since she had pulled Chris's photograph out of the Christmas card the idea of the sea had tugged insistently at her mind, and here she was at last.

The sun glittered on the water and flashed off the guard rails and the wind stung her cheeks, blowing away all her doubts and confusion and leaving her feeling free and invigorated, content to forget about the past and the future and live simply for this moment, with the rustling sound of the waves against the hull and the deep blue water spangled with sunshine and the diamond-bright light all around them.

A bigger wave sent up a spray of foam, and Phyllida felt the tingle of salt water against her skin. Hooking her arm more firmly round the winch, she smiled at Jake with the sunshine in her eyes, and he smiled slowly back. She watched the crease deepen in his cheek, the heart-stopping curve of his mouth and the flash of his white teeth, and sheer joy went fizzing along her veins like champagne.

'Look,' he said, and pointed. A dolphin was curving and rolling through the waves beside them, playing in the blue-white froth of their wake.

Thrilled, Phyllida craned her neck to watch his sleek grey back dive and surface, with a flash of a bright eye and the absurd smiling mouth, and then there were dolphins all around them, curious about the boat, leaping and twisting and tumbling among the waves, seeming to flow through the water with effortless speed, criss-crossing the bow to spin slowly through the sparkling blueness with their smiles and their infectious, uninhibited delight.

Phyllida felt as if she had been given an unexpected present. There was something magical about the dolphins, something inexpressibly moving about their grace and joy, and when at last they disappeared, as suddenly as they had come, they left some of their enchantment behind them like a benediction. For Phyllida, they set the seal on a day of shimmering happiness.

The wind had died to a soft breeze by the time they anchored in an empty bay off Reevesby Island. One of the largest of the Sir Joseph Banks Group, it was a long, low sandy island, barely breaking the line of the horizon, with a dazzling white beach curved around the pale green shallows. The *Ali B* was anchored in deeper waters, where the deep turquoise-blue was broken by a patch of crystal-clear apple-green above a sandy hole.

Jake tied a canopy over the boom for shade, tipped a

straw hat over his face for good measure, and threw a fishing line over the side.

He had an incredible capacity for stillness, Phyllida thought enviously. She had been so busy over the last month that she felt as if she had forgotten how to sit still, and for a while she fidgeted around, picking up a book, putting it down, getting herself a drink, starting a letter but unable to get much beyond the date and 'Dear'.

She couldn't even decide who to write to. Friends at home were vague, remote figures. They would be struggling through the traffic, collars turned up against the wind and the rain, hurrying from one place to the next, and here she was, at the end of January, with the sun on her back and the silence broken only by the faint slap of the water against the hull or the plaintive cry of the Pacific gull that bobbed nearby, hoping for scraps from Jake's fishing line.

In the end, Phyllida decided to paint her toenails a deep red. Tongue caught between her teeth in concentration, she was applying varnish very carefully when something made her look up. Jake was watching her with a mixture of bafflement, amusement and irritation and something else—something that made her heart start thumping and thudding against her ribs.

'What's the matter?' she asked, annoyed at her own breathlessness.

'Nothing,' said Jake, turning away. 'Nothing.'

It might have been nothing, but Phyllida's hand was so unsteady as she returned to her nails that she daubed nail polish all over her big toe.

Gradually, though, her tension unwound in the hot peace of the afternoon. When her toenails had dried she left her book and her magazine and her writing pad behind and lay back on the for'ard deck, doing nothing, just feeling the sun on her skin and listening to the breeze sighing over the shallows. Every now and then it would catch the rigging, and the whole boat would hum like a spaceship, but mostly it rocked gently, and the light threw wavering reflections up from the water onto the white hull.

When Phyllida looked up, the rigging bisected the sky into straight lines and shapes; if she turned her head to the side, the guard rails blocked off the sea into rectangles of blue and green, and behind her Jake was a solid figure in the shade, outlined against the light.

Later he went below, and she could hear him talking to the other Sailaway boats on the radio sched. His voice was a deep rumble that seemed to vibrate through the fibreglass deck and along Phyllida's skin. Opening her eyes, she looked up at the mast soaring above her head and let his voice drift over her body, and unconsciously her toes started to curl.

'Now that you've discovered how to relax, it looks as if you're doing it with your usual excess,' said Jake from the hatchway when the radio sched was over.

Phyllida sat up reluctantly, and twisted round to face him across the cabin roof. The dry tone wasn't matched by the glinting humour in his eyes, and the crease in his cheek was deepening in the way that always made her heart turn over.

The breeze had died completely, and for the first time she noticed that the sun had lost its glare as the day slid imperceptibly into evening. 'Come and stretch your legs on the beach,' he invited, and then made it impossible to refuse by smiling.

Phyllida pulled a T-shirt over her swimming costume. As she left her cabin she caught sight of herself in the round mirror that hung above the locker. Her hair was tousled, her T-shirt faded, but her face was glowing with happiness, and, deep inside, a strange anticipation fluttered.

Anticipation? She grimaced at her reflection. Jake had only invited her for a walk on the beach!

'Careful,' she warned herself severely aloud. 'This is a man who despises everything you stand for, a man who represents everything you most dislike. He's been rude and obnoxious and downright disagreeable, and when Chris and Mike come back not only will you never see him again, but you'll be glad. You're going for a walk, not a romantic tryst, so wipe that silly smile off your face and remember how much you dislike him.'

Phyllida frowned dutifully at her reflection, but her eyes were shining, and as she climbed up the companionway to Jake her unreliable, unpredictable heart began to sing.

CHAPTER SEVEN

Jake was waiting in the inflatable dinghy that was tied to the stern. He looked up at her from where he sat by the outboard motor and smiled, and the light bounced off the water and flickered over his face. Phyllida felt her bones dissolve.

'Careful!' he said astringently as she clutched at the guard rail. 'Climb down slowly, and whatever you do don't jump, or we'll both be in the water.' Edging forward, he stood up cautiously to help Phyllida clamber down into the dinghy.

She wasn't doing too badly until he took her hand, and reaction jerked through her, making her stumble. She would have tipped right over the side if Jake hadn't caught her round the waist and held her steady as the boat rocked wildly beneath their feet.

'Talk about clumsy!' he said, but his eyes were warm and smiling, and Phyllida found herself smiling back at him. She was excruciatingly conscious of the hard hands holding her so securely, but made no move to step back. He was very close. She could see the creases at the edge of his eyes, and the dark hairs at the open neck of his shirt, and a gust of stomach-churning desire hit her just as a wave slopped against the dinghy and threatened to tip them both over.

Laughing, they sat down abruptly. Jake pulled the cord to start the little outboard motor and Phyllida was left to wonder whether it was her imagination or had he really been about to draw her towards him before that wave brought them both back to the precariousness of their position? Her sides throbbed where she could swear his hands had tightened against her, and the thought sent a deep, treacherous pulse of excitement racing through her.

You're not supposed to even like him, she reminded herself, but as they pulled the dinghy up onto the shore and walked barefoot along the beach it was impossible to remember why. The light was a soft, silvery shade of purple, and the waves rippled quietly to and fro over the gleaming wet sand.

They climbed up the low dunes covered in sparse, tussocky grass, and when Phyllida looked back she could see only her own footprints next to Jake's. They might have been the first people ever to land here. The *Ali B* rocked slowly at her anchor in the deep turquoise water, and the rubber dinghy made a bright splash of colour on the beach, but otherwise there was no sign of man, only the birds skittering backwards and forwards with the waves on the shore and the vast sky stretching around them in every direction.

Later, Phyllida couldn't remember what she and Jake had talked about as they strolled around the bay on that still, silver evening.

They walked a little apart, not touching. Phyllida felt the magic of the air tangling her into a knot of awareness; she could feel every grain of sand beneath her feet, and every time Jake turned his head or smiled or lifted his hand something tightened around her heart.

The sun sank below the horizon as they headed back to the *Ali B*. They sat out on deck and watched the sky deepen from milky purple to deep gold, from gold to a fierce blaze of red.

'I'd like to keep this moment for ever,' Phyllida sighed, leaning back against the cabin. 'Wouldn't it be nice if we could freeze time and know that we could stay exactly as we are, without having to worry about practical things like visas and paying bills and looking for a job?'

She spoke without thinking, and Jake looked up sharply from where he was barbecuing the fish he had caught on a kettle fixed to the guard rail. 'I thought you had a job?'

'No.' Phyllida kept her gaze fixed on the sunset. 'I was a group account director with an advertising firm called Pritchard Price. I loved it,' she remembered, with a curious note in her voice. Her days at Pritchard Price seemed so remote now that it was hard to recall just why her job had meant so much to her.

'I was young for the job, but I'd worked really hard to get there, and I was good at it. Then Pritchard Price was swallowed up by a much bigger firm, and they gave my job to someone else. They said that there was a clash of interest between their existing clients and mine, and that they'd decided to rearrange the groupings. But the "rearrangement" was just giving all my clients to one of their more junior account directors, who just happened to have friends in high places and the luck to be male.'

She shrugged. 'One day I was called in and told to clear my desk there and then.'

Jake frowned. 'Why did you tell me you were on sabbatical?'

'I don't really know.' She rubbed her thumb absently over her fingernails. 'I suppose I found it hard to accept the truth. My life revolved around my job, and when I lost it, it was as if I didn't exist without it. I swore I'd find myself an even better job, and make Liedermann, Marshall & Jones regret that they'd let me go, but...

'Well, Christmas isn't a very good time to be looking for jobs. I decided to take the opportunity to come out and see Chris and work out exactly what I wanted to do next. In my own mind it *was* a sabbatical, but instead of going back to my old job I'd be changing to a new one.'

'And now?'

'Now?'

'You said that as far as you were concerned, it *was* a sabbatical. Does that mean you've changed your mind about going back to advertising?'

'I—' Jake's question seemed to open up a precipice beneath Phyllida's feet, and she felt as if she was teetering on the edge of a discovery she wasn't at all sure she wanted to make. The truth was that she had been so busy over the last few weeks that she hadn't given her career a thought. She *had* loved working for Pritchard Price, but did she really want to go back to the world of advertising?

It didn't seem nearly so important now as it had done, and yet what else was there? Phyllida thought bleakly. She couldn't stay in Australia for ever. She would have to go back when her visa ran out, and sooner or later she would have to find herself a job. All her experience was in advertising; it would be natural to end up in that field. Only weeks ago all her energies had been focused on her determination to get back; now the prospect left her feeling strangely flat.

'No, I suppose I'll be going back.'

'You don't sound very enthusiastic about it. I thought you were determined to prove yourself again?'

Phyllida pulled herself together. 'I am,' she said, and then, hearing the lack of conviction in her own voice, added in a firmer tone, 'Very determined.'

There was a pause. Jake turned the fish over on the barbecue. 'How long do you think you'll stay in Australia before you have to go back?' He sounded rather strained, and Phyllida glanced at him curiously.

'I don't know,' she admitted. She didn't want to think about leaving Australia. 'Another month, perhaps.'

'Rupert must be a very patient man,' said Jake drily. 'Is he prepared to wait until you decide to come home?'

'No,' said Phyllida, and his head jerked round from the barbecue. 'I wasn't quite honest about that either,' she confessed, not meeting his eyes. 'We were engaged, but I broke it off when I realised that I could never be the sort of wife he wanted.

'He thought I'd be happy to stay at home, warming his slippers all day. I didn't realise until I was sacked that to him my career was just a game, an affectation, something to fill in the time before I got married and became ''Rupert's wife'', without a mind or opinions of my own!'

'I find it hard to imagine that,' said Jake, with a glimmer of humour. 'Phyllida without an opinion?' He shook his head. 'No, I can't see it!'

'Rupert could,' she said bitterly. 'I'm beginning to think that all men would prefer their wives to be docile and mindless!'

Jake hooked the tongs over the side of the barbecue and sat down opposite her. 'You know that's not true,' he said, picking up his beer.

'Isn't it? Isn't that what you wanted? You didn't like being married to a successful career woman either.'

He was silent for a moment, and Phyllida wondered if she'd gone too far, but when he spoke his voice was quite even.

'I didn't mind Jonelle being successful. What I minded was the fact that, after a while, her success was all that mattered to her. You said you didn't want to be ''Rupert's wife''. Well, I can sympathise. As far as my wife was concerned, I was ''Jonelle's husband''.

'That would have been all right if she had been prepared to think of herself as ''Jake's wife'' occasionally, but Jonelle never compromises. It's one of the reasons she's so successful, but it's also the reason our marriage fell apart. In retrospect, it's easy to see that we should never have got married, but it wasn't so obvious at the time.'

'Why *did* you?' Phyllida asked quietly.

Jake turned the beer bottle around and around between his hands, considering the question.

'Jonelle was—is—very beautiful. She's got long blonde hair and green eyes and legs that go on for ever. I knew what she was like—we'd known each other ever since we were teenagers—but I thought we loved each other enough for the differences between us not to matter. It didn't take long to realise that we didn't.' He sounded weary rather than bitter.

'Oh, it was all right at first. We lived in Sydney, and Jonelle was working for an artists' agency. I'd never wanted to be in the city, but my father was very ill, and he wanted me to run the business in his stead. He'd said it would just be temporary, and I didn't feel that I could refuse when I saw how ill he really was.

'Jonelle liked the prestige of being associated with Tregowan's, and she played at being hostess to increase her contacts. She was good at her job, there's no denying that, but the more ambitious she became, the less I saw of her. She worked incredible hours in the office, and if she wasn't there, she was out at some party—''networking'' she used to call it.' He shook his head at the memory, and took a pull of his beer.

'You must have been busy too,' Phyllida pointed out.

'Perhaps she would have been bored waiting for you to come home.'

'That's why I encouraged her to work,' said Jake. 'I suppose if it hadn't been that she would have become obsessive about something else. As it was, I hardly ever saw her. She used to drag me along to parties, but I never really blended with her décor, and in the end she stopped asking me. It wasn't a very good time,' he remembered bleakly.

'I tried to make things work, but Jonelle's heart wasn't in it. She had her eyes set on higher things. I kept a boat on the Pittwater, and sometimes I'd persuade her to spend the weekend up there with me. I thought that if we were alone, we could get back to the way things used to be, but Jonelle didn't like sailing. She complained that it was cold and uncomfortable, and that she felt cut off without a phone or a fax.' He paused, shrugging off the memory.

'I suppose we would have drifted on for longer, but then she achieved her ambition and was offered a job in California. It was the same week my father died. Jonelle wouldn't even consider staying for the funeral. Nothing was going to stop her getting where she was going.' His smile was rather twisted.

'Even then, I tried. I was going to follow her when I'd sorted out my father's affairs, but she wrote to me from the States and told me not to bother as she'd found someone else—an American who was going to be a lot more useful to her than I ever was.'

'I...I'm sorry,' said Phyllida inadequately. She wished she had the nerve to put her arms round him. Jake's voice might have been unemotional, but Jonelle's desertion must have been a bitter blow to a man of his pride.

'Don't be,' he said. 'Just be grateful you and Rupert

discovered that you wanted different things out of life before it was too late.'

Phyllida was silent, thinking about Jake rather than Rupert. It was easier to understand his hostility now. She must have seemed another Jonelle, in her smart suit and her brittle sophistication, talking about her career as if it was all that mattered to her. As it had been, she acknowledged ruefully. She had never bothered to look at her surroundings before, never stopped to smell the air or watch the way the sun cast shadows across the grass. Breaking away to Australia had taught her how much she had been missing.

She looked across at Jake. He was frowning down into his beer, absorbed in thought, but he glanced up to meet her eyes. 'Sorry, it wasn't a very edifying story, was it? Don't let it put you off marriage for good, though. It doesn't have to be like that. Look at Chris. She's got the right idea about marriage. She knows it's not easy, but she works at it. She's not constantly trying to prove herself, she's just the way she is—loyal and honest and kind.'

'She loves Mike,' said Phyllida.

'Yes, she does, and she's happy because she recognises his faults and loves him in spite—or perhaps because—of them. She doesn't expect him to be perfect.'

'I thought Rupert was perfect,' she said a little sadly. 'It didn't do me much good.'

Jake smiled. 'All or nothing?'

'Yes.' She smiled back ruefully. 'I'm afraid I'm not very good at compromises either. If I can't be utterly, completely, madly in love, then I'd rather not be in love at all.'

'Then why did you pretend that you were still engaged to Rupert when I asked you about him?'

The casual question caught Phyllida off-guard. She had tried so hard to forget that evening, but now the memory seemed to glow between them—the tautness of the atmosphere, the flare of anger, that unforgettable, devastating kiss. Was Jake remembering it too? She didn't dare look at him, didn't dare risk him reading the truth in her eyes.

She had held her engagement before her as if to ward off her own weakness. She had thought it would help her deny the attraction to Jake that held her in its coils. Much good it had done her.

She had fought it for as long as she could: she didn't want Rupert, she wanted Jake. She wanted him to take her in his arms again. She wanted to feel his mouth against her skin, his hard hands curving over her body, to let her fingers feel the flex of his muscles and drift on to explore the whole sleek, supple strength of him—

Phyllida caught her breath, aghast at the truth she had discovered in her own heart and passionately grateful for the darkness which hid her expression.

Jake was looking at her enquiringly, and with an effort she remembered the question. 'I...I... It just seemed a good idea at the time,' she said lamely.

She could see the amused disbelief on Jake's face. Did that mean he could see hers as clearly? Phyllida searched her mind frantically for a diversion. 'What brought you to Port Lincoln?' Her voice was so high and artificial that she wasn't surprised at his curious look, but to her relief he accepted the change of subject.

'After Jonelle left, there was no reason to stay in Sydney. I'd had enough of cities for a while. I've kept an interest in Tregowan's, of course, but I handed over the day to day management to my younger brother and bought myself *Ali B*.' He patted the fibreglass affectionately.

'We've been through a lot together. She's taken me round the South Pacific Islands, and all the way round Australia. For a long time I just kept moving, but when I reached Port Lincoln, I felt ready to stay for a while. I started out with a couple of boats, and somehow the business grew and grew. I still go to Sydney regularly, and keep an eye on Tregowan's in Adelaide—hence the plane—but if I'm ever restless, I come out here. This is my real home—on deck, under the stars.'

'Don't you ever get lonely?'

Jake looked across the cockpit to where Phyllida sat, knees drawn up, arms resting on them, her skin luminous in the darkness. 'No,' he said. 'But that's not to say I never will.'

There was a long, long pause. The sea was still, the air warm and quiet, the only sound the *Ali B* creaking gently against the anchor rope. Phyllida was sure she could hear her senses twanging in the silence. Her heart slowed to a painfully sluggish beat, and she discovered that she was holding her breath. She let it out, very carefully.

She wanted to say something to shatter the sudden tension between them, but her mind was a blank, and her tongue felt dry and awkward. She stared out across the water instead, although there was nothing to see but the first faint glimmers of starlight, and every nerve was strained towards the man sitting as still and silent as the night on the other side of the cockpit.

In the end, it was Jake who broke the tension. He got up abruptly to check the fish, and announced that supper was ready. Phyllida went below to collect the salad she had made, perversely disappointed now that the atmosphere had been shattered by practicality. Before, it had been breathless, fraught with unspoken tension and an underlying current of awareness, but now it was simply strained and uncomfortable.

It was the same the next day. Phyllida had lain in the for'ard berth, staring at the closed door of her cabin and wondering what she would do if it opened and Jake came in. Her body had been beating with the desire she had fought so hard against. She'd wished she hadn't acknowledged it, wished she could go back to pretending that it didn't exist and that the hunger pulsing along her veins was no more than a bizarre chemical reaction.

But the door hadn't opened. Jake wasn't interested in *her*, Phyllida reminded herself bleakly. He was attracted to long-legged blondes, not petite brunettes—especially not a petite brunette whose one point of similarity with his beautiful wife was the very one that had caused the break-up of his marriage.

No, it would be as well not to indulge in silly dreams. Even if Jake *did* feel some attraction, what would it lead to? A few nights together? An awkward farewell? All or nothing, Phyllida remembered sadly. That was what Jake had said, and he was right.

In her heart of hearts, she knew that being a temporary diversion for Jake would not be enough. If she couldn't have all of him, she would be better off having none at all. It was all very well to wish that time would stand still, but it wouldn't. Sooner or later she would have to leave, and it would be much easier all round if she left with her heart and her pride intact.

The next morning she was polite but cool, Jake brisk in return. It was as if the warmth they had discovered walking along the beach yesterday evening had never existed. One of the other boats, moored at the other end of Reevesby, called in on the radio to say that it was having trouble with its engine, and Jake took the dinghy down to see if he could sort it out.

At first, Phyllida was glad to see him go, but it wasn't long before she began to miss his acerbic presence. Even a strained, irritable Jake was better than no Jake at all.

Unable to relax, desperate not to think about the unwelcome realisation that had kept her awake for much of the night, Phyllida sat at the table in the saloon and wrote determinedly cheerful letters home. She wrote to her parents, to her brother, to the friends who had been outraged at her treatment by Liedermann, Marshall & Jones, and last, after some hesitation, she wrote to Rupert.

Jake's story of his marriage had made her look at things from Rupert's point of view for a change, and she was sorry now for some of the hurtful things she had said. They had both been in the wrong. Phyllida didn't regret her decision to break off their engagement, but she did wish it had ended less bitterly.

It was a hard letter to write, and she screwed up several pieces of paper before she managed to get going. She was glad they had discovered in time how unsuited they were, Phyllida wrote, but she wanted him to know that she now realised that she had been thinking only about herself, and hadn't bothered to consider how he might feel. She hoped that it wasn't too late to say that she was sorry, and finished by saying that she would like it if they could continue to be friends when she came home.

Phyllida felt much better when she had finished. She was sealing the envelope when she heard the buzz of the outboard engine approaching. Hastily shoving pad and envelopes onto the deep shelf behind the seat, she climbed up on deck to find Jake tying the dinghy to the stern. Appalled at how overjoyed she was to see him again after such a short time, she forced herself to sound bright and brittle. 'Did you sort out that problem?'

'Yes,' Jake grunted, climbing on board with his usual economy of movement.

'What was wrong?'

'Do you know anything about diesel engines?'

'No,' she admitted.

'Then there's not much point in me telling you, is there?'

Phyllida's lips tightened. She was prepared to be polite, but if he wanted to be like that, let him! It just made it easier for her to reassure herself that last night's hunger and desire had been merely temporary aberrations of the mind.

They were snappy with each other as they took down the canopy and made ready to sail. Jake barked orders at Phyllida, and shouted at her if she didn't respond immediately. 'I thought you wanted to learn how to crew?' he snarled when she objected.

'Not if it means being bossed around by a frustrated sergeant major!' said Phyllida tautly. 'I'll stick to the land in future.'

'That's up to you, but in the meantime you're crew— and that means you do as I tell you!'

All in all, it was a tense sail. The breeze was flukey, gusting one minute and dying out the next, and Jake was edgy and scowling. There was no need to balance the boat today, so Phyllida pointedly sat as far away from him as possible.

The sea was in an intense, glittering turquoise, the islands streaks of white sand along the horizon, but yesterday's fizzing joy was missing. Phyllida looked in vain for the dolphins to reappear, and banish Jake's scowl with their enchantment, but it seemed as if they had abandoned her along with her happiness.

The atmosphere was so bad that she half expected Jake to suggest going back to the marina, but instead he announced gruffly that they would head south to Memory Cove, on the cape that jutted out from the mainland on the point of the Eyre Peninsula. 'Chris would expect me to take you there,' he said, as if excusing himself.

Phyllida would have preferred that he'd wanted to take her there himself, but she wouldn't admit as much, even to herself. 'Why's it called Memory Cove?' was all she asked.

'Matthew Flinders moored there in 1802,' said Jake. 'He was a great explorer and navigator, and several of the islands in the Sir Joseph Banks Group are named after places in his native Lincolnshire. He lost eight of his men when a boat overturned. Their bodies were never found, so he named the cove in their memory.'

Phyllida grimaced. 'It sounds a gloomy place.'

But when at last they anchored in Memory Cove, it was anything but gloomy. Hills covered in the dry, dusty green of eucalypts, she-oaks and pines rolled down to a beach that was a perfect curve of dazzling white sand, and where intense turquoise shallows shaded into crystal as they sighed gently against the shore. The colours were so bright, the light so sharp, that they hurt Phyllida's eyes.

Jake took her in the dinghy across the abrupt line that divided the deep blue water from the shimmeringly clear mint-green of the shallows—so clear that Phyllida swore she could see every grain of sand beneath them. He had announced that he wanted to do some maintenance on the boat, but that he would take her ashore if she wanted.

Phyllida had interpreted this as meaning that he didn't want her around. Well, that was fine by her!

Standing knee-deep in the limpid water, she clutched her shoes and her book to her chest and watched rather forlornly as Jake turned the dinghy round and sped back out to the *Ali B*. She would much rather be on her own than sit around being snapped at by Jake Tregowan, she reminded herself, and, with a last wistful look, turned and waded for the shore.

For a while, she sat on the hot sand and tried to concentrate on her thriller, but her eyes kept straying back to the boat in the distance, where she could see Jake's figure moving sure-footedly around the deck. He never so much as glanced in her direction to see if she was all right, she thought crossly. Piqued, she abandoned her book, brushed the sand off her feet and put on her shoes to explore.

A rough, dusty track led inland through the rolling scrub. There had been a bush fire not so long ago, Phyllida saw. Burnt trees pointed their mutilated branches accusingly at the sun, black and silver slashes against the sky. Everything was brown or grey, or a dull, faded green, parched and bleached by the relentless heat and thrown into relief by the overpowering blue above. The sun cast broken shadows into the fine dust beneath her feet. Phyllida crushed some dessicated leaves in her fingers and bent her head to breathe in their sharp, dry fragrance.

She wished Jake were with her. The space and the silence were intimidating without him, the intensity of the light and the colours threatening to overwhelm her. Phyllida stood very still and stared down at the crushed leaves in her hand.

She loved him.

The realisation filtered slowly through her mind, and she raised her head to look blankly at a slender gum tree, its silvery trunk etched as if by a fine pencil against the light. What she felt for Jake was more than mere physical hunger. She wanted him, yes. She craved the feel of his body, the touch of his lips—but it was more than that.

She needed the reassurance of his presence, Phyllida realised with some reluctance. She, who had always prided herself on her independence, was somehow lost without him. It didn't matter whether he was smiling or shouting at her, as long as he was there she felt...*safe*. Jake was her focus, her anchor.

Her life before she met him had been a heedless rush, she saw. He had plucked her out of a whirling circle of activity that led nowhere except back to where it started, had held her between his hands and steadied her. Without him, she would be sucked back into the vortex. Phyllida felt chilled at the thought.

She walked on, without thinking about where she was going, preoccupied with her new knowledge. It had been bad enough admitting that she wanted Jake, but falling in love with him was a disaster! How had it happened? How had she got herself tangled up in this terrible web of need and desire? Panic stole into her heart. How was she going to cut herself free and face life without him?

Phyllida had no idea how long she had walked before she found herself on a headland, looking down on a wild, beautiful bay where the ocean surged onto the beach in line after line of booming surf. She watched as the waves gathered in the dark blue depths, lifted and grew until they broke in a perfect curve of glacier-green and crashed down into the maelstrom of purest, foaming white.

Life without Jake. How was she going to get through

this evening, knowing that she loved him, being with him but not being able to touch him, not being able to tell him how she felt? Now, more than ever, he mustn't know.

The beach below was a sweep of pure white sand, edged by a sheer rock cliff-face on one side and the pounding surf on the other. Like her, stuck between her desire for Jake and the knowledge that he wouldn't ever need her in the same way, Phyllida thought wryly.

At first sight it looked quite inaccessible, but when she looked again she thought she could see a way down after all. And if there was a way down, there would be a way up.

Phyllida was suddenly fired with a determination to walk along the beach and climb back up again. In some obscure way, it would be a means of proving to herself that things weren't as hopeless as they seemed right now. Things might change. Jake might change; *she* might change. If she could only get to the beach, she might not have to live with this despair for ever.

Carefully, Phyllida began to make her way down. It wasn't too bad at first. The scrub caught at her bare legs, but the ground was quite solid. Gradually, though, the slope got steeper and steeper, and the dry earth started to crumble and slip beneath her shoes. Phyllida looked down and swallowed. She hadn't realised quite what a long way it was to the bottom. Perhaps this was a mistake? Perhaps she should just learn to accept loving Jake hopelessly after all?

Biting her lip, she glanced over her shoulder. It seemed as if she had come a long way, and the climb back up looked daunting from this angle. Phyllida wished she had never thought of reaching the beach. It was a stupid thing to try and do on her own anyway.

She turned a little awkwardly on the steep slope, but even as she realised the potential danger of her situation her foot skidded on the loose earth and she lost her balance. The ground dropped away so sharply that her fall gained momentum with sickening speed, and the next instant she was tumbling down through the scrub.

Terrified, Phyllida flailed out with her arms. The bushes were low and brittle here, but at last she managed to grasp one with a sturdier stem to break her fall. For what seemed an eternity, she just lay there with her face pressed into the dry soil, still clinging to the bush, her heart hammering with shock. She didn't dare look down; she didn't dare look up.

And then, miraculously, there was a shout from the top of the headland. 'Phyllida!'

'Jake!' She tried to shout back, but her voice only came out as a dry whisper.

'Don't move!' he shouted, making his way down towards her with careful, controlled ease.

Phyllida didn't think she could anyway. All she could do was lie there and wait for him.

It seemed to take for ever for Jake to reach her. Every now and then he would dislodge a shower of earth, which would rattle past her face, and she would tense, convinced that the whole headland was about to disintegrate beneath her, but at last he was there, and his strong arms went round her, holding her hard against the indescribable comfort of his body.

'Are you hurt?' he asked in a hard, urgent voice, patting her all over as if to reassure himself that she was still in one piece.

Phyllida clung to him, shaking her head into his broad shoulder. 'No. Just a bit scratched.'

'Well, that's something. Can you get up?'

Her legs were still trembling with reaction, but with Jake's arm around her, and his body as an anchor, she made it back up to the top. He was absolutely sure-footed, his shoes never skidding as hers did, and his hold on her was strong and secure.

His face was set in grim, forbidding lines, but he didn't say anything until they had reached the track again, some way from the cliff-edge. Then he let her go, brushing the dust from her cheek where it had lain pressed into the ground. 'Are you sure you're all right?'

'I'm fine,' said Phyllida, but her voice quavered. She knew that she was lucky to have got off so lightly. Her shorts and T-shirt were dusty, and there were a few minor scratches on her arms and legs, but otherwise nothing to show for that terrifying tumble down the cliff.

'In that case would you like to explain what the hell you were doing down there?' She had never seen Jake so angry. He was very white about the mouth and his nostrils were pinched, the green eyes blazing with fury.

'I—I wanted to see the beach.'

'The *beach*?' he echoed incredulously, his voice rising to a shout. 'What for?'

Phyllida shook her head helplessly, which only seemed to make him even angrier.

'What was wrong with the beach you were sitting on earlier?' he demanded. 'Most people would have been quite happy with white sand and clear blue sea, but not Phyllida! No, she has to choose the most dangerously inaccessible beach she can find, and then try and break her neck getting down to it! What on earth possessed you?'

Phyllida couldn't tell him now desperate she had been at the prospect of spending her life without him. She couldn't tell him how the beach had beckoned, like a promise that things would get better, that he might, just might, learn to love her after all. 'I didn't think,' she said miserably, and Jake almost exploded.

'No, you never do, do you? You just see something you want and go straight after it, without thinking about what's involved, or who's going to have to come along and get you out of trouble! What would you have done if I hadn't seen you go over the edge? You could have been lying there for days with a broken neck before anyone found you.'

'I know, I know! I'm *sorry*!' Phyllida pressed her hands to her head. She longed to throw herself against him and cry, to feel his arms close around her and hear him tell her that he was only angry because he'd been so fearful for her, but there was no hope of that, not now.

She might as well have saved her breath. Jake was too angry to listen anyway. 'You're so full of how clever you are, and how you can look after yourself, but I can't leave you alone for five minutes! I followed you when I realised you'd gone from the beach, knowing that anything could happen once you went wandering off into the bush on your own, but I never dreamt you'd do anything as stupid as throwing yourself off the edge of a cliff!'

'I didn't throw myself off!'

'You might as well have done, and if I'd had any sense I would have left you there!' All through the long walk back, Jake kept up a diatribe about Phyllida. She was spoilt, stupid, selfish, criminally irresponsible.

Phyllida didn't say anything. He was right, anyway. She felt sick with shame at her own stupidity. She trudged beside him along the track, head down and shoulders rigid with misery, still shaken from her narrow escape, but more distressed by Jake's blistering anger and contempt. Her throat was tight, and her jaw was clenched so hard in the effort to keep back the tears that it ached, but she refused to cry in front of him.

It was an enormous relief when the grove of feathery she-oaks fringing Memory Cove appeared. Jake had run out of invective at last, but if anything his icy silence was even more terrifying than his anger. Phyllida walked unsteadily down to the shallows and scooped the blissfully cool water over her scratches, cupping it in her hands against her hot, burning face. She wanted to die.

When she lowered her hands, her eyes were huge in her white face. Damp tendrils of hair clung to her cheek and droplets of water still trembled on the end of her lashes, sparkling in the sunlight. She looked shaken and scared and very vulnerable, and when she saw that Jake was watching her she turned away, so that he wouldn't see the misery in her eyes.

The rage faded from Jake's face, and he caught her arm, pulling her back round to face him. 'Phyllida!' he said urgently. 'I didn't—'

CHAPTER EIGHT

SHE never knew what he had been about to say. There was a shout from the water, and they both jerked round to see an inflatable speeding across the shallows towards them, a big, familiar figure at the helm.

'Rod,' said Jake in a flat voice, and his hand fell from Phyllida's arm.

Rod and his party were delighted to see them, and seemed blissfully unaware that both Jake's and Phyllida's smiles were forced. They had come ashore, they said, to get the barbecue going at one of the sites that had been specially provided behind the beach, to minimise the risk of bush fires, and they urged Phyllida and Jake to join them.

There were five of them altogether, all men, and all delighted to see Phyllida. They were thoroughly enjoying their week fishing, with Rod taking responsibility for the boat, but were, they insisted, ready for some feminine company again.

The last thing Phyllida felt like was a party, but she had been dreading the evening alone with Jake even before he was so angry with her, so she smiled and agreed that it was a great idea. To her surprise, Jake was less enthusiastic. She would have thought he would have been just as anxious for some other company, but perhaps he had wanted to spend the whole evening haranguing her?

Refusing Jake's offer to take her across in the inflatable, Phyllida swam out to the boat in her T-shirt, letting the clear water wash away the dust and dirt. Its sparkling coolness soothed her scratches and her sore feelings, and by the time she had rinsed herself off with fresh water, and changed into a soft cotton shirt and cut-off trousers, she was feeling much better.

Jake had had no right to rant at her like that, she decided as she combed out her hair. All right, it had been stupid to attempt to reach the beach, but she would have been perfectly all right if her foot hadn't slipped. Anyone would think there had been a major tragedy, the way he was carrying on!

By the time they went back to the beach for the barbecue, Phyllida had talked herself into a defiant mood once more. At least this afternoon had showed her how hopeless it was even to think of Jake ever falling in love with her. Instead she knew just how much he despised her, and she was more determined than ever that he should never guess how she felt.

The other party didn't seem to notice the tension between Jake and Phyllida. They all sat on the beach in the fading light, looking out at the two boats anchored at either end of the bay. The water was still and milky pale, the sand cool and soft beneath their bare feet. Phyllida placed herself as far as possible from Jake, but made sure that he could see what a good time she was having.

She positively scintillated, laughing and flirting and trying to convince herself that she didn't care that he was ignoring her. The others were blurred figures, only Jake was clear and distinct in the dim light, and Phyllida hated the fact that she noticed every time he turned or smiled or lifted his bottle of beer to his mouth.

He was making an effort to be pleasant to a group who were, after all, his clients, but Phyllida could see a nerve beating in his cheek and sense the suppressed anger in the rigid lines of his body. In spite of her best resolutions, it made her nervous, and there was an increasing desperation to the way she laughed and chattered and exclaimed at how much she was enjoying herself.

It was late before the party broke up. Phyllida wished the others an effusive goodnight and waved defiantly as Jake ferried her, grim-faced, back to the *Ali B* on the far side of the bay.

'Wasn't that a great evening?' she asked provocatively to disguise her nerves as she climbed down the companionway. 'They're nice guys, aren't they?'

'You obviously thought so,' snapped Jake. 'Though I fail to see what's nice about a group of grown men slobbering fatuously over one girl!'

'Don't be absurd,' said Phyllida bravely. 'You were there—you could see we were just talking.'

'I would hardly describe your performance this evening as "just talking",' said Jake savagely. 'All those girlish giggles, those little sidelong looks, those tantalising smiles... I've never seen such a revolting display!'

'I'd have thought you'd have wanted me to be pleasant to your clients,' she said, tossing back her hair. '*You* certainly weren't. Haven't you ever heard of public relations?'

'The sort of relations you were promising were far from public,' sneered Jake. 'They're probably drawing lots for you even now!'

Phyllida's eyes blazed. 'How dare you?'

'You don't like the truth, do you, Phyllida? Must be your advertising background coming out! You'd rather pretend that things are the way you want them to be rather than face the facts as they really are.'

'Better than being prudish and pig-headed and prejudiced!' she flung at him. 'Well, don't worry, Jake! Chris and Mike will be back soon, and you won't have to put up with my offensive behaviour any longer!'

The muscle was still hammering away in Jake's cheek. 'Believe me, it can't come soon enough for me,' he said through clenched teeth. 'I had a pleasant, peaceful life until you arrived. Now I spend half my time wanting to shake you and the other half—' He stopped.

'Yes?' Phyllida demanded stormily.

Suddenly he was standing very close. She glared up at him, but when she saw the look in his eyes the fire and the fury in her bright face seeped away, and she began to tremble deep inside. Jake reached out and drew her to him slowly, deliberately.

'I spend the other half of my time wanting to do this,' he finished quietly, and kissed her.

The world melted around Phyllida, along with all her fine resolutions to save her pride and keep her distance. Pride counted for nothing when Jake held her against him; the future ceased to exist the moment his lips met hers. Resistance was a poor candle in the storm of feeling that swept over her as they kissed, hesitantly at first, as if half expecting the other to pull away in disgust, then with a spinning sweetness that grew into an increasing urgency.

Insistent, bewitching, his mouth explored hers, his hands moved demandingly over her curves, and Phyllida dissolved beneath his touch, gasping his name in helpless pleasure. Desire had them both in its thrall. This was no time to talk, no time to explain or wonder at the way the strain and tension of the day had led them to this point, where they clung to each other with a wild desperation, kissing and touching, half smiling, half awed by the sensations that tangled them closer and closer.

Jake's fingers were deft and sure as he peeled off first

her clothes, then his own, and led her, still without words, to the wide berth with its hatch open to the moonlight. Smiling, she reached for him as he stretched out beside her, and he smiled back as he rolled her beneath him and bent to explore her silken warmth.

Phyllida shuddered with a deep, wrenching excitement at the feel of his naked body against her own, his skin against hers, the fierce hunger of his touch. It was so wonderful to be able to run her hands over that sleek, solid strength. She could feel his muscles flex and ripple beneath her fingers, and lovingly traced the bumps in his spine, dizzy with relief at being able to touch him and taste him and hold him at last.

A sigh of breeze sent the *Ali B* swinging gently on her anchor, and the sea rustled responsively against her hull, but neither Jake nor Phyllida noticed. Intent on each other, and the rhythm of love that was beating between them, they clung together, whispering endearments like secrets, murmuring breathlessly at each caress, each piercingly sweet kiss.

Phyllida was molten wax in Jake's arms, fluid desire beneath his demand, and as the urgency rolled and surged into a turbulent, unstoppable tide she dug her fingers into his back and cried out her need and her hunger.

She felt Jake smile against her breast, heard his muffled promise against her throat, and then, at last, she could welcome his hard heat and look into his eyes for one long, unforgettable moment as they paused together on the edge of time itself before the tide lifted them up and over and on together.

Caught up in the urgency of the rhythm, they let the tide carry them, plunging onwards and upwards in a frantic quest for fulfilment where there was nothing but the pulse of need and their bodies moving together in the light of the moon, and a final starburst of release and unimaginable delight.

Phyllida woke to the gentle creak of the boat, rocking almost imperceptibly from side to side and sending the marbled shadows that reflected up from the water wavering across the ceiling in time with the waves.

Stretching, filled with the boundless contentment of a dream, she rolled over to find Jake propped up on one elbow, watching her. The sunlight flooding the cabin made his eyes look very green, the grey flecks almost gold. For a long moment they gazed at each other wordlessly, while memories of the long, sweet night whispered over their skin.

Inexplicably shy after all they had shared, Phyllida felt faint colour tinge her cheeks and wanted to look away, but Jake's green-gold eyes held her.

'Hello,' she said.

'Hello,' said Jake, and dissolved all her awkwardness with a sudden smile. He leant over to kiss her, and Phyllida melted against him, sliding her arms around his neck and letting his possessively drifting hands snarl up all her senses again.

'Do you still want to shake me?' she murmured as she kissed his throat.

Jake smiled against her breast. 'I'm sure I will at some stage, but right at this moment I have other plans in mind!'

Satisfied, Phyllida stretched luxuriously beneath him, her fingers playing over the powerful shoulders. She loved the contrast between steely muscle and warm, sleek skin. She loved his lean, compact strength and the supple, unexpected grace in the way he moved. He was never blundering, never hurried, just slow and sure. She loved to bury her face into his throat and breathe in the scent of him, to touch her tongue to his skin and taste him, to feel his weight pressing her down into the cushions.

She loved *him*.

Awash with the enchantment of the night, Phyllida had forgotten yesterday's resolutions. She had buried the knowledge that she would have to say goodbye, ignored the fact that Jake had said nothing of how he felt. Reality meant nothing with the sunlight pouring over her and Jake's strong brown hands on her body.

Reality, though, was determined not to be dismissed that easily. Their kisses were just beginning to deepen out of control when there was a thump on the side of the boat and a voice called, 'Ahoy, there! Anyone awake in there?'

Jake stiffened in Phyllida's arms, and sighed. 'I suppose I'd better go,' he said reluctantly, dropping a last kiss on her shoulder. 'Otherwise they'll be climbing aboard to investigate!'

Phyllida stretched again and watched the reflections rock over the ceiling. She could hear Jake conferring with someone on deck, but was too lazy to listen. She wanted to lie here all day, enveloped in sunlight.

'They want us to go over to breakfast,' said Jake, reappearing fully dressed in the doorway. 'I'm afraid I couldn't think of a good reason to refuse—and your jealous swains are determined not to let you go without seeing you again!'

She coloured and laughed, remembering her desperate attempts to persuade Jake that she wasn't interested in him. Why had she bothered? she wondered happily as she pulled on shorts and a shirt and splashed cold water over her face. She had come a long way from the days of suits and full make-up.

When she emerged, glowing, from the cabin, Jake was tidying up the saloon. 'Making everything ship-shape?' she teased, and ran her hand down his back as he bent to retrieve her shirt from the floor where it had fallen unheeded last night.

He grinned as he straightened. 'Messy crew get put on short rations,' he said, handing her the shirt.

'I can't think how it got there, Captain,' said Phyllida with an innocent look. 'But I'll make sure it doesn't happen again!'

Jake laughed, and tugged at her hair. 'We don't need to take tidiness too far,' he relented with mock reluctance. 'Here,' he went on, picking up her shorts and pants and piling them into her arms, 'you'd better take these as well... And while you're at it, you can get rid of these, too.'

He reached into the shelf for the notepad and the letters she had written yesterday morning, and balanced them precariously on the top of the pile. 'They were sliding around all over the place yesterday.'

'Aye, aye, Cap'n!' Phyllida attempted a salute, dislodging the top letter from the pile. It fluttered to the floor at Jake's feet, and as he picked it up his smile faded. He handed it back to her, his expression suddenly quite blank, and she felt a cold feeling trickle down her spine.

Phyllida glanced at the envelope, and the name sprang out at her in her bold black writing: Rupert Deverell. 'I...er, wrote to Rupert,' she said uneasily, unsure of why she had to acknowledge it.

'So I see.'

'You see, I wanted to explain—'

Jake held up a hand to interrupt her. 'You don't need to explain anything, Phyllida,' he said, in the same crushingly cool voice.

'No, I meant to Rupert. I just—'

'I don't want to know,' he said flatly.

'But Jake, you don't understand!' To Phyllida's intense frustration she was interrupted again, this time by a shout from the other boat.

'Coffee's ready! Come aboard!'

Without a word, Jake turned and climbed up on deck. In silence, they buzzed across in the dinghy to join the others.

Phyllida couldn't believe how swiftly the atmosphere had changed, how utterly the joy had drained from the morning. All her doubts came rushing back. If Jake had loved her, he wouldn't have turned cold on her like that, with no provocation. He could hardly have made it clearer that last night hadn't changed anything between them.

'You look as if you're suffering a bit,' Rod said to her sympathetically. 'Regretting all that wine last night?'

For a fleeting moment, Phyllida's eyes met Jake's. 'I'm regretting a lot of things about last night,' she said evenly, and Jake's face tightened as he looked away.

They left as soon as they could, in spite of urgings to stay. Jake made some excuse about having to get back to the marina, and Phyllida smiled brightly and agreed. They didn't look at each other as they went back to the *Ali B*, and Jake began preparing the boat to sail with a brisk efficiency that chilled Phyllida to the bone.

It was ridiculous to let things sour so completely, she decided. 'Look, Jake, about Rupert—' she began as he unlashed the mainsail. But he was in no mood to listen.

'I don't want to hear about Rupert,' he said. 'Who you write to is your affair. I'm not interested in how you feel about your engagement or what you do when you get back to England. It's got nothing to do with me.'

He went forward before she could answer, and began hauling up the anchor. Sick at heart, Phyllida waited until he came back and started the motor.

'Didn't last night mean anything to you?' she asked quietly.

'It was great,' he said with chilling indifference. 'I'm not going to pretend it wasn't. But it didn't change the fact that your life's in England, Phyllida, not here. If you want to have a fling while you're away, well, that suits me fine—but a fling is all it is. I learnt my lesson with Jonelle. I don't want to be part of your life, juggled between your job and your other commitments. You can keep Rupert for that.'

'Jake, it wasn't *like* that,' Phyllida pleaded, but he only hunched a shoulder irritably.

'Let's leave it, shall we?'

Phyllida gave up. 'I don't want to be part of your life'. Well, what had she expected? That last night's breathtaking joy would be enough? That the glorious, spiralling passion would somehow change all the facts? Jake was right. She didn't belong here, with the wind and the wide sky. She was just having a fling.

Phyllida remembered his description bitterly. It might have been a fling for him, but for her it had been the source and the fulfilment of love. Hadn't he heard her, murmuring 'I love you' against his skin? Couldn't he read it in her eyes?

Numbly, she stared out across the waves and felt misery settle itself, cold and leaden, in the pit of her stomach.

The wind was light today, blowing from right behind them, so that Jake let the mainsail right out until it was almost at right angles to the boat. In front of it, cut off from the breeze, the jib flapped frantically, as if gasping for air.

Jake frowned. He had been sitting morosely at the helm, glancing automatically from sea to sail, checking the wind, his face closed, his mouth set grimly. Running before the wind like this, there was nothing for Phyllida to do, but she would even have welcomed some of Jake's abrupt commands to break the silence that grew tauter and tighter with every passing minute. When Jake did speak, she jumped.

'Take the helm, will you?' His voice was harsh.

Phyllida edged back and took the helm nervously. 'What are you doing?'

'I'm going for'ard to goosewing the jib. If I can pull it round, and brace it with the spinnaker pole, it'll catch the wind on this side and we'll get on a bit faster.'

'What do I have to do?'

Jake pointed to the compass. 'Just hold this course, and don't let the boat swing across the wind. OK?'

She nodded. It didn't mean much to her, but he would only bite her head off if she asked questions.

Jake unlashed the spinnaker pole and climbed out of the cockpit to make his way forward. Phyllida's gaze followed him automatically. She hadn't been able to look at him all morning, but now that his back was turned she could let her longing stare rest on the broad shoulders, the lean hips and the strong brown legs. Fatally, she took her eyes off the compass.

Preoccupied with memories, she didn't notice that her grip had slackened on the helm until the *Ali B* swung round into the wind, and the heavy boom went crashing across the boat. It caught Jake across the shoulders with a terrific blow, and would have knocked him overboard if he hadn't fallen against the guard rails where he lay ominously still.

'Jake!' Phyllida dodged the still wildly swinging boom

and scrambled up beside him. 'Oh, Jake... Oh, my God... Jake, *please*, are you all right?'

For one black, terrifying moment she thought she had killed him, but he stirred and groaned, and she burst into overwrought tears. 'Jake, I'm so sorry...I didn't realise...are you hurt?' she sobbed incoherently.

With an immense effort, Jake pulled himself groggily into a sitting position and pushed her away. 'What happened?' he groaned, dropping his head into his hands.

'It was the boom...it swung round before I could stop it.'

'I *told* you to keep the wind behind you!' Somehow Jake got himself down to the cockpit, where he collapsed on the lockers, wincing as he held his chest.

The boat had rounded up into the wind, and both sails were flapping aimlessly. 'What shall I do?' asked Phyllida in panic, looking around her wildly for another boat. If Jake was badly hurt, there was no way she would be able to sail the *Ali B* back single-handed. Never had she felt so useless.

'Don't...touch...anything,' Jake ground out, eyes tightly closed.

'But we're drifting!'

Jake grimaced as he dragged himself up to look around them. The sea stretched glittering off into the distance and the nearest land was miles away. 'We're not going to run into anything,' he said with difficulty and, lying down, closed his eyes once more. 'And I'd feel safer if you just sat completely still and didn't do anything!'

It was some time before he sat up again. He wouldn't even let her do anything for him, refusing to let her even touch him. Rejected, guilty, desperately worried, Phyllida sat miserably hunched in the corner and watched him grit his teeth and force himself to recover enough to take the helm again.

'Shouldn't you go and lie down below?' she asked timidly.

'And who's going to sail the boat? You?' Jake's voice was justifiably scathing. 'If I'd been knocked overboard, unconscious, I would have drowned, and you wouldn't even have been capable of turning the boat round to pick me up!'

'I'm sorry—'

Jake ignored her attempt to apologise. 'All you had to do was hold onto the helm and keep a steady course for two minutes, but you couldn't even concentrate for that long!'

'I didn't know what you meant!' said Phyllida tearfully. 'I only got on a boat for the first time two days ago, and you expect me to be Captain Cook already!'

'If you didn't understand, why didn't you ask?'

'Because you'd just have been unpleasant about it!' A mixture of guilt and relief was curdling her temper. 'How am I expected to learn, when all you ever do is shout at me?'

Later, Phyllida couldn't remember just how they got themselves back to the marina. All she knew was that she never wanted to go through another experience like it.

She was frantic with worry about Jake, who stubbornly refused any help. He was obviously in pain, but seemed to find some relief in a savage denunciation of Phyllida's character, actions and all she stood for, and by the time they finally tied up at the marina she was white with rage, shock and humiliation.

Scorning her assistance, Jake took himself off to the hospital, and Phyllida was left miserably cleaning the boat. It seemed to be all she was good for nowadays, she thought wearily. She found Jake back at the house when she had finished.

'What did the doctor say?'

'Three cracked ribs, heavy bruising and a touch of concussion,' said Jake. 'Although it feels more like a bloody great whack than a touch! He's told me to rest, so I'm going to bed.'

'Can I do anything?' she asked in a small voice.

He turned at his bedroom door. 'Yes,' he said with brutal frankness. 'You can keep out of my way for a while!'

Phyllida sank down into a chair and buried her face in her hands, letting the hot tears course down her cheeks. Only this morning he had held her and kissed her and whispered sweet words into her skin; now he was a bitter stranger again.

Her heart felt as if it was full of pebbles, scraping and rasping painfully against each other like shingle on a beach, as wave after wave of misery swept over her. Memories of last night mocked her. What a naïve fool she had been, to place such trust in love to make everything right! Love had been all that mattered last night, and now everything was wrong—terribly wrong.

She sat dully all evening, thinking about the night before, and all the lonely nights to come when all she would have would be memories of Jake's lips and Jake's hands and Jake's hard, exciting body. When the phone rang she was tempted to ignore it, but roused herself to answer listlessly.

'Phyllida?' It was Chris's voice. 'What on earth's the matter?'

'Nothing,' said Phyllida with an effort. 'I'm just tired.

It's been a long day. How's Mike?' she added quickly, before Chris could pursue the subject.

'A bit wobbly, but on his feet at last. That's why I've rung: we should be home next week!'

She chattered on for a while, and Phyllida was so pleased to hear her bright and happy again that she forced herself to sound cheerful in reply. Chris wasn't fooled, though. 'Something *is* wrong, isn't it?' she said suspiciously.

Phyllida hesitated. She couldn't tell Chris about Jake. She would be distressed if she knew just how miserable Phyllida was, and anyway, her feelings for Jake were too raw and painful to talk about just yet. On the other hand, she would have to tell Chris something, or she would bully the truth out of her anyway.

'I...I'm missing Rupert,' she improvised.

'Rupert? But I thought you were the one who broke off the engagement?'

'Yes, I was but...' Phyllida trailed off helplessly, then rallied. 'I've had some time to think about things,' she said. 'I didn't realise how much I'd miss him.' None of it was true, she thought bleakly, but it didn't seem to matter. Nothing seemed to matter any more.

Chris was surprised, but so sympathetic that Phyllida began to feel guilty about misleading her. 'I didn't mean to unburden my problems on you,' she said, trying to stem the flow.

'Don't worry. It makes a nice change to worry about somebody other than Mike,' said Chris cheerfully.

Jake was stiff and surly for the next few days, snapping at Phyllida when she suggested he go back to the doctor. Hurt, wretchedly unhappy, she retreated behind a barrier of frigid hostility, and kept out of his way as he wanted.

It was impossible to avoid him completely, of course. She had to pass him in the office when she went to collect fresh linen, or edge past him on the narrow pontoons, and her heart was so sore she wanted to cry out with the need to touch him.

Jake himself spoke to her as little as possible, and, to rub salt into the wound, spent much of his time with Val, who always seemed to be around, spotting places Phyllida had missed with the polish or dealing competently with the radio.

Phyllida gritted her teeth and carried on doggedly. She didn't cry.

Alone at night she would lie in bed and stare at the ceiling, remembering how the moonlight had poured through the hatch on the *Ali B*, but even tears seemed frozen up in the cold bleakness inside her. She tried to think positively, and make plans for the future, but it was as if her world had shrunk and it was impossible to imagine a life without Jake or the cheerfully rocking boats in the marina.

Mike's progress was still satisfactory; he and Chris would be home soon. Phyllida didn't know whether she longed for this nightmare situation to end or dreaded the time when she would have to say goodbye to Jake.

Three days before Chris and Mike were expected, Phyllida was cleaning *Valli* again. She knew each boat like an old friend by now, and she would miss them as much as she would miss the huge sky and the dazzling light and the soft slap and sigh of the water against the jetty.

Gathering up the dirty sheets and pillowcases into a huge bundle, she took them along to the office. Jake was there, scowling over some accounts, and, although he didn't look round, she could tell from the stiffening of his body that he knew she was there.

Phyllida looked at the back of his head and wished that she could slip her arms around his neck and bend down and whisper 'I love you' in his ear. She wished he would turn his head and smile, and pull her into his lap so that she could kiss the lines of strain from his face...

What was the point in wishing? Phyllida remembered bleakly. Wishing hadn't made things right before. So, instead of putting them around Jake, she tightened her arms around her bundle of dirty washing and headed into the back room, where she dumped them in the basket and began pulling out clean sheets from the store.

In the other room, she heard the creak of Jake's chair as he swung round the way he did when someone came to the door of the office. 'Can I help you?' His voice was preoccupied, not overly welcoming.

There was a murmur, and then Phyllida heard him call her name. Puzzled, she went to the door, her arms full of sheets which went cascading to the floor as she saw who was standing in the office waiting for her.

'Rupert!'

CHAPTER NINE

RUPERT smiled. Next to Jake he looked cool and pale and patrician, and somehow insubstantial. 'Phyllida, darling!' he said.

Jake looked from Rupert's handsome face to Phyllida's stunned expression, and his face hardened. 'This is obviously a personal call,' he said coldly.

'It is,' said Rupert smugly. 'Very personal.' He turned back to Phyllida. 'Is there somewhere we can be alone, darling?'

Her eyes flicked helplessly to Jake, who was looking thunderous. His chair scraped across the floor as he got to his feet. 'You can stay here,' he said curtly. 'But don't be too long. Phyllida's got a lot to do, and I don't pay her to stand around gossiping all day.'

Rupert glanced at him with ill-concealed dislike. 'We've got better things to do than gossip,' he said. 'I haven't seen Phyllida for more than two months, and we've got a lot to talk about.'

'In that case, I suggest you talk about it in her time, not mine,' said Jake. 'You can have five minutes now, but otherwise you'll have to postpone your touching reunion until Phyllida's finished work.' He looked stonily at Phyllida. 'I'll be on *Calypso* if anyone needs me.'

I do, Phyllida wanted to cry after him. She watched him walk out of the office and along the jetty, his stiffness almost gone, and it seemed as if he was walking out of her life without a backward look.

'He's a bit grim, isn't he?' said Rupert, shutting the

door after Jake. 'How on earth do you come to be working for a rough type like that?'

'It's a long story.' Blankly, she bent to pick up the sheets she had dropped, and clutched them to her chest as she faced Rupert. His image had become blurred in her mind over the last few weeks, but she could see now that he was just the same.

His hair was the same dark gold she had once loved, his eyes the same blue, and there was the same faint arrogance in his expression. He had been the best looking man she had ever met. He still was, Phyllida considered fairly, but he didn't make her heart leap or her senses tingle just by standing there, like Jake did.

'This is a surprise,' she said with an effort. She felt oddly disorientated by his sudden appearance. 'How on earth did you find me?'

Rupert looked rather taken aback, as if he had expected her to throw herself into his arms. 'I've just flown out from London,' he said. 'I thought you'd be at your cousin's address, but when I got there a neighbour said I'd probably find you at the marina. So—' he smiled and spread his hands '—here I am.'

'You always used to be so rude about Australia,' said Phyllida, putting the sheets down on a chair with an awkward laugh. Once, when they had just got engaged, she had suggested that they come out together, so that she could introduce Rupert to Chris, but he had poured scorn on the idea, saying that it was a barbaric country and that he had better things to do with his holiday than stand around in a lot of dust, photographing kangaroos. 'Don't tell me you're out here on business?'

'Personal business,' said Rupert, walking towards her and taking her hands. 'I came to find *you*, Phyllida. I want you to come home. I was angry after that awful argument, but after you left I realised how much I missed you. I've been thinking about things, and I know that I should have been more sympathetic when you lost your job. I realise now how much it meant to you, and if you want to go on working after we're married, I won't mind—I promise.'

Phyllida stared at him in astonishment. 'You mean, you still want me to marry you?' She couldn't believe he thought it would be that easy.

'Of course I do!' Rupert put his arms round her, evidently expecting her to be speechless with joy, and he looked hurt when she wriggled free. 'What's wrong, darling?'

He wasn't Jake, that was what was wrong. Phyllida hugged her arms together in an unconsciously defensive gesture.

When she had thrown Rupert's ring back in his face, she had sworn to make him regret his lack of sympathy. Well, now he did. Her wish had come true. He had said that he loved her and understood her need for a career, just as she had longed for him to do. It should have been the perfect ending, a fairy tale come true, but all Phyllida could feel was panic at finding herself in the wrong scene, with the wrong hero.

How could she tell Rupert that? She hesitated, wanting to tell him the truth but reluctant to hurt him. He had just flown all the way from England to see her. It wasn't fair to tell him that he had wasted his time as soon as he had arrived. She should let him explain himself properly; she owed him that at least.

She glanced around the office. 'We can't discuss this here,' she temporised. 'You're tired. Why don't we talk about things when you've had a chance to sleep?'

'Of course,' said Rupert with a smile, certain that she

would come round to his point of view eventually. 'I've sprung this on you without warning, haven't I? No wonder you're behaving strangely!'

It was on the tip of Phyllida's tongue to inform him sharply that there was nothing strange about *her* behaviour, but she bit back her retort. She didn't want to start an argument here.

She found Jake on *Calypso*, savagely polishing the guard rails. He looked up as she approached and wiped his hands on the rag. 'So that's Rupert!' he sneered. 'Very aristocratic! Was he offended because I forgot to tug my forelock?'

Phyllida clenched her hands. 'He didn't mention you.'

'What's he doing here, anyway?'

'I don't think that's any of your business,' she said steadily.

'Let me guess!' said Jake with bitter sarcasm as he went back to his polishing. 'He's come to sweep you out of this ghastly hovel and carry you back to the family mansion, where you can use your famous executive skills organising all the old retainers? No more cooking and cleaning for you! I can't help feeling you'll be a little bored, though, Phyllida. Rupert's not man enough for a girl like you.'

'He's man enough to apologise, which is more than you are!' said Phyllida before she could stop herself. She took a deep breath and counted to ten. 'Rupert's tired,' she went on in an even tone. 'I'm going to take him back to Chris's house so he can sleep. He's hired a car, so I might as well collect my things and go back with him.'

'Very cosy!' jeered Jake. 'Sure you'll be able to manage without a butler?'

Phyllida ignored him. 'I'll get a taxi back later this afternoon.'

'Don't bother,' he said. 'Far be it from me to wrest you from the arms of your lover, who's come so far to see you!'

'I thought things were supposed to be too busy to allow me more than five minutes off?'

Jake dug his rag into the tin of polish and attacked one of the uprights. 'The business isn't going to fall apart without you. I've managed without you before, and I'll manage again.'

Would *she* manage without *him*? 'I'll be here tomorrow morning, then.' When Jake didn't reply, or look up from the guard rails, Phyllida sighed and walked away, but when she glanced back from the end of the jetty, she saw that he had put down his rag and was staring at her.

While Rupert slept Phyllida sat out on the shaded veranda and watched some pink and grey galahs settle with a lot of squawking and fussing in the tall gum tree across the road. She had managed to persuade him that she needed time to think, and he had agreed not to press her for an answer yet.

She *did* need to think, she told herself. She had been wrong before; might she not be wrong again? Perhaps Jake was right, and this *was* just a temporary madness that would fade as soon as she got back into her old routine. She ought, in fairness, to give Rupert the chance to remind her about the things that had once been so important to her.

Phyllida had cleared out the fridge before she went to Jake's, so they had to go out to eat. Knowing how snobbish Rupert could be, she took him to the best restaurant in town, but found herself wincing at his carrying cut-glass tones and patronising glances.

'Liedermann, Marshall & Jones have been asking

round about you,' he told Phyllida when they had ordered. 'Rumour has it that they want you back. In fact, Barry Shillingworth asked me to tell you to get in touch as soon as you got back.' He reached out and covered her hand with his own. 'You see, darling, we all want you!'

Jake didn't, Phyllida thought wistfully. Tugging her hand away as unobtrusively as she could, she looked desperately over Rupert's shoulder in search of a diversion, only to find herself staring into familiar green, grey-flecked eyes.

Phyllida felt jarred and breathless, as if she had tripped at the unexpected end of an escalator, or missed the last step on the stairs. For a shocked moment she wondered if her thoughts had conjured him up out of thin air, and then she saw that he was with Val, and that they were already embarked on their meal.

So this was where he brought her! Sick with jealousy, Phyllida looked defiantly back at Jake over Rupert's shoulder. Her eyes were bright and hostile, his cold and accusing.

'Well, I must say you don't look very enthusiastic,' Rupert was complaining, and with difficulty she brought her attention back to him. 'I thought you'd be over the moon! You always used to be obsessed with that damned job of yours.'

'I'm sorry, Rupert.' Phyllida shrugged her shoulders helplessly. He was right. She should be ecstatic at the idea of having her old job back. 'I suppose it's all happened too quickly. It's going to take some getting used to.'

'I don't see why,' he said a little sulkily. 'It's not as if you have to think about anything new. It'll just be going back to exactly the way you were before. I thought that's what you wanted.'

'I've had a lot of time to think since I came to Australia,' she tried to explain. 'Don't you see? I can't just pretend that LMJ never sacked me, or that we never had that argument!'

Rupert looked at her in disbelief. 'You won't get another chance like this, Phyllida. The way Barry was talking, you might even be up for a promotion if you go back now. You never used to be slow about taking opportunities to get on!'

'No,' she admitted ruefully. 'I know I built my life around my job. But now that I've had a chance to stand back and think about things, I don't know if I want to go back to advertising.'

His face lit up. 'You mean, you don't want to work after all? We can get married as soon as we get back, then!'

'I didn't mean that,' said Phyllida quickly, before he got carried away. 'I'm just not sure what I want at the moment.'

'You've changed,' said Rupert, staring at her as if he'd never seen her before, and, over his shoulder, Phyllida's eyes met Jake's unwillingly once more.

'Yes,' she said. 'I have.'

Rupert was happy to accept her change of heart about her career, but refused to believe that she wasn't just being coy in refusing to give him a direct answer. 'We could be on our way home in a couple of days!' he pointed out. 'There's nothing to keep you here now that you've made your point.'

'This isn't a game,' said Phyllida wearily. 'Let me sleep on it, Rupert. I don't want to rush into another decision.'

The meal seemed to last for ever. Phyllida tried everything to keep her gaze on Rupert, but her eyes kept sliding over his shoulder and jarring with Jake's with such a clash that she half expected Rupert and Val to twist round in their chairs and demand to know what all the noise was.

All in all, it was a relief when Jake and Val got up to go. Phyllida relaxed back in her chair, only to jerk upright when she realised that they would have to pass the table on their way out.

Val stopped in surprise at the sight of Phyllida. 'Hello! I didn't know you were here.'

'Small world,' said Phyllida with a brief smile. She glanced at Jake. 'Hello,' she said coolly, as if they hadn't been glaring at each other for the last hour.

'This is Phyllida's fiancé,' said Jake, managing to turn the description into a sneer. 'It's Rupert, isn't it?'

'Rupert Deverell.' Rupert looked as if he didn't know whether to be pleased at Jake's description or offended by his tone.

'I'd have thought you two would have wanted to be alone tonight,' Jake went on nastily. 'Surely the reconciliation's not over already?'

'Of course not,' said Rupert, looking down his nose. 'One must eat.'

'If I hadn't seen my fiancé for over two months, food would be the last thing on *my* mind!' said Jake. 'But then, if I had a fiancé—especially one like Phyllida—I wouldn't let her go away for months on end.'

Rupert half rose from his seat. 'What do you mean by that?' he demanded angrily.

'He means that he hasn't got a fiancée because no girl would ever consider marrying anyone with his kind of suspicious and possessive attitude,' said Phyllida, with a vengeful look at Jake as she pulled Rupert back into his chair where he subsided, muttering.

'I didn't know you were engaged, Phyllida,' Val put in quickly, before the argument could develop any further.

'Didn't you?' Phyllida glanced at Jake in frustration. Why had he called Rupert her fiancé? She had told him the truth at Reevesby Island, but she could hardly deny it in front of Rupert before she had had a chance to tell him in private that she wasn't going to change her mind.

'If I'd known you were here, I'd have asked you and your fiancé to join us,' Val went on, running her hands through her blonde mane. 'We've been planning a round-the-world trip and could have done with your culinary advice—neither of us know the first thing about cooking, do we, Jake?'

Phyllida felt as if she had been struck. Jake and Val, planning a round-the-world trip together? Jake and Val, lying together night after night in the for'ard berth, with the stars shining down on them? Jake and Val, strolling along empty beaches in the still evening light? She wanted to stand up and scream No!, to wipe the smug smile from Val's face and tell her that Jake belonged to *her*.

Her lips were stiff, her throat tight and dry. 'I'm sure Jake will tell you that I'm no good for anything on a boat.' She looked at him, daring him to remember how they had braced themselves against the side and watched the dolphins leaping through the water, how they had sat and talked while the sunset flamed and faded, how they had made love in the starlight.

Jake looked back at her, his eyes dark and angry, and she knew that he remembered only too well, and resented her for reminding him.

Rupert was laughing indulgently. 'Don't tell me you've been sailing, darling? It's obviously high time I took you home, before you become a real outdoor girl!' He put his hand over hers. 'And I like you firmly indoors—and preferably in bed!'

Jake's expression was so murderous that for one moment Phyllida thought he was going to hit Rupert, but in the end he only took Val's arm in a grip that made her wince. 'We'd better not keep you, then,' he said, his voice like a steel trap. 'You'll want to get back there as soon as possible!'

'Well!' Rupert stared after him in outrage. 'Who does that chap think he is?'

Phyllida's eyes followed Jake out of the restaurant. She had longed for him to go, and now the room felt cold and empty without him. 'He's not always like that,' she said, thinking of Jake laughing, Jake smiling, Jake whispering endearments against her skin.

'I don't know why his girlfriend puts up with him,' huffed Rupert, still much put out by the whole encounter.

His girlfriend. Val. Lucky Val, who would be able to wake up every morning in her berth and turn to find Jake there. 'I expect she thinks he's worth it,' said Phyllida quietly. It didn't matter how unpleasant Jake was, she would think so too.

'I was beginning to think there might be something going on between you two,' Rupert confessed. 'It's the way he looks at you—and at me! If looks could kill, I'd be splattered all over the wall. But if he's going round the world with that girl, I suppose he's got other interests.' He hesitated. 'There *isn't* anything going between you, is there?'

'No,' said Phyllida sadly. 'There's nothing going on.'

* * *

She took a taxi to work the next morning. 'But I'm here!' Rupert had protested, peeved, when she'd announced her intention. 'This Tregowan chap won't expect you in.'

'The boats still have to be cleaned,' Phyllida had said, although the frantic rush was over, and none of the boats going out that weekend wanted catering. 'And there's no point in my hanging around while you sleep off your jet lag. You can come and pick me up later.'

Rupert had grumbled, but she'd insisted. The marina was the only place that felt like home at the moment, and her need to be near Jake was a physical ache. There might be nothing between them any more, but she still needed to see him. It didn't matter if all she could do was watch him; knowing he was there was enough.

She had lain awake long into the night, torturing herself with thoughts of Jake and Val together. Would it have made any difference if she had known how close they were? Why had he made love to her if he had been planning to go away with Val? Phyllida's tired brain couldn't come up with any answers. All she knew was that even the dream of a future with Jake had died, along with all her other dreams.

Jake's expression was even more forbidding than usual, and he avoided Phyllida until she was putting the buckets and scrubbing brushes away at the end of the day. 'Chris rang a little while ago,' he said flatly. 'She and Mike are coming home a day early. They'll be back tomorrow.'

Tomorrow? Phyllida was overwhelmed with panic at the thought that the end might be so close. 'That's good news,' she muttered.

'I'll pick them up from the airport,' Jake went on. 'You'd better be at the house to meet them. There's no need for you to come here. We're not busy, and I can manage on my own until Chris is ready to come back.'

'I see.' She didn't even have tomorrow. The end was today. Now. Numbly, Phyllida picked up her bag. 'So this is goodbye?'

Jake got to his feet. 'I...yes, I suppose it is.' He hesitated, as if he wanted to say more, but when he did speak, his words were stilted and formal. 'Thank you for your help.'

'That's all right.' Phyllida's body felt as if it didn't belong to her any more. She couldn't go like this, without telling him how she felt! She swung round. 'Jake?'

'Yes?' His tone wasn't encouraging.

'Jake, I...' Phyllida faltered and stopped. It ought to be easy to tell him that she loved him and needed him, that her heart was breaking at the thought of never seeing him again, but the words stuck in her throat. He would laugh in her face. He would snap his fingers and tell her that she could keep her love and go back to her precious career.

Jake's eyes were suddenly alert as she hesitated. 'Well?' he prompted urgently.

Let him laugh, Phyllida decided. At least she would have told him. 'I just wanted to tell you—'

An imperious blast of the horn interrupted her. Through the window she could see Rupert at the wheel of his hired car, and her shoulders slumped. Jake's face hardened.

'You'd better go,' he said. 'You don't want to keep his lordship waiting.'

Phyllida bit her lip, then nodded. She couldn't tell him with Rupert peering through the window at them. Perhaps it wasn't meant to be. Perhaps in time she'd be glad she hadn't said anything. 'Goodbye,' she said in a low voice, and walked quickly out to the car.

Rupert was still feeling aggrieved at having been neglected all day. He complained all the way back to the house. 'I just don't see why you had to go into work,' he continued as she unlocked the door. 'It's not as if the fellow's even paying you!'

'That's not the point,' said Phyllida tiredly.

'Well, what is? He's not a charity, and I don't like the idea of my fiancée spending her days acting as an unpaid char—especially not for a man like that.'

'I'm not your fiancée,' she said, dropping her bag onto a chair and turning to face him. 'I haven't been since I gave you back your ring.'

Rupert frowned. 'I thought we'd decided we'd put all that behind us.'

'*You* decided that. I didn't.'

'Are you trying to tell me that I've come all this way for nothing?' he demanded incredulously.

She sighed. 'I was upset after that argument. Of course I was. If you'd come round to see me the next day, and told me what you told me yesterday, I'd probably have fallen into your arms and we might have been able to carry on as before. Now I'm glad that you didn't.'

'*Glad?*'

'I know now that it would have been a terrible mistake for us to get married,' she explained, as gently as she could. 'We didn't know enough about each other, Rupert. I didn't realise until that argument just how different we are.'

'We're not different,' he protested. 'We lead the same life, have the same interests, share the same friends... What's different in that?'

Phyllida looked at him helplessly. 'We think differently.'

'What nonsense!' said Rupert, with a dismissive gesture. 'Australia seems to have gone to your head. You'll soon change your mind when you're back home again.'

'I don't want to change my mind.' She took a deep breath. 'I'm sorry, Rupert. I can't marry you because I don't love you. I don't think I ever did.'

Rupert's expression clouded with gathering fury. 'Do you realise what I've given up to come running after you, Phyllida? It wasn't an easy time to leave the firm, you know. God knows what's happening while I'm not there!

'I've had a ghastly trip that's cost me an arm and a leg, I've been stuck in this benighted place for two days, and my back will probably never be the same after the most uncomfortable bed it's ever been my misfortune to sleep upon...all for you! And now you calmly turn round and tell me you won't marry me after all!'

'I didn't ask you to come,' Phyllida pointed out, annoyed by his assumption that this was somehow all her fault. 'I'm sorry you've had a wasted journey, but you could have written. I did.'

'I never had so much as a postcard from you!'

'No,' she admitted. 'I never got round to posting the letter.' She took it out of her bag and smoothed the crumpled envelope between her fingers.

Rupert was forgotten for a moment as she looked down at it and remembered how it had fallen to the cabin floor, how Jake's face had changed as he'd picked it up, how the happiness of the morning had crumbled. She hadn't changed her mind about anything she had said in the letter, but her heart had been too sore to do anything about it until now.

She handed the envelope to Rupert. 'Here, you might as well read it. It's addressed to you.'

Rupert took it with a suspicious look and ripped open the envelope. 'I see,' he said heavily when he had read it. 'So I might as well have saved myself the trip? You'd already made up your mind?'

She nodded. 'I had no idea you'd come out here.'

'Obviously not,' said Rupert bitterly. 'Why didn't you tell me all this as soon as I arrived, instead of letting me get my hopes up and make a complete fool of myself?'

Rupert hadn't just had hopes, Phyllida reflected. He had been convinced that she would fall in with his plans—just as she had always done before. She sighed. 'I'm sorry,' she said again.

'I just don't understand you,' he went on petulantly. 'I'm offering you the chance of everything you've always wanted and you turn it down! It's not as if there's anything to keep you here—this is hardly your kind of place, is it?'

Phyllida thought of the inky blue of the sea, of the sunshine dancing on the waves and the intense turquoise shallows sighing onto wide white beaches. She thought of the sky and the wind and the sound of the boat shushing through the water. And she thought of Jake, and the hard green eyes that could melt into a smile that set her heart swinging with happiness.

'I like it here,' was all she said.

Rupert snorted. 'You won't be able to stay here for ever. You know that, don't you? What are you going to do then?'

Phyllida's heart contracted. 'I don't know.'

She might have felt more guilty about Rupert if she hadn't sensed that his pride was wounded as much as his heart. He had always been fond of grand gestures, she remembered, and flying out to Australia had been the grandest of them all. Unfortunately, things hadn't worked out as he had planned, and he was not amused.

Phyllida had had her chance, he informed her petulantly, and he sincerely hoped she would live to regret it. In the meantime, he couldn't wait to shake the dust of Port Lincoln from his shoes.

All in all, Phyllida was relieved when he managed to get a place on the last flight back to Adelaide that night. He left announcing that since he had come this far he might as well do some business, visiting the vineyard in the Barossa Valley.

Phyllida hated herself for wondering cynically whether that hadn't been his intention all along, and whether coming to see her had just been a side-trip on impulse, to make the most of his ticket which he would undoubtedly manage to claim off his tax.

She spent that night alone in Chris's house, wondering whether Jake was sitting on his veranda looking out over the sea. Was he thinking about her? Did he ever remember that night they had shared? Or was he out with Val, planning their romantic round-the-world venture?

Jake's image circled round and round in her mind: Jake rolling his eyes in exasperation, Jake holding out his hand to help her onto the boat, Jake leaning down to kiss her. She tried to hold onto those memories, but darker ones kept intruding. She thought about how he had pushed her away from him, how cold and angry his eyes had been last night.

'I don't want to be part of your life.' His words echoed bitterly through her thoughts. He was part of Val's life, not hers.

It was just as well she hadn't had the chance to tell him how much she loved him, Phyllida thought bleakly.

She had been so desperate at the thought of saying goodbye to him that she had forgotten Val. She couldn't have borne the thought of the two of them laughing together at the silly English girl's infatuation. How could she even have dreamt of being a rival to Val, who belonged here?

Phyllida was up early the next morning. She had slept badly, disturbed by dreams of Jake drawing her towards him with a smile only to thrust her aside in disgust when he realised at the last moment that she wasn't Val. Misery felt like a great weight pressing down on her shoulders and Phyllida found that she was moving stiffly like an old woman as she cleaned the house and made everything look nice for Chris and Mike's return.

She was just placing a vase of agapanthus lilies on the table when she heard a car draw up outside. Her hands shook as she set the vase down. Jake would be there. She would have to greet him coolly, as if nothing had happened between them. Nothing must spoil Chris and Mike's homecoming.

Taking a deep breath, Phyllida went to the door. She saw Jake first of all. He was helping Mike out of the car and onto his crutches, but he looked up as the door opened and his eyes met Phyllida's along the length of the veranda. His expression was intense, searching, and, without thinking, Phyllida took a step towards him.

The next instant Chris had emerged round the back of the car and rushed towards Phyllida with a cry of delight, enveloping her in a hug. 'You look so different!' she exclaimed, holding Phyllida at arm's length to study her properly. 'I can't put my finger on it...maybe it's because you've been out in the sun? Or have you changed your hair? No, it's something else...'

Phyllida looked at her cousin in some dismay. It was

just like Chris to spot the truth at once! She forced a laugh. 'I haven't had time to dry my hair properly, but otherwise I'm just the same, I promise you!'

She moved forward to greet Mike with a smile, carefully avoiding Jake's eye. Mike was a tall, lanky man, and was having trouble manoeuvring his crutches, but he kissed Phyllida warmly and thanked her for taking Chris's place at work. 'It made all the difference to her not having to worry about her job,' he told her gratefully.

'Won't you come in, Jake?' Chris pleaded, obviously continuing a conversation that had begun in the car. 'We haven't had time to thank *you* yet.'

'No, I won't stay,' Jake said with a brief smile. 'You'll want to settle in, and besides, this should be a family occasion. Phyllida has some news for you about Rupert.' And he got back into the car and reversed out of the drive without waiting to see what the reaction would be.

CHAPTER TEN

'WHAT on earth did he mean by that?' Mystified, Chris looked after Jake as he drove away. 'And what's all this about Rupert?' she added to Phyllida.

'Nothing important,' said Phyllida hastily. 'I'll tell you later.' She bent to pick up one of the cases. 'Come on, let's go inside.'

It was some time before they were settled with a celebratory drink under the pergola in the back garden. Phyllida was careful to steer the conversation away from what she had been doing, and for a while they were happy to tell her about Mike's stay in the hospital and how kind everyone had been to Chris.

'I did a lot of thinking when I was lying in that bed,' Mike said. 'I realised a lot of things I wished I'd realised sooner—like how selfish it was of me to drag Chris around from place to place, and how all my schemes fell through because I lost interest before they had a chance to work.' He covered Chris's hand with his own and smiled at his wife. 'That's all changed now, hasn't it?'

Chris nodded happily. 'We had a long talk one day,' she told Phyllida. 'We've decided to start afresh, but this time we're going to work together to make a real success of it. Mike found a small charter company in the Whitsundays whose owner wants to sell up, so we're going to sell our house here and use what's left of the money Jake paid us to start again. We're going to go upmarket, like Jake has, and although things will be tight at first, we're determined to make it work.'

'That's right,' Mike confirmed. 'The accident sorted out all my priorities for me. I was always restless, always thinking things would be better if only I was somewhere different or doing something different. Now I know what's important—and the most important thing of all is that I've got Chris, and she's got me.'

He smiled lovingly at his wife as he spoke. They were so happy, so confident that everything would be all right as long as they were together, that Phyllida felt tears sting her eyes.

Jake would never look at her the way that Mike looked at Chris. She would never be able to smile like Chris and know that everything would be all right because Jake would always be at her side. They wouldn't share the doubts and the worries along with the laughter, or look forward to a bright future, secure in the knowledge that they would share it together.

Phyllida blinked the tears away furiously. This was no time to waste in what-might-have-beens. It was Chris's happiness that mattered now, and no one deserved it more. 'I'm so pleased for you,' she said warmly.

'Now, tell us about Rupert!' Chris commanded. 'What did Jake mean by saying that you had some news?'

'Rupert turned up here a couple of days ago,' said Phyllida, and laughed at the look on Chris's face.

'He came all the way out to Australia to see you?' she asked excitedly.

'Me and a few vineyards,' Phyllida said with a dry look.

'But Phyllida, that's wonderful news! How have you managed to keep it to yourself while we've been boring on about our news?' She paused, puzzled by her cousin's expression. 'I suppose he *did* come to beg you to go back to him?'

'He said he still wanted us to get married.' Phyllida chose her words carefully. Rupert hadn't done much begging. Assuming was more his line.

Chris was looking bewildered by Phyllida's restrained manner. 'Isn't that what you wanted? You told me you were missing him.'

Phyllida flushed. She had forgotten that she had told Chris that. She had only said it was Rupert she was missing because she couldn't say that it was Jake she longed for.

'I was just feeling down about…something else… then,' she explained awkwardly. 'I'm afraid Rupert was just an excuse. When he turned up here, I didn't feel anything for him at all. If anything, it just made me more certain than before that I'd been right to break off our engagement.'

'I see,' said Chris, but she didn't look as if she did.

Phyllida hoped her cousin wasn't about to ask why she had been feeling so down that she'd felt the need of a broken engagement as an excuse. 'When are you planning to go up to the Whitsundays?' she asked brightly.

'As soon as we can sell the house,' said Mike. 'The only problem is letting Jake down. We feel bad about the fact that he's kept Chris's job open for her, but when we told him our plans in the car he was great about it.'

'Frankly, I'm not sure he even took it in,' Chris put in after some reflection. 'He seemed very preoccupied, didn't he, Mike?'

'Perhaps he's got other problems,' Mike suggested. 'Phyllida probably knows. She's the one who's been working with him, after all. What do you think, Phyllida? Has business been good?'

'As far as I know,' she said in a colourless tone. 'It

hasn't been so busy this last week, but I think that was expected.'

'How did you and Jake get on, anyway?' asked Chris with interest.

'Fine.' Phyllida's throat was tight, her voice high and brittle.

'Funny, that's what Jake said too,' said Mike humorously. 'He didn't sound as if he meant it either! There's nothing going on between you two, is there?' He laughed heartily at the idea.

'Of course not.' Phyllida tried to smile, but it went rather astray.

Chris had been watching her cousin's face. 'Mike,' she said suddenly, 'don't you think you should go and rest?'

'I'm not tired,' he objected, surprised.

'You've had a long journey, and you haven't been out of hospital long,' said Chris firmly, hauling him to his feet.

While she was chivvying him into the bedroom Phyllida had a chance to rearrange her face and get herself under control again. By the time Chris reappeared, she was sipping her drink with a determinedly cool expression.

Chris sat down beside her. 'Well?'

'Well, what?' said Phyllida, with a fine assumption of nonchalance.

'Well, what's going on between you and Jake?'

'Nothing.'

'Come on, Phyl! I saw your face just now. I can tell something's wrong, and my guess is that it's the same thing that's wrong with Jake.'

'Nothing's wrong,' Phyllida insisted, with an edge of desperation.

'Then why do you look as if you're trying to pretend that your heart's not breaking?'

'It isn't,' she said, but the glass rattled against her teeth as she put it down unsteadily.

'I thought it might be Rupert,' Chris continued inexorably, 'but you tell me it's not. Which leaves Jake—who, coincidentally, is also looking as if he's had a hard kick in the stomach!'

'If he is, it's n-nothing to d-do with m-me,' said Phyllida, and her face crumpled as she lost her battle to control her trembling mouth. 'H-he h-hates me!' Horrified, she put up her hands to cover her face, but it was too late to stop the tears. 'I'm s-sorry,' she sobbed. 'I didn't mean to cry and s-spoil everything for you, just when you're so happy again.'

Chris handed her cousin a tissue. 'I think you'd better tell me all about it,' she said.

Gradually, she coaxed the whole story out of Phyllida. How they had met, how they had argued, how Phyllida had fallen more and more in love with him without knowing it. How the atmosphere had kept changing on that fatal sailing trip and how Jake had been furious with her for walking off on her own. How disagreeable he had been that evening, and then how everything had changed suddenly again.

Phyllida glossed over that night, but presumably Chris got the message, for she nodded understandingly when her cousin told her how devastated she had been by Jake's reaction to the letter he had seen.

'One thing—he sounds even more confused than you were,' she said comfortingly.

'He didn't sound very confused to me,' wept Phyllida. 'He said he didn't want to be part of my life, and then when the boom hit him he was furious!'

Chris had to suppress a smile when Phyllida explained about the goosewing incident. 'If you'd been hit by a boom, you'd be cross too!' she said. 'On the other hand, Jake was probably even angrier because he realised that it was partly his fault for not explaining properly. I don't know what you're worrying about, Phyllida. It sounds to me as if the poor man's out of his mind with jealousy!'

Phyllida shook her head miserably. 'He couldn't wait to get rid of me when Rupert arrived, and anyway—' she sniffed '—he's planning to sail round the world with Val.'

'*What*?' Chris stared at her. 'Who on earth told you that?'

'Val did.'

'Well, I wouldn't believe it until I heard it from Jake,' said Chris stoutly. 'Val's all right, and I dare say Jake's fond of her in his own way, but abandon his business to sail off into the sunset with her? No!'

Phyllida scrubbed her face furiously with the damp and crumpled tissue and refused to be comforted. 'He was there. He heard her say it and he didn't deny it.'

'He probably thought *you* were going to swan off into the sunset with Rupert!' Chris shook her head with mock severity. 'Really, Phyl! I can't believe that two smart, intelligent people like you and Jake could get themselves in such a muddle! You were both wonderful when *I* was in a state, but it doesn't sound to me as if you've the least idea about your own affairs!'

Phyllida opened her mouth to protest, but Chris wouldn't let her speak. 'If you'll take my advice, you'll go straight down to Jake now and tell him what you've just told me.'

'I can't!' she said in panic.

'You can,' said her cousin implacably. 'Do you love him?'

'Yes,' she whispered. 'Yes, I do.'

'Then tell him.' Chris got to her feet. 'If we had a car I'd drive you to the marina, but as it is I'll have to call you a taxi. You go and wash your face.'

'Chris, I don't think—'

But Chris was deaf to Phyllida's flustered objections. She bullied her cousin into getting ready, and personally instructed the taxi driver to take her to the marina and not dare drop her off anywhere else.

Phyllida was borne along by Chris's determination, but as she paid the taxi driver and got out at the marina her courage began to fail her. It had sounded easy when Chris had said that all she had to do was tell Jake she loved him. Now she had no idea where she would begin.

She stood for a while by the wall, looking down over the marina. The sunlight danced and glittered on the water, just as it had done when she had first seen it. The boats still rocked beside the jetty, their gay pennants fluttering proudly in the breeze. The air was as sparkling clear as it had always been. Only she had changed. Slowly, Phyllida walked down the steps to the office.

Jake wasn't there. As she stood there the telephone shrilled loudly, making her jump, but when she moved towards it the answer machine cut in. Jake's voice echoed eerily round the empty office, and Phyllida's heart sank. He only ever put the answer machine on if he was going to be away for a while. Had she come down here for nothing?

From force of habit more than anything else she wandered down the jetty, past the familiar boats rocking comfortably against the pontoons, their mooring lines creaking and the halyards rattling against the masts as the wind caught them. She passed *Valli*, *Persephone*, *Dora Dee*, *Calypso*...all gleaming clean in the sunshine. Their decks were scrubbed, their woodwork shining, the guard rails flashing silver.

And then she saw Jake.

He was sitting alone on the *Ali B*, his expression so bleak that Phyllida's heart almost failed her. He had obviously been polishing the brass around the compass in the cockpit, but the rag was forgotten in his hand as he stared out to sea, wrapped in bitter thoughts. He didn't hear Phyllida's footsteps along the pontoon, or know that she was watching him until she spoke.

'Jake?'

His head swung round and he stared at her incredulously, the grey-green eyes ablaze with an emotion Phyllida couldn't identify but which left her tongue-tied and breathless.

'Phyllida,' he said, getting uncertainly to his feet.

There was an agonising silence. It was the first time Phyllida had ever seen him unsure of himself, and she didn't know what to do. She was trapped in a straitjacket of nerves, unable to do more than look helplessly back at him.

She cleared her throat. 'Can I come aboard?' Her voice sounded high and silly to her own ears—too brittle, too English.

'Yes...yes.' Jake seemed to realise that he was still holding the rag and wiped his hands with it as he watched Phyllida step over the guard rails. 'You learnt how to get on board a boat, anyway,' he said.

'Yes.' For want of anything better to do, Phyllida sat down in the cockpit, and Jake subsided slowly opposite her. They didn't seem to be able to do anything but look at each other.

'Where's Rupert?' said Jake, breaking the silence at last.

'He's gone.'

'I thought you were going with him?' He sounded strained, and Phyllida moistened her lips.

'He asked me to, but I...I decided to stay.'

'Why?' he asked harshly. 'You want to go back to your career in England. You want Rupert. He's perfect for you...successful, sophisticated, prepared to come all this way to apologise to you.' His voice was very bitter. 'You belong together.'

'That's what I used to think, but I don't belong with Rupert any more.' Phyllida drew a deep breath and looked directly at Jake. 'I belong here,' she said.

Jake went very still. He stared back at her as if her words were filtering slowly through to him, and then the defeated look drained from his face as an incredulous smile lit his eyes. 'You want to stay?'

She nodded, and he reached for her hands and drew her to her feet with him. 'You want to stay here?' he asked, still sounding as if he couldn't quite believe what he was hearing.

'Yes.'

'With me?'

'Yes...if you'll have me.'

'Have you?' Jake gave a sudden, exuberant shout of laughter. 'I've been sitting here in black despair because I thought you'd gone and that I'd never see you again, and you ask if I'll have you!' His hands tightened around hers and he smiled down into her eyes.

'I've been cursing myself as every kind of fool for letting you go to Rupert, and wondering if I'd be too late if I followed you to England and begged you to come back, but I thought you'd refuse. I'd have been asking you to give up your career and your flat and your smart lifestyle, and I knew I couldn't give you any of the things you'd said you wanted.'

'I don't want them any more,' said Phyllida as the cold stone of misery and despair shattered and dissolved in an explosion of exquisite relief that the pretence was over and she could tell him the truth at last. 'I only want you.'

And then she was in his arms, and he was kissing her, and she clung to him and kissed him back, as if afraid that the wondering happiness would vanish if she stopped. It was Jake who drew back first, and Phyllida caught her breath at the expression in his eyes. He took her face between hands that shook slightly, and looked down at her as no man had ever looked at her before.

'I love you,' he said seriously, although the smile still glimmered. 'Do you really love me, Phyllida?'

'Yes,' she said on a half-sob, tears of happiness trembling on the ends of her lashes. The sudden release from the tension and distress of the last few days had left her feeling quite dizzy. 'Oh, yes, I do!'

'And you'll marry me? You'll stay for ever?'

'Yes, yes,' she said, half laughing, half crying, and pulled his head down so that she could kiss him again.

Much later, she leant back against him as they sat close together in the cockpit, and sighed happily at the feel of Jake's arms wrapped securely around her. 'I've been so miserable,' she told him. 'I thought you despised me.'

'I tried to,' Jake admitted. 'The first time I saw you, in that smart suit of yours, I thought you would be like Jonelle—obsessed with your image and your career. I didn't want to get involved with anyone like that again, and all the alarm bells went off whenever you mentioned your job, but no matter how hard I tried not to, I couldn't help noticing that you *weren't* like Jonelle.' He stroked her hair, a tousled mop now, rather than an immaculately swinging bob, but still soft and still shining.

'Jonelle wouldn't have given up her plans for anyone, and she certainly wouldn't have got down on her hands and knees to scrub decks. I worked you much harder than I should have done, I know. I think I almost wanted you to give up, and convince me that you were like Jonelle after all, because then it would have been easier for me to ignore how bright your eyes were and how your whole face lit up when you laughed.'

He smiled, twisting a strand of hair round one finger. 'But you wouldn't give up, would you? There was something gallant about the way you refused to let yourself be beaten. I was rude to you, I bullied and provoked you, but you just stuck your chin in the air and glared right back at me.

'Jonelle was much more subtle. She used to rely on feminine wiles to get her own way. She could be sweetness itself when it suited her, but it was only to disguise her iron will. You were so much more honest. At first I told myself that I secretly admired your defiance, and then I realised that what I felt for you was a lot stronger than admiration.'

'I was convinced you thought I was absolutely ridiculous!'

'I have to admit that you *did* amuse me. You were so stubborn, so determined to be contrary.' Jake's voice changed, and he ran his finger caressingly down her cheek. 'And so beautiful.'

Phyllida shivered beneath his touch. 'I didn't think I was your type. I thought you liked long-legged blondes?'

'Not any more,' said Jake, kissing the sensitive spot just below her ear. 'My taste is for small, fiery brunettes, with elfin faces and the sweetest kisses...' His lips drifted along her jaw and she turned her head with a smile so that they could claim her mouth.

'The first time I kissed you was just an impulse,' he murmured after a while. 'I wasn't prepared for the effect it would have on me, or for the fact that I couldn't get it out of my mind. I was falling more and more in love with you, but I fought it every inch of the way. Jonelle made me very wary of love.'

'I didn't want to fall in love either,' Phyllida said, snuggling closer against him. 'After Rupert, I was determined to be independent.'

'That's what I thought,' he said. 'You talked about your career, and what you would do when you got home, and it made me realise that Australia was just a temporary phase for you. I kept forgetting, though. When I kissed you, when we walked along the beach, when we sat together in the darkness...it seemed so *right*.

'I nearly gave in that night at Reevesby, but you started talking about going home to your job, and I decided it was pointless. I didn't want a temporary affair, and I thought that the more involved I got, the more I'd regret it in the end. It didn't stop me feeling extremely frustrated, though!'

'Is that why you were so foul to me the next day?'

'I'm afraid so. I even shunted you off to the beach at Memory Cove because I was terrified I wouldn't be able to keep my hands off you any longer. And then, of course, I lost control completely when I looked round to see that you'd disappeared! If it had been anyone else, I'd have assumed they'd gone for a walk and left them to it, but, because it was you, I rushed off to try and find you and make sure you were all right.'

'I'm glad you did,' said Phyllida. 'It was so stupid of me to try and get down to that beach, but it was a sort of test for myself, to see if I'd be able to live without you...and I failed it dismally. I knew then that I was stuck with loving you, but of course you were furious with me, and it all seemed more hopeless than ever.'

'I said a lot of things I shouldn't,' Jake apologised with a rueful grin. 'But I was so afraid when I saw you lying down there. Everything went black until I got you back on the track and saw that you really were all right, and then I lost my head. I was furious with you for giving me such a scare, and even more furious with myself for caring so much if you were even slightly scratched.'

'I wish I'd known,' sighed Phyllida, resting her head back against his shoulder. 'I was so miserable that evening!'

'Is that why you spent the whole time flirting with everybody except me?'

She blushed faintly. 'I didn't want you to guess how much I loved you,' she explained, and he kissed her.

'It worked,' he said, raising his head. 'I was so jealous I couldn't think straight! I couldn't think about anything except how much I wanted you, and when we got back on the boat... Well, I just lost what little self-control I had left.'

She smiled at the memory, and felt his arms close more firmly around her. 'It was so wonderful,' she remembered softly. 'Couldn't you tell how much I loved you then?'

'I let myself hope you did. I even let myself think that everything would be all right after all—and then I saw that you'd written to Rupert, and I decided I'd been making a complete fool of myself. I was angry with myself for falling so deeply in love with you, and humiliated at the idea that I'd let you see it when it seemed as if you were still interested in Rupert.'

Phyllida sat up in surprise. 'I had no idea,' she protested. 'All I knew was that you'd suddenly gone cold on me.'

'I thought it would be easiest if I put a stop to things there and then,' said Jake. 'It served me right when you knocked me out with the boom!'

'I didn't do it deliberately!'

'I know.' He grinned. 'And anyway, it didn't hurt nearly as much as when I overheard you telling Chris that you were missing Rupert. I'd got up to answer the phone and was just about to open the door when you started talking.

'I'm ashamed to say I listened, hoping against hope that I'd learn something about what you felt after that night, but you know what they say about eavesdroppers...! I was devastated when you said that it was Rupert you were thinking about, not me. It just confirmed everything I was most afraid of.'

'I only said that because I didn't want to tell her I was crazy about you.'

Jake pulled her back into the circle of his arms. 'Why didn't you tell me?'

'Why didn't *you* tell *me*?' countered Phyllida, and he gave a wry smile.

'Stupid pride, I suppose. I avoided you as much as I could, certain that you were making plans to go back to Rupert, but then, when he turned up, I was poleaxed with jealousy! He was just the sort of man I'd expected you to have, and he fitted your image in a way I knew I'd never do.'

Phyllida touched his cheek lovingly. 'Maybe he did once, but I've changed since I met you. Even Chris noticed that I was different!'

Jake held her away from him slightly, as if comparing the career girl he had met at Adelaide airport, in her gold shoes and her matching accessories, with the girl smiling at him now, careless of her appearance, her only ornament the wide eyes that were shining and starry with love. 'Maybe you have changed, at that!' He smiled.

'Or maybe I was like this all along, and I just didn't know it,' said Phyllida. 'I knew as soon as Rupert arrived that I'd never really loved him—not the way I loved you—but I didn't think it was fair to tell him five minutes after he'd got off the plane.'

'Is that why you told Val you were engaged?'

'I didn't,' she said indignantly. '*You* were the one who told her that, not me!'

Jake shifted uncomfortably. 'Well, you didn't deny it.'

'How could I? I'd promised Rupert I'd think about it, and I could hardly smash his hopes in front of an audience. Anyway,' Phyllida went on, remembering, 'I didn't think it would make much difference to you. I thought you'd been involved with Val all along, and had just been amusing yourself with me.'

'With *Val*?' Jake looked astonished. 'What on earth made you think that?'

'Well, what was this round-the-world trip you were planning together?' she asked accusingly, and his brow cleared.

'The only thing we were doing together was the planning, you idiot! Val's determined to sail round the world single-handed, and I was just supposed to be giving her advice about the supplies she'd need—not that I made a single sensible suggestion once you and Rupert appeared! I could hardly eat, I was so choked with jealousy.' Jake gave another wry grin.

'I hadn't realised I had such primitive impulses. Jonelle made me feel sad and bitter, but I'd never felt the sheer rage I felt seeing you and Rupert together. I wanted to choke the life out of him for daring to touch you, and then drag you off so that I could somehow manage to beat you and make love to you at the same time!'

He shook his head. 'And all the time you thought I was interested in Val! How could you even *think* that?'

'She's got long legs,' Phyllida explained, slightly on the defensive. 'And she knows all about sailing.'

'True, but the ability to tell a boom from a bilge pump isn't much competition for a pair of stormy brown eyes,' Jake pointed out, amused. 'Val's a nice girl, and I like her a lot, but I wouldn't want to spend a year in a boat with her.'

'That's what Chris said,' she admitted.

'Oh, you've talked to Chris, have you?' he teased.

'I was busy denying everything, but she wormed the truth out of me in the end. She sent me down here with strict instructions not to go back until we'd both stopped being so silly!' Phyllida smiled. 'She said it was obvious that you were in love with me.'

'Wise Chris!' said Jake, kissing her hair. 'Shall we go and tell her how right she was?'

Phyllida disentangled herself from him with some reluctance and got up, stretching with sheer delight.

The sky was a deep cobalt blue, and the sunshine dazzled her eyes. Everything was brighter, sharper, more distinct—as if glinting with reflected joy—and even the water murmuring against the boats and the breeze chinking the rigging seemed like a chuckling echo of her happiness.

Smiling, she kissed Jake again, and they walked hand in hand along the jetty to break the good news to Chris and Mike.

Less than three hours later, they were back at the marina. A delighted Chris had urged them to stay and celebrate, but Jake and Phyllida had had other plans, and as the afternoon light softened into evening gold, the *Ali B* nosed her way out of the marina, unfurled her sails and headed south towards Memory Cove.

Modern Romance™
...seduction and passion guaranteed

Tender Romance™
...love affairs that last a lifetime

Sensual Romance™
...sassy, sexy and seductive

Blaze
...sultry days and steamy nights

Medical Romance™
...medical drama on the pulse

Historical Romance™
...rich, vivid and passionate

29 new titles every month.

With all kinds of Romance for every kind of mood...

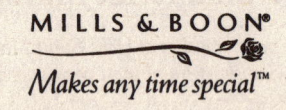

MILLS & BOON®
Makes any time special™

MAT4

Treat yourself this Mother's Day to the ultimate indulgence

3 brand new romance novels and a box of chocolates

= only £7.99

Available from 15th February

Available at most branches of WH Smith, Tesco, Martins, Borders, Eason, Sainsbury's and most good paperback bookshops.

0202/91/MB32

MILLS & BOON

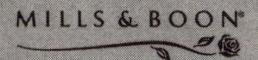

Modern Romance™

THE SECRET LOVE-CHILD by Miranda Lee

Rafe wanted Isabel. But his job was to photograph the bride-to-be, not seduce her. Then he discovered the wedding was off and Isabel boldly asked him to accompany her on what would have been her honeymoon!

AN ARABIAN MARRIAGE by Lynne Graham

When Crown Prince Jaspar al-Husayn bursts into her life, Freddy realises he has come to take their nephew back to his Arab homeland. Freddy refuses to part with the child she's cared for and loved, so she proposes marriage to Jaspar!

THE SPANIARD'S SEDUCTION by Anne Mather

Cassandra had been married to Enrique de Montoya's brother for less than twenty-four hours when she was widowed. Now Enrique has had a letter from her son. But all that time ago Enrique had tried to stop Cassandra's marriage to his brother by seducing her himself...

THE GREEK TYCOON'S BRIDE by Helen Brooks

Andreas Karydis had women falling at his feet, so Sophy was determined not be another notch in his bedpost. But Andreas didn't want her as his mistress – he wanted her as his English bride!

On sale 1st March 2002

Available at most branches of WH Smith, Tesco, Martins, Borders, Eason, Sainsbury's and most good paperback bookshops.

MILLS & BOON

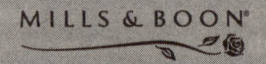

Modern Romance™

SOCIETY WEDDINGS BY KENDRICK & WALKER

PROMISED TO THE SHEIKH by Sharon Kendrick

The only way Jenna can get out of the wedding to Sheikh Rashid of Quador is to pretend she is no longer a virgin, but what happens when sizzling attraction overwhelms them and Rashid discovers she's lying?

THE DUKE'S SECRET WIFE by Kate Walker

Just when Isabelle thinks their secret marriage is over, Don Luis de Silva, heir to the dukedom of Madrigal, asks her to return to Spain. But what does Luis have to gain from this reunion?

RYAN'S REVENGE by Lee Wilkinson

Jilted at the altar. No one can do that to Ryan Falconer and get away with it. That's why, two years later, Ryan's back, convinced their passionate love isn't dead. He's determined to lead Virginia down the aisle – willing or not!

HER DETERMINED HUSBAND by Kathryn Ross

Kirsten discovers she must work intimately with Cal McCormick, her estranged husband! Only a few years before, tragedy had ripped apart their young marriage, but now Cal seems set on making her fall in love with him all over again...

THE RUNAWAY PRINCESS by Patricia Forsythe

Marriage to a man who would love her was Alexis's most cherished dream. But how would Jace react when he discovered the truth about her? That the beautiful substitute teacher was actually a princess...

On sale 1st March 2002

Available at most branches of WH Smith, Tesco, Martins, Borders, Eason, Sainsbury's and most good paperback bookshops.

MILLS & BOON

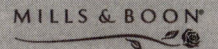

Tender Romance™

THE BOSS'S DAUGHTER by Leigh Michaels

Being the boss's daughter is tough—and now Amy's temporarily in charge of the company! Worse, her 'assistant' is the extremely handsome, dynamic Dylan Copeland. He's intent on keeping an eye on Amy, but is he getting close to her for professional or personal reasons...?

THE BABY QUESTION by Caroline Anderson

Laurie thought she and Rob had the perfect marriage—and a baby would make their happiness complete. But years later she still isn't pregnant and things have changed. For better or worse, Laurie is forced to put her cards on the table and their love to the test...

HIS SECRETARY'S SECRET by Barbara McMahon

Millionaire tycoon Matt Gramling has rules for avoiding love-struck secretaries. Outraged, Karla Jones is determined to become his PA—even if it means disguising herself. But she knows it's only a matter of time before Matt discovers her true identity...

A SPANISH HONEYMOON by Anne Weale

When Liz moves to the idyllic Spanish village of Valdecarrasca, she's stunned to find herself living next door to the infamous Cameron Fielding. He has a string of glamorous female visitors, so Liz is amazed to discover he was contemplating marriage—to her!

On sale 1st March 2002

Available at most branches of WH Smith, Tesco, Martins, Borders, Eason, Sainsbury's and most good paperback bookshops.

MIRANDA LEE
Secrets & Sins
revealed

SEDUCED BY HER BODYGUARD AND STALKED BY A STRANGER...

Available from 15th March 2002

Available at most branches of WH Smith, Tesco, Martins, Borders, Eason, Sainsbury's and most good paperback bookshops.

MILLS & BOON

FOREIGN AFFAIRS

*A captivating 12 book collection of sun-kissed seductions.
Enjoy romance around the world*

DON'T MISS BOOK 6

western weddings—
*Untamed passions,
way out west...*

Available from 1st March

*Available at most branches of WH Smith,
Tesco, Martins, Borders, Eason, Sainsbury's,
and most good paperback bookshops.*

FA/RTL/6

Starting Over

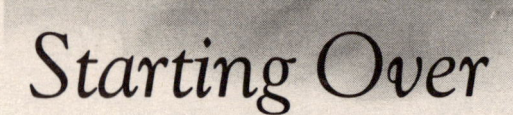

*Another chance at love...
Found where least expected*

PENNY JORDAN

Published 15th February

*Available at most branches of WH Smith,
Tesco, Martins, Borders, Eason, Sainsbury's
and most good paperback bookshops.*

MILLS & BOON®

STEEP/RTL/11

The STEEPWOOD Scandal

REGENCY DRAMA, INTRIGUE, MISCHIEF... AND MARRIAGE

A new collection of 16 linked Regency Romances, set in the villages surrounding Steepwood Abbey.

Book 11
The Guardian's Dilemma
by Gail Whitiker

Available 8th March

Available at most branches of WH Smith, Tesco, Martins, Borders, Eason, Sainsbury's, Woolworths and most good paperback bookshops.